What Love Feels Like

F. Y. Dawn

Dawn2Dawn Publishing

Dawn2Dawn Publishing

8810c Jamacha Blvd #136

Spring Valley, CA 91977

Published by Dawn2Dawn Publishing 02/2014

ISBN-13: 978-0991400041(sc)

ISBN-13: 978-0991400058(e)

Library of Congress Control Number: 2012917990

Alicia lay sound asleep on the couch as Marlon arrived home from work. With the night he'd had, an outlet was desperately needed for the tension built during his shift. He thought of waking her, but lately, her attitude toward him hadn't been the greatest. Conversing with her had become like pulling teeth. When he'd address her, contempt would plaster her face. His very presence and voice had grown, for some reason, recently unbearable. This was the last thing he wanted to deal with after the hellish night he'd just had.

As the executive chef of Pavoli's, an upscale Italian eatery, Marlon had his hands full with the restaurant's daily operations. He was a chef down to his soul and could never stand by and merely supervise others. Cooking was his passion and oftentimes, he would chop and mix food in the kitchen just like a line chef. His primary responsibilities were maintaining order, handling personnel issues, and approving dishes. Although he wasn't required to do much cooking, the quality and taste of the food lay on his shoulders. He was more hands-on than most executive chefs and he was a perfectionist. When he set the menu, there were certain details that had to be followed. He didn't mind showing other chefs how to do it right.

Executive chefs seldom lacked experience, but God had shown Marlon favor. His instructors from culinary school sang his praises and a prominent restaurant owner accepted their recommendations and hired him immediately. Marlon's confidence and demand for perfection set him apart from competition; he quickly advanced. When he was finally allowed to tweak a few recipes, the owner, who was also the executive chef at that time, was repeatedly called to the front by customers who complimented Marlon on such wonderful cuisine.

The owner had taken Marlon under his wing—teaching him the ins and outs of the restaurant business. Alicia had failed to see the blessing of Marlon's career success; she felt neglected. Marlon worked tirelessly, pushing himself far past his limit. He would go in early and stay late just to learn more. When the owner announced that Marlon would be taking over, everyone was floored. The kitchen was turned over so the owner could operate solely as owner. Some lacked the education that Marlon had; therefore, they couldn't complain about his promotion. A sous chef and a line chef were livid, but others didn't want the added stress. The sous chef walked out immediately, cursing and calling the owner an idiot. Marlon looked the line chef, Cole Monroe, in the eye and said, 'You are an excellent chef, but if you doubt my ability, you can follow him out. If you are a team player, willing to support my decisions and follow my lead, then I would be happy to have you as my sous chef'.

That particular night, Cole was out sick and there was a new line chef. Trying to be executive and sous chef on a Friday night with a new line chef was a recipe for disaster, but Marlon held it together. When the night was over, all the chefs and the owner applauded him for the night's success. One even stopped to say, 'I wasn't sure if you were the right man for the job until now'. Over the six months they'd been working together, they'd forged an impenetrable alliance.

Marlon accepted the compliment, shook the man's hand, grabbed his keys, and left. He tried to relax during the drive home, but adrenaline still raced through his veins.

He stood watching his wife sleep and knew exactly what would take his edge off, but he also knew she wouldn't be up for it. As she lay awkwardly, Marlon decided to carry her to their bedroom. Before Marlon could take two steps, angry eyes popped open.

"What are you doing?"

Marlon placed her on her feet and sighed.

"You looked a little uncomfortable; I was carrying you to the bed."

"I was fine. It took me forever to fall asleep, why would you come in here and wake me up?"

"You know what?" Marlon shook his head. "I was just trying to help you out. I apologize for waking you." Marlon turned to walk away, but Alicia's stopped him.

"So, you woke me up and now you're just going to leave?"

"What I'd like to do is come home and talk to my wife about the horrible day I had and her actually care. I would even like to make love to my wife and relieve some of this stress, but my wife hasn't touched me in over a month." Marlon rubbed his hands across his face and plopped down on the couch. She was becoming more irritable each day and he was praying for strength.

"Well, let me tell you what I want. I want my husband to care more about me than his stupid job. I want my husband to be home at night so that I am not always alone. I would also like to be taken out on a date every once in a while, but I can't because my husband works seven nights a week."

"Is that what your problem has been these past few weeks? You want to go out more? If that will get you to chill out, go get dressed. There has to be something open this late. Tomorrow is Saturday and you don't have to work, so let's go."

"I don't want to go anywhere with you acting like this."

"Acting like what? I just got home from a bad night at work, but if you want to go out, let's go. Now go get dressed."

Alicia hesitated for a moment, then hastily grabbed her purse off of the couch and dashed past him, "Fine!"

Marlon waited for her to get dressed. *I should have let her sleep on the couch.* He had long outgrown the club scene. The loud music, crowded, confined space, and rubbing up against strangers no longer appealed to him. Marlon nodded off while he waited for Alicia. He fought to stay awake, but his eyelids had grown too heavy.

"I knew we weren't going anywhere." Alicia tossed her purse on the couch and flopped down next to it. The sight of him sleeping deeply irritated her. She had actually gotten excited about going out, but as quickly as the good mood had came, it left.

"No, I'm up. Let's go." Marlon jumped up and led the way to the door and Alicia hesitantly followed.

Marlon bought an energy drink at a gas station before they got to the club. He hopped back in the car, popped the top, and guzzled it down. She watched him out the corner of her eye, *how can a man younger than me, act so old?* He was always tired, always concerned about money, never took a day off, and rarely did anything exciting or spontaneous. Alicia had made up her mind; she was going to enjoy life with or without her husband.

They stepped into the club and the music thumped so loud that no conversations could be heard. It instantly gave Marlon a headache. It was the same pathetic scene he had once loved. Women were dressed to tease and men were eager to please. No reality, just false promises and misrepresented intentions. All around the room, cleavage hung out and there was always a keen eye available to ogle it. Grown men gawked as women dropped it on the danced floor—mesmerized and salivating like they'd never seen beautiful women before. Marlon shook his head and chuckled.

"This is sad."

He tried to ignore the look Alicia flashed him when he complained about the noise, but couldn't. "Why do you want me to take you out if you can't stand me?"

"Marlon, don't start. Let's just have a good time. Will you buy me a drink?"

"A drink? When did you start drinking?" He couldn't believe it. They didn't drink, or at least he didn't.

"I will buy my own drink." There are a lot of things I do that you don't know about," she said, walking away. She smiled with satisfaction as his face drew up like a withered crop.

Marlon tried to grab her before she walked away, but she had jumped behind someone and he didn't want to make a scene. They'd just arrived at the club and in less than ten minutes, he was seeing a different side to Alicia that pissed him off. He was a good Christian man and was determined to live a life that pleased God. Although they had no children, he still expected her to live right. Now she was drinking and doing God knows what else. He watched as she swayed her hips into the crowd.

Alicia ordered a double shot of tequila, downed it, and then gyrated her way back to the dance floor. A strange man slid his arm around her waist and whispered in her ear.

"I've seen you here before and I told myself the next time I saw you, I would holler at you. Will you dance with me?" Alicia's eyes roamed the length of his body, quickly assessing his financial worth. Bling on each hand, diamonds on his ears, very well-groomed, high-end wardrobe, and muscles cut to perfection. *Very nice*, she thought. Alicia was totally in her element as they stepped onto the dance floor to a slow tempo jam. She leaned her back suggestively against his chest.

Unbeknownst to her husband, she'd been frequenting the night club scene. The first time she'd gone, it was for a bachelorette party of an old friend. Like Marlon, Alicia couldn't stand the noise, but all the attention she received from men had made it worthwhile. They'd offered to buy her drinks and asked her to dance. At first, she simply flashed her wedding ring and smiled, until one guy smiled back, and asked, 'What does that have to do with me'? Then, he grabbed her hand and led her to the dance floor.

That next morning, Marlon asked if she enjoyed herself; she lied and said no. The truth was she had the best time she'd had in a long time and it worried her. She had always been known as a good Christian woman. She was faithful to church, payed her tithes, fasted often, and prayed every day. It made Alicia uneasy to be enjoying a place forbidden by her faith. Alicia had every intention of not returning, but the lonely nights were getting the best of her and she found herself back at the club behaving in an ungodly manner.

Twenty minutes had gone by and Alicia still hadn't returned. Marlon was so busy examining his life and the direction his marriage was heading that he hadn't really noticed the time. *She has been gone for a long time*, he thought while checking his watch. He finally found her on the dance floor grinding on some man. Marlon stood in the background for a minute watching.

His blood was boiling and if he approached them before he thought things through, someone was going to get hurt. Alicia was suggestively grinding her butt against the man's crotch. Marlon was seething and veins nearly protruded from his temples. Alicia leaned her head against the man's chest, now totally cradled in his embrace. Marlon had seen enough. He flung his keys out of his pocket and approached her on the dance floor. Alicia snapped away from the man and froze as Marlon headed her way. She was terrified, but to her surprise, Marlon simply gave her a hug and yelled over the music.

"Why cry about me taking you out and when I finally do you spend the night dancing with someone else? I am not going to compete with another man for my wife's attention. I don't know what kind of game you are playing, but you better decide if want to lose your marriage over it before I make the decision for you." He placed the keys in the palm of her hand and whispered through clenched teeth, "Drive yourself home, I will find my own way." Marlon stormed out of nightclub.

"Marlon relax," Alicia said, trying to follow behind him. Unfortunately, the stride of his long legs was too much for her; she had to run to keep up. "I was just dancing, why are you so upset?"

Marlon ignored her and marched on, despite her protests. Alicia watched in disbelief.

"No he didn't just walk off like that," she mumbled. There were people standing around watching and she was embarrassed that he'd ignored her in front of them.

Alicia strutted back into the club, determined to teach him a lesson. Alicia downed two shots she'd ordered from the bar and quickly headed to the dance floor. As the alcohol surged through her, she loosened up. Moments later, she was dancing seductively by herself. The rhythm of each song flowed through her body and she gyrated her curves the best she knew how.

Then, a beautiful woman approached her. They were complete opposites. Alicia was shorter with a creamy, light-brown complexion, curly golden-brown hair with voluptuous curves to match. This woman had long, silky black hair, was tall and slender, and had deep brown skin. The woman slid her hands around Alicia's waist and pulled her close. Alicia was startled by her aggression, but went with the flow. The woman matched the sway of Alicia's body and they danced seductively against each other. Suddenly, the woman aggressively slid her tongue into Alicia's mouth and she stopped dancing to savor the kiss. She returned the oral exchange until it occurred to her that it was another woman who was arousing her. She staggered backwards, confused as to how a woman could have such an effect on her. Alicia abruptly left the dance floor in search of the man she was dancing with before Marlon had interrupted. She found him at the bar with a drink in hand. Alicia stepped into the space between his legs, rubbed her hands across his chest, and pressed her chest against him.

"So, are we going to pick up where we left off?" She purred against his ear.

"I don't know, ma, you seem to have a little drama in your life." He grinned as he lifted his drink to his lips. His bad boy swagger and deep raspy voice enticed her dark side.

"Well, he is gone now and I just want to have some fun." She returned his naughty grin and leaned in to nuzzle her face against his neck. Her whinny purrs against his neck quickly persuaded him to oblige. He roamed up and down her thigh, then firmly gripped her backside.

"If you really want to have fun, come with me." His kisses silenced the still voice telling her to go home to her husband.

The thumping of the music, the shots of tequila, and this man's sex appeal were all spellbinding. An intoxicated sigh escaped Alicia's lips, "Lead the way."

He led her outside to his Escalade. When he hopped into the backseat, Alicia hesitated. She looked around at all the people standing outside.

"Is this all I am good for, a quick screw in the backseat of your car, at the club? My car is right over there. Why don't I follow you back to your place?"

"We could do that, but you said you wanted to have fun. Fun is spontaneous and in the moment. Hop in, I promise you won't be disappointed."

Alicia cautiously accepted his extended hand and stepped up into his truck. She quietly sat and allowed him to remove her clothes. Her mind was running wild. One second she thought, *stop, don't do this; you are married*. The next was, *forget Marlon; he walked out on you*. Alicia dishonored the man she had vowed to love till death in the back seat of a stranger's Escalade. The sex was so impersonal and unemotional—the complete opposite of what she had experienced with Marlon.

This high-energy romp was full of excitement and fear. The noise of people nearby was stimulating. The windows were fogged up, so no one could see in or out. Alicia's raw animalistic instinct—one she didn't know she possessed, had taken over as she took the lead. Thoughts of the woman she danced with floated through her mind, making her even more curious. She closed her eyes to remember their encounter and allowed her imagination to run wild. When her body released its essence, she sat dazed and confused while her heart struggled for understanding.

Alicia threw her clothes on, dramatically ran to her car, and sped off. She didn't want to exchange numbers or even names for that matter. She just needed to get away to think. The reality of what had taken place hit Alicia as she drove home. She was shocked at the rush of excitement she'd received by being with a perfect stranger. She was taught that a woman was to be reserved and docile in the bedroom. That is what she gave Marlon and whenever he attempted to spice it up a bit, she would quickly shut him down. The first few times he had complained, but he eventually accepted it for what it was. And now, she'd had sex at the club, in a car, with a strange man, while fantasying about a woman.

The mere thought of that night's experiences sent waves of emotion throughout her mind and body. At one point on the way home, she'd gotten so consumed in thought, she sat at a green light while people honked behind her. Not once did she regret betraying her husband or the Lord. Her heart had already been so far removed that she had no will to resist temptation. Satan had set the trap, and Alicia walked right in with eyes wide open.

Alicia tiptoed into her house, trying not to make a sound. She didn't want to wake Marlon. She wasn't up for another argument. She just wanted to shower, crawl into bed, and sleep all day. She slowly opened their bedroom door and surprisingly, the bed was still made. Marlon was nowhere to be found. She stomped around the house searching every room for him, neglecting her own betrayal just minutes ago. *How dare he not be home*, she thought, as she headed toward the last bedroom.

Alicia barged through the door and there he lay asleep. She quietly backed out of the room; however, Marlon wasn't sleep. He called her name before she could close the door. A lump formed in her throat, robbing her body of the oxygen needed to speak. She tried to swallow it and nearly chocked in the process. Alicia stepped back in to the room coughing. Marlon sat up, looked at the clock, and shook his head. It was 2:00a.m., and she was just now creeping into the house.

"Come here. We need to talk."

"Marlon, I am tired; can we do this in the morning?" She froze. The scent of another man was on her skin. One whiff and Marlon would go ballistic.

"What I have to say won't take long." He had been going over his speech since he left the club and knew he wouldn't be able to sleep until he got it out. "I am a man of God first and foremost and that is how I choose to live my life. If you are choosing to turn your back on the Lord, that is your choice and does not affect how I love you. I will stand by your side and help you through this, but what I saw on the dance floor was more than a woman having a good time. I want to be absolutely clear: if you step out on me, I am gone."

"You're clear." She shut the door and dashed to the shower, praying Marlon didn't follow her. Her heart raced as she fumbled to turn on the water. She hopped into the shower after frantically undressing. The hot water finally ran across her body, and she sighed with relief. She had to get the smell of the night's events off of her. She enjoyed herself and was also unhappy with her marriage, but wasn't sure if she was ready to give up on it.

Marlon slid straight out of bed to his knees. Alicia's behavior was becoming intolerable and the only thing he could do was pray. Everything about her seemed different—the way she talked, dressed, even her attitude. It had all changed.

2

During the next few weeks, Marlon and Alicia barely spoke to each other. He finally came to the conclusion that Alicia had been sneaking off to the club and couldn't help but wonder what else she was doing. Marlon began waking up to have a cup of coffee with her before she went to work. He was determined to salvage their marriage. He would prepare coffee and a light breakfast while she showered, but she refused it every time. He even started calling her at least once during the night while he was at work, but when he called she was curt and rude. She'd answer the phone saying, 'What do you want'? Alicia saw all his efforts, but wasn't fazed by them. *Too little too late*, she thought. His gestures were more aggravating than comforting and she wished he'd just leave her alone.

Alicia couldn't shake the woman she had danced with that night and even went to a gay club a few times hoping to run into her. The soft kiss and gentle caress vividly invaded her mind and sent her emotions racing. Even her dreams were haunted by this woman's touch. One night, she woke up so besot with sexual desire that she woke Marlon and gave him everything she dreamed of giving that woman. He was so surprised at her forwardness and so thrilled she wanted him, he didn't notice how emotionally detached she was. That night was the first time she had ever initiated sex during their marriage and Marlon waited for the next time so he could give her everything he'd been holding back.

Marlon surprised Alicia by taking a night off from work. It was the middle of the week and he wanted to take her to one of the finest restaurants in the city. He was beginning to make a name for himself in the restaurant community and didn't need to make reservations months in advance. He could simply call a few hours ahead of time to notify them that he needed a table.

He spent that entire morning shopping for an outfit she could wear to dinner. She had a classy, but sexy style. Choosing the right outfit would take time. Marlon looked through endless racks of clothes, and eventually found the perfect little black dress. Next, he bought the perfect pair of shoes and picked up a little something for himself before heading home. He anxiously waited for

Alicia to come home and prayed all his efforts would pay off. He was hoping she would welcome his embrace and end the days of silence. One thing was certain: that night was crucial—either they'd work everything out or he was done trying.

He'd drawn her bath, laid her new dress out along with two dozen roses, and nervously went over his speech as he waited for her to arrive. The front door opened and he stood to greet her. Their eyes met and Alicia let out a deep sigh.

"What are you doing here?"

"I don't want to live like this." He was determined not to let her negativity sway him and timidly made his way toward her. "I still love you and want our marriage to work, but it is going to take work from both of us. I took the night off to take you out. I see how I was wrong in not doing so in the past. I was being inconsiderate; please forgive me."

Alicia walked away without responding and Marlon followed her into the bedroom. Her eyes scanned the bed and Marlon waited for her reaction, but there was nothing. His heart sank into his stomach, but he was still focused on reconciling.

"Will you go to dinner with me?"

Alicia saw the dress and flowers on the bed and they did not phase her one bit. With a cynical grin, she turned and gave him the same response he had given her many times. "I just got home from work and I am tired, maybe some other time."

A smile spread across her face as she rejected him. Seeing the pleasure she received from denying him was infuriating. Marlon stormed into the bathroom and slammed the door. He didn't know what she hoped to accomplish by playing these games, but his ego was hurt. He vowed to leave the situation in the Lord's hands and stop chasing behind her.

Alicia had previous plans that evening and was furious that she would have to cancel, but practically leaped for joy when Marlon came out of the bedroom dressed for work and walked out of the house. She listened for his car to start, then immediately called her date back.

She bathed in the water Marlon had drawn and put on the dress he'd bought. Then, Alicia grabbed the roses and headed out the door. She was having fun playing Marlon for a fool. Her victim had been reluctant in the past to fulfill her desires, but Alicia had a plan to have her desires fulfilled.

Marlon walked into work fuming. He was so pissed that he didn't speak to anyone. He inspected every chef's work station, hoping for something to be out of place so he'd have just cause to gripe, but everything was in order. Everyone expected him to be out for the night, but by the look on his face, they knew something had gone wrong. He was a time bomb waiting to explode. If anyone dared to speak, he was going to tear them apart. The walk to his office seemed to take forever. He could see all the chefs avoiding eye contact as he walked by and knew he'd soon be the talk of the kitchen. Marlon plopped down in his office chair. A lump formed in his throat and tears singed the corners of his eyes, but he refused to let them fall. Over the past few days, he had feared his marriage was over, but somehow had convinced himself there was still hope. After tonight, he wasn't too sure if they would be together much longer. Although he'd spoken the words, he couldn't honestly say he still loved her. Divorce was forbidden in the church and that alone was the reason he came home every day.

Meanwhile, Alicia waited in a parking lot for her date to arrive. Tonight was actually their first date outside of the house. They had bumped into each other at one of the clubs she visited while in pursuit of answers to her budding curiosity. The Golden Stone catered to gays and lesbians, and Alicia hoped to figure out why she couldn't get over a simple kiss. About two weeks prior, curiosity had driven Alicia there. Meme, on the other hand, had been living on the down low for a year.

Alicia was so embarrassed that someone she knew had actually seen her in such a place that she didn't ask why Meme was there. She simply turned around and walked right out the door. About ten minutes after getting home, the doorbell rang. It was Meme wanting to make sure Alicia wouldn't reveal her secret and promised secrecy in return.

They conversed for hours, more than they had ever talked since meeting years ago. When it was time to leave, Alicia leaned in to kiss her goodbye, but Meme pulled away.

"I don't do married women.

We can be friends and hang out, but nothing like that will ever go down between us." Alicia felt foolish, but agreed. Meme had to admit, the chemistry between them was amazing, but she wasn't a home wrecker.

After days of hanging out, watching movies, talking, laughing, and long moments of awkward silence and staring in each other's eyes, Alicia once again made her move. Her kiss was hesitantly received and returned. It was only the second woman Alicia kissed, but it didn't take her long to realize a woman's kiss was gentle and more sincere than a man's could ever be. Meme taught Alicia how to kiss all over again and with each sample of Alicia's lips; she was drawn further under a spell.

Meme told herself that Alicia was off limits and after their kiss she tried to stay away, but Alicia had gotten into her system. She only lasted two days before calling to arrange a date. The chance of Meme's family finding out about her secret life style was much greater when dating someone they knew, but Alicia was worth the risk.

It was dark and cold out and the wind sent chills throughout Alicia's body as she stood outside her car. Common sense told her to wait inside the car, but jittery nerves had her out pacing around. If tonight turned out the way she hoped, her life would never be the same. She was about to cross a line from which most marriages never recover. The moral voices within her conscience had long been silenced and she was now being fully led by sexual desire.

Alicia's heart raced with excitement as she watched the black Nissan Maxima pull into the parking lot. Meme's long slender legs stepped out of the car and Alicia rushed over to give her the roses. Meme grinned when she saw Alicia approaching. She accepted the flowers and offered a kiss to say thank you.

"I missed you so much," Alicia mumbled through their kiss.

Meme leaned into Alicia, pressing their bodies together. She used her hands to discover Alicia's curves while their lips connected. Their tongues cautiously introduced themselves, and when a soft moan escaped Alicia's mouth, Meme deepened their kiss. They took their time kissing and enjoying each other. Cold air swirled around them, but the intense fire heated every inch of their bodies. Reluctantly, they separated—chests heaving and emotions spinning out of control.

Meme rested her head on Alicia's. "Alicia, we have to talk. I do not want to be the reason your marriage breaks up. Honestly, I don't want to be involved with you. I shouldn't be involved with you, but I can't stop thinking about you." She grabbed Alicia by the hand and led her into the club so they could get out of the cold. "I want you to be sure you know what you are getting into. This lifestyle is not a cake walk. If your family and friends find out, they will turn on you. Marlon will leave you. Are you ready to accept that?"

Marlon leaving didn't concern her. She saw the sad, sappy expression on his face as he left for work and knew he was too much in love to go anywhere. As for family and friends, Alicia didn't plan on anyone finding out. She told herself that she wasn't a lesbian; she was just having a little fun. There was nothing wrong with having fun. Refusing to respond to the question, Alicia gripped Meme's hand a little tighter and tugged her toward the entrance.

They walked through the doors holding hands. A rush of excitement raced through Alicia in anticipation over what would transpire. She was up for anything and wasn't going to allow Meme's warning to deter her pursuit of pleasure. They headed toward the section deemed for couples. Off to the right of the dance floor, there was a cozy corner with tables, chairs, and a few love seats. It was a low-key spot where every man could snuggle with his special guy and every woman, her little lady. Some of the couples had defined male and female roles in the relationship, but not Meme and Alicia. They were both soft and feminine with glossed lips, polished nails, high heels, and tight skirts. The sight of them together would fulfill any man's fantasies.

"Don't worry, just about everyone in here knows the struggle of coming out of the closet and it is an unwritten rule that you don't out anyone. Our secret is safe," Meme laughed. "Most don't say anything because to tell that you saw someone at gay club you'd have to admit that you were there too."

Alicia tried to smile, but she'd been so focused on having a good time that she hadn't considered someone recognizing her and snitching. Suddenly, that tough resolve to fulfill her desires had a crack in it. Meme saw apprehension cover Alicia's face and asked her to dance before it could fully set in. She started out dancing wild and off beat which completely embarrassed Alicia. Meme jerked and wiggled her body and danced circles around Alicia. Looking around at everyone watching, Alicia couldn't help but laugh. Meme laughed right along with her; seeing Alicia loosen up was worth the momentary embarrassment. They danced wildly together until the music slowed. Meme pulled Alicia close.

"I am glad you are loosening up; I was going to take you home if you didn't."

Alicia chuckled, "You wouldn't be able to get rid of me that easily."

They danced entangled in each other's arms. A few people tried cutting in to dance with Meme, but she turned them all down. Alicia nervously watched as woman after woman walked by trying to get Meme's attention and couldn't help but wonder how many of them she had actually been with. When she asked, Meme replied, "Don't worry about them. I am with you."

"Why are you with me? It looks like you could have just about any woman in here."

Well, look at them. I want a woman, not a man. Most of them are manlier than the men I know. "When I look at my woman, I want to see her curves. When I kiss my woman, I don't want to feel the stubble of a beard." Her hands trailed up the front of Alicia's dress. "When I caress my woman I want to feel the soft swell of her breast." Her hands slid around to the back of Alicia's head. "And when I make love to my woman, I want my fingers to get lost in her long hair." Alicia was everything Meme had been searching for.

Alicia closed her eyes and enjoyed the sensation of Meme's touch. She was completely under Meme's control and would've done anything Meme asked at that point. Every erogenous zone on her body was alert; the sensation made her weak.

"Please take me home with you tonight."

"I can't…" They pressed their foreheads together and Meme paused to collect her thoughts. "We both have so much to lose by being together and I am not willing to risk it for a sexual fling. I want us to be sure this is what we want." Although frustrated, Alicia agreed.

Meme sealed her words with a kiss as they swayed to the rhythm of the music. The background noise and people around them faded. They were totally lost in each other's presence. Their hearts' sentiment was not relayed through verbal conversation, but their mouths spoke each time their lips connected. Each kiss spoke of their desire for each other. Meme usually frowned at such displays of affection on the dance floor, but she now understood. A slow dance with someone who caused your heart beat wildly made it impossible to exercise self-control. The music sped up to club tempo, but they still danced slowly with lips connected totally oblivious to the world around them until a voice shrieked behind them.

"I know that is not my girl Meme all hugged up on the dance floor," a random voice said.

Alicia turned to see who was talking and bit her lip to keep from laughing. A grown man, who looked like he'd invaded his little sister's closet, sashayed over to where they were dancing. With hand on hip and lips pursed together, he scanned Alicia from head to toe. He scrutinized her appearance just as she did his. Finally deciding Alicia had his approval; he leaned toward her and jokingly whispered. "You must really be something if you can get my girl on this dance floor." He turned and sashayed away. He then waved his hand at Meme, "Call me." His tight jeans and bad wig disappeared into the crowd. His over-the-top femininity was straight off the movie screen. Alicia couldn't believe people acted like that in real life.

As he walked away, Alicia had a better understanding of what Meme said about wanting a real woman. If a man wanted to be with a man, why be with a man trying to be a woman. She turned to ask Meme who he was, but didn't have a chance. Meme instantly smothered her with intense kisses. She held Alicia firmly against her body. Her kisses trailed down Alicia's neck, feathering across her collar bone.

Alicia placed her hands on Meme's cheeks and lifted her head to stare into her eyes. "Please, take me home with you."

"You have no idea how bad I want to, but we have to wait," Meme stepped back to put distance between them. "Let's go home before we go too far and maybe I will come over on Sunday. You have to promise that you will behave if I come over." Alicia smiled innocently as they exited the dance floor hand in hand.

Alicia made it home and was glad to see that Marlon hadn't yet made it home from work. Beating him home would prevent her from having to answer his questions. She showered and washed her hair to remove any hint of where she'd been, and then climbed into bed at the same time as Marlon's keys hit the door. Alicia lay in bed pretending to be asleep as she waited for Marlon to crawl into bed, but he never did. The flickering light from the TV glared into her room and she crept into the living room to see what he was doing. Their eyes met as she stepped further into the room. He had been flipping through the channels until he noticed her. His intense stare halted her footsteps and a nervous lump formed in her throat. The dim light of the TV made him look extremely tired and stressed and she could see the toll stress was having on him.

"Are you coming to bed?" She asked, with a hint of remorse. She was hoping to break the intensity of his gaze. Marlon examined her from head to toe. The light from the TV shined through her shear night gown revealing everything she'd been keeping from him. He knew it was a long shot, but he beckoned for her to come to him. Her compliance made him want her even more.

As she stood before him, he admired her beauty while she trembled under the intensity of his gaze. Marlon stood and removed his shirt. He didn't want there to be any confusion as to what he wanted. He stood in front of her, silently giving her one last chance to deny him. When she said nothing, he laid her on the couch and pursued his desire.

Alicia planned to just let Marlon get what he needed to ease her conscience, but Marlon knew how to arouse her. Before long, Alicia squirmed beneath him with desire. She tried to control herself, but Marlon wasn't having it. Marlon made love to his wife in ways she'd never allowed and she enjoyed every minute of it. The moans of pleasure escaping her lips were music to his ears. His name breathlessly rolling off her lips stroked his wounded ego.

"I am your husband and don't you ever forget it," he scolded her. Her nails scratching his back and the outcry of his name intensified their pleasure. Marlon tried to look into her eyes to gauge her true feelings, but they were closed. He laid perfectly still waiting for her reaction. When he saw her breathing slow and realized she was falling asleep, a satisfied grin spread across his face. He adjusted his weight so he wouldn't hurt her and for the first time in weeks they slept in each other's arms.

Morning came and with it came clarity. Alicia looked at the man lying next to her and felt foolish for betraying him. He was better to her than anyone had ever been. He was faithful, hardworking, and most of all he loved her. *You are a fool*, she thought. *You have to fix this.* She made up in her mind that when Meme came over tomorrow she would end the games. But, as for right now she was going to enjoy the man lying next to her.

Alicia filled their oversized garden bathtub, added some bubbles, and lit a few candles. Since the bathroom had no windows, it was as dark as night when the door was shut. She brushed her teeth, put on a little lip gloss, and went to wake Marlon. She nearly jumped out of her skin as she exited the bathroom. Marlon was standing right outside the door.

"I'm sorry." He didn't mean to sneak up on her, but he was curious about what she was up to. He had hoped their encounter last night had changed some things, but by the looks of it, it hadn't. She was trying to bathe and get dressed before he woke up. Before he could ask any questions, Alicia grabbed his hands and led him into the bathroom. Marlon laughed at himself when he realized it wasn't what he had suspected. He helped her into the tub and followed behind her. Marlon sat in the hot water and cradled Alicia between his legs. Alicia nestled back into his chest, savoring their embrace.

There had been so much distance between them these past few weeks that Marlon readily accepted the closeness. He tried to stay positive and was hoping that the change would last, but in the back of his mind, he knew something wasn't right. Less than twenty-four hours ago, she had joyously smirked at denying him and was now giving herself to him without reserve. He hoped for the best, but instinct told him not to get too comfortable.

<u>3</u>

Alicia sat nervously on the couch waiting for Meme to arrive. She had told Marlon she wasn't feeling well and convinced him to go to church alone.

She had to end things with Meme as soon as possible. She rehearsed over and over again what she was going to say. Their little fling had to end. If they continued, too many people would be hurt. She planned to break things off with Meme, and then clear the air with Marlon when he returned from church. The things she had to confess could destroy their marriage, but she couldn't move forward with lies looming over her.

The doorbell rang and Alicia's heart practically stopped. "Come on you can do this," she mumbled to herself, as she walked to the door. She opened the door and the sight of Meme took her breath away. The parts of Meme she had grown to appreciate were enhanced by a tight tank top. The skirt she wore stopped just below the crease of her butt which made her long, trim legs look even longer. Alicia stood dumbfounded and her speech went right out the window; lust had taken over.

The things Alicia had opened herself up to would take more than just a change of heart to get over. Her parents had told her that time and time again, but now she was learning it the hard way. Her new found appreciation for the beauty of the female body was going to make this conversation a little more difficult.

Alicia took a deep breath and stepped aside, allowing Meme to enter. She was persistent on keeping control. Meme seductively smiled and stepped past Alicia and gave a playful pull to the belt of her bath robe. Alicia grabbed the robe before it slid open. Meme was in the mood to play. She had decided that if Alicia made the same proposition she did Friday night, it would not be turned down.

Alicia attempted to collect her thoughts. Meme's heart instantly sank as the dreaded words, "We need to talk," rolled out of Alicia's mouth.

Alicia led her to the couch, but before she could even speak, Meme was all over her. Meme was intent on using passion to deter Alicia's news. They kissed and caressed passionately. Meme slid her hand between Alicia's thighs, trying to reach the spot that would change Alicia's mind.

Alicia shot to her feet and pleaded, "We have to stop. We can't do this." There it was: the words were out there. Silence seemed to suck the oxygen out of the room. Meme dropped her head and forced herself to breath.

"That's what I said weeks ago, but you kept coming on to me," she said, frantically. "Now that I am in love with you, you're pushing me away. Please don't do this to me."

Love, when did love get involved? Alicia thought.

"I'm sorry, but I have a good life, and a good husband who doesn't deserve this. You of all people should understand that." Alicia paused, backed toward her bedroom, and then pointed toward the front door. "Please leave and lock the door on your way out." She disappeared into her room, leaving Meme speechless sitting on the couch.

Meme hesitated, then followed Alicia into her room and shut the door behind her. Before Alicia could respond, Meme rushed her, knocking her onto the bed in the process. She ripped through Alicia's robe and passionately kissed each breast as if her life depended on it. Alicia bucked and squirmed for freedom, but Meme was a woman on a mission. "Let me make love to you," Meme pleaded. "And, afterwards, if you still want me to leave you alone, I will."

Alicia was losing the fight and there was only so much one's willpower could withstand. Her spirit was willing, but the flesh was weak and at that moment, every ounce of her flesh wanted Meme. The tension left her body, and Alicia sighed in submission. Meme removed her clothes and slipped under the sheets. She worked all that she knew to do hoping it was enough to win Alicia's heart. Meme's aggression slowly foiled into tenderness, which helped Alicia relax.

"You are so beautiful," Meme whispered, as she stared deep into Alicia's eyes. Meme trailed Alicia's body slowly, making sure to savor every inch of flesh she kissed. She wanted to make the most of her last chance to hold Alicia.

Alicia was subdued with pleasure and couldn't believe how well Meme knew her body. Every man she had ever been with, including her husband, took weeks—sometimes even months to properly ignite her body. Meme knew exactly where to kiss and where to put her hands. She also knew the amount of pressure to apply. She knew when to lick and when to bite. Alicia gripped the sheets and pulled them around her face hoping to muffle the euphoric shrills coming from her mouth. Alicia laid there trying to wrap her mind around what she was experiencing. She tried to focus, but with Meme, it was virtually impossible. It would be an hour before Marlon returned, so she abandoned logical thinking to do things she never imagined.

Marlon couldn't shake the guilt he felt for being at church while Alicia was sick. He decided to stop at a local diner and buy her a bowl of her favorite, split pea soup. He was certain she'd appreciate this gesture. He flew home and in a moment's time, was at his bedroom door ready to surprise his life. He heard noises of nasal congestion which again jilted his conscience for abandoning a sick wife. Marlon's heart rate came to a standstill at the scene he beheld when he walked in. He quickly jilted the door shut, insisting he was seeing things. After a few desperate breaths, he gripped the doorknob and turned it slightly— convincing himself he needed to look again to be sure. He peeked through the crack in the door and sure enough his sick wife was tussling under the covers like a professional wrestler.

"Alicia!" He roared as loud as he could. The baritone of his voice echoed through the room and the movement under the covers ceased. "What is going on?"

Her inability to respond confirmed in his heart his worst fear had become reality. Rage surged through him and he stormed toward the bed. As he reached out to grab her, fear on her face stopped him. He spun away from her, picked up perfume bottles off the dresser, and hurled them at the wall. Sweat poured from his body and veins bulged on his temples as the room spun in circles while he violently threw punches to the air. Marlon marched toward the door, and with every ounce of strength within, punched a hole in the wall before walking out.

Tears saturated Alicia's face as she watched Marlon stomp around in a rage. She had never seen him so angry and wanted to grab him and plead for his forgiveness, but fear immobilized her. Her entire being flinched when he punched the hole in the wall. Drops of blood ran down the wall and she knew he'd hurt himself. Alicia grabbed her robe off the floor and chased after her husband. Marlon was moving so fast, by the time Alicia got to the door he was already in his car. Alicia ran toward the car as fast as she could, but Marlon screeched off before she reached him.

Alicia cried hysterically, pounding her fists into the grass which now stained her terrycloth robe. She didn't care who saw her nor what her neighbors might've thought. Her only concern was the man she loved and the marriage she had now ruined.

Meme had gotten dressed and stood in the doorway telling Alicia to come into the house. For a while, she watched Alicia with regret. Her selfish actions had hurt the people that she cared about. When her phone rang she answered, trying to hold back the barrage of emotions she was feeling. She managed to have a level-headed conversation and when she hung up, she went to bring Alicia into the house. Placing one arm around Alicia's waist, Meme tried to help her to her feet, but Alicia pushed her away

"Get away from me. This is your fault. Why couldn't you just leave when I asked you to?" Alicia tried to run into the house, but Meme was right on her heels and jumped into the house before Alicia could shut her out.

"Get out!" Alicia wildly screamed, as she lunged toward Meme pulling her hand back to slap her across the face. Meme tumbled to the ground while clutching the side of her face. Alicia dropped to the floor next to Meme to caress her cheek, but Meme grabbed her hand and pushed it away

"I am fine."

Meme stood to her feet and helped Alicia to her feet while they both were wiping tears. "I know you are upset, but you need to take some responsibility for this mess and stop putting it all on me. We don't have time to fight each other. You need to figure out what you are going to do." They tried to come up with an explanation, but Alicia was an emotional wreck. Meme didn't want to be the cause of a marriage being destroyed, but couldn't fight the excitement she felt over the possibility that Alicia could soon be hers.

Marlon weaved erratically in and out of traffic while speeding down the street. He flew through two red lights before realizing how fast he was driving. He pulled into a shopping center parking lot and took out his cell phone. He needed to talk to his sister. She was always the voice of reason and helped him to remain calm and make wise decisions. She was the only one who could help him think straight when he was this upset. Tears filled his eyes as he waited for her to answer, but he refused to let them fall. The phone seemed to ring forever before she answered.

"Hey Marlon, what's up?"

"Where are you? I need you."

"What's going on?"

"You will never believe what just happened! I just walked in on Alicia in bed with someone else. Can you believe that?" It was becoming harder and harder to hold his tears back. "We stood before God and vowed to love, honor, and cherish each other. Yeah, I know things have not been perfect between us, but she could at least be woman enough to ask for a divorce instead of cheating." Marlon was now yelling into the phone. His temper was rising and he wanted to destroy everything in sight.

"So, what are you going to do?" She was a bit taken back by the tone of his voice. She had seen her brother angry before, but what she felt coming through the phone scared her.

"I don't know, but I can't believe I left before finding out who she was in bed with. That little punk was just hiding under the sheet; too scared to come out. I should go back over there and find out who he is. Yep that is exactly what I am going to do." Marlon popped his car into reverse and sped out of the parking lot.

"No!" She yelled into the phone, "You are upset, and if you go over there, it is not going to end well for anyone. Go to mom's house and I will go to your place to get you some clothes. Being at mom's will give you time to think. Now calm down and drive safely. I will meet you there later." She hung up the phone before he could respond.

Marlon was speeding toward his house when he looked down and saw blood dripping from his knuckles. The sight of blood made him recognize how much pain he was in and he pulled over to tend to his wounds. He rested his head on the steering wheel he reached into the glove box for napkins. Marlon continued to rack his brain for a sign of when things went wrong as he dabbed blood from his hands. *He gave her exactly what she wanted in the bedroom, so what would make her cheat on him? Had she been faking it? How long had she been cheating? Is she cheating with someone I know*? Unanswered questions flooded his mind.

After driving around for a while, Marlon made his way to Jaleel's house. His hand was throbbing and he realized that going home to feud with some man wasn't wise. He thought maybe a man's point of view would help him see things a little clearer. Jaleel, his cousin who was more like a brother had been married for a while and had made it through some rough times; surely he could help. As he stood on the porch waiting for someone to answer the door, Marlon tried to encourage himself, but every scripture he remembered was overshadowed by the image of his wife making love to someone else. Although he hadn't seen the person, his mind played tricks on him and he had a vivid image of Alicia with some muscle-bound steroid using man tangled between the sheets.

Marlon flashed a phony grin as Jaleel opened the door. Jaleel had company and Marlon wanted to leave, but the only other place he could go was his mother's and he wasn't ready to deal with her. Marlon tried to hide turmoil with smiles and pleasantries as he greeted everyone, but they all saw right through him.

Delisa watched Marlon while everyone else continued their meal. "Marlon, you are more than welcome to pull up a chair and join us."

"Thanks, but I'm not hungry." Marlon leaned against the counter and patiently waited for them to finish.

"So," Jaleel chose his words carefully. "Didn't you leave church early to check on Alicia? Is she feeling better?"

"She is at home…" Marlon's voice cracked and all his emotions rushed to the surface. His eyes flooded with the tears he could no longer suppress. He turned his back toward everyone and unsuccessfully tried to pull his self together. He firmly gripped the sink to quell the tears from falling, but they poured down his face like a waterfall. He felt a rub across his back and turned to hide his face, but Sheena was persistent. She grabbed his shoulders and turned him toward her.

"Marlon, you came here for a reason; now talk to us. We can't help you if you don't talk." Sheena dried his face with a napkin and grabbed his hand to escort him to an empty seat, but when her hand tightened around his knuckles Marlon flinched and snatched his hand back.

"What happened?" Sheena asked, looking down at his hand.

"I punched the wall." Marlon grumbled, as he made his way to the table.

Marlon cleaned his face and gathered his thoughts while everyone sat quiet, yet concerned. He looked around at Paul and Sheena who had been married for almost as long as him. They still looked happy and more in love than he and Alicia ever did. Then there was Tim and Camilla, who loved each other before they really knew each other. Finally there was Jaleel and Delisa, who loved each other enough to overcome every obstacle that had stood before them. Camilla and Delisa were sisters and Sheena was their cousin; they were all beautiful amazing women who took pride in tending to their husbands. Paul and Tim were brothers who were confirmed bachelors until they met their wives and still managed to give more of their heart to their wives than he ever considered giving Alicia. How could they get it so right while he had it so wrong? What did they do to keep their women faithful?

Marlon forced himself to talk after taking a deep breath. He told them about the lie Alicia had given him before he left for church and how he had sat through service feeling bad for leaving her alone. He explained what he saw, how he reacted, and how she just sat there without offering any explanation. He explained why his knuckles were swollen and gladly accepted the ice pack Delisa offered. Then, he finished with all his questions, insecurities, and self-doubt.

When he finished talking, the table was silent. No one spoke and no one moved. Each one waited for the other to respond.

"So, you just left?" Tim finally spoke up. Finding your wife cheating is the ultimate blow to the male ego and Tim did not think he would have handled it that well. "I don't want to minimize what you're going through, but if it were me I would still be over there wrecking shop." Paul and Jaleel nodded in agreement.

"Marlon, I am so sorry you have to go through this." Delisa reached across the table to grab his hands as she kicked her husband under the table for not speaking up. "If there is anything we can do to help, let us know. If you want to stay here for awhile, so you can get your head together, you can."

"Thanks, I might just…" Marlon paused when April and Candice came into the room.

April was Sheena's little sister and Candice was Paul and Tim's little sister. Together, the two of them brought a whole new meaning to the term party girl. Every weekend they did it big. To be young, drop dead gorgeous and arrogant was a deadly combination.

"Um, it ought to be illegal for one room to be full of so many fine men," April chuckled, as she walked into the kitchen.

"That is disgusting; these men are family." Candice slapped her across the shoulder.

"No, Paul is my sister's husband. Tim and Jaleel are married to my cousins, which makes them unavailable, but it doesn't make me blind. I would give Marlon a run for his money if he wasn't married."

"April!" They all yelled in unison.

"What?"

"You guys it is okay. I am going to head out to my mom's. She is waiting on me. You all have a good evening and I will lock myself out," Marlon said, trying to ignore the prick April's words left in his heart.

Sheena waited until she heard the front door close, "April you really need to learn how to control your mouth. You can't just say any and everything that comes to your mind."

"I was just messing around. I was not trying to upset anyone. Is Marlon alright or should I run out and apologize?"

"No, he will be alright; he's just had a rough morning."

"Didn't he go to church this morning? How rough could it have been?" April chuckled.

Everyone had been trying to get her back into church, but she was young, having fun, and felt the Christian lifestyle was too boring.

"Don't worry about if he went to church. Why weren't you at church?"

"Oh Lord," April sighed, and rolled her eyes "I am not about to have this discussion. Candice, I told you it was a bad idea to eat with them on a Sunday. Call me later." She rolled her eyes as she stormed out of the house.

After driving around for awhile, Marlon finally made it to his mom's house. He pulled his car up to the curb behind his sister's car and saw the awesomeness of God in the sky. The sun had moved across the sky, leaving trails of orange streaked clouds. He sighed and whispered to the Lord as he stepped out of the car. "What did I do to deserve this?"

Marlon's mother, Gloria, met him at the front door. As he stepped onto the porch she flung her arms around him. "Where have you been? Your sister called hours ago telling me what happened. I have been worried sick. Are you alright?"

"It's all good; I just had to clear my head."

"Boy, don't give me that macho attitude. I am your mother and I know you are hurting. You loved that girl."

Marlon shot his mother a disturbed look and walked past her into the house. He did not like to burden her with his problems and made a mental note to say something to his sister about telling his business. Marlon tried to ignore his mother's probing eyes as he searched for food in the kitchen.

Gloria watched her son sulk around the house. His shoulders hung so low it appeared he was bearing the weight of world. He was a proud man and she had raised him to be such and he usually handled his own problems. She could see the pain and anger in his eyes and desperately wanted to help him. Gloria tried to signal his sister to get her to talk to him, but she was keeping her distance from him, which was unusual. She had been sitting quietly on the couch trying to avoid making eye contact. Although Gloria wanted her to help her brother, she totally understood why she was avoiding him. He was a handful when he was angry and would lash out at anyone in his path.

"So, this is what's up." Marlon saw his mother trying to force his sister to talk to him. He was not in the mood for her interfering and was going to stop it before it began. "I am going to stay here tonight. If Alicia calls, I don't want to talk to her. I don't want to talk about what happened, so don't ask me a whole bunch of questions, understood?" Marlon looked them in the eye and waited for them to nod in agreement. "Good, I am going to bed." He stormed out of the room before they could say anything.

Marlon checked his cell phone and angrily slammed it on the bed. Alicia still hadn't called. He felt she should have been blowing up his phone with apologies. Marlon lay back, pulled the pillow over his head, and tried to get some sleep. *Maybe I should've gone to work, at least my mind would be occupied.* He tossed and turned for what seemed like hours. Then, he slid out of bed and dropped to his knees. He kneeled in silence for a few minutes. He didn't know what to say to the Lord. What he wanted to say was, 'Lord, take Alicia out for doing me like this'. But instead, he spoke what he knew was proper. "Father, humbly I come to you. You are all-knowing and all-seeing. I know you see the situation I am in right know and I know you have a purpose for allowing me to experience this test. I ask that you help me endure and keep me in my right frame of mind until you see fit to bring me out." His words were not heartfelt and were void of conviction. This was the most emotionally frustrating draining day of his life. He was determined to leave all of his rage at the feet of the father. If it took all night, he was prepared to do so.

As he prayed, he heard a soft voice whisper. "Marlon?"

"What are you doing here?"

"We need to talk, don't you think?" She slowly made her way toward him. "I was waiting for you to come home and when you didn't I went looking for you."

"You should not be here right now, leave!" The very sight of her heightened every emotion he was on his knees praying against. His head was pounding, his palms sweating, and his breathing deep and labored.

"Marlon please, I am sorry." Alicia moved closer and reached out to stroke his arm. "I was not expecting you home so early…"

"What do you mean not expecting me home so early?" He jumped into her face, eyes bulging with rage. Spit landed on her face as he barked and yelled. With every word he spoke, his balled fist jabbed in her face. Alicia shook with fear. Marlon matched every step she took. It looked as though they were connected at the hip. No matter where she went or how she moved, Marlon was all over her. Alicia stumbled against the dresser. There was no way of escape. Marlon's six-foot frame towered over her.

"How about you shouldn't have been cheating in the first place? I don't know what made you think you could come over here to apologize and everything would be all right. I don't want to see you, I don't want to talk to you, and you have about five seconds to get out of my face or I am going to choke you." Marlon immediately grabbed her by the arm, slung her out of the room, and slammed the door shut with such force the house shook.

The room was spinning, and Marlon's heart raced. "How dare she come here? How dare she cheat on me? I was good to her. I gave her everything and this is how she repays me. She better hope I don't find out who this punk is. Nope, he better hope I don't find out who he is. How is he going to disrespect me like that by sleeping with my wife in my bed?" Marlon continued in his tirade not noticing that his sister had entered the room.

"Marlon…"

"What!" Marlon spun around and yelled so loud that she flinched and left the room. She was his soft spot and would never hurt her. She had been there for him more times than he could count. Marlon ran after her. "I'm sorry. I told myself I was not going to take my anger out on you guys. I am sorry for yelling, but I do need a little space. I am going to stay at a friend's house for a few days. I don't want anyone to know where I am, but you can reach me on my cell." Marlon grabbed his things and headed back to Jaleel's house.

4

Deciding to get a divorce wasn't an easy decision. It was a slap in the face to be cheated on, but it was also difficult to just concede to divorce. At least that's how Marlon perceived it. He had played the field strategically before getting married. He had slept with just about every semi-attractive to gorgeous woman during culinary school, along with several women from his church. He was clear and up front about what his intentions were and all of them readily accepted his proposals. Settling down and starting a family was far from his mind; he was having fun being young and wasn't ready to be tied down.

Marlon's mom always said he would reap what he had sown if he did not change his ways. At the time, he saw no wrong in what he was doing. Yes, fornication was a sin and he knew he'd have to answer to God, but those women had consented to having sex with him. There were no hard feelings, no resentment, no broken hearts—just sex. A few of the women he'd slept with never told a soul and neither did he. He respected their need for privacy. Some had even gotten married, but if they ever decided to tell their husbands, Marlon would lose a few close friends.

Pentecostal Player' was the term used to describe him amongst his peers at church. When he decided to start seriously living for the Lord, he changed churches to get a fresh start. He was not proud of the way he'd persuaded the sisters into giving up what they were taught to save for their husbands. And no matter how hard he tried to change, his reputation always preceded him. Whenever he spoke to a sister at the church, the older members would give him a disapproving look, even though he was just being friendly.

Alicia walking into his life was Marlon's saving grace. She had confronted him on all his mess and refused to give in like all the other women had. Her resistance to his advances fueled his desire to be with her. The game he played and the drag he ran was futile; he had to change his whole approach. Alicia, who was four years his senior, was done playing games. She had a 'been there, done that' attitude and was ready to settle down. Marlon chased her tirelessly. Every Sunday, he would get a stern look from her father, warning him to stay away, but Alicia was a thirty year old woman who no longer needed daddy's approval.

Before long, Alicia would look for Marlon to pester her. He had gotten under her skin and she couldn't get enough of him. His good looks, his scent, and charm had become harder and harder to resist. She heard the rumors and had been warned to stay away from him, but when she saw him mature right before her eyes, she was a goner.

The church had thrown a fourth of July picnic and Alicia had volunteered to facilitate all the games. Marlon sat watching as she interacted with all the children. The sight of her solidified his feelings for her. For the first time, a woman had stirred his heart as well as his sex drive. Occasionally she'd look over and catch him staring and he'd wave; he wanted there to be no question of whether he was looking or not. His gaze made Alicia blush like a school girl. Marlon's eyes were fixed on her and the girls who sought his affection faded into the background.

The final activity was the basketball tournament. Alicia had watched Marlon the entire time, enraptured by the sight of his physical strength. The muscles in his calves flexed while he jumped to make shots. Every ripple of the muscles in his arms was etched into her memory. Alicia tried to hurry away when the game was over, but Marlon pulled her toward him pressing her against his sweaty chest, and had whispered, 'I am really into you. Let me take you out tonight. I want to prove to you that I am not the man everyone says I am'. The depth of his voice vibrating against her ear captivated her and all she could whisper was 'okay'. Their courtship was short and in a mere six months they were running down the aisle in matrimony. He'd convinced her to change churches with him in order to leave all the rumors behind and for a while they were really happy. Now, only five years later, what once seemed so perfect was breaking apart.

Some marriages go through hell and love prevails, but there is a point where love can't even survive. Marlon was at that point. When he slept at night all he could see was his wife making love to some strange man in their bed. Though he had only seen movements under the sheets, vivid images raced through his mind. He envisioned the man's blissful face as his wife bucked wildly on top of him. She had let the wild side, a side she had always been too timid to show him, loose. Her head was thrown back and she was giving and receiving more than she ever had with him. The thought of Alicia enjoying someone more than him made Marlon sick to his stomach.

Trust was the main component of marriage to Marlon. After Alicia had cheated and lied to be with her fling, he knew he'd never be able to trust her again. He refused to live in constant uncertainty. Staying together would make both of them miserable. A divorce would bring misery for a short time, but a dejected marriage was a lifetime of misery.

Marlon invited Alicia to dinner after finalizing his decision of divorce. He was not thrilled about seeing her, but they needed to talk face to face. Some conversations were not meant for the phone. He wanted her to see his face so there would be no mistaking his plan for their relationship. There wouldn't be a false hope for reconciliation and he was not going to surprise her with divorce papers months down the road. He wanted the split to be as amicable and brief as possible, and then he never wanted to see her again.

Dinner with Alicia sounded like the right idea, but Marlon's stomach twisted and turned into knots as the hour approached for them to meet. He sat waiting for Alicia to show up at the restaurant; everything he'd eaten was on the verge of coming up. Jaleel had warned him that it might be too soon for them to meet alone in public and had offered to join them, but Marlon thought he was overreacting. Alicia walked toward him wearing a black dress that hugged every curve. Every man took turns looking at her backside. He then knew Jaleel was right. Marlon stood to greet Alicia and gave her a peck on the cheek. He was faced with the daunting task of keeping his anger in check. Marlon pulled her seat out before taking his.

"I went ahead and ordered for you. I hope you don't mind. You usually order the same thing when we come here. I got that out of the way, so we could talk while we waited for our food." Marlon forced a half-smile. The real reason he ordered for her was because he wanted to spend as little time with her as possible.

"I don't mind at all. You have always known me so well." Alicia reached across the table to grip his hand. Despite Marlon's tone, she was hopeful when he'd called inviting her to dinner. They hadn't seen or spoken to each other since the night of the incident. A month seemed plenty of time for shock and anger to have worn off and she had every hope that he'd come home.

"Well, lately that hasn't been the case." Marlon pulled his hand away as Alicia lowered her head in shame. "I don't want to beat around the bush. I invited you here to let you know that I want a divorce."

"What?" She stared at him in unbelief. She tried to grab his hand again, but a look on his face said, 'don't touch me'. "Marlon, I made one mistake. Please don't throw our marriage away."

"One mistake?" He asked—his temper now escalating. He paused to get his emotions under control. He watched with no sympathy as tears rolled down her face. "Look, I didn't come here to argue. I would like our split to be cordial. We don't have any property, bills, or children to fight over. I will pay for filing the paperwork. And if you want to change your name, I will pay for that too. We both work, so there should be no need for alimony."

"Wait, can we at least discuss it first? Marlon, I was lonely. You work at night and I never get to see you. She was there for me when you weren't." Marlon's face contorted into sheer terror.

"She? I know you did not just say she." Not a day went by where Marlon didn't wonder what kind of man just hides under the sheets and now he had his answer. "So, you're gay now?"

"No, that is something that just happened. I want to be with you. I love you." Alicia was crying hysterically and the people around them were starting to stare.

"How can you love someone, yet lie and cheat on them?" Tears had begun to well in Marlon's eyes, but he refused to let her see him cry. He leaned forward and rested his elbows on the table and his head in his hands as he massaged his temples. The pressure of the situation was building up inside of him and he was on the verge of erupting. "For our entire marriage, I've loved you and in return you've ridicule my dreams, you accuse me of stepping out on you, and now, you've dishonored our wedding vows. I can't trust you and I can't stand to look at you."

Marlon dug in his wallet, slammed a fifty on the table, and stormed out. The waitress stood patiently, holding a tray of food. She'd witnessed Marlon's entire outburst and tried to hide the look of disgust on her face as she passed Alicia her plate. Alicia wiped the tears off her face and took off after Marlon. She did not let her high heels, tight dress, or anything else stand in her way. She was on a mission to get her man back and caught up to him just as he was putting his hand to the car door handle.

Marlon turned after hearing high-heels clicking behind him.

"Please, just hear me out." She was not going to give up on her marriage without a fight. "You said you wanted our divorce to be cordial. Well, I am not agreeing to anything unless you agree to marriage counseling. Two months with one session a week, and if you still want a divorce after that I'll sign the papers."

Marlon sat in the driver's seat. Straightforward and unemotionally replied, "Two months with Pastor Hawkins and if I catch you in any more lies, the deal is off and you sign the papers anyway." He then slammed the door in her face.

Alicia's mental wheels were in immediate motion trying to concoct a plan to win Marlon back. She wasn't too keen on counseling with the pastor. There would have to be the whole confession of sin with scrutiny and a quest for restoration which she wasn't really in the mood for. But she would put on a good front if it meant getting Marlon back. If she could get Pastor Hawkins to side with her, he could definitely persuade Marlon to go home.

Marlon floored it all the way back to Jaleel's house. He had no intentions of taking Alicia back, but the last thing he wanted was a nasty divorce. The more he thought about having to sit next to her and listen to her give excuses why she cheated, the more irritated he became. He was fuming by the time he walked into the house. He stormed into the kitchen to make a sandwich and Jaleel was at the table with his family making ice cream sundaes.

Jaleel took a look at Marlon and shook his head. He knew what it felt like to be betrayed by the woman you love; he'd been there before. Just the very sight of her could send you into a rage. "Why don't you grab a bowl and join us?" Jaleel asked.

Marlon slumped into a chair. The stress of that evening had taken its toll and his head was pounding. Suddenly, DJ's little fingers tapped him on the shoulder. Marlon lifted his head to see what he wanted and DJ shoved a spoonful of ice cream into Marlon's mouth. Delisa gasped and grabbed DJ to scold him, but Marlon stopped her. "You're right little man; I do need some ice cream." He grabbed a bowl, scooped two big scoops of ice cream, and let DJ pile it high with caramel, chocolate sauce, nuts, and whip cream.

DJ always put a smile on Marlon's face. He wanted to have children of his own, but was now glad that Alicia had wanted to wait. A child would've made his decision of divorce more complicated. The emotional turmoil scars children for a lifetime. When Marlon was in culinary school, his parents had decided to separate. Although they were still legally married and he was grown, he still hated the fact that they weren't together.

Jaleel signaled for Delisa to take DJ out of the room after they finished the ice cream. He waited until they were out of earshot before addressing Marlon. "You know I love you, man. You are like a brother to me and I can't stand to see you hurting like this." Jaleel was an only child and Marlon was the closest he ever came to having a sibling. "I hope you have thought this whole divorce thing through. Can you, or are you willing to live without this woman. I have been in your shoes before—on both ends of the spectrum. No matter how I looked at it, I loved my wife and did not want to lose her. Right now, your ego is a little bruised, but don't let male pride ruin your life."

"There is no forgiveness for breaking the wedding vows and besides, she admitted to sleeping with a woman."

Jaleel's mouth almost hit the floor, "What, do you mean, a woman?"

"Exactly, when I walked in on her she was in bed with a woman. If that is what she is in to then there is no place for me. To be honest, things weren't all that great between us in the first place. We rarely spent time together, and honestly, I enjoy going to work more than spending time with her. I've worked hard to get where I am and she resents me for it. The more she complains about my work the more I want to work. Does that give her the right to cheat on me?"

"You know it doesn't, but if you know you weren't giving 100%, maybe you should take more time to think things over before rushing into a divorce."

"Whatever man..." Marlon stood and paced around the kitchen. His mind was made up and he was not going to allow Jaleel, Alicia, Pastor Hawkins, or anyone else to change his mind.

"Look, I am not trying to upset you. I just want to make sure you have thought this through. Being hotheaded and making decisions while you're angry is not wise. I am speaking from experience. When I found out Jalisa wasn't my biological daughter, I was heated. I accused my wife of being a liar, being deceptive, and trapping me into marrying her. After Jalisa passed away, grief helped me calm down and I really thought things over. I needed my wife to help me get through the mourning and she needed me. If I hadn't calmed down, I would've never heard Delisa explain why she assumed I was Jalisa's father. I would have turned my back on her and this great life we have together." Jaleel hoped he was getting through to Marlon. He was sympathetic to his situation and would have probably responded the same way had the shoe been on the other foot, but the last thing Marlon needed was someone hyping him up to leave his wife. Jaleel said his peace and left Marlon alone in the kitchen to think.

Meme showed up at Alicia's house looking beautiful. Alicia had asked her to stay away to give her the opportunity to work on her marriage. Meme respected her wishes, but it had been a while since they'd talked or seen each other. She rang the doorbell, nervously waiting for Alicia to answer. *Even if she slams the door in my face at least I had a chance to see her*, Meme thought.

Meme adjusted her clothes and jewelry. She desperately wanted a relationship with Alicia and hoped today's visit would sway Alicia into her arms.

It had been only about a year since her first lesbian encounter. She'd always been attracted to men, but after a horrific night with a man she trusted, she had shut all men out. Then, one day she went out for drinks with Wayne, a friend who also owns the salon she'd worked at, and he took her to a gay club. It was awkward at first, but she started to relax and have fun without being hit on. She made a few female friends and started hanging out with them. One of them made a move and when their lips touched, the chemistry she felt was undeniable. Although she'd been dating women for a while now, her family was still unaware of her sexuality. Fearing her family's reaction, she kept all of her romantic relationships at a distance, but with Alicia she was happy and willing to be with her at all cost—even if that meant losing her family.

Meme's heart raced as the door slid open. The sight of Alicia standing in the doorway wearing a skin-tight black dress took her breath away. Meme fumbled for the right words to say, but came up with nothing. Alicia chuckled at her nervousness and stepped aside, allowing her to enter.

They stood in silence each waiting for each other to speak. Meme had so much to say before she'd arrived; now her mind was blank. Alicia was still frustrated over her dinner with Marlon. She wasn't in the mood for foolishness, but had to be honest with herself. Her heart fluttered when she'd seen Meme through the peephole. The last time they were together it ended so disastrously when Marlon walked in on them, but until that point their sexual connection had been the greatest encounter of her life. Alicia shook her head to keep those thoughts from racing through her mind. "Is there something you wanted to say?"

"I just came to let you know where I stand." Meme threw her shoulders back and looked Alicia in the eye. "I should probably feel bad or guilty about what I am getting ready to say, but I don't. I love Marlon and what I have done to your marriage is wrong, but again, I don't care." Meme stepped into Alicia's face and placed her hands on Alicia's waist. "I can look in your eyes and see that you want me. I can tell by the way your breath speeds up when I touch you that you feel the electricity pulsating between us."

Alicia swallowed hard and tried to stand her ground. "It doesn't matter what I feel or what could have been. I want to be with my husband and you have to respect that." Alicia stepped away. She had to sever their physical connection if she was going to be successful at resisting Meme. "I admit, messing around with you was fun and exciting, but I was never serious about being with you. Please accept that and don't come back." Alicia opened the front door, signaling for Meme to leave.

Meme choked back tears and rushed past Alicia. She kept her eyes low to avoid eye contact. She ran to her car and balled like a baby. If anyone found out what had happened with Alicia, her family would disown her and her friends would turn their backs on her. Meme was still willing to take that risk.

Meme stopped the tears and steadied her breathing; ultimately, she was satisfied with just being able to see Alicia alone. Alicia had refused to admit it, but Meme knew there was more than fun and games between them. The moment their naked bodies had touched, Meme knew Alicia was the only woman she could be happy with. She wanted to settle down with one woman and have a baby or adopt one. She prayed Marlon never forgave Alicia—her happiness depended on it. When Alicia came to the realization that her marriage was over, Meme planned on being there with open arms.

5

Marlon listened to another voicemail from Alicia. He wouldn't be able to avoid her forever. Two months had now passed and Marlon still hadn't filed for divorce nor made any attempt to start counseling. Her calls were becoming more frequent and her messages more irate. For a while, he'd thought about skipping counseling. If she wanted to contest the divorce then let her. How bad could it be? There was nothing to fight over, but with every threatening message she left, his decision waned. He had no idea what she'd hoped to accomplish by forcing him into counseling. Threatening to wreak havoc on his life was not the way to get him back.

His phone buzzed again; this time she was texting. Marlon shook his head and showed his phone to Jaleel.

Marlon please talk to me. I love you.

"Just talk to her," Jaleel said, repeating what he'd been telling Marlon for weeks. "I know your mind is set on divorce, but you don't want to look back years from now and regret not hearing her explanation."

"I hear you. Maybe I'll call after the game. I just didn't know love felt like this. If I had known, I would've left it alone." Marlon tossed his phone into his gym bag and got out the car. Jaleel followed him into the gym.

"Sometimes love hurts, but true love is worth fighting for. I could have lost my wife because I was chasing after a fantasy. I hurt her and she had every right to leave. Finding out Jalisa wasn't my daughter hurt me and I could have left, but we kept fighting." Jaleel abruptly stopped right as they entered the basketball courts. "Yes, love can hurt, but with true love you feel so much more. Love feels like that rush of adrenaline pumping through your veins after a good workout. It hypes you up and gives you that energy you need to make it through the day. Sometimes it even feels like that cold shower right after a workout; it washes away all the dirt, soothes your aches, and refreshes you."

"Why you tryin' to be all deep?" Marlon laughed, trying to hide the fact that he'd never felt any of that for Alicia. Maybe everyone was right when they

38

told him not to marry her. If they'd taken time to really get to know each other, they may have realized they were wrong for each other.

"Late as usual," two brothers announced in unison as Marlon and Jaleel arrived on the basketball court. Their monthly Saturday morning basketball game had grown from just him and Marlon playing to Paul and Tim joining them once they had married into the family. Jaleel had mentioned to Pastor Hawkins that they played monthly and he wanted to join. So Jaleel, Marlon, Paul, Tim, Pastor Hawkins, and Cole met at the gym one Saturday a month for a friendly game of basketball.

Sometimes the games weren't so friendly. The most intense games were the ones when Paul and Tim or Marlon and Jaleel were on opposite teams. They always insisted on guarding, pushing, and fouling each other. Trash talking sometimes got out of control and a few times Pastor Hawkins had to step in as spiritual counselor and referee. Today seemed like it was going to be one of those games. They pulled numbers to make sure the teams were separated fairly; Paul and Tim were already on separate teams. When Marlon pulled the same number as Tim, Pastor Hawkins and Cole sighed. They knew the game was definitely not going to be friendly.

Marlon and Jaleel had that same competitive sibling rivalry as Paul and Tim. With Marlon and Tim being younger, they always felt they had something to prove and would push themselves to the limit trying to win.

Cole wound up being on Marlon and Tim's team and they couldn't have been happier. It wasn't that Pastor Hawkins couldn't play, he just wasn't as aggressive as the others. Marlon pulled his team to the side to lead a little pre-game pep talk.

"I say we switch it up a bit. Tim you guard Richard."

"For what? I know Paul's game like the back of my hand," Tim questioned.

"Exactly, he knows yours too and has been wiping the floor with you every time we've teamed up against them," Cole laughed out loud.

"If we switch up on them, we force them to play off of skill which we both have more of," Marlon said. With a fist bump they agreed Tim was on Richard, Marlon on Paul, and Cole would guard Jaleel.

When they joined the other team at half-court, Paul was the first to talk trash. "What's wrong little brother you too scared to guard me today?"

Marlon shot back, "What's wrong old man, afraid you can't keep up?" He smiled and nudged Paul off balance as the ball was passed in to Tim. Tim shot Marlon a bounce pass which he grabbed and bolted down the court, scoring an easy right-hand lay up for the first point of the game.

"So, that's how you want to play?" Paul smirked, as he checked Marlon hard. "Don't start what you can't finish." Paul caught the ball and dashed down the court. Marlon was faster and was all over him before he got too far. Rounding in front of Paul, he planted his feet and braced for the charge. Paul tried to spin around him, but Marlon reached in and snatched the ball out of his hand. The ball bounced across the court and Jaleel and Cole both dove for it. After a brief struggle, Jaleel came up with the ball and Tim immediately ran over, leaving Richard wide open under the hoop. Jaleel found him with a brisk, chest pass. With a dribble and pivot, Richard took the jump shot and tied up the score.

"It is going to be a short game if you don't stick your man." Cole hissed, as he walked passed Tim.

"If you step up your game, I wouldn't feel the need to help." Tim shot back without missing a beat.

The score fluctuated throughout most of the game. Everyone was drenched in sweat and the energy they started with had severely dissipated. They were well passed the required twenty-one points needed to win, but their self-imposed rule of having to win by four points was wearing them out. Neither team wanted to be the one to say forget the rule unless they were in the lead. At this point, Marlon, Tim, and Cole were leading by two points; they'd called a quick time out to regroup. There weren't timeouts in three-on-three, but Paul was so out of breath he didn't protest. He was feeling every year of thirty-nine and knew that a hot bath with some Epsom salt was in order.

Marlon, Tim, and Cole decided that the ball should go to Tim. They hated to play dirty against the man of God, but Tim could muscle past Richard and make a painless layup. Tim hesitated, claiming that Paul was so tired that Marlon should take the shot. However, Marlon had been fighting Paul the whole game and barely had the energy to stand up straight. Agreeing to take out the pastor, Tim grabbed the ball and headed for the top of the key. Tim checked the ball and tried to trample over Richard, but he wasn't having it. Richard leaned into the charge and surprisingly deflected Tim to the ground.

The court was shocked into silence as everyone watched Tim get up off the ground. Richard helped him to his feet with a warning.

"Don't underestimate me again," Pastor said. They broke out into thunderous laughter. Even his teammates were doubled over laughing.

Before Tim could absorb what had happened, several phones chimed from gym bags on the side of the court. Jaleel, Paul, and Tim ran over to answer their phones. The calls meant one thing: their wives were together and it was time for them to come home. It was a silent pact that when the wives called, the game was over. Whoever was in the lead was the winner. Cole had yet to meet these women, but knew that they had to be something to woo these grown black men into immediate submission. He laughed to himself. *Not in a million years would I ever be that sprung.* He enjoyed lots of women and had the looks to get anyone he wanted and he used it to his advantage. Monogamy was not for him, but his boys seemed to enjoy it.

Marlon and Tim were well into their victory dance when they heard Paul and Jaleel begging their wives for ten more minutes.

"The rule is when they call, game is over. There's no asking for more time. Besides, I already hung up and I am not calling back, so I still have to leave," Tim protested.

Paul smirked and tossed his phone back into his bag, "I asked her for you so stop whining and get back on the court."

Tim was just about to rush Paul when Richard stepped in. "A rule is a rule and we can't just change it to benefit us. Besides, I wanted to run something by you guys real quick."

Paul conceded to the loss with an eye roll. Marlon, Tim, and Cole congratulated each other on a game well played, and then everyone tuned their ears into Pastor Hawkins. "Marlon and Jaleel do you guys remember Jason, the young man that had a scholarship to play basketball in college, but got caught in some drama before he left and was sent to prison?" They responded with nods. "Well as you know, because of him, my dad started a prison ministry before he passed away. The older brothers at the church have been doing a wonderful job with this ministry, but Brother Jason is getting out soon. I think it best that some of us build a relationship with him so when he gets out he will have someone his age to relate to." Before Pastor Hawkins finished pleading his case everyone agreed to help out however they could—even Cole who hadn't stepped a foot in church since he was a child and adamantly refused all invitations.

Before they left, Pastor Hawkins extended the same invitation to Cole as he did after every game. "I hope to see you at church this Sunday; and you too, Marlon." Marlon's head dropped in shame. He'd almost made it through the day without that awkward moment with the pastor. Since he'd left Alicia, his church attendance had been shoddy, but he wasn't quite ready to talk about it. He simply nodded his head and turned toward the car. Having a young pastor had its benefits, but when your pastor was also your boy, he could flip from friend to pastor at the drop of a dime. It's easy to tell your boy to mind his business, but it's hard to say it to the pastor.

Marlon plopped in his car seat and heard his phone buzzing; he knew exactly who it was. Answering it would only put an end to his good mood that Pastor Hawkins had already started to dampen.

Alicia wanted to scream. Marlon had ignored yet another one of her phone calls. Things were not going as she had planned and it was starting to piss her off. They should have at least started counseling by now. There, she would've been able to explain her side of the story and with Pastor Hawkin's help, Marlon would see his role and fault in their failing marriage. Then, the pastor would convince Marlon to go home to make it work. When he did come home, she was going to be so good to him that he'd never again think about leaving. None of that would happen if he didn't talk to her.

A change in game plan was definitely in order. First off, she'd issue no more threats, because they obviously weren't working. She thought about seduction, but that could only work if she saw him. Instead, she'd be more soft and vulnerable when she left a message, which she always had a hard time doing. She was head strong, feisty, and lived by the phrase 'never let them see you sweat'. This was one of the reasons she'd had such a hard time telling Marlon how miserable she was. Every time she broached the subject, he would jump on the defensive and her hard exterior would well up, but all that was going to change.

After giving herself a pep talk, Alicia determined that not hearing from Marlon was a good thing. It meant that he hadn't filed for a divorce, so there was still hope. A ray of hope brightened her face, but was quickly dimmed when she looked down at the text message that popped up on her cell phone screen.

I miss you please call me.

Alicia rested her elbows on her knees and her head in the palms of her hands. The whole situation was draining. Marlon was ignoring her and she was ignoring Meme. Life would be so different if she had the strength to kick Meme out of her bed that day, better yet, if they hadn't have gotten involved in the first place. It would've been even better if she'd accepted Marlon's attempts to work things out. *Hindsight is 20/20*, she thought.

Meme clung to her cell phone all day waiting for Alicia to respond to her text. Her mind was so focused on Alicia that she burnt a client on the ear while flat ironing her hair. The client jumped swiftly out of the chair and turned around like she was getting ready to backhand Meme. Meme apologized profusely and offered the woman a discount which seemed to appease her anger, but did nothing for Meme's wandering mind.

Meme forced herself to focus. If there was one client she didn't want to alienate, it was this one. As a hairstylist, Meme was used to women sitting in her chair and unloading their baggage, but not this one. She was usually friendly and conversational, but kept her business to herself. The only personal thing Meme knew was that her husband paid everyone good money to cater to her every Tuesday.

He dropped $2,000 a month on the salon and her services never came close to totaling that much. The one time Latrice had opened up to her, Meme was floored. She revealed that she was in an abusive relationship and that her husband would fly off the handle at any given time over something insignificant. Once she heard that, Meme figured his generosity was hush money for any bruises they may have seen or anything his wife allowed to slip.

"I can't apologize enough, but I can fix your hair so he doesn't notice." Seeing the worry on Latrice's face, Meme felt the need to do something.

"I'll be fine. What's up with you? You seem a little preoccupied."

"I think I have finally destroyed my life beyond repair," Meme sighed, as she plopped down on the stool next to Latrice's chair. "Let's just say I slept with someone I shouldn't have and I kind of got caught. To top it off, I fell in love." Meme shook her head at how ridiculous she sounded.

"What do you mean 'someone you shouldn't have' and 'kind of got caught'?"

"Well, this person is married," Meme was not about to come out the closet to a woman whose life was just as unstable as hers she still didn't even know why she was telling a client all this. "And the spouse caught us in the act, but never saw who I was. However, when everything comes out in the open, the shit will hit the fan and I will lose everything that's important to me."

"Maybe if you tell on yourself it will soften the blow." Latrice wanted Meme to work and talk. She was on a tight schedule, but knew how it felt to need someone to talk to so she didn't rush her. Meme gave her a look that said I am not confessing anything.

"I know I am the last person to give advice, but sex doesn't just happen. If you knew sleeping with this person was going to be so detrimental to your life, why did you do it?"

"Because I have never felt something so strong for a person in all my life and I am an idiot."

Meme suddenly jumped up. "But enough about me; let's get you all fixed up." Latrice sat back to enjoy the rest of her salon treatment and thanks to the call from her husband earlier, a few added minutes of freedom.

6

Latrice sat at the salon enjoying her freedom. It was the only time Calvin let her out on her own. She thoroughly enjoyed her four hours of independence and hated when it ended. Every move she made was controlled by her husband, but salon time was her time and she did as she pleased. As long as she came home looking beautiful with her hair whipped into place, nails trimmed and polished, feet soft, and Brazilian wax smooth, Calvin had no complaints. She only got the waxing done every six weeks and normally scheduled her appointment for early in the morning. The pain was unbearable, but Calvin didn't care if she was hurt. He liked to have sex the same day and she figured the earlier she got it done the more time she'd have for the skin irritation and pain to subside.

Having gone through the worst part of her day, Latrice would pop a pain pill and then enjoy a manicure and pedicure. She felt sheer pleasure as her feet were fully submerged in hot water. The stream of water coming out of the jets in the footbath always seemed to be the hottest, but Latrice didn't care. She pressed her feet right up against the jets, making sure the high-powered stream sprayed between each toe. Then, she'd lean back in the massage chair to get comfortable.

The rollers in the chair glided up and down her back, working out all the knots. She tried to convince Calvin to add a massage to her weekly ritual, but he'd refused, stating that he didn't want anyone rubbing their hands all over his woman. This made no sense, because he allowed someone to wax her most prized possession without complaint. Latrice settled for the spa pedicure instead to keep the peace. Although it wasn't as intense as a real massage, it still helped her to relax and temporarily escape the horror of a marriage.

During her manicure, she got a little surprise from her husband. The manicurist had just begun polishing Latrice's nails when her phone rang. Latrice frantically asked the woman to grab the phone from her purse, but she didn't speak English. Fearing she'd miss Calvin's call, Latrice plunged into the purse, wet nails and all. The manicurist furiously mumbled something in her native language, but Latrice didn't care. She answered the phone before it went to voicemail, which would spare her a slap across the face.

Latrice eyeballed the woman, who had suddenly started being rough with her hand, as she listened to Calvin rundown the evening's events. He gave explicit instruction on what she needed to do.

"I have a business dinner tonight with a client and his wife. I called the store you like at the mall and reserved you a dress. Go to the mall, get the dress, and get out. I don't want you walking around the mall by yourself. Do you understand?"

"Can I get a few extra things from that store?"

"If you need to go shopping I will take you this weekend, but as for right now, get the dress and get out."

"Okay and thank you."

Latrice hung up the phone, thankful for the extension of freedom. She laughed as she thought about the conversation. She should've known better than asking that question, but occasionally, she'd have a bold moment—they always shocked her. She would've loved to go shopping alone, but settled for what she could get. Calvin was always generous with his finances and would buy her anything she wanted. He had to watch her every move and also stared down every man that looked her direction. When they were dating, his protectiveness was a turn on; now, it was her worst nightmare.

She left the salon that day with her hair washed, blow dried, straightened, and styled to cover the burn on her ear. Next, Latrice was off to the mall. She gave Meme a hug, told her to keep her head up, and sashayed out to her car.

Latrice ran into a little problem after arriving at the store. The dress Calvin picked out was too small and they didn't have another in her size. Knowing this would mean another extension of her freedom, Latrice smiled and called Calvin. Just as expected, he gave her an hour to find something else. He had to talk with the saleslady to prove Latrice was telling the truth first, but embarrassment was a small price to pay for another hour away from a controlling, abusive husband.

Latrice had plenty of dresses that were perfect for that night's occasion, but Calvin was too competitive. He had no idea what his client's wife would wear and refused to let anyone out shine his wife. Nonetheless, Latrice was enjoying herself and wouldn't dare remind him of her wardrobe. She had seen the dress she wanted soon as she walked through the door, but took her time combing through racks of clothes. With ten minutes left to shop, Latrice picked up the dress she wanted and headed to the register.

Latrice informed Calvin that she was leaving the mall and would be home in about twenty minutes. She pulled out of the parking lot, hopped on to the freeway, and merged into traffic—which happened to be bumper-to-bumper. She hadn't realized what time it was until she ran into traffic, but the freeway seemed unusually backed up, even for rush hour.

Latrice called to tell Calvin there was horrible traffic and it was going to take her a little longer to get home.

"Don't play games. I am leaving the office now; you better be home when I get there." He hung up the phone before she could respond.

Latrice tried to stay calm, but he was pissed and she would have to pay for making him angry. The traffic was not moving. Latrice racked her brain for an alternate route home and decided on exiting the highway and taking the scenic route. Traffic was just as bad there. She missed just about every light and when she finally pulled in the opened garage her heart sank as she saw Calvin's car. She didn't want to face him. For a minute, she thought about turning the car around and driving away, but the repercussions alone terrified her.

Calvin had only been home for fifteen minutes, but was angrily pacing back and forth. When he told Latrice to do something, he expected her to obey despite the obstacles standing in her way. He'd called the traffic information hotline to make sure Latrice was being honest, but couldn't care less that there was an accident. He figured if she hadn't been playing games at the mall, she would've been home on time.

He glared at Latrice as she came through the door. He placed his hands in his pockets as he walked toward her. Calvin wanted to slap the stupid look off her face, but didn't want to risk leaving a bruise before dinner. He kept his hands balled in his pocket in order to control his rage.

His muscular frame towered over her and she froze. Her mind said, *walk away,* but her feet were paralyzed. Instead, she braced for the blow that she thought was coming.

"Get dressed," Calvin barked. Latrice shuddered, jolted from her paralytic state, and sprinted into the bedroom. He followed behind her, watching her every move, and when she was done, he practically dragged her to the car.

They drove all the way to the restaurant in silence and when they pulled up to the valet Calvin whispered,

"Don't say anything to embarrass me," then exited the vehicle. Latrice accepted Calvin's extended elbow, miserably displayed her best pageant smile, and followed his lead into the restaurant. Relief washed over her when the host informed them that their guests hadn't yet arrived. She knew Calvin would definitely slap her around if his client had been there waiting.

Latrice was far more stunning than Calvin's client's wife and was absolutely brilliant during dinner conversation. The client was taken by Latrice's intelligence and knowledge of the business. She smiled, laughed, and spoke when spoken to—giving everyone her undivided attention. She followed Calvin's cues to engage the client's wife in conversation to allow the men a private moment. When Calvin placed his hand under the table and slid it up her dress, she sighed with relief, knowing that she'd escaped a beat down later.

They had finished their final course and were sipping on coffee. Latrice was feeling pretty good about herself and how great the night had turned out. Calvin had already taken care of the bill and now they were discussing politics and current events. The waiter had refilled her coffee and spilled coffee all over the table and her new dress. He frantically tried to clean the mess, but Latrice gripped his hands and innocently told him, "It's alright."

Latrice was still holding his hand and smiling while he profusely apologized. Calvin rose to his feet, trying to keep his anger in check.

"We were just leaving," he said, and extended a handshake to the waiter holding Latrice's hand.

Oblivious to Calvin's anger, Latrice looped her hand around Calvin's elbow and followed him to the car. During the ride home, Latrice rambled on and on about dinner, business, and how much she had in common with the client's wife. The more she talked, the angrier Calvin became. By the time they arrived home, Calvin was seething. Once the garage door was fully closed, he grabbed her by the hair and pulled her across the seat and into the house.

He flung her onto the floor and kicked into her ribs. "Don't ever put your hands on another man." He kicked her again, this time in the stomach. She instantly vomited onto the floor. She moaned in pain, trying her best to get up without getting kicked again. She gripped the island in the middle of the kitchen to steady herself. She heaved to cope with the pain, but the deeper she breathed, the more it hurt. She cried out with agonizing intensity, but Calvin's mind was given to total rage.

Calvin punched her in her face repetitively. Blood splattered everywhere as he beat and tossed her around the kitchen. She pleaded for mercy, but inwardly her spirit lamented, *God, if you are who I have heard people say you are, then make him stop.* As they completed a full circle around the kitchen, Latrice slipped in her own vomit. She cried hysterically and blood and tears rolled down her face. She could see Calvin towering over her through her swollen eyes and braced herself for another kick, but he just stared at her, then calmly walked away.

It took every ounce of strength to get up, but she knew her life depended on it. Latrice stumbled to the bathroom, then shut and locked the door. Blood gathered in the back of her throat and she spit it into the sink. She turned on the hot water and began the painful process of tending to her wounds. Latrice looked at her reflection in the mirror. Her swollen, bloody lip and eyes distorted her image. She barely recognized herself.

Her face ached from the beating it just endured. She was no stranger to abuse, but this was the worst it had ever been. Over the past two years, she'd spent many nights in the bathroom tending wounds. On nights like these she always asked herself, *how did I get into this situation*? She'd always prided herself as being an independent woman. She'd never believed in monogamous relationships—only casual sex and sexual friendships, until she met Calvin.

She'd spent weeks preparing for a meeting with the client of an account she had taken over. She went over every detail of the account. The rumors of the client's cut-throat demeanor had made her paranoid. As she sat in the conference room waiting for his arrival, her heart pounded uncontrollably. When he stepped into the room, he exuded power and his good looks took her breath away. Calvin had flirted with her throughout the entire meeting, but she remained professional— resisting his advances. Every day, for two weeks following their meeting, he sent her a dozen white roses. She gave him the same cat and mouse chase that she'd given many times before, but Calvin was relentless in his pursuit. He presented himself to be different than the men in her past. His kind words, expensive gifts, and intensity between the sheets eventually captured her heart. For the first time, she'd given a man her all, and when he asked her to be his wife, she was overjoyed.

Everything seemed perfect; Latrice finally had the love and the life that had engrossed her friends. A man who worked, paid the bills, and took pleasure in providing for his woman was more than she had hoped for. She enjoyed playing the submissive housewife. All he required of her was keeping the house clean and cooking meals.

Then one day, about six months into their marriage, Latrice was feeling a bit under the weather and decided not to cook dinner. Latrice lay on the couch and took a nap, hoping they could order takeout. A short time later, she was awakened by Calvin ranting and raving about his dinner being on the table when he gets home from work. Her response, "Calvin calm down, I wasn't feeling well," changed their lives forever. His eyes squinted as rage wrinkled his brow and with one quick movement his hand smacked across her face knocking her to the ground in the process. Her body spun around and she landed flat on her stomach.

With the coldest voice she ever heard Calvin whispered as he stood over her. "Don't make me have to hit you again. Now get up and cook my dinner."

She never told a soul, but that slap had claimed the life of their unborn child. A few hours after he knocked her to the ground, she got severe cramps in her stomach. Thinking that a hot bath might ease the pain Latrice made her way to the bathroom. As she placed one foot into the tub she felt a small pop and blood ran down her leg. The cramping and bleeding intensified, but she remained in the bathroom. She dealt with it on her own; cleaned the mess on her own, and struggled through the depression on her own. Sometimes she felt that she should've told Calvin about the baby and miscarriage, but she was terrified of his response.

In a short time, Calvin had managed to destroy Latrice's self-esteem and self-respect. He verbally abused her and blamed all of his anger on her stupidity. There were times when she thought about leaving, but where could she go? Because of him, she had no job, no friends, and hadn't spoken to her family in over a year. Every time she thought of leaving, fear would convince her to stay. Calvin would be furious if he came home and she was gone. He would not rest until he found her and forced her to return; then, he would probably kill her.

Latrice stood in the bathroom mirror nursing a bloody lip. She wondered if things would have been different had she fought back that first day. Would he have thought twice before hitting her again? But now, two years into their marriage, the beatings still persisted. Each one was worse than the one before and was always followed by some extravagant gift or a weekend getaway. Each time, she would fall for his lies. She loved him and feared him, but their love dwindled with each beating.

Latrice was too ashamed to deal with the reality of her abusive relationship. She forsook her friends and family fearing they'd ask about her bruises. She was isolated and the house, in which she once gracefully roamed, now held her captive. No one called and no one came to visit. Occasionally, she'd go to the store, shopping, or Calvin would take her on a trip, but he was always there questioning her about what she was doing, what she was looking at, or thinking about. She had no freedom, no friends, and no life of her own. She felt so alone and desperately needed someone to talk to.

Swift thuds on the door startled Latrice back into reality. "Latrice open this door. How many times have I told you not to lock doors in my house?" The gruffness in Calvin's voice brought tears to her eyes. The door rattled as the force of his fist pounded against it. "Latrice don't be stupid; open this door."

Latrice fearfully stepped toward the door, bracing herself for the collision of Calvin's fist. The click of the door unlocking echoed through her heart and the door flung open. "I am sorry; I don't…" Latrice tried to apologize, but her apology was halted by Calvin's hands squeezing her throat. The impact of his hand slamming against her neck caused her to gag and gasp for air. She squirmed in an attempt to break free. She grabbed his hands and tried to pull them away from her, but he increased the pressure. The desperation in Latrice's eyes pleaded for her life. She tried to caress his cheek to calm his rage, but no longer had the strength to lift her arms. She was losing the fight and drifted off into unconsciousness.

Panic rushed through Calvin and his rage quickly subsided when he felt Latrice's body go limp. He jerked his hands away from her neck and she slumped to the floor, banging her head against the cabinet. Calvin pounded on his head as he tried to gather his thoughts.

"Oh God Latrice, look what you made me do. Why do you always have to get me so upset?" Heat rushed through Calvin and sweat poured from his body as he tried to determine his next move. He never considered his own anger; the problem was always attributed to being with the wrong type of women. At first, Latrice seemed different, but after they married she'd turned out to be like all the rest. Everything she did pissed him off and he had to slap her around every now and then to keep her in her place. He stood over his wife's lifeless body and the promising future that once awaited him was now destroyed. If anyone found out what he did, he would more than likely spend the rest of his life in jail.

The only thought he had was to get her out of the house, and without thinking twice, Calvin swooped Latrice up into his arms and raced through the house toward the garage. After fumbling to open the car door, he carefully placed Latrice in the back seat. Backing out of the car he gave her one last glance and her wide eyes staring back at him nearly gave him a heart attack. Calvin jumped back, bumping his head in the process.

"Calvin, where am I?" Latrice whispered; her voice was raspy and she winced with pain as she spoke.

"What?"

"Where am I?"

"I-I-um…Are you okay?" Calvin closed his eyes and took a deep breath trying to get over the shock of her being alive. "You're in the car I was just taking you to the hospital to make sure you were okay." Calvin extended his hand, trying to help Latrice out of the car.

"I don't feel well. I think I should still go to the hospital." Latrice tried to slide further into the car, but Calvin firmly gripped her arm.

"No, you are fine. I will help you get in bed and I will take care of you." Latrice knew better than to protest. She exited the car, carefully following his every direction. His mood was becoming more and more unpredictable and she could not take another beating tonight. She stood in the bathroom and undressed as he prepared her bath. Every muscle in her body ached. The pain was practically unbearable and she clenched her teeth to keep from screaming.

As he washed her body, it took all her remaining strength to keep from cringing at his touch. When he smiled, she smiled back. When he kissed her, she pretended that it hurt her swollen lips to bad to kiss him back. The look in his eye warned her that he wanted sex and her stomach turned at the very thought. He lifted her from the tub and laid her across the bed. Tears filled her eyes as she watched him undress and she quivered with repulsion as he slithered his body on top of her and entered her.

She buried her head into his chest hoping to hide her tears as she put on the act of enjoyment. She'd been beaten before for not being actively involved in sex and that is one memory she didn't want to revisit. She faked an orgasm to coincide with his climax and heaved with relief that the experience was over; he gasped with satisfaction.

Latrice lay stiff as a board while Calvin rolled off of her and fell asleep. Instead of sleeping, her mind raced. She'd reached her breaking point and knew she had to get away from Calvin before he killed her. For whatever reason, God had chosen to spare her tonight, but it was proof that Calvin was now going too far. She lay awake all night calculating an exit plan. Her first thought was to call Camilla, the only person she knew that would be there unconditionally.

When the sun gleamed through the curtained windows, Latrice slid her aching body out of the bed, tiptoed to the kitchen, and began preparing breakfast. Her swollen eyes made it nearly impossible to see, but cooking breakfast for Calvin before he left for work was part of her normal routine. Being sore from a beating was never a sufficient excuse for meals not being prepared.

As she stood cooking bacon, she ran over her plan in her mind. *I have to call Camilla as soon as he leaves; I know she'll let me stay with her. Then I'll immediately file for a restraining order, and I have to get some type of weapon just in case he comes after me.*

"Good morning, baby." The sound of Calvin's voice made the hair on the back of Latrice's neck stand up.

"Good morning," she forced. She'd watched his smile fade and his head drop in shame. The shame, regret, and apologies were soon to follow.

"I am sorry. I can't believe I did this to you." He caressed Latrice's swollen face. "I just love you so much and it makes me crazy sometimes. Do you forgive me?"

She'd heard this all before, but Latrice smiled, nodded, and accepted his kiss just as she normally did. Her near death experience had opened her eyes and for the first time she saw her reality with clarity. Calvin was a wife-beater and would always be one. The love she thought she'd had was a delusion. She was a prisoner in her home and her husband was the warden.

"Of course I forgive you. I know better than to lock the bathroom door. I wasn't thinking straight. Do you forgive me?" She purposely left out the main reason the beating even started hoping to change the subject. She began pulling out plates and utensils for their meal.

Calvin smiled as he pulled a chair out and sat at the table. He never answered when she asked him to forgive her. He simply smiled and went on about his business.

"You know, while I was showering, I was thinking maybe we should go out of town this weekend."

Latrice accidentally knocked a plate onto the floor while trying to hide a look of disgust on her face. She pivoted back toward Calvin with fear in her eyes. She knew the consequence for breaking things. She eyed the knife sitting on the counter next to her and was mentally prepared to cut him if he came near her. He got up from the table, wiped his mouth, and calmly placed a napkin on the table. Latrice watched his every move as he walked across the kitchen. To her surprise, he grabbed the broom and dust pan. The closer he got to her, the closer she got to the knife. By the time he'd stepped in front of her, Latrice had a firm grip on the handle and was ready to plunge the blade into his chest.

Fully prepared to pounce on Calvin, Latrice's entire being sighed when Calvin smiled, kissed her on the forehead, and started sweeping up the glass. "So, what do you think about going away this weekend?" Calvin continued the conversation, unaware that his life was almost cut short.

"Um…" Latrice searched for an excuse. She hoped to be gone before the weekend, but if she wasn't there was no way she was going anywhere with him. "My face," Latrice blurted out, as she rubbed fingers across her lumps and bruises. "It looks pretty bad and I don't want people to see me like this."

"So, you don't want to go away with me?" Calvin stopped sweeping.

Latrice gripped the knife again. "Of course I want to go away with you. I just want to look my best while we are out. Can we wait until the following weekend?"

"You're right." Calvin walked away to dump the dustpan leaving Latrice with an astonished look on her face. "There is this spot up north, that a friend of mine told me about and I want to check it out. I will make reservations for next weekend."

Latrice faked a smile, and then joined him at the table for breakfast. Breakfast took seemingly hours. Carrying on and pretending to enjoy a conversation with a man who had almost taken your life was sheer torture. Whenever his voice even suggested aggression, she made sure her knife was still on the counter. Latrice had thoroughly scanned the kitchen and mapped out an escape route from the table to the counter just in case. It was either her life or his, and she'd resolutely affirmed that it wasn't going to be hers.

Latrice fidgeted as she watched Calvin eat the last few bites. She brought him his final cup of coffee and gathered his things for work. She rushed back into the kitchen carrying Calvin's briefcase and suit jacket and was sorely disappointed to see him still sitting sipping his cup of coffee.

"Calvin, honey you are going to be late."

"Yeah, I am just really enjoying this time we are spending together. I was thinking maybe I will call in sick." Latrice's eyes widened and she raised her eyebrows in an attempt to hide her disappointment. "And besides, I want to keep an eye on you today, just to make sure you are feeling okay."

Just like that, Latrice's plans were put on hold. *Don't panic*, she told herself. *This is only a minor setback*. Latrice cleaned the kitchen. She searched for any and everything that could possibly need cleaning, doing all she could to avoid joining Calvin in bed.

7

A s he waited for Latrice to join him in the bedroom, Calvin's mind ran wild with thoughts from his childhood.

There had been many nights where he fell asleep to the sound of his father ranting and raving about his mother being disrespectful and stupid. They argued well into the night and at the breakfast table the next morning Calvin would ask questions about what happened to his mother's face and she'd make up some lame excuse to pacify his curiosity.

He had always believed her until one night, his parents had been arguing for hours. He'd become so numb to it that he continued his nightly routine of getting ready for bed without pause. His mother tried to explain to his father that he didn't hear or see what he thought he did, but it only made matters worse. His voice escalated as he called her a stupid whore. Calvin checked on is little brother, who he shared a room with, making sure he was sleep. He then climbed back into bed, putting the pillow over his head forcing himself to fall asleep.

No matter how hard he tried, he couldn't sleep. Calvin, who was only ten years old, lay in bed listening to his mother defend her actions and in mid-sentence she'd stopped talking altogether. The house was dead silent and the sudden silence worried him more than the arguing. Calvin climbed out of bed, tiptoed into the living room, and stopped dead in his tracks when he saw his father with both hands wrapped around his mother's neck. He made eye contact with his mother and her eyes pleaded for help. Calvin was terrified, his feet were frozen, and even if he knew what to do, he wouldn't have been able too. His father instantly dropped his mother to the ground and marched out of the room without a word when he saw Calvin watching with a tear streaked face. Calvin never asked questions or mentioned that night, but it gave him nightmares for weeks. He was glad his little brother and sister always went to bed early and seemed to be oblivious to what was going on.

Calvin's father was always a good dad and after that night, he tried even harder to be the dad that every little boy wanted. They went to San Diego Padres and Charger games, camping, and fishing—building a relationship that made Calvin over-look what was being done to his mother. On the mornings she served breakfast with a swollen eye or busted lip, he no longer asked questions; he would just wonder what she'd done to make his dad so upset. He'd just stared across the table hoping his siblings didn't notice what was going on.

One night a few years later, Calvin woke up to use the bathroom and was greeted by the flashing lights of police sirens. He ran into the living room just in time to see his father being escorted out the door in handcuffs. His mother sat on the couch crying. Calvin was confused, scared, and angry as he watched his father being taken away and his mother doing nothing to stop it. He ran over to her pleading for her to do something and she replied, "I am, I'm protecting myself," then walked away.

His father received a four-year sentence for assaulting his mother, but for a while, it seemed as though he was the one in prison. His mother slipped into a depressive state. She rarely got out of bed, the house was a mess, and Calvin stopped attending school to take care of her. He'd get ready for school, dress his siblings and get them out to the bus stop, then go to her room to say good bye. The sight of her sprawled out across the bed with empty beer bottles and used tissues all over the nightstand tugged at his heart; he couldn't bring himself to leave her. So, skipping school became a habit as he took over as head of the house. He cooked the meals and forced his mother to eat; he cleaned the house, did the laundry, and even persuaded bill collectors to work with their limited income.

After missing three weeks of school and ignoring all their phone calls, one of Calvin's favorite teachers showed up. She took one look at his mother and called the police. Calvin knew what would happen when they got there, he'd be taken away and his mother left alone. He grabbed his mother by the face and desperately pleaded for her to snap out of it.

"Mom, they are going to take us away then you will be all alone. You have to get better!" Calvin cried.

She sat up, her head pounding from a case of beer she'd ingested the night before. Calvin helped her to her feet and guided her to the bathroom where he made her brush her teeth and wash her face. Then, *he made a pot of coffee which his mother guzzled down while they waited for the police to arrive.*

Calvin had done such a great job at cleaning the house, and had used his father's ATM card to buy food, that when the cops arrived the only information they had was the teacher's account of his mother's physical state and the school's report of his absences. They warned his mother that she had better get her act together because their next visit would not go so smoothly. They also warned her that if Calvin did not start attending school she could get jail time. The revelation that he had not been attending school hit her hard and it was just the reality check she needed to pull herself together. They suggested counseling and she took their advice joining a support group where she made lots of new friends and received the help she needed

As the days went by Calvin saw a different side to his mother. She'd wake him up for school with a song and a smile; at first, he thought she was losing her mind. Soon he'd realized she was happier than he had ever seen her. She found a job and made some friends. The insecure fragile women, she'd become, no longer existed. There was a self-help book that was given to her from the support group. She read it from cover to cover, over and over again. She tried to live her life based on the concepts of that book and it transformed her into an assertive motivated woman in a short period of time.

As Calvin, entered high school he began to miss his dad. He missed the guy stuff they did. Although his mom was great and he enjoyed hanging out with her, he wanted his dad back. He was starting to notice the pretty girls at his school. One in particular made his stomach do flips, and he had questions that he did not feel comfortable asking his mom. His hormones were out of control and the late night erotic dreams were becoming more frequent. He'd experimented a little, but too many failed attempts of intercourse left him fearful of trying again. Then during the summer before his sophomore year, his dad was let out early. He showed up at their door step surprising them. He wanted to come home and be a family, but his mother stood her ground. She loved her freedom and was not about to allow him back into her life. He demanded she let him in, and when she refused, he slapped her across the face. Calvin rushed into his father's face, shielding his mother from another blow, and told his father, "I love you and I am glad you are out, but if you put your hands on my mother again, I will kill you. She doesn't want you back and I don't blame her. Find somewhere else to live." His dad backed down, only out of fear of going back to jail, but constantly called begging for another chance.

His mom filed for divorce, got an order of protection, and bought a stun gun. When the divorce was finalized his dad moved on, found a new girlfriend, and occasionally made time to be a father. He was all too enthusiastic about teaching Calvin about relationships, which did more harm than good. Calvin would leave their conversations more confused and eventually decided he'd be better off learning on his own without asking his father questions.

Calvin tried to shake the thoughts of his mother and father out of his head. The demons from his past would always haunt him after he'd been abusive to Latrice. He told himself that he would never harm a woman, no matter what she did. His father had told him, 'If a woman picks a fight with a man, she deserves everything she gets'. The women his father dated after his mother, met the same fate, but Calvin vowed to be different. He'd promised to treat his woman like a queen, but when he started dating, everything was great until he developed serious feelings for her. Then, the slightest disagreement or suspicious action would send him into rages that became harder for him to contain.

The previous night, he'd become further caught up in the whirlwind of rage than he ever had. He'd gone from dragging a woman by the hair, to punching her in the face, and now almost choking her to death. For the first time, he realized that it was he who had the problem and he needed help before he went too far.

Calvin had planned to spend the next few days trying to erase all of the pain and bad memories from Latrice's mind with love. In the back of his mind, he knew he'd promised to change and miserably failed in the past, but swore this time would be different. Calvin grabbed his laptop and made reservations for their upcoming getaway—arranging for two dozen roses to be delivered every day until they'd left. He then sat back and waited for Latrice to join him.

Calvin headed downstairs to see what was taking Latrice so long. He walked into the kitchen and she was unloading the dishwasher. Every time she lifted her arm to place a dish in the cabinet, he could see her wincing from pain. A lump formed in his throat as he watched her suffer through the injuries he'd inflicted. He whispered her name and the mere sound of his voice startled her. She spun around and immediately started explaining what she was doing. Her voice was incoherent as she fumbled for the right words to say.

Calvin went to comfort her, but as he lifted his hand to caress her cheek she ducked. This wasn't the first time she had ducked when he was being affectionate, but today it bothered him more than it ever had. Calvin softly grabbed her wrist and pulled her close.

"I am not trying to hurt you. I promise I won't hurt you again. I will go to counseling, anger management, or whatever else it takes. I don't like hurting you."

Latrice was at a loss for words. The sincerity of his words and the compassion in his touch had been absent through every beating of the past. She watched tears well in his eyes and his struggle to hold them back. Calvin could always put on a good show of remorse, but there was more to it this time. He actually took responsibility for his actions, which had never happened before. 'you made me angry' or 'look what you made me do', were familiar phrases Calvin used. Even in his apologetic regret, Latrice was always to blame for his inability to control his anger.

With an unforgiving heart, Latrice watched as a tear rolled down Calvin's face. It was too late. His change of heart met her hardened heart and she refused to be swayed by his tears. She stood silently still as he continued to ramble off his apology, but disgust and hatred ran through her mind.

Latrice could only see the expression he wore less than twenty-four hours ago. His brow was furrowed and beads of sweat had resided on his forehead. His eyes were dark and distant as if he was blind to his surroundings and his cheeks sucked in and out while he drew in deep breaths. His face was void of compassion and full of wrath. The distortion of his face made him nearly unrecognizable.

Latrice was so caught up in the vision of the previous night's beating, she didn't realize he'd asked her a question. When she snapped out of it, Calvin had a firm grip on her arm and a frustrated expression on his face. The tone of his voice as he called her name and the pressure from his hand squeezing her arm confirmed in Latrice's heart that he was never going to change. No matter what she did or said, the slightest misstep would upset him. It was just a matter of time before he'd lose control again and kill her.

"I am sorry I am not feeling well and I spaced out; please forgive me." She'd made up her mind to do whatever it took to get through the next couple of days. Even if that meant lying, she was willing to do it, but as soon as he left the house, she was leaving.

Calvin loosened his grip on her arm and compassion returned to his face. "Well, let me help you to bed."

Calvin lifted Latrice off the ground in an attempt to carry her to bed, but when he grabbed her Latrice screamed out in pain. He instantly put her down and ran to the cabinet, grabbing zip lock bags to fill with ice. He then escorted Latrice to bed. Calvin helped her into bed and placed a bag of ice on her ribs and face. Finally, he curled up next to her.

Latrice heard the soft rumble of Calvin snoring and turned to watch him sleep. All the repulsion and contempt she felt surged to the forefront. Tears stained her face while she attempted to restrain emotion. Homicidal thoughts ran through her mind as she watched his chest rise and fall with each breath. She wondered if he would wake up if she smothered him with a pillow. Would she be strong enough to hold him down? She envisioned herself going to retrieve that knife from the kitchen and plunging it in to his chest.

What story would she tell to the police? *Self-defense or extreme emotional distress would surely let me off the hook,* she thought. She thought it even better for him to wake up and fight back; that way, she could most definitely claim self-defense, but Calvin was bigger, faster, and stronger. He would over power her and she'd be the one dead.

Tears flowed as she contemplated her next move. She was willing to risk her life for her freedom. Living in captivity was driving her crazy and desperation was now her driving force. Her hands continued to shake uncontrollably as she battled her conscience. Although she was willing to risk her life to be free, she wasn't a killer. Freedom would come soon enough without resorting to violence and she'd be truly free without his death looming over her head.

Latrice finally crawled out of bed. She sobbed hysterically into the pillow she'd just thought about smothering Calvin with. The physical pain, the distortion of her face, and the emotional distress was overwhelming and she rushed to find something to take the pain away. She was in the bathroom frantically fumbling to open a pill bottle when the deep vibration of Calvin's voice sent chills down her spine.

"What are you doing?"

Latrice dropped the bottle of pills, causing the lid to pop off and pills scattered to the floor. She shuddered in fear as Calvin picked up the bottle. He read the label, scooped the pills off the floor, and flushed them down the toilet.

He stood in front of her, pulling her close; Latrice could have sworn she saw tears in his eyes.

Calvin released his embrace and asked with all sincerity, "Were you trying to kill yourself with those pills?"

"No!" Latrice screamed. "I am just hurting really bad, and need something to help me get comfortable."

Calvin studied her face for any sign of deception, but could barely stand to look at her. The bruising and swelling was evidence of the man he had become and he was ashamed of what he had done. Calvin grabbed a couple of pain killers out of the medicine cabinet and escorted Latrice back to bed.

Latrice lay in bed stared at the ceiling. She tried to block out Calvin's smell, the feel of his hand on her thigh, and the kisses he placed on her shoulder. Her stomach churned when he climbed on top of her and she closed her eyes to endure what Calvin must have saw as therapy. Again, she moaned when appropriate. It had been almost a year since she'd had an actual orgasm, but Calvin hadn't noticed nor did he care. She'd perfected the fake orgasm, which stroked his ego. By the time he was finished, the pain killers had kicked in and Latrice drifted off to sleep.

hree days had gone by since Latrice had decided to leave Calvin and she was on the verge of losing her mind. Faking her way through sex and pretending to be in love with her abuser was chipping away at her sanity. He wanted sex three times a day as if his lovemaking was a healing balm miraculously taking all of her pain away.

On the morning of the fourth day, she'd had enough. She woke early and ironed his clothes for work and prepared his breakfast. She tiptoed into the room and kneeled on his side of the bed. He could get up, shower, and head to work, or he could beat her senseless for waking him up. At this point, she was willing to take the risk for her freedom. She patted him on the back and whispered his name.

"What do you want?"

His tone was chilling, but she was not giving up that easily. "I know you said you were not going to work today, but I was thinking." Calvin turned around and glared at her.

"I am feeling much better and I'd hate to be the cause of you getting any further behind in work. That would be so selfish of me to take up all your time. So I was thinking, maybe you could go into work and when I finish my chores around the house, I could come down there and help you. Maybe I could make copies or type some things up for you." Latrice held her breath as she waited for his response.

"Is my breakfast ready?" Calvin rolled over, revealing his finely cut torso. He kept a rigorous workout schedule and demanded Latrice do the same. Her flawless body was one of the only benefits she'd received from their marriage. If Latrice was going to get him to leave, she was going to have to lay it on thick. At that point, she was willing to do whatever it took to get him to leave. She placed a trail of kisses across his chest as she spoke.

"Yes it is. Do you want to eat first or shower?"

Calvin chuckled while stroking the back of her head. "I will pass on breakfast if you take those kisses a little lower." He guided her head below his waist. Latrice knew better than to protest.

Staying focused on her freedom allowed her to get through the act. She'd have to play nice for another hour and hopefully she would never see him again. The thought alone had a smile on her face and a song on her lips. The past few days had been torture and there was finally a ray of hope. Calvin was going to work and she would be packed and gone before he made it to his office. She wished she could see the expression on his face when he came home and realized she'd left. *He will probably bust a blood vessel*; the thought alone put a smile on her face.

Calvin stepped out the shower and watched as Latrice danced and sang around the bedroom. She twirled around dancing with his suit jacket before carefully laying it on the bed. He loved her more than he ever loved a woman and couldn't believe how close he came to killing her. Every time he hit her, he'd vow to never hurt her again. Then one day she'd make him angry and he would lose control. It was easy to say what he was going to do the next time, but when that anger showed up he lost his mind.

Calvin made his way toward Latrice and grabbed her by the arm. Her reflexes kicked in and she ducked. "I am sorry. I did not mean to scare you. I don't like you being scared of me. Please help me to not be this person anymore," he pleaded, as he pulled her close.

Latrice was not moved by his emotions. These were all things she had heard before. It had become more frequent over the past few days, but she was done falling for it. She was not allowing his guilt to deter her plan and had to think quickly before he decided to stay home. "Baby, I know you feel bad, but there is no need. I feel much better and I am anxious for us to get back to our regular lives. Maybe going to work will take your mind off what happened. I love you." Latrice ended her speech with a long deep kiss just to seal the deal and make sure he left the house.

With suppressed excitement, Latrice walked Calvin to the door. She chewed on her bottom lip to keep from smiling as she handed him his briefcase. She whispered that she loved him, but in her mind said, *goodbye, you bastard*. Freedom was the most underrated luxury in the world; never again would she take it for granted.

Latrice shut the door and rushed to the window to watch Calvin walk to the car. He hopped in his car, pulled out of the driveway, and drove off. She watched until she could no longer see his car. When the coast was clear, she threw on some sweats, a hat, filled two trash bags with clothes, and headed to the car. She knew she had an hour before Calvin started calling to check on her and wanted to at least make contact with Camilla by then.

Latrice decided to head in the direction of Camilla's job. She knew her husband had opened an accounting firm and hired her as the administrative assistant. She'd look there first and then go to Camilla's house if needed. They were good friends at one point and Latrice was sorry for letting Calvin ruin it. They'd become even closer when Latrice remembered details about a night they had gone out. Camilla had gotten so wasted that she had a one-night stand. When she woke the next morning, she was so ashamed that she'd left the hotel without getting the guy's name or a good look at his face. A few weeks later, Camilla found out she was pregnant and had no way of locating the guy she slept with. Latrice did not drink quite as much that night and had gotten a real good look. There was no doubt in Latrice's mind that Camilla would help her. She had been foolish to allow Calvin to isolate her from her friends and family, but now it was all over.

Latrice sped through the city and had to force herself to slow down several times. The last thing she wanted was a ticket, but she was anxious to get to her destination. She neurotically checked the rearview mirror for Calvin's car. She never saw it, but couldn't shake the feeling that Calvin was somewhere near.

After Latrice arrived at the office building, she circled the parking lot three times to see if any cars were following. Panic set in and she trembled while she searched for a parking space. She pulled into a parking space, threw the car into park, hopped out, and took off running toward the building. She ran at full speed, never looking back, nor slowing down. She burst through the door and slammed it shut as fast as she could. Her chest heaved as she struggled to breathe. She plopped down onto a chair in the waiting area.

The receptionist looked perplexed, but patiently waited for her to pull herself together. "May I help you?" The receptionist finally interjected, amid Latrice's heavy breathing.

"Yes." Latrice gasped for air as she spoke. "I am looking for a friend of mine who used to answer the phone and run the office for her husband. Her name is Camilla, do you know her?"

"Yes, but they are in a meeting right now. Would you like to wait or come back later?"

"I will wait, but is there somewhere else I can wait; like a conference room or something."

As the receptionist escorted Latrice to a conference room, Camilla and Tim stepped out of Tim's office giggling and chatting lightly. The sight of her brought tears to Latrice's eyes, she ran up to Camilla, and threw her arms around her.

Camilla slowly retreated from the embrace. "I am sorry, can I help you?" She glared at the receptionist for allowing a strange woman to get so far into the office.

You don't recognize me?" Latrice pulled off her hat and Camilla gasped.

"Latrice, oh my God! What happened to you?" Camilla traced the bruises on Latrice's face with her fingers. "Who did this to you?" Camilla draped her arm around Latrice and guided her into Tim's office.

Once behind closed doors, Latrice broke down. "My husband did this to me."

"Your husband did this to you?" Tim waited for her nod then turned his back on them and immediately made a phone call.

"He has been beating me since the beginning, but this time he almost killed me. He choked me until I passed out. He thought I was dead and put me in the car to get rid of me." Latrice collapsed to the floor—at this point she was crying hysterically. Camilla attempted to comfort her, but her wails grew more out of control. The anguish she'd endured over the past few days came rushing to the surface. Camilla held Latrice's hair back as her stomach convulsed; she'd cried herself into vomiting. It pained her to see her friend in such distress and she cried with her.

By the time they calmed down, Tim was off the phone and had already set a plan in motion. Tim instructed Camilla to drive directly to Delisa's house and he drove Latrice in her car. By the time they arrived, Paul was there along with Delisa and Jaleel. Tim backed Latrice's car into the garage and they joined everyone at the kitchen table.

Paul was the first to speak. "First, you need to do exactly what we tell you to do. If you are not completely done with him get up and leave. We are all family. We have children and do not want anyone to get hurt because you are playing games. Are we clear?"

Latrice looked around and every eye was pinned on her waiting for her response. "Yes we are clear, and you do not have to worry about me ever going back."

"That's good. So, first of all give me your cell phone. He is going to call you and I do not want you to be tempted to answer. You can use this prepaid phone if you need to contact one of us, but even that has to be limited." Jaleel slid it across the table and Latrice willingly gave up her old one. Paul continued with his list of demands. "You will stay here with Delisa and Jaleel. Calvin knows where Camilla and Tim live. After your family, that will be the next place he checks. You can never leave the house without some form of disguise and when you leave, you cannot drive your car. Do not go to any of the places he frequents. Avoid even simple places like restaurants, malls, or supermarkets. The last thing you need is for him to spot you and follow you. Finally, I have a judge friend who can rush an order of protection. This piece of paper is not to be taken lightly. Follow it to the letter. It pretty much gives you license to protect yourself at any length should Calvin come near you. Now, when Calvin gets home today he is going to be pissed that you are not there."

"Actually," Latrice interrupted. "He is expecting me to show up at his office in a couple of hours."

"That just means he is going to be calling and calling." Paul waved her phone in the air. "And when he doesn't get a hold of you, he will leave work to look for you. He will threaten or even bribe your family to tell him where you are. Some may be persuaded to give you up, that's why it is important that you do not contact them. When he is served with the restraining order, he will be fuming. So you need to lay low for the next few weeks."

"Consider it done," she replied. Paul passed her some papers to sign and pulled out a camera. Latrice started to protest being photographed, but decided against it. She remembered that Paul was a big shot lawyer and was grateful he was willing to help. She didn't want him to think that she wasn't fully on board. They took shots of her face from every angle imaginable. They lifted her shirt to take pictures of her ribs; every bruise great or small was photographed. When it was all said and done, Delisa escorted her to the guest room. They passed Marlon in the hall and Latrice tried to cover her wounds. Her attempt might have worked if Delisa hadn't stopped to introduce them.

"Marlon, this is Latrice. She will be staying here for a while. Latrice, Marlon stays here also. I know it is going to be a little crowded, but bear with us, please. The rooms you guys are in have a connecting bathroom. There are locks to keep anyone from entering your room through the bathroom, but if either of you are uncomfortable, we could switch DJ's room."

"It's not a problem, I'm just grateful you had a place for me to lay my head."

"Yes, me too," Latrice chimed in.

Marlon noticed she was trying to cover her face and pulled her hands down; his sudden movement caused her to flinch.

"You are beautiful; there is no need to hide your face." He turned and walked away thinking that something terrible must have happened for her face to be so bruised. When he stepped into the kitchen and saw Jaleel, Paul, Tim, and Camilla all there so early in the morning, he knew his assumption was correct.

"Hey Marlon, did you see Latrice in the hall? She is a friend of mine from college."

"Yes I did. Delisa introduced us."

"Good, please try to make her feel welcomed. She has been through a lot and anything you could do to help would be great."

"Sure, just let her know that I am here during the day. So, if she needs anything she can knock on my door." Marlon did not ask any questions and he wasn't quite sure he even wanted to know what was going on.

"What time do you go to work tonight?"

"I go in around four."

Do you think you can hang around the house until I get here at about three?"

"Well, I was going to run by my house and get some more clothes, but I guess I can just go later."

"Thank you so much; this really means a lot to me." Camilla informed Latrice that Marlon would stay with her during the day and she would be back as soon as she could. Everyone went back to work leaving Marlon and Latrice home alone.

Marlon had made himself a light breakfast and watched a movie while he washed clothes. Latrice still hadn't come out of the room. He kept telling himself she was a grown woman and if she wanted to stay locked up in the room all day that was her prerogative, but now he was beginning to worry. He made her a turkey sandwich and grabbed a bottle of water. He called out her name and tapped lightly on the door, but there was no answer. Marlon opened the door and peeked inside. Latrice was bawling into a pillow. He grabbed some tissue from the bathroom then kneeled on the side of her bed.

He pulled the covers back and whispered her name. She turned to face him, and the tears on her face caused her hair to stick to her cheeks. The pillow was soaking wet and her eyes red and puffy. Marlon offered her the tissue and pulled the hairs out of her face.

"Are you hungry? I made you a sandwich. I really think you need to eat something."

"I don't want anything, but thank you."

Marlon paused, allowing her to blow her nose, and then continued insisting that she eat.

"Just take a few bites." Marlon picked the sandwich up and placed it on her lips. Hesitantly, she took a bite. "It's good, isn't it?" Marlon smiled, as she sat up and finished the sandwich. He tried not to stare as she ate, but being closer to her, he could see the bruises more clearly. She had a massive black eye that looked like she had been kicked in the face by a horse. The corner of her mouth that had been split open was now crusted shut. There were even bruises on her neck that looked like finger prints.

"You know, you don't have to stay locked up in this room all day. You are more than welcomed to come downstairs with me. I am going to watch another movie and I would love some company." Marlon watched hopefully as she contemplated whether to join him or not.

Latrice slid out of bed, which was high off the ground. Marlon placed his hand on her side to help her slide down and she winced in pain. He instantly backed off. Latrice lifted up the side of her shirt and revealed an enormous bruise on her ribs.

"Are you okay?" Marlon sympathetically asked, but seeing tears build up in her eyes, he didn't force the issue. He escorted her downstairs where they silently watched movies until Camilla arrived.

Marlon nodded off to sleep during the movie and the doorbell ringing startled Latrice. She franticly tapped Marlon until he woke up then whispered, "There is someone at the door." He got up, confused as to why she did not answer it herself and why she was so jumpy. When Camilla came in with bags of wigs and sunglasses, Marlon was even more confused.

"Okay, I was trying to respect everyone's privacy, but there is obviously something serious going on. If I'm going to be here with her during the day, I would like to know if she is in danger."

"You are absolutely right." Tears filled Latrice's eyes, but she fought to hold them back. "You noticed all the bruises. Well, my husband did this to me. A few days ago, he beat the hell out of me like he has been for the past two years. I went in the bathroom to clean up my face and locked the door. I know how he feels about locked doors. It was so stupid of me to lock the door." Her voice cracked. "He came to check on me and was furious that he could not get in. I unlocked the door bracing myself for another beat down, but he put his hands around my throat. I couldn't breathe. I struggled to get free, but nothing worked. The more I fought, the harder he squeezed. I guess I passed out, because I woke up in the garage on the back seat of the car. Calvin said he was taking me to the hospital, but I knew he thought I was dead and was getting rid of my body." Latrice hung her head in shame.

"I know it shouldn't have taken this long, but that night was an eye-opener. I realized that he would actually kill me during one of his fits of rage. So,

I made up my mind that the first time he left the house, I was gone. Camilla was the only person I could think of that would help me."

"I am so sorry," Camilla said, gently embracing Latrice. "I had no idea all that was going on. But, you hold your head up. It's not your fault. Calvin has a problem and I'm glad you had the courage to leave. Some women aren't that lucky."

Marlon silently watched Latrice. He didn't even know her, yet he was enraged. "Does he know where she is?"

"No, that is why we felt it was better for her to stay here than at my house, but…" Camilla grabbed Latrice's hand to comfort her. "He has called your cell phone. We knew he would call, but Paul said his tone was lethal. He felt it was best to have him served with the restraining order immediately."

Marlon sat next to Latrice and grabbed her trembling hand. "Don't worry. I will sit here with you every day. I will not let anything happen to you."

"Thank you, but I do not want my problems to inconvenience anyone."

"It's not an inconvenience. I work late and don't really go anywhere during the day. If I need to run an errand or something, I'll take care of it and come right back, or you can go with me." Seeing what she was dealing with made him realize his situation wasn't that bad. He was happy to help. "But I do have to go to work soon. Will you guys be okay by yourselves?"

"Yeah, we should be fine. Tim stopped to get dinner and will be here shortly."

"Okay, I am going to take a quick shower; holler if you need anything."

Camilla wrapped her arms around Latrice and prayed for her strength and healing. She had always felt guilty for not telling Latrice about the Lord when she had a chance, but when they were in college she was rebelling against the Lord and did not want to seem like a hypocrite. Now that the Lord had given her another opportunity, she was not going to blow it. "Lord we need you. I know you see this woman that you created. You see all that she has endured and only you can heal her. I ask, in the name of Jesus, that you remove all pain and discomfort, heal every emotional as well as physical wound. Lord, she also needs your spirit. Oh God, let her feel you inside and out. Take charge of her life and let her feel your love in Jesus name."

Latrice listened intently as Camilla prayed. She wanted to believe God was that powerful, but her faith was limited. As soon as the prayer was over she had questions.

"Camilla, if God can do all the things you asked him to, then why did He allow this to happen to me? Wouldn't it have been easier for him to make Calvin treat me right than to come behind him to clean up his mess? It would have been easier for me." Latrice didn't wait for a response, she simply stormed up the stairs to her room, brushing pass Marlon on the way. He tried to speak, but it was in vain. He wanted to check on her, but he had to get to work.

Shortly after, Tim arrived with dinner. Latrice came out of isolation, but didn't have much of an appetite and went back upstairs to rest. The day had been full of life-altering decisions and the reality of her choices was overwhelming. Despite her fear of the repercussions from leaving Calvin, she felt surprisingly safe. Marlon seemed nice and if he was willing to keep her company during the day, she wouldn't stop him. What bothered her most was Camilla's prayer. Latrice believed in God, but wasn't taught to depend on him or live for him. If he had the power Camilla claimed he did, why didn't he spare her the pain and heartache of the past two years?

Calvin sat behind his desk seething with anger. He ended a phone call and hurled his cell phone across the room; it shattered as it hit the wall. His secretary rushed in to make sure he was alright and he snapped at her. The fact that a man had answered his wife's phone pissed him off, but finding out she was leaving him enraged him. One after another, he picked up the vases and decorative statuettes that Latrice had purchased for his office and hurled them at the wall. He stormed around in a rage throwing and breaking things, flipping over his desk, and tipping over bookshelves.

When his rage had finally subsided, his office was left in shambles. Books, paper, broken glass, and ceramics were all over the floor. Calvin tiptoed around the mess, searching for his broken phone, put it in his pocket, and headed out the door. He stopped by his secretary's desk and grumbled, "Have my office clean before I get back," and left.

If Latrice wanted to play games, he was willing to play, but she wouldn't like the outcome. Calvin's mind was already full of plots to locate her. He was even more pissed when he realized how she had schemed to get him out of the house so she could leave. His efforts over the past few days to convince her he'd changed were in vain. In his mind, Latrice running off nullified his vow to never to hurt her again; when he found her he was going to make her pay.

Calvin was approached by a black man as he left the building. He wore sagging pants and his hat was cocked to the side. Calvin brushed quickly passed the man. He had no time for some street thug, but the man stood in his path, forcing him to stop.

"Are you Calvin Stewart?" Calvin studied the man's face and knew they'd never met. "I am; who's asking?"

"Mr. Stewart, you have been served." He handed Calvin an envelope and walked away.

Calvin ripped the envelope open and knew exactly what it was. Latrice had gotten a restraining order. A muscle twitched at the base of his jaw and he mumbled several obscenities under his breath. Calvin quickly made his way to his car. He forced himself to stay calm. Being angry and destroying things was wasted energy and he'd already wasted enough on his office. He needed to direct all his energy to tracking down his wife. If he had any chance of finding Latrice, he had to stay focused and not be controlled by anger.

2

Marlon was dead tired after work. The Saturday night drive was always rough, but tonight was worse than usual. The effects of stress were starting to manifest in his work performance. He raked over his marriage with a fine-tooth comb, looking for both his and Alicia's true motive for marrying. A hot shower and sleep was all he wanted. He dragged his tired body up the stairs, grabbed his robe, and headed toward the shower. He turned the doorknob and realized it was locked.

"Great, a perfect ending to a perfect night," he said, shaking his head in frustration. Latrice had probably locked the door when she showered and forgot to unlock it when she was finished. Knocking would do no good; she was usually asleep when he came home from work. He thought about banging on the door until she woke up, but figured that would scare her to death.

He usually liked to wash the smell of food off before going to bed, but tonight he'd have to deal with it. They had church in the morning, so hopefully Latrice would be up early enough for him to shower. Marlon landed face down on the bed and was fast asleep. His body was shutting down from the lack of sleep; neither stress, nor anger could keep him awake.

He hadn't realized how accustomed his body was to sleeping with someone. Even though he was barely speaking to Alicia before he left, he'd still find his way toward her body heat in the middle of the night. The past couple of weeks without someone laying next him had made it almost impossible to fall asleep. Given his current mental state, sleep was always a battle.

Marlon's alarm soon was going off. He dragged himself out of bed to check the bathroom door and it was still locked. Marlon tapped on the door, hoping Latrice was awake. He waited a few seconds, and then tapped a little harder. Shortly after, the lock clicked and the door creaked open.

"Sorry, I must have forgotten to unlock it after I showered last night," Latrice apologized.

"It's okay. I managed to sleep pretty good without a shower."

Latrice gasped, "Why didn't you knock? I was still awake when you came home."

"I assumed you were sleep and didn't want to bang on the door."

There was a moment of awkward silence. Latrice was still standing in the doorway and Marlon needed to get into the bathroom. He didn't want to ask her to move, but if he didn't get into the bathroom soon, they were going to be late for church. He took a step toward the door, hoping she would get the hint, but she didn't.

"Do you mind if I..." Marlon asked.

"Oh, I am sorry," Latrice interjected, realizing she was still preventing him from showering. "I can be such an airhead at times. Let me get out of your way."

"No problem. I'll be just a few minutes, then the bathroom is all yours."

Latrice stepped out of the bathroom and Marlon was finally able to shower. The water washed away the grogginess and helped his mind to get through another day. Marlon's church attendance had been sporadic since leaving Alicia. No matter what scripture he quoted to motivate himself to go to church, when the time came for service, he just didn't have the enthusiasm. He was angry with God and couldn't help but surmise his luck with Alicia as a spiritual reward. This morning was no different, but Delisa had asked him to give Latrice a ride because they had to go early for a meeting. Marlon thought that if anyone needed the Lord, it was Latrice and agreed to give her a ride.

Marlon's chief excuse for not going to church was the fact that Alicia would be there. Although her attendance had been shoddy before they split, Marlon knew she would come to church just to force herself on him. He was not ready to talk with her. The thought of being in the same room with her upset him and he was afraid of what he might do to her. He agreed to counseling, but didn't think he could make it through the sessions.

Marlon finished getting dressed, gave himself one last pep talk to ignore Alicia if he saw her, and he and Latrice were out the door. The ride to church was quiet. Marlon studied Latrice out the corner of his eye. She kept looking at her face in the visor mirror. The swelling in her face had gone down considerably, but there was still some bruising. She wished she didn't have to go to church, but the alternative was staying home alone and she wasn't ready for that.

Last Sunday was her first time in church in years. There were a few people who said hello and introduced themselves, but for the most part everyone just stared at her. She would have preferred that they had asked her what happened instead of gawking at her as if she had leprosy.

Marlon parked in the church parking lot and Latrice checked her face in the visor mirror again, ensuring her bruises couldn't be seen through makeup. Latrice shook her head. No matter how much makeup she put on, she always felt disgusting. She put her sunglasses on, grabbed her purse, and tried to exit the car, but Marlon stopped her.

"Latrice, you have nothing to worry about." He had seen her checking her face and knew what was bothering her. "You are beautiful."

Latrice sighed as tears formed in her eyes, "You don't have to say that, but I appreciate you trying to make me feel better."

"I'm not just trying to make you feel better." Marlon took off her sunglasses to look directly into her eyes. "You forget I see you every day without the wigs and makeup; you are a beautiful woman. So what, your face is a little bruised. Most women on their best day don't look as good as you do right now." Marlon compassionately kissed her on the cheek.

"Thank you." Latrice took a few moments to allow Marlon's words to sink in. It's amazing how the kind words of a good looking man could lift your spirits.

"Now, let's go in here and praise the Lord."

Marlon scanned the sanctuary for Alicia and was relieved when he did not see her. The praise team was singing, the musicians were rocking, and the praises were going forth. Marlon wasn't one of those pretty boy brothers who thought he was too good to praise the Lord. He came to church to give the Lord his all, but today was a different story. He didn't feel like praising the Lord and sat cemented to his seat. Something deep within him told him to get up, but his body wouldn't cooperate. Even lifting his hands was a chore. Marlon felt like an outsider watching everyone else singing and clapping. He closed his eyes and tried to focus on the goodness of the Lord while his mind ran wild with random thoughts.

Pastor Hawkins came to the podium to deliver the morning sermon and instantly, Marlon's mind checked out. He thought about Alicia and what woman she could have been sleeping with. He thought about work and the new dishes he was working on. When his mind strayed too far, he'd shake the thoughts away and try to focus on what the pastor was saying. Marlon struggled to pay attention during the entire sermon and when it was time for altar call, he knew he should have gotten in line for prayer, but couldn't make himself get up.

After service was over, Marlon took Latrice by the hand and made a beeline for the car. He didn't want to talk to anyone. He didn't want them asking where he'd been the past few Sundays or asking where Alicia was. He was in such a hurry to leave and was one of the first cars to pull out of the parking lot. The ride home was quiet. Latrice sensed that something was bothering Marlon, but couldn't find the words to make him feel better.

Marlon opened the front door to the house, and then stepped aside allowing Latrice to enter. Latrice whispered, "I don't know what is bothering you, but it is going to be okay. Look at me, if I can get through this, surely you can handle what you're going through."

Her hug was sudden and awkward. Uncertain of how to respond, Marlon wrapped his arms around her and hugged her back. The warmth of their embrace was comforting and neither wanted to let go. Latrice leaned her head on his chest and ran her hands up and down his back, inhaling his strength. Marlon rested his head on the top of hers, pulling her close to bask in the neediness her fragility created.

Prior to their embrace, they'd only been strangers sharing a living space. Some days they ate breakfast together and had short conversations, but Latrice spent most of her time in her room. Occasionally, she'd accepted his offer to watch a movie, but when she did, they watched in silence. They were now more than two people living in the same house; they were friends.

After Marlon left, Alicia tried to forgo the lifestyle that had gotten her into so much trouble. She stopped drinking, going to the club, and turned her back on Meme. All she did was work and come home to wait for Marlon's call. For a brief second, she thought about going to church to see him, but her life was such a mess, she wouldn't dare step a foot in church. She even thought about going to see him at work, but didn't really know where his restaurant was. She had spent so much time hating his job that she never bothered to visit. Even if she did go see him, showing up uninvited and unannounced might make things worse.

She had one of her nosy, non-working neighbors watching her house. Alicia had given the woman strict instructions to call immediately if Marlon showed up. Every day at work she could barely concentrate, because she was anticipating a phone call. She planned to race home, strip down to nothing, and ravage his body until he gave into her. When her monthly cycle would show up, she would plead to God that he not come home that week. Afterwards, she was grateful, but now the days were ticking by and she was getting a little restless. She wanted to be touched and made love to and that need could only be satisfied by two people. She wanted it to be Marlon, but as the days went by, it was becoming harder and harder not to call Meme. Loneliness is what had gotten her caught up with Meme in the first place and she told herself it wouldn't happen again. Alicia wanted Meme almost as bad as she wanted her husband. Several times she picked up the phone to invite her over for a little fun, but knew Meme wanted more. What Alicia felt for Meme was new and she didn't completely understand it. If she admitted that she wanted more than sex, she'd be admitting that she was a lesbian. In all the confusion, there was one thing she was certain of: she was not a lesbian. Alicia looked at the clock it was just after four.

"Marlon should be on his way to work," she whispered to herself. At the beginning of their marriage, she'd rush home just to see him before he left. Toward the end, she would poke around at work, hoping he would be gone before she got home. Now, she wished she could do it all over again. She'd support him and give him the attention he truly deserved. Alicia decided to just come clean, put her heart on the line, and beg him to put an end to her yearning. She bit her fingernails as she waited for him to answer. She'd called him just about every day since he left and he had yet to answer. She was anxious for their counseling to begin just so she could be close to him, but he repeatedly rejected her call.

When she finally heard his voice coming through the phone, chills ran down her spine. Alicia was so excited that he answered that she lost her train of thought. Marlon had to say hello several times before she responded.

"Hey," was all she could come up with.

Marlon's head dropped in frustration. He'd neglected to check the caller ID. "What do you want?"

"Marlon, I miss you like crazy. I know I screwed up and you may never forgive me, but I need you. Please, come be with me tonight—no strings attached and no promises. I want to make love to you the way I should've been doing these past five years."

Marlon had to admit, a sexual yearning had been riding him all week, but his hatred for Alicia outweighed his desire; her offer was appalling. "So, just like that I am supposed to forget about everything and hop into bed with you?"

"You don't have to forget anything. I know I messed up and things may never be the same, but I am offering my body to you. You can have me any way you want me."

"That's just it," Marlon spoke slowly to make sure Alicia got the point. "I don't want you. If we were the last two people on earth, human life would cease because I'm never going to touch you again. The thought of you makes me sick. Lose my number and don't ever call me again. If I have something to say I will call you."

Marlon was both shocked and offended by her proposal. She'd freely given away what belonged to him. He didn't care that it was a woman. He would never come behind someone else and make love to his wife. He should've been Alicia's last lover and she'd ruined that. The spots she loved for him to touch, she allowed someone else to touch. Her body was tainted and he would never touch her again.

Tears streamed down Alicia's face as she clutched the phone long after Marlon had hung up. Her heart was broken and Alicia realized she'd never be the woman Marlon fell in love with. She pulled a bottle of wine out of the refrigerator and poured herself a glass. Before long, the bottle was empty along with Alicia's good judgment. She had a buzz and was feeling even more sensual than before. Without another thought, she called Meme. If she couldn't have who she wanted then she'd settle for the next best thing.

Soon thereafter, Meme showed up. She was heartbroken the last time they'd been together and couldn't believe that Alicia was giving her another chance. By the sound of her voice, Meme could tell this was just a booty call, but she didn't care. Whatever the driving force behind the invite, Meme was going to take advantage of the situation. All she wanted was to be close to Alicia. She changed into something a little more revealing to allow her femininity to radiate.

Meme arrived at Alicia's house hoping to be greeted by a woman who was ready to give in to her every desire, but what she encountered was a blubbering mess. Alicia had pulled out a half-empty bottle of vodka and started chugging it down. She was hurting and wanted anything to numb the pain. She'd gone from a playful buzz to sloppy drunk. Tears saturated her face and instead of a kiss, she greeted Meme by crying out, "He doesn't love me anymore." Alicia fell into Meme's arm sobbing. Meme helped Alicia into bed and climbed in next to her.

"He may not love you, but I do." Alicia continued to sob into Meme's chest until she fell asleep. Although she had hoped for more, being able to hold Alicia was more than satisfying. Meme pulled the blanket over them and brushed her lips across Alicia's, then snuggled up to go to sleep.

Morning came and with it sobriety. The blaring siren from the alarm clock echoed through Alicia's head. The alcohol she'd drank magnified every sound; a hangover was an understatement. She vowed to never get drunk the night before work again. Alicia made her way to the kitchen hoping a few cups of coffee would get her mind right for work and quell her pounding head.

Alicia's heart sank when she walked in the kitchen. Meme was standing in front of the stove making breakfast. She'd completely forgotten that she invited her over.

"So, you stayed the night?"

Meme didn't reply, but placed a cup of coffee and a plate with toast and scrambled eggs on the table. She pulled out a chair and motioned for Alicia to sit.

"Did we have sex?"

"I wouldn't take advantage of you like that. You were drunk and upset; I just held you until you fell asleep." Meme was offended by Alicia's sigh of relief. "Is having sex with me that repulsive?"

"You know I don't feel that way."

"I don't know how you feel. The last time I came over you hurt me, and then you call last night asking me to soothe your fire, but when I get here you're crying over Marlon. So please, enlighten me; how do you feel about me?"

"Well, I was crying because my husband made it pretty clear that he never wants to touch me again. He is still my husband and although I screwed up, I still love him. You have to understand that regardless of how I feel about you, I will keep fighting for my marriage until the divorce papers are signed."

"I am sorry, but you have to realize that I am twenty-seven years old, and I have never felt what I am feeling for you. You can't jerk me around."

"I'm not jerking you around. I am trying to be honest. I want you, but I also want my husband. If you can't discreetly be with me knowing there is a chance you might lose me, then we can't be together at all."

Meme reflected on Alicia's words. Deciding she'd rather have something rather than nothing, she timidly asked, "Can I come over when you get home from work?"

A victorious smirk spread across Alicia's face as they kissed to seal their arrangement. Heat surged through Alicia and she remembered exactly why she'd invited Meme over. Their kiss was profoundly obsessive. It enticed the yearning that had been plaguing Alicia. Kissing was no longer enough. They headed to the bedroom to more thoroughly enjoy each other.

10

Latrice was getting stir crazy sitting around the house doing nothing. She was used to days filled with cleaning, laundry, and preparing meals which was a huge contrast to her current situation. Since she'd been living with Delisa, someone else cleaned the house, there was no husband calling with his to do list, and every meal she ate someone else prepared. Most women would love the change from over worked housewife to pampered princess, but not Latrice.

There was too much on her mind and she needed something else to focus on. When she would close her eyes to sleep, her dreams would be filled with Calvin's wrath. Some nights she would wake in a cold sweat. She was free from Calvin, yet fear still held her captive. Fear kept her in the house, fear kept her from making phone calls, and fear kept her from interacting with the people around her. She'd escaped the abuse, but Calvin still controlled her. Latrice wondered if she would ever really be free from him.

Latrice snuck passed Marlon's room down to the kitchen. She had decided she would beat him to making breakfast. The house was quiet and she tiptoed across the cold kitchen floor. She quietly pulled out pots and pans, so she wouldn't wake him. She hoped she didn't offend him by cooking for herself, but she'd had enough of being waited on hand and foot. Latrice loved to cook and felt right at home in the kitchen. She opened the refrigerator and dove in, grabbing things off the shelves. Then, she walked to the counter with arms full of goodies. Before long, she was chopping and mixing away.

She got so caught up in her cooking that she didn't hear Marlon sneak up behind her. He tapped her on the shoulder and she froze. He chuckled at her reaction and reached around and grabbed the spatula out of her hand. As she turned around to beg him to let her finish, Latrice's eyes met Marlon's glorious chest. *My god,* she thought. *I thought Calvin had a nice chest, but his is ridiculous.* Her eyes roamed across every muscle from chest to abs.

Marlon was shocked that she was checking him out, and he flexed his chest to give her a little show. Latrice gasped as Marlon smiled. She spun around to tend to her breakfast.

Marlon laughed and waved the spatula back over her shoulder. "Aren't you going to need this to cook?" Latrice snatched the spatula out of Marlon's hand. "Was that a smile?" He teased. "Your smile is beautiful. You should do it more often." Latrice blushed, trying hard to contain another smile. She was unsure if he was flirting or making fun, but she enjoyed it.

Marlon stepped next to her, inspecting the pots on the stove. He lifted every lid, deeply inhaling the aromas that came spiraling out. With every whiff, his stomach growled. Alicia had stopped cooking for him a long time ago, and although he was a chef, soul food was not his forte. He could do a little something, but it just didn't taste the same.

Latrice smiled as Marlon savored the aromas of the food she'd cooked. It felt good to cook just for the fun it, instead of having to cook to avoid a beat down. Latrice turned to Marlon and blew the heat off of a spoonful of grits she'd scooped. "Are you hungry?"

Watching her blow on the grits turned Marlon on. All of the swelling and bruising had left her face and he could finally see just how stunning she truly was. Her lips were puckered as she blew on the food and her hair was slightly disheveled, which he loved. He placed his hand on her hip as he leaned in to receive the spoon she offered. Their eyes connected as he opened his mouth. He knew he was flirting, but couldn't help himself. She hadn't touched him and had barely said three words to him, but she had excited him and he was glad he'd put on a pair of jeans instead of a flimsy pair of basketball shorts that would have exposed his excitement.

"Well, how is it?"

"It's good." Marlon's voice was deep and husky with desire that he was no longer trying to hide.

"Good," Latrice smiled. "You get the plates and we can eat."

Marlon took a few deep breaths and forced himself to calm down. He attributed his overactive libido to the past few of months without sexual contact.

"Get a grip," he whispered, before returning with the plates.

Latrice piled his plate high with grits, country potatoes with peppers and sausage, strips of bacon, homemade biscuits with country gravy, and two eggs cooked over medium. Marlon carried their plates to the table and waited patiently while Latrice poured them a cup of coffee. She joined him at the table, and paused, allowing him to bless their food, which she was growing accustom to doing. It felt strange the first time he grabbed her hands to pray, but she was now more at ease with it.

For a few minutes, they ate in silence until Latrice asked the question that had been bugging her since she moved in. "Marlon, why are you here?" Latrice instantly regretted asking the question. "Sorry, I know it is none of my business."

"It's okay. I know why you are here; it is only fair that you know why I am here. A couple of months ago I came home early from church and I caught my wife in bed with someone else."

"I am so sorry; you don't have to talk about it."

"There is no need to apologize. Things had been pretty shaky between us for a while, but I never would've guessed she would cheat on me. So, I have decided to get a divorce and I am staying here until things are settled." Marlon placed his fork on the table and leaned forward to whisper as if someone may have been eavesdropping. "To be honest with you, I don't love her and the more I think about it, I don't know if I ever did. I look at Jaleel, Paul, and Tim; they have given so much of themselves to their wives." Latrice knew exactly what he was talking about. Their devotion and love were a few of the reasons she rushed into marriage. "I have never been like that with Alicia. We rushed to get married and didn't really know each other. For awhile, we made the best of what we had, but in the long run it wasn't enough. She wanted me to give up my career. I wasn't willing and she resented me."

"What kind of work do you do that would make her so adamant about you giving it up?"

"I don't think it is what I do; it is the hours I work. I am a chef and I can only work when people are eating. Alicia wanted me to lower my standard and cook at a restaurant that serves breakfast and lunch so that I could be home with her in the evening. I didn't ask her to quit her job and work at night, so why should she ask me to change hours?" Latrice's body language changed and Marlon paused.

"Am I offending you? If so, we can stop."

"I'm sorry," Latrice looked around at all the food she had made. "I hope the food was okay. I didn't know you were chef; you're probably used to eating extraordinary food."

"There is no reason to apologize; you did your thing. Everything was better than anything I make. I can't make soul food to save my life."

Latrice smiled, "What kind of food do you cook?" Marlon's face lit up as he talked about cooking. As she saw the joy on his face, Latrice wondered how his wife could ask him to give up something that he loved so much.

"There are so many things I enjoy cooking, but I'm currently the executive chef at an Italian restaurant. So that is my primary focus right now, but I am working on a dish with the rich flavors of Italian cuisine fused with the techniques of Asian cooking. When I'm done, I would love to cook it for you. But as for right now you finish eating while I get started on the dishes," Marlon smiled.

Latrice grabbed Marlon's hand before he walked away and whispered, "I think you are an incredible man, and your wife must be crazy to walk away from you."

"And I don't see why a man would raise his hand to hurt a woman as amazing as you." Marlon kneeled to look directly in Latrice's eyes and caressed her cheek.

Latrice closed her eyes and leaned her cheek into the palm of his hand, savoring the warmth of his touch. It felt good to be touched by a man who she knew would never do her harm. Marlon fought the overwhelming desire to kiss her. Her full lips were enticing, but the last thing she needed was to be taken advantage of. She needed to be loved, not used to relieve his sexual tension.

Latrice fluttered her eyes open, embarrassed by how long her face had lingered in his hand. She turned to finish her food and Marlon walked away silently, cursing himself for the things he wanted to do to her. Latrice ate in silence and watched Marlon as he cleared the table and washed the dishes. His close-cropped hair was laid down with waves rippling evenly across the top. His smooth, bronze skin accentuated the whites of his eyes, making their dark centers seem even darker. His body looked like he'd been chiseled from stone. Even his back muscles were etched to perfection. *An amazing body with a kind heart; he is too good to be true,* Latrice thought. When he refused to let her finish washing the dishes and insisted she relax, she thought again, *too good to be true.*

After the kitchen was cleaned, Marlon headed upstairs to shower. He was seriously contemplating resorting to self-gratification. Being around Latrice was testing his will-power and he could see no other way to pull his hormones under control. Marlon walked into the bathroom with his mind set on taking care of business and there stood Latrice. Her naked, chocolate skin glistened with water as steam from the shower still hovered around her. *Oh my god,* Marlon thought, as he examined her body from head to toe. He had to bite his lip to keep from blurting out what was going through his mind, but his facial expressions gave it away. He had never seen a woman's body so physically toned and voluptuous at the same time. Latrice's body sent Marlon's into overdrive and now, more than ever, he desperately needed a release.

"Get out of here," Latrice screamed, hurling a towel at Marlon. She couldn't believe how long he'd stood there staring at her. For the first time, she thought maybe the joined bathroom was going to be a problem. Their hearts raced as they now stood on opposite sides of the door. Latrice was embarrassed that a man she barely knew saw her naked, and Marlon was embarrassed that he had stared for so long.

The thought of knocking on the door to apologize crossed Marlon's mind, but he figured it was way too soon and she might not want to see him. Instead of knocking, he stood at the door hoping she'd say something and when she didn't, he knelt on the side of his bed to ask the Lord to keep his mind from wandering. Maybe if he'd been on better terms with the Lord, his attempts at prayer would've been more successful. Conceding defeat, he got up from his knees, threw on some sweat pants, and headed toward the front door; if he couldn't pray exercise was the next best thing.

Marlon didn't see Latrice in the kitchen when he walked pass, but when he opened the front door she most certainly saw him. She hastily sat a glass of water on the table and rushed to him.

"Are you leaving me here by myself?" Her voice trembled with fear.

"I won't be gone long. You will be fine." Marlon avoided eye contact with her.

Latrice grabbed him by the arm and pleaded "Please don't leave." Tears welled in her eyes, "I don't want to be alone."

Her touch reignited his desire and he needed to escape before he pounced on her body. "I'm just running a few laps around the block. You will be fine." Latrice's tears affected Marlon more than he let on, which is why he persisted on leaving. He barely knew her, yet she was touching places inside him that his wife never could. When he left, the sobbing behind him nearly broke his heart.

Before starting his run, Marlon had taken a few moments to stretch. The sun had already burned off the early morning haze and it was starting out to be a beautiful day. Marlon tried to rid his mind of Latrice. A man jogging down the street waved and Marlon nodded at him. A car drove pass and the man behind the wheel just stared at Marlon as his car slowly rolled by. Then, it dawned on him that he didn't even know what Calvin looked like. He could have been either of those men and Marlon would've never known. Without second thought, he went back inside the house.

Latrice was still standing in the spot where he had left her. Tears were flowing down her cheeks. Marlon wiped them off with his sleeve, wrapped his arms around her, and held her until her sobs tapered off. Holding her was exhilarating and before he could stop himself he swept his lips across hers. The contact was brief, but electrifying and Marlon was glad when she allowed him to continue holding her.

"Are you alright?" He wiped the remaining tears from her cheeks.
When she nodded yes, he took her by the hand and led her to the sofa where he held her tight. Marlon pulled her close and their bodies molded effortlessly together. The gentle running of Marlon hands through Latrice's hair put her fast to sleep; he was asleep soon, also.
Hours later, music blared from Marlon's cell phone and they both jumped up. Marlon fumbled to grab his phone and Latrice yawned. He turned off the alarm on his phone and sat up.

"I can't believe we slept that long. It's time for me to get ready for work. Will you be okay down here by yourself?"

Latrice nodded and Marlon walked away. A smile spread across her face as she watched him leave. She hadn't slept that well in almost two years. The comfort and safety she felt in his arms was priceless. In Latrice's eyes, being able to rest was worth more than jewelry, nice clothes, and fancy cars. She had all that with Calvin, but didn't feel safe enough to sleep soundly. With just a few hours in Marlon's arms she felt rejuvenated, strong, and energized.

The couch was calling Delisa's name when she came home from work. Everything in her hands was thrown in a corner in the living room. She kicked her shoes off, and curled up on the couch opposite Latrice. Chaos was all around her today and she needed a moment to herself before Jaleel came home with DJ. She was just about to close her eyes when she saw Latrice smiling on the other couch. Delisa looked at the TV to see if she was watching something funny, and she wasn't. "It's good to see you smile. I don't think I've seen you smile since you've been here."

"It feels great to be able to smile. I just took a nap and it was the best sleep I've had in a long time."

"That's good I am glad you feel comfortable enough to rest."

Latrice thought about telling her the real reason she was able to rest, but thought it best to keep her mouth shut. After all, she and Marlon were both still married and she didn't want anyone getting the wrong idea. Something innocent could've easily turned into something outrageous when the wrong assumptions were made, and she did not want to put Marlon through anymore stress.

"I feel rejuvenated and you look like you could use that same kind of nap." She ended the conversation before she blurted out something she wasn't supposed to. "I saw that you had some steaks in the refrigerator; I can cook them for you so you can rest."

"Would you, please? Jaleel likes to eat as soon as he gets home and I just don't have it in me to get up and cook right now."

"Not a problem. Is there any special way you want them cooked?"

"Cook them however you'd like."

Latrice made her way to the kitchen without hesitance. Another opportunity to cook made her even more excited. Just as she was entering the kitchen, Marlon was coming down the stairs.

"What's got you so excited?" Marlon asked, as he made his way toward her.

Latrice smiled like a kid on Christmas morning. "I get to cook dinner. Delisa had a rough day, there were steaks in the refrigerator and I offered to cook them." Latrice grabbed him by the hand and pulled him into the kitchen. "Do you have any pointers for me?"

"I can cook a mean steak, but you cooked breakfast so perfectly I am sure you can handle it."

"As a matter of fact, I can; too bad you won't be here to taste my steaks."

Marlon laughed at her cockiness, "You better save me a piece." Without a second thought, Marlon had both arms around her and had fully embraced her. Before he could correct himself and apologize, Latrice slid her arms up and returned the embrace.

"I really want to thank you for helping me get some sleep." Latrice looked in his eyes. He would never fully understand how much she appreciated him.

"Don't mention it. It's the least I can do to make up for my little mishap up stairs." Just mentioning her nakedness sent Marlon's hormones raging. He instantly let her go, hoping she did not feel the sudden bulge in his pants. "Are you going to be up when I come home?"

"Do you want me to wait up?"

"It would be nice, but I understand if you are too tired." Marlon started backing away toward the door. He had sense enough to know that this conversation was heading in the wrong direction. Going to work was his chance to get away from her to get his mind and hormones under control.

Latrice busied herself with preparing dinner. She sliced onions to caramelize and mushrooms to sauté for the steak. There were tons of fresh veggies in the crisper and she chopped them up for a salad. She chopped a few potatoes for mashed potatoes, and then put the steaks on the indoor grill. The aroma filled the house and when Jaleel walked through the door his stomach was growling. Just as Delisa said, he was ready to eat. The food wasn't quite ready and Latrice was beginning to feel a little nervous. Dinner being late was a guaranteed slap across the face with Calvin. She knew Jaleel wasn't going to hit her, but she couldn't help apologizing continuously.

Jaleel grabbed her shoulders to put her mind at ease. "Latrice I am not upset. Please stop apologizing. Take your time. I am going to take a shower so you have plenty of time to finish okay?"

"Okay. Old habits die hard, I guess." She exhaled and continued mashing the potatoes.

Fifteen minutes later, dinner was on the table and everyone was indulging. Watching everyone enjoying their meal reminded her of Marlon and the way he'd wolfed down breakfast. The mere thought of Marlon and his invitation to be up when he got home almost took her breath.

Time dragged while she waited up for Marlon. She'd cleaned the kitchen, taken a shower, and played blocks with DJ until he went to bed. Then, one of her favorite shows came, but it couldn't quite keep her attention. After Delisa and Jaleel went to bed, time seemed to move even slower. She put in a movie hoping it would make time go by faster, but it didn't. Butterflies fluttered in her stomach when it was time for Marlon to come home. She heard his keys enter the lock and jumped up to greet him. Half way to the door, she abruptly stopped. "Why are you in such a hurry to see this man, Latrice?" She asked herself. She pivoted and returned to the couch, but not before Marlon walked through the door.

Marlon looked exhausted, but when he saw Latrice his face lit up. She had her hair pulled into a loose bun with a few strands hanging down. Her white tank top and spandex shorts radiated against her dark skin. Her clothes clung to every curve. Marlon had to contain his impulse to grab her and press that immaculate body against his. Latrice stretched out her arm to hold his hand. They walked hand-in-hand into the living room. She wanted to do something special for him to repay him for being so nice to her. Since he worked on his feet all night, she thought he'd appreciate a good foot massage. She returned to the living room with a bucket of hot water and placed it in front of him. He sat up to protest, but Latrice wouldn't hear it. She grabbed his feet and proceeded to take off his shoes and socks.

"Latrice, you don't have to do this," Marlon whispered, as she rolled up his pants legs.

"I know, but you helped me relax and get some much needed rest. The least I could do his help you relax after a long night at work."

Hot water covered his feet as he submerged them into the bucket. A soft moan escaped Marlon's mouth as He rested his head against the back of the couch to unwind. He had never been given a foot massage before. He knew a few brothers that went to the nail salon and got pedicures. He even knew a few whose wives hooked them up, but he had never been blessed with the experience.

"Okay." Latrice patted his leg as she finished rolling up his pants. "You enjoy the hot water, I will be right back.

"Wait." Marlon placed his hand on her waist and guided her toward him. "I made this for you." He passed her a small bag from the restaurant.

Latrice smiled. "I love cheesecake. You serve this at your restaurant?"

"No, but I was thinking about you and thought you would like something sweet."
She skipped into the kitchen to grab a fork to dig in her cheesecake. Latrice plopped down on the sofa next to Marlon. Each bite of the cheesecake tasted like heaven. It was rich and creamy with swirls of raspberry jam.

Marlon watched her mouth as she moaned with each bite. She licked the front and back of the fork, making sure she ate every bit before digging in for another bite. He had to force himself to look away. There was a rise in his pants and she was way too close not to notice. Less than half way through, she surprised Marlon by offering him a bite. Initially, he refused, but Latrice insisted. They alternated bites until it was gone. After each bite, Marlon licked the fork searching for the taste of her mouth that lingered. He wanted to knock the cheesecake out of her hand and get a taste of her mouth firsthand, but he had to settle for what he was getting.

"That was so good," Latrice sang. Not only did it taste good, but he'd made it just for her. Knowing he was thinking of her made it taste even better. "Now, you relax while I finish what I started. She rushed off to grab a few things and quickly returned. Latrice knelt in front of Marlon and grabbed each foot and dried it off. She was surprised at how well kept his feet were. All the nail tools she borrowed from Delisa were laid out and ready for some serious scraping, but there was barely any dead skin. Instead of cleaning, she focused on the massage. She applied a generous amount of foot cream, and then proceeded to massage it into his skin. Each toe was given special attention as she worked in the cream.

When the first foot was complete, she looked up to see if he was enjoying, and he was asleep. She was pleased with her success of helping him relax.

Despite Marlon being sleep, Latrice finished the foot massage, dumped the bucket of water, and covered him with a blanket. She shook her head in disbelief. How could any woman in her right mind throw out such a wonderful man? Besides the fact that he was gorgeous, he was thoughtful and caring. He was the type of man that women dreamed of. Calvin, with his smooth talking and expensive gifts had fooled her into believing he was a good man, but Marlon was genuine. Looking back on things, there were signs that Calvin wasn't what he appeared to be, but she had ignored them and married him anyway. *"Life lesson learned,"* she thought, as she headed to bed.

11

Marlon sat at the kitchen table listening to the rain. The weather outside matched the way he felt in his spirit. There was no power within, just a slow continuous trickle. The storm in his life was slow and continuous, and he was powerless to stop it. Today was to be his first counseling session with Alicia. He'd put it off long enough. Because of his commitment to look after Latrice, he'd convinced Pastor Hawkins and Alicia to come to Jaleel's house. He didn't want Alicia to know where he was staying, but did not want to hurt Latrice by leaving her home alone. He had made her cry once and he refused to do it again.

Marlon did not want to go through the deception of marriage counseling. Reconciliation was not an option he was willing to consider. There was nothing Pastor Hawkins could say that would convince him to give Alicia another chance. This meeting was a waste of his time, but if it spared him more heartache in the long run, he was all for it.

The meeting was scheduled for one o'clock, but Marlon asked Pastor Hawkins to arrive at 12:30. He wanted to make sure they had an understanding. When the doorbell rang, he escorted Pastor Hawkins into the kitchen and got straight to the point. "Pastor, I asked you to come a little early, because I wanted you to know where my mind is. I should've come to you weeks ago, but I guess I was embarrassed. I understand that you have a job to do; certain things you are obligated to say and won't be persuaded by anything I say. I also don't want to waste your time. If you are here to get Alicia and I to reconcile, then I need to inform you…"

"Hold on," Pastor Hawkins said, leaning back in the chair, hoping that Marlon would follow suit to relax. "I have no idea what is going on between you and Alicia. You called me and asked for marriage counseling and that is all I know. I have not spoken with her at all. So calm down and tell me what happened."

"Well long story short, I came home early from church a couple of months ago and caught her cheating on me. I told her I wanted a divorce and she threatened to make it a nasty one if I didn't agree to counseling."

"Did she say why she cheated?"

"Is there ever an acceptable excuse for cheating?" Marlon asked, shooting the pastor a look which reflected his irritation.

"No there isn't, but it is helpful to see when and how a marriage unravels. Most marriages are dead and heading south long before the infidelity begins." Marlon shook his head in frustration as he thought about what Alicia had said at the restaurant. She'd accused him of working too much and never having time for her. It still wasn't an excuse. He was in the same boat and wasn't out cheating, but Pastor Hawkins did shine light on the situation.

"She claims that she was lonely and tired of being home alone every night."

"Do you understand how she could feel that way? Forget about the cheating for a second. Do you see how lonely she might have been?"

"I understand she was lonely. I was home all day without her and you don't see me laid up with someone." Marlon's voice was beginning to escalate and he had to apologize. He knew going through with this counseling was going to try his patience and when he heard the doorbell ring, he clenched his teeth and grumbled in frustration.

Alicia sauntered through the kitchen in a mini-skirt and high heels. She looked a mess. She was switching so hard, she could've broken her hip. Marlon sensed her motives and it made him sick to his stomach. He rolled his eyes and showed her to her seat. While she settled into her seat, Marlon whispered in her ear, "You look ridiculous." He could practically see steam coming from her head. She was furious and he could sense that she wanted to curse him out, but she bit her lip.

Alicia scooted her chair closer to the table and turned toward Pastor Hawkins. "I am ready when you are." She smiled in an attempt to hide her frustration. The outfit she wore had taken hours to put together. She wanted Marlon to see what he would be giving up. All of her effort was in vain. She looked over her outfit. Her skirt was so short you could practically see her panties. The push-up bra made her breasts bulge out the top of a low-cut shirt. She felt like an idiot. She'd been so busy thinking about catching Marlon's eye that she never considered Pastor Hawkins was going to be sitting there too.

For the first five minutes of the meeting, Alicia pulled and tugged at her outfit. She thought about crossing her legs, but that would further expose her. Her fidgeting kept Marlon amused, and he was barely listening to anything Pastor Hawkins said. He even chuckled out loud, and then tried to pretend he was clearing his throat when the pastor looked at him.

After a while, Marlon was finally able to focus on Pastor Hawkins, but his attention was interrupted when he saw Latrice step into the kitchen. Marlon excused himself and followed her, because he knew she was thrown off by what she had walked in on.

"Hey, did you need something?"

"I am starving, but I didn't realize you had company. I can wait."

"That is not necessary. You can make you something to eat."

"It's okay, I will be fine. I do not want to interrupt." Latrice smiled and walked away. She did not know who the woman was, but she was gorgeous and did not want her or the pastor to see her looking a mess.

Marlon went to the kitchen and whipped up one of his croissant sandwiches and brought it to Latrice in the living room. "You see how fast that was?" He knelt in front of her and handed her the plate. "You eat up, and if you need anything call my cell phone. I could use another break from this meeting." He smiled as he wrote his cell number down.

Marlon was incensed when he heard the nonsense coming from Alicia's mouth. She was accusing him of neglecting his marriage to pursue his career. Marlon marched around the table and stood in her face. "What are you talking about? I didn't neglect anything. I went to work every day, just like you did."

Alicia jumped in his face. She felt safe and bold with the pastor there. She was trying her best to play the role of a neglected wife that so desperately craved affection and had no other choice but to seek that affection outside her marriage. She hoped the pastor would side with her and make Marlon come home. "You know exactly what I am talking about. I would sit at home all night by myself. You never called to check on me or even to say hi. I'd stay up late just to see your face and half the time you didn't want to be bothered. The other half you'd come home so late, I'd be sleep. How was I supposed to know you weren't cheating on me?"

"What? That is crazy and you know it." Marlon's anger was spiraling. "Don't sit here and make up stuff to make yourself sound better. I never cheated on you. And so what you were home alone and I never called. You go to work all day and never call me. I am at home all day by myself and you don't see me sleeping around. Grow up and take responsibility for what you did and stop trying to blame me."

Alicia was now yelling back. Pastor Hawkins stepped between them, but neither of them backed off. "You are to blame. You loved that job more than you ever loved me. I needed your affection. You're a man and don't have the same needs as a woman. You didn't give me what I needed, so I found it elsewhere."

Alicia saw the look on Marlon's face and wished she could take it back. His brows knitted together with a scowl that barely hid the sorrow in his eyes. Although his mask of anger was securely in place, she knew she was driving a wedge further between them, but she couldn't shut her mouth.

Marlon opened his mouth to tell her where she could go and how fast she needed to get there, but his cell phone rang. He checked the caller id, and then went into the living room. As soon as he stepped into the room Latrice started speaking. "I didn't want anything. I just heard you yelling and figured now would be a good time for a break. Maybe you should pray before going back inside. I don't know much about praying. I only know what I have learned in these few weeks that you guys have been making me go to church. I will try my best if you want me to pray with you."

Marlon didn't respond, he just paced back and forth. He didn't want to pray. He prayed the majority of his life and look where it had gotten him: renting a room from his cousin, arguing with his wife, and on the verge of divorce. No, prayer was not what he wanted. He wanted to go back into the kitchen and wring Alicia's neck.

Latrice blocked his path, giving him no choice but to stop. She took his hands in hers and started praying before he could protest. "God help Marlon. He seems to be having a rough time handling the situation that is going on. Allow him to think clearly and keep him and everyone else involved calm. Amen."

"Amen, Sister Latrice has the right idea. Prayer is exactly what I was going to suggest."

"Pastor Hawkins, I did not hear you come in. I would have stopped and let you pray." What she wanted to say was, "I would have stopped and ran out of the room." She was wearing some baggy sweats that Marlon had given her to lounge around the house in and didn't want to be seen.

"Oh no, your prayer was sincere and to the point. I couldn't have said it better myself." He turned to Marlon and shook his head. "I sent Alicia home. From what I just saw, you guys are not ready to be in the same room. What I suggest is a week of prayer and fasting. When we meet next week, it will be through a conference call." Marlon nodded his head in agreement; then he escorted Pastor Hawkins to the door.

Before leaving, he paused and looked Marlon in the eye. They'd been friends before he had become his pastor—back when they were two little boys wreaking havoc on the girls in the church. He couldn't stand to see him hurting and was upset that Marlon hadn't come to him before now. Pastor Hawkins was even more upset with himself for not noticing that Marlon was dealing with all this chaos. He knew Marlon had missed a few church services, but was clueless as to why. Now he knew and truly felt his brother's pain.

Without words they communicated. *I am here if you need me.*

I know. They hugged and Pastor Hawkins left.

Latrice waited for a few minutes for Marlon to return. She'd heard the shower start and figured he was too upset to talk. She put a movie on, but he never came down. She checked the time and it was a few hours before he normally left for work. She went upstairs and knocked on his door.

"Who is it?" Marlon snapped.

"It's Latrice. Can I come in?"

"Yeah." Marlon took a deep breath and sat up. He knew how horrible he could be when angry and didn't want Latrice to see that side of him.

Latrice gripped his hand. "Are you okay? I was waiting for you to come back."

"I'm sorry. I just needed some time to myself. I didn't want you to pay for the way she makes me feel."

"Lay down on your stomach and I'll help you get rid of some of the tension." Latrice slid her hand up and down his back

"That is not necessary." Marlon tried to ignore her caress.

"Just relax." Latrice gently pushed him to lie back against the bed and waited with her hands on her hips until he turned over. Marlon gave into her request and lay on his stomach. He was really beginning to relax when she climbed on his bed and straddled him. He was going to protest, but she put both hands in the middle of his back and rapidly shifted her weight on to his back in a forward pushing motion, causing his back to crack. Marlon moaned in comfort as Latrice worked every bit of tension out of his muscles.

Latrice rocked back and forth as she dug her knuckles into Marlon's back. His moans united with her straddling and rocking over him kindled a flame between her legs. Unsure how to process her body's untimely response, Latrice abruptly hopped off of Marlon and dashed for the bathroom. Marlon chased after her. He tapped on her door and she didn't answer. "Latrice, I am coming in." He tried to open the door, but she was sitting up against it. He pushed harder, eventually sliding her out of the way. "Don't hide from me like that. I am not going to hurt you." He placed his hands under her arms and lifted her to her feet. "Now tell me what's wrong."

Latrice sighed and plopped down on her bed. "I am just a little embarrassed that's all."

Marlon placed his arm around her shoulder. "Embarrassed about what? Did you pass gas or something?"

Latrice laughed and playfully punched him in the chest. "No, I did not pass gas. I was on top of you, you were moaning, my mind started wandering, and I got a little aroused." She cringed at her admission and waited with eyes closed for his rejection.

"Why are you embarrassed about being aroused?"

"It's been a long time since I've had that feeling. After my husband beat me the first time, he stopped having that affect on me. There was nothing sexual going on between us and it kind of just crept up on me."

"A massage is very sensual to the giver and the receiver." Marlon slid his hands under her sweat shirt. Rubbing his hands up and down her back he gently kneaded his fingers against her bare skin. "It is the warm hands almost touching the most cherished parts of you. It's the intimate close encounter with a person's body. It's the thought of being only inches away from making love that makes a massage so arousing."

The age old battle of good and evil warred in his mind. His conscience yelled, *stop!* Yet his desire for her, his hatred for his wife, and his anger toward the Lord silenced that voice. He slid his hands up to her neck and lifted her sweat shirt over her head and tossed it to the floor as he went to shut the door.

Latrice covered her bare breast with her hands. She regretted not wearing a bra. Marlon glared passionately into her eyes. His towering presence was intimidating. Her chest tightened with fear and anticipation as she awaited his next move. He undressed on his way back to her and lifted her to lie on the bed. "What are you doing?" she whispered as he nuzzled the erotic zones of her neck

"I'm giving you the love you deserve." She needed to be loved and he needed to be wanted to erase all the anger, hatred, and rejection that he'd felt over the past few weeks. What had started as a quest for healing had escalated as their bodies connected. All apprehension dissipated and they ignored the warnings blaring in the back of their minds. He wanted her and the look in her eyes said she wanted him too. Marlon reacquainted Latrice with love making. With every flick of his tongue she exhaled with enjoyment.

Latrice squirmed seductively, possessing a dire need for fulfillment. Without hesitation, he honored her request. Their eyes reflected their blissful connection. Latrice's body quivered to her core. Marlon was awakening parts of her that hadn't been stimulated in years. She rocked her hips to engulf every single one of his thrusts. Her hands slipped around his neck, pulling him close to envelop his lips with hers. At first, they were hesitant about sharing something as intimate as a kiss, but the intensity of their connection made it impossible to resist. What he intended to be a quick, comforting experience had exploded into something more. They both received more than they ever had with their spouses. The passion flowing between them calmed the beast that raged within him. Marlon looked into Latrice's eyes and saw the fear that was once there had been replaced with delight. She had mastered faking her arrival to ecstasy, but Marlon guided her there and they'd disembarked together.

Latrice lay quietly next to Marlon waiting for his reaction. He had rolled off of her and was inaudibly still. She did not have to be deep into the church to know that what they just shared was unacceptable, and assumed that was his dilemma. She sat up, looked into his eyes, and caressed the side of his face. "Are you okay?"

"I should be asking you that." Once again, he'd silenced that voice. It went from warning to accusatory, and he still had refused to listen. He pulled Latrice close and rested her head on his chest. "You deserve better than what I just gave you. You deserve a man that can commit to you, love you, and give you his whole heart."

"What you just gave me was the greatest experience of my life. My husband and I had sex at least three times a week and it has been over a year since I've had an orgasm. It had gotten to the point to where even his intimacy was abuse. I know you are unavailable and this is just sex to you…"

"Shh." Marlon placed his finger over her mouth. "Don't put words in my mouth. You have been arousing me since the day you arrived and today is no different. You are so beautiful, and the fact that you don't know it makes you even more beautiful."

Marlon was pleased she'd accepted his excuse as to what was bothering him. He didn't really understand it. He'd just succumbed to a cycle that took years to break free from. There should've been remorse or shame, but there was none. Latrice smiled up at him and his heart skipped a beat. How could a woman he barely knew have his heart beating so wildly? Marlon watched her mouth and wanted to overtake it and make her body re-surrender, but he forced some restraint. Knowing that he'd given her a long overdue orgasm made him anxious to give her another.

Latrice hugged him tightly. His love making and kind words were soothing to her bruised emotions. She wished the moment didn't have to end, but on the other side of the door awaited real life—a life where they were both legally attached to someone else. Latrice eased off the bed. She didn't want to read anymore into what they had shared.

"Where are you rushing off to?" Marlon sat up and grabbed her by the wrist. He flashed that sexy smile and pulled the covers back on the bed, slid underneath them, and waited for Latrice to join him. When she finally did, he pulled her close and they cuddled and talked until it was time for him to go to work.

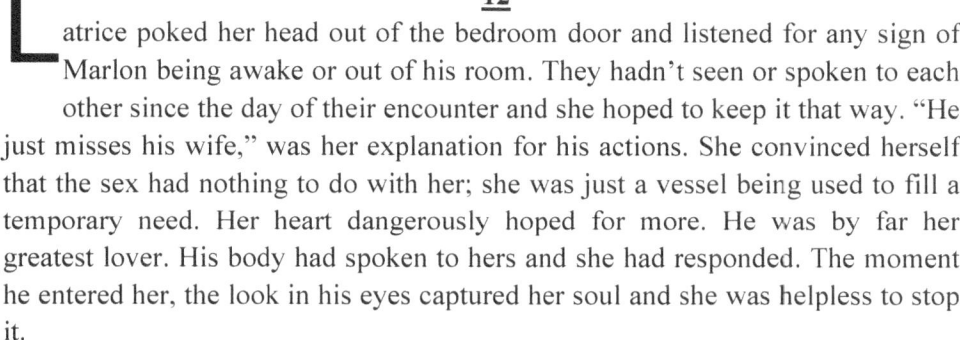

12

Latrice poked her head out of the bedroom door and listened for any sign of Marlon being awake or out of his room. They hadn't seen or spoken to each other since the day of their encounter and she hoped to keep it that way. "He just misses his wife," was her explanation for his actions. She convinced herself that the sex had nothing to do with her; she was just a vessel being used to fill a temporary need. Her heart dangerously hoped for more. He was by far her greatest lover. His body had spoken to hers and she had responded. The moment he entered her, the look in his eyes captured her soul and she was helpless to stop it.

Even now as she ran past his room, she was drawn to him. It took all the strength she had not to knock on his door. Sometimes she hoped he would hear her and come rushing out to be with her, but it had been days since they'd spoken and she continued to avoid him to prevent further rejection. She had established the perfect time to get breakfast. Just after Delisa and Jaleel left for work, she'd rush down to the kitchen, fix breakfast, and take it up to her room before Marlon woke up. She made sure she grabbed enough food to hold her until dinner. She didn't want to chance coming out of her room for lunch.

With food in hand, Latrice trekked back up to her room. Then, she laid a towel on the floor and had her own private picnic. Even as she ate, her mind wandered to Marlon. The meals and conversations they shared had become the highlights of her day. The past few days without his company had been lonely, but she convinced herself she was doing the right thing.

She heard Marlon fumbling around in the restroom and then the shower popped on. Just the thought of him standing in the shower naked caused blood to surge through her veins. She tried to focus on something else, but it was impossible. Her imagination ran wild with memories and fantasies. By the time the shower cut off, Latrice had worked herself up into a sweat.

"Latrice, baby, open the door." The knocking startled Latrice out of her fantasy. "I don't like the distance between us. Tell me what I can do to make this right." Her avoidance was killing him. The guilt Marlon carried was bad enough to bear, but knowing that she was now uncomfortable around him was torture.

Not to mention, his actions had wedged more distance between him and the Lord. His lack of self-control was appalling and he felt so ashamed, he couldn't even face the Lord in prayer. The shame didn't show up right away, but when it did it hit him like a ton of bricks.

Most of all, he missed her. Her laugh, her conversation, her cooking, and just looking at her face, he missed it all. He knocked on the door again. He wanted to tell her how much he'd missed her, but didn't want to risk making her more uncomfortable. Instead, he waited for her to answer and when she didn't, he went down stairs to spend another day without her.

Marlon flipped through hundreds of channels and nothing caught his interest. He knew where he wanted to be and what he wanted to be doing, but convinced himself to just let it go. He tried, but for the life of him he couldn't. His mind couldn't focus on anything else until she forgave him. The hours dragged by and Marlon found petty chores around the house to occupy his time. He organized the DVD collection in alphabetical order with the spines facing out. The pantry was in desperate need of some organization and he took care of that. He then cleaned out the refrigerator and folded some towels Delisa had left in the dryer. With all that done, he still had three hours until he had to leave for work.

Marlon decided to do what would definitely take the edge off: he cooked. There was lots of good stuff in the refrigerator and he knew exactly what he wanted to make. He quick-thawed some Cornish hens and Italian sausage in hot water. The sausage was removed from its casing, browned in olive oil, and then stuffed into the cavity of the hens. Marlon then rubbed the hens with a little olive oil and seasoned them with rosemary, salt, pepper, garlic, basil, and Old Bay seasoning. He placed the Cornish hens into a roasting pan, slid it into the hot oven, and went to work on his side dishes.

Within minutes, a heavenly aroma filled the kitchen, reminding Marlon that he hadn't taken the time to eat breakfast or lunch. He hoped Latrice smelled it as well and that it would withdraw her from hiding. Placing the cornbread in the oven, Marlon began chopping the onions, celery, and bell peppers for the stuffing.

Thirty minutes later, the cornbread was out and chilling on the counter, and he was preparing to sauté the veggies when he felt her presence. Her scent fought through the aroma of the food and wafted up his nostrils. Blood rushed from his head to his groin; even without visual proof his body knew she was in the room. "Latrice," he whispered before turning around. The second he turned, their eyes connected. Without a word, Latrice flanked and fled from the room as if her life depended on it. She'd tipped into the kitchen just hoping to catch only a glimpse of him in his element. Whether it was a big or small meal, the sight of him cooking was enthralling. She figured he'd be so caught up in cooking that he wouldn't notice her. *Wrong!*

Marlon was right behind her. Taking the stairs two at a time, he made it to her room just in time for her to slam the door in his face. "Latrice, I am sorry. I didn't mean to hurt you." He turned the door knob and it was locked. When she didn't answer, he balled his fist to bang on the door, but thought better of it. If she needed to stay away from him, he'd give her what she needed. He immediately returned to the kitchen. He put the stuffing together and threw it back into the oven. Then, he prepped a basic Sicilian broccoli, steamed with black olives and covered with melted butter, fresh garlic, and parmesan cheese.

While he waited for the food to finish cooking, Marlon wrote Latrice a note, apologizing for his selfish actions. He offered to move out if that would make her more comfortable and ended it with how much he missed her company.

Over the next hour, Latrice tried to convince herself to go back down stairs and talk to Marlon. Until Calvin, she had never been afraid of a man. She met every challenge they'd issued with enthusiasm and even issued a few of her own. She wished she still had that same back bone; then she would be able to handle whatever rejection Marlon had to dish out. Latrice pretended to feign that same confidence as she marched toward the door, but in the end, she chickened out and plopped down on the bed.

Marlon finished up dinner later than he had anticipated, but took the time to set the table. He presented the food on platters and set them on the dining table. He placed settings and drinks out as well, then put the sealed envelope with Latrice's letter in it on the table hoping no one other than her would read it.

The front door opened and closed, and Latrice knew it was Delisa; she was home from work. When it opened and closed again she knew that Marlon had left. She drifted down stairs, silently berating herself for being a coward. She found Delisa standing in the kitchen next to the table with the most delectably enticing food she'd seen in a long time. "I don't know if he made all of this for you or not." Delisa handed Latrice the note. "But I am going to make me a plate."

As Delisa dug into the food, Latrice sank down in her seat and read the letter.

Latrice,
I will never be able to apologize enough for taking advantage of you. I can't lie to you, I wanted you and I enjoyed every minute that we spent together. I should

have continued to fight my desire for you, but you touching me and my finally being able to touch you proved to be more than I could handle.

I don't want you to feel uncomfortable around me and I am willing to move out if that is what you need. I must say this, I have been miserable without your company over these past few days. I miss talking to you and if I move out I know it will only get worse. I hope we can get past this; I need you.

Marlon

Latrice blinked back the tears, hoping Delisa hadn't noticed, and joined her in partaking of the meal Marlon had prepared. Jaleel came home with DJ, saw them eating without him and was ready to complain, but when they explained that Marlon had cooked, they didn't have to say anything else. It was a smaller spread than what he normally prepared when he decided to make a family meal, but still delicious.

Latrice tried to focus on the dinner conversation, but her mind kept going back to Marlon's note. She wanted to take it at face value and not over analyze it, but was scared. *He wanted her, enjoyed her, missed her, and needed her—not his wife.*

Alicia was really beginning to like having someone to spend her evenings with. Every day, after she got off work, Meme would come over and they'd laugh and talk as they prepared dinner together. After their meal, they usually ended up in bed, vigorously working off everything they'd just eaten. No matter how good the sex was or how much she was enjoying Meme's company, Alicia always made sure she was gone by the time Marlon normally came home from work, just in case he decided to stop by. Although he never did, tonight would be no different; she wasn't willing to risk it.

As she stood at the sink rinsing off the lettuce for a salad, Alicia racked her brain for what her next step with Marlon should be. Their one attempt at counseling had been a disaster. Alicia's own behavior perplexed her. She'd spent hours coaching herself to own what she did, but before she could stop herself, she had strayed so far off script there was no turning back. She was yelling, arguing, and pointing the accusing finger so strong that it angered him. It angered him so fiercely it looked like his head might explode.

Her biggest regret was not suggesting counseling before her infidelity. If she had, none of the other stuff would have happened. They would've worked through their issues, she wouldn't have cheated, and they would still be happily married. Maybe if she had gotten over her fear of being a mother and given him a baby, it would be harder for him to walk away. She had seriously entertained the idea of faking a pregnancy to get him to come home. Knowing the kind of man he was, he would want to be there for her during the pregnancy and wouldn't hesitate to move back in. She figured he'd come home, she'd stop birth control, get pregnant, and all would be good. The more she thought it through, the more she realized it wasn't such a great idea. Yeah he'd probably come home, but there was no guarantee he'd sleep with her. If he did and by some stroke of luck she got pregnant, the timing would be off. He'd expect the baby to be born in six months; how could she explain a three-month delay? Her lies would be exposed, and she'd be in a deeper ditch than she was now. One thing for sure, she wasn't finished fighting for her marriage.

"You're thinking about him again, aren't you?" Meme's voice sliced through Alicia's mental ramblings. Meme rejected the denial before it even left Alicia's lips. "I know I agreed to be your second choice, but you promised that when we were together, I'd have you a hundred percent."

This wasn't the first time they'd had this conversation and probably wouldn't be the last. Alicia moved from the sink to the table where she mindlessly began chopping the rest of the veggies, hoping to block out Meme's ranting. The cutting board was cluttered with carrots, cucumbers, mushrooms, tomatoes, red onions, and banana peppers. Alicia hoped she had enough chopping to do to keep her mind occupied for the entire conversation.

"I know he is your husband and, since you constantly remind me, I know you want him back, but have you ever thought about where that is going to leave me?" The lack of response broke Meme's heart. Tears built up in her eyes as she watched Alicia chop cucumbers without so much as a glance in her direction. She wanted to flip the whole cutting board onto the floor and force Alicia to respond.

Since Alicia had invited her back into her life, Meme had tried to be everything she needed and more. She had even accepted being dismissed from her bed every night. Although she knew the reason and it hurt, she accepted it. Some nights, she wanted to scream out, "He's not coming home," but she held her peace and left without complaining. Her conscience told her to get out before everything blew up in her face, but the magic she felt with Alicia outweighed rational thinking.

"Do I really mean that little to you that you could just use me and not consider my feelings?" Her voice cracked and up until that point, Alicia hadn't noticed she was crying. Her head snapped up from her cutting and the pain she saw in Meme's eyes touched her more than she expected.

Unsure of how to respond to her tears, Alicia went to her and kissed them away. Between each kiss she wiped the residual tears with the pads of her thumbs. "I am sorry." *Kiss* "I know this is hard for you." *Kiss* "I'd be miserable if I didn't have you." *Kiss.* This time she lingered, brushing her lips back and forth across Meme's mouth coaxing her to open. For the first time, Meme had received what she needed emotionally from their relationship. The emotional support always seemed to be one-sided, with Meme always comforting Alicia over something Marlon said or did. Although Alicia had once again thwarted her inquiry about feelings, she let it slide in exchange for emotional comfort. Pinning Meme against the wall, Alicia's kisses turned ravenous. "Do you mind if we eat later?" She hungrily savored Meme's lips.

Meme broke free of their oral exchange. She was not letting Alicia off the hook that easy. No matter how bad she wanted it, Alicia was going to have to work for it tonight. Without responding to the question, she stepped around Alicia to check on the meatloaf and finished prepping the mashed potatoes. Alicia shook her head and returned to her seat to finish preparing the salad. The kitchen was quiet as they finished cooking and even quieter when they sat down to eat. Alicia scooted her chair closer to Meme and placed a hand on her thigh. Meme swiftly swatted it away. She nuzzled the sensitive spot on the side of Meme's neck and Meme sat as stiff as a board. Alicia laughed. "Are you still going to sit there and act like you don't want me?" Taking the silence to mean yes, Alicia scooted to her side of the table to finish her meal.

13

Marlon came home from work at around 11:30 PM to find Latrice sleeping on the couch. The TV was on and the volume cut low. She was balled up with her arms tucked into her shirt and she was shivering. Her beauty captivated him in a way he did not understand. He wasn't a stranger to beautiful women. His wife was gorgeous, but there was a soft, feminine vulnerability that Latrice exuded. Since the day they'd made love, he could not get her out of his mind. It wasn't a conquest or a daily chore. It was passionate and invigorating—something he'd never experienced with any woman, not even Alicia. He could not shake the feeling of their connection and even though he knew he shouldn't, he desperately wanted her again. Even after the note he'd written, she'd yet to let him back into her life and this was his first time seeing her in over a week.

He knelt in front of her, gazed at her lips, and imagined kissing them until she was fully awake, aroused, and ready to give herself to him. Inhaling her scent was driving him over the edge. She wore the same alluring fragrance the day they'd made love and each day since. It would crawl under his door, enticing him to take her.

He brushed his hand across her cheek and she screamed. A bewildered wail erupted from her mouth and she lunged forward, knocking him off balance as she beat on his chest screaming, "Get away from me!"

He grabbed her hands, clutching them to his chest as he flipped her over to lie on her back. The quick movement jolted her body, her eyes popped open and she became fully aware of who she was with. *Marlon not Calvin* Her pulse raced and she tried to apologize, but before she could finish, Marlon covered her lips with his. It was better than anything he had dreamed about all week. He savored the sweetness of her lips with each nibble. He released her hands and they slid underneath his shirt to caress his back. Their kisses intensified as he tried to get his fill of her, but deep down he knew that would be impossible. He would never get enough of her; she had gotten into his system and now he was addicted. Her hands slid further up, effortlessly removing his shirt. His mind kept saying, *Marlon what are you doing? Stop*! However, desire had already overridden rational thinking.

He wanted her and no longer had the strength to fight it. Marlon carried Latrice to his room. He lay her on his bed, removed her clothes, and sat on the bed next to her. He kissed each leg from ankle to thigh while Latrice purred in enjoyment. His fingers explored her body as his mouth set fire to her flesh. Each lick drove her further into sexual madness as her body thrashed in search of fulfillment. Sensing her aching desire, Marlon stood to remove his pants. Latrice sat up to assist him, leaving a trail of kisses down his leg as she pushed his pants down. Sex with his wife had always been one-sided. She just lay on her back, acting as if being inside her was all the satisfaction he needed. He needed more, wanted more, and Latrice was giving him all he craved.

"Finding you makes all the hell I've been through worthwhile," Marlon whispered in her ear.

"You make all my hell nonexistent."

"I've wanted you all week."

"I've needed you all week."

"I've missed you all week."

"I've craved you all week."

They went back and forth, reassuring each other of their need until they had pushed each other over the edge. Together they erupted, sending shockwaves of orgasmic bliss throughout each others' bodies. Latrice tried to contain the sounds coming out of her mouth. The last thing they wanted was for Jaleel and Delisa to find out. Marlon flipped her over to continue their escapade. Selflessly, he made love to her denying his own gratification, drawing her deeper into his soul.

When her body quaked beneath him again, Marlon lost control. His body shuddered with overwhelming pleasure. In unison, their moans echoed throughout the house. Latrice panted through labored breathing. "What are you doing to me? No one has ever made me feel like this."

To keep from blurting out what was running through his mind, Marlon covered her mouth with his. He couldn't believe the thoughts and emotions he had for this woman he barely knew and chocked it all up to him being a little vulnerable.

Marlon looked deep into her eyes and, with a sincerity that grasped her heart, whispered, "I can't get enough of you." He then lowered his lips to meet hers.

They made love through the early morning hours; sleep did not find them until the sun rose. Light peeked through the blinds as they finally separated.

Latrice begged, barely able to breathe. "We have to stop. You have to get some sleep."

Marlon flipped her on her back and smiled. "I can sleep later." He lowered his head to silence the objection perched on her lips, but was interrupted by a knock on the door. They froze, hoping whoever it was would think he was asleep and go away. Silently, they waited. The knocking stopped, but Latrice lifted her hips and rolled from under him. He tried to stop her, but she shook her head no. He rested his head against hers and sighed.

"I am sorry." Latrice saw his disappointment and regretted denying him.

"You have nothing to be sorry for. I should be apologizing for being so greedy and keeping you up all night."

"Please, you haven't forced me to do anything I didn't want to do." Latrice began making her way toward the foot of the bed and Marlon stopped her.

"Don't go; stay with me, please?" *What in the world just came out of my mouth?* Marlon questioned his sanity. He did not need to beg a woman for anything, but the thought of being away from her did not sit well with him.

"I would love to, but answer this, what is going on between us? If it is just sex to you, then I am cool with that at least I know up front. But if that is all it is to you, let's not complicate things by cuddling." They cuddled the last time, and being in his arms felt so right. She felt safe and comforted, like she had finally found the place she had been looking for all her life. Although it felt right, she didn't want to get her hopes up.

Marlon contemplated what she was asking and the impact his response could have on their lives. Neither of them was in a position to be in a relationship and he knew sex out of wedlock was forbidden. He had been in church since he was a child, and after he'd turned fourteen, sex had been his downfall. None of his prior sexual partners had given him the thrill Latrice did.

"I hope you will accept 'I don't know', because I truly don't. All I know is you are the first person I think of in the morning and the last I think of at night. That is all I can admit to right now. I hope it is enough to convince you to sleep in here."

"Let me ask you this. When you make love to me are you thinking about your wife? I don't want to be used."

"Like I told you in the letter, it's you I want. Since I walked in on you getting out of the shower, your body has driven me crazy. Every curve was etched into my memory and being able to touch you was a dream come true. If I was thinking about my wife, we would have been asleep a long time ago. My hatred for her would've hindered my performance." Marlon feathered kisses across her shoulder. "Now let me ask you something. Are you going to stop avoiding me? I can't take it anymore."

"I am sorry. I guess I was just afraid of being rejected. I am kind of feeling you and this is more than sex for me."

"You're kind of feeling? Well, I guess I'm kind of feeling you too." Smiling, Latrice slipped under his covers, turning her back toward him they snuggled as close as possible and spooned as they fell asleep.

Latrice kicked her way out of the covers. The sun was heating up the room, and along with Marlon's body heat, sleeping was unbearable. She slid off the foot of the bed to gather her clothes that Marlon had strewn across the room. Flashbacks of their night together sent chills throughout her body. Being around him made everything she'd been through almost nonexistent.

She looked at the clock it read 2:30 PM. She couldn't believe they had slept so late into the afternoon. If Marlon did not get up soon, he wouldn't have time to eat and shower before going to work.

"Marlon," she whispered as she rubbed his chest. Gradually he opened his eyes, squinting at the light shining into the room. "If you want to eat and shower before work you better get up."

"I am going in late."

"Are you okay? Is there anything I can get for you?" Latrice asked, her voice laden with concern.

"Will you take a shower with me? I promise I won't try anything."

Latrice dropped the clothes she was carrying, placed her hands on her hips, and seductively grinned as she questioned, "Are you sure you want to make that promise?"

Marlon scanned every inch of her naked beauty. The room was dark when they made love, but his mouth and hands had surmised the exquisiteness of her body. The sneak peak he'd had a while back had been nothing compared to the mental video he was taking now. Her deep brown skin was well toned and there wasn't an ounce of fat. She was curved to perfection with beautiful, round breasts, a slender waist, and a slight arch at the hips. "I can see you like what you see."

Marlon smiled; her cockiness was cute. He lunged forward and tried to grab her, but she anticipated his move and swiftly stepped away. Marlon stood tall and walked toward her. "You keep trying to seduce me and you are going to miss out on the surprise I have planned for you." He brushed his lips across her ear and walked away.

A shudder of desire rolled through her and she followed behind him, contemplating which she wanted more, him or the surprise. She stood, watching his every move, and when he effortlessly lifted her into the shower, her desire for him was heightened. It took all the strength they had to keep from indulging in another round of mind-blowing sex. Latrice turned to face him and backed into the water, causing a stream to trickle all over her body. Marlon almost broke his promise of not trying anything.

Once they parted ways to get dressed, Marlon sucked in a deep breath. He needed to calm his libido and get his mind in the right place. He had committed fornication, adultery, lust, and you could even throw greed in there. He was greedy for a woman who was not his wife. "You know better than this. You have to get it together," he mumbled to himself. He looked at his reflection in the mirror and was disgusted. He pointed at himself and declared, "Despite everything that is going on, God has been too good to you for you to turn your back on Him now."

Marlon knelt on the side of his bed to talk to God, but every time he closed his eyes, his mind flashed to his late night rendezvous with Latrice. Each image was as vivid as if it were happening all over again. He sighed in frustration and the only words he was able to speak were, "Jesus, help me."

He decided to continue with his plan to take her out; getting out of the house would be good for both of them. The last thing he needed was to sit around the house, cuddled up, inhaling her perfume. They needed to be out in public where they would be a little apprehensive about touching each other. Marlon finished dressing and stepped into the hall and a big gust of Latrice's raspberry vanilla perfume hit him in the face. He was the type of man that loved the scent of a woman and Latrice's scent was easily detectable.

Latrice smiled when she looked up at Marlon, but the somber look on his face made her smile fade. "What's wrong? Do you have to go into work earlier? Because if you do, we can cancel; it is fine with me."

"No. Are you trying to get out of spending time with me?"

"Are you kidding me? I have been in this house for weeks besides my time at church. I think I might have cried if you had changed your mind."

"Good, we can go as soon as you put on the wig and sunglasses. You look gorgeous, but I am not taking any chances."

Latrice rolled her eyes, but she complied. She practically drug Marlon out of the house. He surprised her with a trip to a salon where she was able to get a weave and forego the wig. She stepped out of the salon and pranced around in a circle, modeling her hair for Marlon who had been waiting in the car. "Thank you so much. Going to the salon is so relaxing." She sealed her gratitude with a soft kiss.

"There's no need to thank me. You deserve that and so much more."

"And your friend was really nice." Latrice eyed him suspiciously. "She seemed to know a lot of personal details about you. Is she an ex?"

"Yes, I tried to get you in with someone else I know, but she is not returning my phone calls. I hope you're not upset." Marlon placed his lips on hers to draw her mind to a different subject. He then drove her to the mall to buy her a new outfit for their date later, but their outing was cut short when his cell phone rang.

Hearing the urgency in Delisa's voice, Marlon stepped away from Latrice so she wouldn't over hear. "What's up Delisa?"

"Is Latrice with you?"

"Yeah, what's going on?"

"Okay, we have to really start being careful. Calvin just came by Camilla's house looking for her. Tim wasn't home and he threatened to hurt Camilla if he found out she was hiding Latrice. Camilla is freaking out, Tim is heated, and you need to be careful. It might be better if you bring her back here."

"I hear you, but we kind of had plans. I assure you she will be out of harm's way. Besides, the last thing Calvin wants is to show up when I am around." The thought of someone coming after his woman pissed him off. He did not have time to analyze the possessiveness he was feeling; he had to get to a safer place.

Latrice saw the look on his face and immediately came toward him. Marlon abruptly ended the call and shoved his phone into his pocket. "Marlon who were you talking to? Why do you look so upset?" He ignored her question, grabbed her hand, and led her out of the mall. Once outside, Latrice snatched her hand away and asked, "It's Calvin, isn't it? Did he come looking for me?" The look on his face answered her question and she began to hyperventilate. "Oh my God," she cried repetitively.

Marlon pulled her close and covered her lips with his. "Don't be afraid. He has to get past me. I won't let him hurt you."

Just as her lips parted to return his kiss, Marlon heard someone call his name. The hairs on the back of his neck stood and his stomach churned. It was Alicia. He turned to greet her, pulling Latrice behind him.

Alicia stepped up to him and smashed her hand across the side of his face. "Who the hell are you out here kissing?"

Latrice tried to come from behind him, but Marlon gripped her firmly and she stayed put. "Alicia, it is no longer your concern."

"What do you mean not my concern? I am still your wife," she screamed, jabbing her finger into his chest.

"Only on paper," Marlon roared back, matching her intensity.

"How could you have found someone already? It has only been three months. Were you cheating on me with her?" Alicia kept trying to get around Marlon to get a look at Latrice's face, but Marlon refused to let that happen.

"I told you time and time again that I wasn't cheating on you, now get out of my face." Marlon rushed Latrice to the car, ensuring Alicia didn't see her face.

Alicia continued to scream as she punched Marlon in the back. "You bastard! How can you do me like this?"

Marlon passed his keys to Latrice and whispered, "Please wait for me in the car." She shot him a dirty look, but did as he said.

Marlon waited until Latrice was out of earshot before he addressed Alicia. "Let's get one thing straight; you cheated on me. I can't just forget something like that." The coldness in his voice brought tears to her eyes. "I don't know what you hope to accomplish by acting like this or by insisting that we go to counseling."

Alicia interrupted him, pleading for another chance. Seeing him with someone hurt more than anything she'd ever experienced. She had foolishly sacrificed her marriage for some fun and was now so tangled in adultery that if he ever found out about, he would never forgive her. Now, some other woman had taken his affection. She was nowhere near ready to accept the fact that she'd lost him forever and she begged him to continue loving her. Her pleas fell on deaf ears and Marlon walked away, leaving her standing in the middle of the street.

By the time Marlon got into the car, Latrice had plenty of time to get her anger under control. She couldn't believe he had put her to the side for the woman that broke his heart. She was even more livid that Alicia had the nerve to put her hands on him. All lingering anger dissolved when Marlon asked with the sincerest voice if she was all right. It was then that she realized he wasn't hiding her from his wife; he was trying to protect her. "Did she hurt you?" Latrice caressed the side of his face.

"No, I just wish all this was over with." Marlon knew what he had to do. He hadn't fasted or prayed like Pastor Hawkins had told him and that was the only way they could continue the counseling. Fasting meant no more Latrice and although he knew he should fast to get his sexual desires under control, he wasn't quite ready to give her up.

Marlon headed toward the next part of his surprise for Latrice. He was taking her to a place that he'd never taken his wife. He parked behind the building; it was dark and isolated.

"Where are we?" Latrice asked, scanning her surroundings.

Marlon laughed at the worried look on her face. "We are at my restaurant. I want you to see what I do." Latrice was flattered. Through their conversations, she knew Alicia had never been to his restaurant and she felt honored that he'd brought her there.

Marlon walked Latrice through the kitchen, introducing her to everyone they passed. They all smiled and said hello, but they could hear whispers as they walked away. There were debates over who she was. The majority of them thought she was his wife, the others swore he wasn't married. Latrice didn't mind being called his wife and was even more flattered that Marlon didn't correct them.

Once they entered his office, Latrice placed her arms around his waist and rested her head on his chest. The past twenty-four hours with him had been amazing. From the way they made love and slept in each other's arms to Marlon bringing her to his restaurant, Latrice was falling for him. She didn't know whether to praise God for bringing Marlon into her life or to be angry with Him for allowing them to meet while neither of them was available. She attributed her ability to quickly get over what Calvin had done to Marlon being so kind. Now, his kindness had turned into an insatiable infatuation and she loved being desired by him.

Although she liked the attention he was giving, she knew it would end soon. After his divorce was final, he would move out and probably never think of her again. There was also the matter of her own marriage; she couldn't stay in hiding forever. Calvin was getting closer to locating her. It was time she took charge of her life.

Latrice's solemn mood worried Marlon, "Baby, are you okay?" The endearment refuted her interpretation of their relationship and overwhelmed her heart. Tears flooded her eyes and she fought to hold them back. "Do you not want to be here? I can take you home." Marlon feared her answer and was relieved when she shook her head. "Is it Calvin? Because you know I will never allow him to hurt you again."

Marlon waited for her response, but there was no response. Latrice placed her hand on his neck to guide his lips to hers. Her kiss explained her thoughts and her tears. Marlon understood the message she was trying to relay. He let his tongue explore the depths of her mouth, hoping she understood that he reciprocated her feelings.

A knock on the door ended their kiss and Marlon was sorely disappointed. There was a problem in the kitchen that needed his immediate attention. He excused himself. "Feel free to roam around and watch." At first she hesitated, then shyly made her way into the kitchen. Unbeknownst to Latrice, Marlon had already sent a message to everyone asking them to make her feel welcome and if she stopped by their station, feel free to show her what they were doing. She caught his eye as she exited the office. Marlon smiled and motioned for her to go further.

Latrice stood amazed, watching the hustle and bustle of the kitchen. Everyone was busy chopping, mixing, preparing plates, or carrying plates. They moved systematically throughout the kitchen. Everyone was focused on their task, yet aware of their surroundings. She watched as Marlon moved someone out of the way to show them how he wanted things done. The plating design was off and Marlon, being a perfectionist, had to correct it.

Latrice was overwhelmed by the aromas as she walked by each station. There was olive oil and garlic along with a mixture of other spices simmering in a pan. The smell was heavenly and she couldn't help asking the chef what he was making. He tossed in some shrimp and thinly sliced red peppers, then squeezed fresh lemon juice over the skillet. Latrice's stomach growled when he plated the dish.

Marlon saw her watching and made his way over to instruct the chef to make another plate for her, but she refused, stating, "I want you to make it for me." Without hesitation, the chef excused himself and Marlon stepped up to the stove. The sight of him engrossed in his cooking was exciting. He took his time preparing Latrice's meal, making sure every single detail was perfect. When he was finished, he escorted her to his office where she was able to eat in private.

"Marlon this is wonderful. You are really great at what you do."

"Thank you, that means a lot coming from you." Marlon kissed her forehead. "I really have to get back out there. Will you be all right in here by yourself?" Latrice nodded yes and continued to enjoy her food. She ate the entire dish and curled up on the small loveseat for a nap when she was finished.

In what seemed like only minutes, Marlon was waking her up for them to go home. The drive seemed longer than usual and Marlon could barely keep his eyes open. They walked into the house, both worn out from their long day and the events that took place before daybreak.

They climbed into bed together. Although they were tired, Marlon knew they needed to talk. "Latrice, can we talk for a minute?" His altercation with Alicia at the mall and the fact that Calvin was getting closer to finding Latrice had been weighing on his mind. "First, I want you to know that I am more than feeling you. You are a beautiful woman both inside and out. At a time where I should be angry and bitter, you put a smile on my face."

Latrice put her finger over his mouth to stop him from talking. She heard the 'but' coming and thought she'd be less affected by his rejection if the words came out of her mouth instead of his. "You have done the same for me and I will always be grateful for you." Her voice cracked and she paused to reign in her emotions. "I know your heart is unavailable and that you have business to take care with your wife. This is the moment I have been trying to avoid all week."

"You are right; I do have business to take care of with my wife. As for my heart, it is unavailable, but it's because you have it. I want us to stop sleeping together so we can get closer to the Lord, but there is no rule that says we can't be together." The words echoed through the room. His words ran across her skin and Latrice rested her face against his chest in an embrace which symbolized their journey to purity, together.

"Will you make love to me one last time?" She'd lost control of her tears and they streamed down her face.

Marlon groaned in frustration. His body said yes, but he knew he had to make a clean break while his mind was still strong enough to resist. He slid out of bed before she could kiss or caress him; it would be all over if she did. Where he got the strength to resist was a mystery, but he held on to it. He rose to his feet and backed away from the bed. "As much as I want to I can't, but please know my heart is with you." The tears rolling down her cheeks broke his heart and almost destroyed his resolve.

"And mine is with you." Latrice wiped the tears from her face, blew Marlon a kiss, laid her head on the pillow, and watched as he left the room.

14

Calvin was still up in arms over Latrice's disappearance. He sat up late many nights seething. The private investigator he'd hired had located her family and Calvin called them all. Everyone claimed they hadn't spoken to Latrice in almost a year and were quick to chew him out for isolating her from her family. Calvin hired someone to follow Latrice's mother and siblings; he didn't believe a word they said. After weeks with no sign of Latrice, he focused his attention on Latrice's friends from college.

The investigator tracked down Camilla, and this time Calvin personally went to her house to talk. Her response to his presence assured him that she knew where Latrice was. Camilla was intentionally unfriendly. "What do you want?" She had barked through a cracked door.

"Tell my wife that if she doesn't come home soon, she is going to make things worse for herself and anyone hiding her."

It had been over a week since then and the guy he hired to follow Camilla reported no sign of Latrice. He even followed Camilla to church, but she hadn't shown up there either. Calvin decided to pay Camilla a visit at church. He knew if Camilla was involved in hiding Latrice she would most definitely bring her to church. He had to check for himself, just in case Latrice was wearing a disguise; he would recognize her even with a changed appearance.

Calvin deliberately waited until the middle of service and walked into the church. He bypassed the ushers who'd greeted him at the door and walked straight to the front. Calvin strolled to the front like he owned the place. As he turned around to face the congregation, Latrice firmly gripped Marlon's leg.

She was trembling, beads of sweat formed above her upper lip, and tears now flooded her eyes. She tried to avoid making any sudden moves that would draw his attention to her. She slowly leaned toward Marlon and whispered, "That is Calvin."

The terror in her voice was evident. As Marlon turned to look, Calvin spotted her and made his way toward her. Marlon jumped to his feet and flashed Calvin a look that dared him to make a move. Marlon tried to move forward, but

113

Latrice had wrapped her arm around his leg and was holding on for dear life. Rubbing his hand through her hair, Marlon pressed her head against his hip. Fire ran through Calvin's veins as he watched Latrice respond to this stranger's caress.

Camilla recognized Calvin and was shocked he'd shown up at church. She pointed him out and Tim instantly jumped up, blocking Calvin's path and warned him that he did not want to do this here. If they had met on the street, Tim would have laid Calvin out for threatening his wife, but Tim had respect for God's house.

Paul had no idea who Calvin was at the moment, but saw the anger in his little brother and ran over to assist. Tim's face was set like flint as he breathed down on Calvin. Paul could see he was seconds from losing control. He tried to push Tim to the side, but he wouldn't budge. He looked to Camilla for a clue as to what was going on and she whispered, "That is Calvin."
Paul knew how pissed Tim was behind Calvin's actions and knew if he didn't do something soon, it was going to go down right there in the middle of the church. Paul alerted the deacons and they surrounded Calvin, daring him to make a move.

Marlon grabbed Latrice by the hand and ran out of the church. Calvin chuckled as he pulled out his cell phone and called the investigator that was waiting in the parking lot. "The woman that just left the church is Latrice; follow her."

Paul followed suit and pulled out his cell to call Marlon, "Don't go home you are being followed. Let him follow you, then pull into a well-populated area, tell him to give you his camera, all the notes he's taken, and I will pay him triple what Calvin is paying." He hung up with Marlon and called the police to have Calvin arrested for violating the order of protection.
Marlon followed Paul's instructions and as usual, money talked. The P.I. accepted the deal. Calvin was wealthy, but his fortune was a drop in the bucket compared to Paul's. He followed Marlon to the bank where he withdrew all the money from his savings. The P.I. took the money and disappeared.

After the cops took Calvin away, the rest of the family left church and met up at Jaleel and Delisa's house. They needed to decide where to go from here. It was obvious they needed to move Latrice, but none of their houses were safe. "We have to do something and quick." Paul knew Calvin would have a high-priced attorney who knew the ins and outs of restraining orders. They would argue that church was a public place and that Calvin couldn't have possibly known Latrice was going to be there.

Marlon and Latrice sat at the table listening to everyone talk. She was still pretty shaken up and he was trying his best to comfort her. Her head rested on his shoulder as his hand caressed her back. No one noticed how close they had become until Marlon spoke up to offer a suggestion. Before he could complete his thought everyone was looking at him cross-eyed with mouths hanging open.

"What?" Marlon asked. It had become natural for her to be in his arms and it hadn't dawned on him that no one had ever seen them so close.

"What do you mean what?" Camilla snipped. "Look at you guys. Do you really need to make either of your lives more complicated right now?"

Latrice realized what she was talking about and immediately sat up. Marlon pulled her back to rest against him. "I know you are frustrated right now, but you of all people should understand what we feel." Marlon looked around the table at Paul and his wife Sheena, Tim and Camilla, and Jaleel and Delisa. "Every single one of you knows how it feels to have your mind consumed with thoughts of someone. You know what it's like for your phone to ring and you hope it's them, but are disappointed when it isn't. I used to watch all of you thinking that Alicia and I were never as committed or as in love as you guys. I told myself not everyone has that kind of relationship, but the past couple of months with Latrice have proved me wrong." The house was silent as Marlon waited for someone to respond, and when they didn't, he redirected the conversation to the issue at hand: Latrice's safety. "My suggestion for Latrice is to move her into my mother's house. I will move in to keep an eye on her. What do you guys think?"

"That is actually a good idea. If you think you can handle it, then I am all for it." Camilla flashed Marlon a look, warning him to be careful.

"You guys wait," Latrice chimed in, tired of the fuss everyone was making. "I can't hide forever. I want my life back. Calvin is still controlling me and I am tired of it. One of the things I have learned at church is that God is the giver and taker of life. If Calvin is going to kill me there is nothing that any of you can do about it. I am going to get a job, take self-defense classes, and move out on my own. I appreciate everything you guys have done for me, but it is time to stand on my own two feet." She was terrified of what Calvin might do and did not like putting her friends in danger.

Marlon whispered in her ear, "I hear you, but first we have to get you to a safer location and then I promise I will help you with everything else. So go pack up your things so we can go."

Without question or hesitation, Latrice left the kitchen to pack and Camilla, Delisa, and Sheena, followed closely behind her. Once in the room they shut the door for a private conversation.

"Latrice, are you all right?" Camilla approached her first. "I know I haven't been coming to visit, but I knew Calvin would eventually look for me and follow me."

"I know and that is one of the reasons I have to stand on my own. Because of me, you haven't been able to visit your sister. Everyone has rearranged their lives for me and all I am doing is putting everyone in danger."

"Latrice, we consider you family. Family is there to offer support when standing on your own is a little rough. You can lean on us for as long as you need us. We love you."

"Thank you. You guys and Marlon are the most amazing friends anyone could have." Latrice patted the tears gathering in the corners of her eyes.

"Now that you mentioned Marlon, what is going on with you two?"

"It's not really clear. I do know that he is a wonderful man. He set aside his own issues and made me feel like the most important person in the world. Being around him has helped me see how horrible Calvin was, even before we got married. I should be depressed with low self-esteem and no confidence in myself. I was headed that way, but Marlon's kindness started chipping away at the wall of self-pity I was putting up, and before I knew it I was getting out of bed every morning just to see him." Everyone watched Latrice's face light up as she talked about Marlon. They were all familiar with falling victim to love at unexpected times, but Latrice and Marlon had inexcusable circumstances which made such love forbidden. "I know you guys may not understand this," Latrice continued to unload her feelings for Marlon, unaware of the scrutinizing eyes that were on her. "And I hope you are not angry, but I am in love with him."

Camilla's eyes bulged as Latrice finished divulging her emotions. "We are not angry. We are just concerned that you guys are rushing in to something that neither of you are ready for. Both of you are extremely vulnerable. Just promise me you guys will take things slow and not get too seriously involved until your divorces are final."

Latrice silently hoped there was no pressure for a response to Camilla's plea. They'd already gone too far and it was too late to turn back. "Thanks for your concern, but if anyone knows what love is or isn't, it's me and Marlon. We both rushed into our marriages. If we'd waited, we would have seen that what we felt wasn't true love. True love feels like the first ray of sun that breaks through a cloudy day giving you a sudden rush of heat and all you want to do is stand in its warmth. True love doesn't try to control you or shape you into something you are not. It enhances the greatest part of you and makes you feel like you can conquer the world. I loved Calvin, but I overlooked his need to control me because of his money. Now that I have a chance at something great, you can't expect me to just walk away from it."

"That would be asking the impossible." Sheena knew firsthand how sudden love could be and so did Camilla. She couldn't believe Camilla was asking Latrice to take love slow. "I think it is okay to love him, but if you love him, you will do what is best for him."

"So, you think staying away from him is what's best?"

"No, in fact I think that is the worst thing you could do. We all saw how attached he is to you. If you turned your back on him now, that would destroy him. I am just saying keep it holy. I am not sure how you feel about God and living for Him, but Marlon loves the Lord. If you love him, help him stay holy. It will not be easy. Keeping your hands off the man you love is one of the hardest things you will ever have to do."

Guilt was overwhelming Latrice and she had to change the subject. "I was going to get baptized today. Marlon has been explaining some scriptures to me and helping me understand why the Lord allowed these horrible things to happen. I decided to give the Lord a try." Just as she hoped, everyone's focus shifted from her relationship with Marlon to her relationship with the Lord.

Downstairs Paul, Tim, and Jaleel all hemmed Marlon up on the same topic. Marlon didn't break a sweat, flinch, nor did he care what they thought of him. When he fell for Alicia, there was nothing that could've stopped him from having her. The feelings he once had for Alicia were merely a fraction of what he now had for Latrice. He was going to be persistent in making her love him.

"Marlon, what are you doing?" Jaleel was not going to take the passive approach; he got straight to the point. "Did you not learn from your marriage to Alicia that rushing things never works?"

"Wait a minute," Tim had to protest. He and Camilla were married after just weeks of knowing each other and Paul and Sheena were engaged within a few months of dating. "Time has nothing to do with it. You just have to be in the right frame of mind to accept love. Your mind has to be right, so you know what you're feeling is not tainted. I wasn't around when you met Alicia, but I think it is safe to say that right now your mind is a little cluttered."

"I appreciate what you guys are doing, but you just don't understand. I am not sad or upset about Alicia. At first, I was livid, but Latrice helped me work through all that. What I feel for Latrice has helped me realize that I never truly loved Alicia. I used to watch you guys with your wives wondering why you were all up under them. Now, I totally understand it." Marlon didn't dare tell them why he understood.

"Well, just be careful. Latrice has been through a lot and the last thing she needs is to be hurt again by someone she trusts." Their conversation was cut short when Latrice and the other women came back into the kitchen carrying her bags. Marlon stood and shook everyone's hands and then grabbed her bags. Latrice hugged everyone, thanking them for all their help. As instructed, she drove Marlon's car, while he drove hers, and followed him to his mother's house.

Latrice was terrified to drive alone, but kept telling herself, "This is part of standing on your own two feet." And she prayed for strength. When she pulled up in front of the house, she sighed with relief and thanked God for getting her there safely.

Marlon had called ahead to let his mother know what was going on and she was more than willing to help. Gloria took one look at Marlon and Latrice together and knew he hadn't given her the whole story. No matter what they did, they never broke contact with each other. Either he was touching her or she was touching him. What she noticed most of all, he looked happy. She hadn't seen him since the day he caught Alicia and expected him to be depressed. The joy on his face was a pleasant surprise and she knew this woman was the cause.

Marlon escorted Latrice to his room and she was shocked to find out they were going to be sharing rooms. The room was huge with two twin sized beds. There was plenty of space, but she had a hard enough time sleeping in the next room. How were they going to sleep in the same room and keep their hands to themselves?

"This is your home now, so relax." Marlon saw the nervous look on her face.

"This scares me. We decided to stop having sex. It has only been a few weeks and I have to force myself to stay out of your room. I wake up in the middle of the night aching for you and have to grip the side of the bed to keep from going to you. I can't guarantee that I will have that same strength with you in the next bed."

"I am sorry, but your safety is my main priority. We will just have to help each other. Hopefully, on the days your feeling weak, I am strong and on the days I am weak, you are strong."

"I think you are going to have to be strong enough for the both of us." Latrice plopped down on her bed laughing.

Marlon lay on the bed behind her and pulled her close. "That's because you are relying on your own strength. You have to lean on the Lord."

"It's harder for me. I don't know the Lord the way you do," Latrice whined as she snuggled her face against his neck. "I don't know what is right and what is wrong."

"The closer you get to the Lord, the easier it is to hear His voice. Just trust Him; He won't lead you astray. We have to be honest about how we are feeling. If I tell you that I want you, then you have to pray and help me get my mind right."

"So, if we are being honest about how we feel; then I have to tell you that I love you." Lifting her head to look in his eyes, Latrice unloaded her heart. "I know it sounds crazy. After all I have been through, how could I possibly love again? I tried to deny my feelings at first, but I can't anymore. I love you more than I ever loved my husband and if it is wrong in God's eyes for me to love you, then…"

"Shhh." Marlon ran his fingers through her hair. It felt good to be loved with a pure love that wasn't overshadowed by infidelity and lies. "I love you, too," was all he could utter before succumbing to the overwhelming desire to kiss her. At first, he just brushed his lips across hers, but his hunger for her wouldn't let him stop there. They tried to refrain from deep passionate kissing, because it made abstinence even harder, but today neither could resist.

Marlon abruptly pulled away, apologizing for almost losing control. Latrice, sensing his turmoil, laughed as she went to lie in the other bed. "You see," Marlon laughed. "You can be strong when I am weak."

Latrice rolled her eyes and tossed her pillow at him. It landed right on his face. She gasped and then busted out laughing, "I am sorry."

"You think that's funny. I am going to show you what's funny," he playfully threatened, as he held her down and tickled her. She bucked and screamed underneath him, laughing to the point of tears.

Latrice picked up the pillow and tauntingly asked, "Do you want a piece of me?"

Marlon grabbed a pillow and tossed it at her. "You better ask my sister who the pillow fight champion of this house is."

"Well, this is a new day," Latrice chuckled as she swung the pillow hard as she could.

Marlon blocked it and stripped it from her hands. Latrice screamed as she ran to get the pillow he'd tossed at her, but he grabbed it before she could reach it. There was one more pillow on each bed, but she had to get past Marlon to get them. He saw her eyeballing the pillows and picked them up.

"You have to play fair. Give me a pillow," Latrice whined with a pouty face.

"What? Fairness doesn't exist in pillow fights." Marlon teased her with the pillows, and then one by one sent them hurling into her face. The first one she tried to catch, but the others hit her in the face causing her to stumble backward, trip over her bags, and fumble onto the floor.

Marlon rushed over to see if she was all right and she was laughing so hard she had tears in her eyes. He couldn't help but join in. The more she loosened up, the more he fell in love with her. They lay on the floor talking and laughing. They were so caught up in each other's presence that he forgot he had to go to work.

15

Calvin sat in the jail cell, waiting for his lawyer to arrive. The smell of urine and other foul body odors were turning his stomach, and if he did not get out of there soon, its contents were going to come up. He sat in a corner, off to himself, trying to keep up a hard exterior. He appeared to be a tough guy who wasn't fazed by his current location, but inside he was falling apart. He had called his lawyer three times to find out why he hadn't shown up, and each time he'd come up with some lame explanation.

Just as Calvin was heading to the phone to contact his lawyer for the fourth time, he heard his name being called. One of the arresting officers let him out of the cell and apologized, stating that he was sorry for having wasted his time and that he was free to leave. He was so happy that he didn't ask any questions. He completed the necessary steps to receive his confiscated items and rushed out before anyone could change their mind.

Getting into his lawyer's car, Calvin wanted to slap some sense into him. He flashed him a furious glare to let him know that he had screwed up and with an incensed growl commanded, "Take me home!"

When he arrived home, his mind was already burning with his plot for revenge. His scope of interest had expanded past Latrice. She was his ultimate goal, but since Paul and Tim wanted to jump in the middle, Sheena and Camilla would have to pay. He was a little hesitant about hiring someone to carry out his plan, but the things he was going to do would surely land him in jail again. That was one risk he wasn't willing to take. He knew a few people who had mastered the criminal lifestyle and could pull off just about anything you could ask without being detected. Breaking and entering, arson, car thefts for insurance fraud; they'd done it all. He was contemplating the final details of his plan when his phone rang.

"Calvin, this is Paul." He had a friend of his at the police station who called as soon as Calvin was released.

"What do you want?"

"It is time for all of this to be over. Latrice doesn't want to be with you anymore."

"She doesn't have a choice."

"You are crazy if you think you can make this woman stay with you. You have spent the past two years terrorizing her. You almost killed her and you think following her around is going to show her you've changed or convince her to come home? She wants a divorce and I am prepared to make it worth your while if you agree to stay away from her."

"What is going on between Latrice and I has nothing to do with you. Instead of being in my business, you should be more concerned about Sheena. There are some crazy people in this world and I'd hate for something to happen to her."

Paul's hand tightened around the phone as his jaw clenched. Taking a second to calm his anger, Paul smoothed his free hand across his goatee, and with a commanding intensity warned, "That's what you don't want to do. Come near my wife and jail will be the last thing you have to worry about. I will see to it that you disappear. That's not a warning or a threat. It is a promise."

Calvin chuckled; he knew he had hit a nerve with Paul and was amused. "I'm just saying, accidents happen all the time. Make sure your own wife is safe before worrying about someone else's."

"The divorce papers will be at your office in the morning; be a man and sign them." Paul hung up the phone before Calvin could respond.

Calvin paced back and forth in his bedroom. He hated to be hung up on. The conversation wasn't over until he said it was. Paul had some nerve to call his house, interfere in his marriage, and then hang up. Pacing was an attempt to stay calm and not allow Paul to get a rise out of him, but Calvin's temper was raging and his mind was in a whirlwind state. Rage was taking control and he was unable to collect his thoughts. He stared at his reflection in the mirror and, with all the strength he could muster, punched the mirror. Pain instantly shot up his arm. Rage was replaced with agony and he rushed to the kitchen to get some ice.

He picked flecks of glass out of his hand and stopped the bleeding. Calvin took a pain killer and plopped onto his bed. The conversation he had with Paul replayed clearly in his mind. Disrespect was one thing he did not tolerate from anyone. He canceled the plan of hiring someone; it was now personal and his last thought before drifting off to sleep was, "I will take care of Sheena myself."

Paul had ended the call with Calvin and wasted no time setting up a demonstration to let Calvin know who he was messing with. There was one thing about Calvin that Paul knew for sure: he was crazy. Crazy people needed a little more convincing than most. Paul would lay down his life, or even take a life, to protect Sheena, and Calvin needed to understand the validity of the threat to make him disappear.

Within the hour, Paul had contacted a few acquaintances and persuaded them to pay Calvin a visit. They waited until the sun had completely set and assembled at the corner of Calvin's block. Paul's car pulled up behind them and, on cue, the men slithered out dressed in all black with ski masks. One by one, they raced across the lawn and hopped the fence into the backyard. Picking the lock to the back door, the men inconspicuously crept through the house, searching for Calvin. He was still lying in bed asleep. With one swift movement, each man grabbed a limb.

Terrified, Calvin woke up instantly fighting for his freedom, but they had a firm grip on him. He had no clue what was going on and pleaded for mercy. The men said nothing in response to his plea. They carried him down stairs and tied him to a chair in the kitchen.

Paul had been waiting in his car for the call that they were ready for him, and when they called, he drove around to park in front of Calvin's house. He strolled up to the porch and the front door opened for him. He stepped into the kitchen and smiled at the scowl that spread across Calvin's face when he realized what was going on.

Paul pulled a chair up to sit in front of Calvin. "There are some things you don't know about me." His words coldly drawled out of his mouth. "I haven't always been the nice church boy that you know…"

"Then why don't you dismiss your boys and untie me so we can handle this man to man?" Calvin huffed.

Paul flashed a look of annoyance to his associates and without words being exchanged they pulled out a roll of duct tape to shut Calvin up. "I don't like being interrupted." Paul firmly pressed the tape across Calvin's mouth. "I was saying, don't let my current life fool you. The nice guy that you see now only exists because of my wife. These men here are friends from my past. We run in separate circles, but because of things I helped them out of, they have pledged to be there for me when I need them. They have an explicit instruction that if anything happens to my wife or anyone in my family to take you out." Paul had left this cutthroat life style alone and wasn't proud that he resorted back to it, but he loved Sheena and would do whatever he had to do to keep her safe.

"Now my friend here is going to leave you with a little friendly reminder to stay away from my family. I hope I'm clear, because I don't want to have this conversation again." Just as calmly as he had entered; he left. Paul hoped Calvin heeded the warning, because he had every intention of following through.

One of the men untied Calvin's arm and slammed his hand down on the table. He tried to squirm free, but the other men surrounded him to hold him still. They rolled up his sleeve and pulled out a knife. Sweat flowed down Calvin's face as the knife approached his arm. A muffled scream rumbled out of his duct-taped mouth as the blade pierced his skin. They carved a 'P' into his arm. Paul wanted this day to be a constant reminder of who not to mess with.

Calvin groaned from the pain. Sweat, tears, and snot mingled above his lip then slid down the tape. Every attempt he made to free his arm only caused the knife to dig deeper. Panting heavily, his fingertips went numb from hyperventilating and before they could finish carving, he passed out.

When Calvin came to, he was alone, still sitting at the kitchen table with one arm and both legs tied to the chair. The pain in his free arm was excruciating, but he gathered up enough strength to untie himself. Every movement sent waves of pain rushing through his body. He grimaced with the slightest flick of the finger. Once he'd finally freed himself, he took two more pain killers, bandaged his arm, and gently laid himself on the bed.

In the morning, Calvin woke with a pounding headache next to a puddle of blood. His wound had soaked through the bandage and stained the sheet. The pain pills had long since worn off and the pain was just as evident as the night before. He was pissed and revenge weighed heavily on his mind, but the throbbing in his arm made him terrified to retaliate.

While waiting for the bleeding to stop, Calvin redialed his last incoming call. As soon as he heard Paul's voice answer the phone, Calvin flatly stated, "You were clear."

"Good," a satisfied grin spread across Paul's face. "Like I said before, there will be divorce papers waiting at your office; be a man and sign them."

"Let me be completely clear, your wife is your business and my wife is my business. You have no say where Latrice is concerned."

"Well, let me further clarify things for you. Latrice is like family; if you touch her, the same fate awaits you." Paul waited for a response, but all he heard was the click of Calvin hanging up the phone.

The night's events had scared Calvin out of his mind. He considered women to be weak and fragile and had no problem over powering them. Going up against a man was a different story. He talked a good game, but when it came down to it, he was nothing but a punk. His mouth always got him into trouble and he cowered away from many physical altercations by throwing his money around. Lucky for him, most men would rather get paid than beat him down. He'd laugh it off like he was too good to fight and pull out his wallet saying, "Let me make it up to you." This situation was different. Paul wouldn't be swayed by his money and had proved he was capable of following through with his threats.

Although he did not want to go up against Paul, Calvin couldn't leave Latrice alone. He loved her and refused to let someone else have her. She was his wife and only death could keep him away.

Alicia checked the caller ID on her cell phone. She signaled for Meme to be quiet and smiled as she answered the phone. "Hey Marlon." Meme heard Marlon's name, rolled her eyes, and walked away.

The sound of Alicia's voice turned his stomach. Marlon did away with all the small talk and got straight to the point. "It is time for us to stop messing around. We have an appointment this Saturday at noon with Pastor Hawkins at my mother's house. Are you able to make it?"

Her smile faded. "Of course I can." She was holding on to hope that one day he'd call saying that he wanted her back. She could hear the coldness in his voice and knew today wasn't that day.

"Good, I am going to make us lunch and we can have a civilized adult conversation. Also, he told us to fast before we meet again. I will be fasting Tuesday, Wednesday, and Thursday. It would be nice if you could do the same." Before she could ask any questions, Marlon hung up. Alicia tossed her phone back into her purse. Every time they spoke, he gave her the same distant, disgusted attitude. Each time it hurt as if it were the first time.

Meme walked back into the room with her shoes on, carrying her purse. Her eyes were glossy and she was fighting to hold back the tears. "You are waiting for Marlon to come home. I am done being your second choice. We both know him very well. He is not coming home. I am tired of waiting for you to face reality. You said yourself that you saw him kissing some woman. He has moved on and it is time for you to move on too." Burrowing through her purse for her keys, Meme walked toward the front door, and before leaving snapped back, "I can't believe I am ruining my life to be with someone who doesn't want me." Meme stormed out of the house, refusing to let another tear drop for Alicia.

Over the course of their relationship, Meme had cried herself to sleep many nights. Her feelings for Alicia were overwhelming and she desperately wanted them reciprocated. Day after day, she'd listen to Alicia ranting and raving about Marlon ignoring her, seeing him at the mall with some woman, or about how much she missed him. Meme waited patiently, hoping that she'd realize he had moved on. Any hour of the day, she would drop whatever she was doing to tend to Alicia's needs. From running errands, to emotional support, to sex, Meme gave Alicia her all. Now it was clear, she was being used and she was tired of it.

Even after she was gone, Meme's words raked over Alicia. Her heart was breaking over the dissolution of her marriage and she had begun to find solace in Meme's presence. When she was lonely, Meme was there with companionship, laughter, and sexual comfort. She was so self-absorbed; not once had she considered what Meme was risking to be with her. The truth was that Meme was fun, but Marlon was her life. The thought of Marlon not wanting her was painful and Alicia made one last attempt to prove Meme wrong.

Alicia waited for Marlon to answer the phone. She knew he was at work and getting him on the phone would take a miracle, which was part of the reason she had the nerve to call. Just as she suspected, he didn't answer. When the voicemail beeped for her to leave a message, she tried to make her voice peppy and full of life, but failed. Her voice shook with nerves as she rambled, "I was just calling to tell you how great it felt to hear your voice today. I was thinking that maybe you could stop by after work and we could talk. I really miss you." A lump formed in her throat as she struggled to contain her tears. "I totally understand if you don't want to. Okay, I'll talk to you soon." She ended the message before she became a blubbering mess.

Marlon saw her name on the caller ID and intentionally sent the call to voicemail. Then, he waited to see if she had left a message. When it came through, he rolled his eyes in frustration and checked his voicemail. Listening to her voice, the anguish was apparent. For the first time, he'd acknowledged her pain. He could sense she was miserable and on the verge of a meltdown. He no longer wanted her to hurt the way she had hurt him.

His compassion for her almost made him grant her request. He was on his way over until he thought about Latrice. Even though he was just going to talk, he thought about how it would look to Latrice, made a u-turn, and headed to his mother's house. Alicia was his past; Latrice was his future. Going to Alicia would only give her false hope and hurt Latrice in the process.

It was one AM before Alicia accepted the fact that Marlon wasn't coming. She balled like a baby as she realized her marriage was over. Meme was right, Marlon would never come back. Before they married, she had heard the rumors about all the women who tried to catch him by freely giving themselves to him. He felt that loose and easy women were untrustworthy. "They used sex to try to lure me in and would use it again when it suited them," was what he said when she asked him why he never exclusively dated women in the past. He had fallen hard for Alicia, because he trusted her. She stood for what she believed in and didn't let down her principals just to get what she wanted. She violated that trust the moment she started clubbing; he would never trust or love her again.

Time ticked by and Alicia sank deeper and deeper into the sofa. The reality of losing Marlon was weighing her down. She tried to move herself from the couch to the bed, but each limb felt like a ton of bricks. Over the past month or so, Meme had been her sounding board and it was times like these when Alicia would lean on her for support, but the way Meme had stomped out of the house, there was no way she was coming back. Alicia had to tough her way through this one on her own.

Alicia cradled and cried herself to sleep. Her body was drained from crying and sleep wasn't a problem. The fun she had stepping out on her husband was nothing compared to the pain of losing him. If she knew then what she knew now, she would've bore the lonely nights and done everything she could to mend their relationship.

In a few hours, the alarm on her phone to get up for work would go off, but she was not in the mood for work. She'd hit the snooze button four times before she decided to just turn it off. Sleeping the day away would become her pattern for the next few days.

16

After four days of lying around the house, crying, and wallowing in self-pity, Alicia tried to shake off the depression. She hadn't eaten or showered during that time, and her body was in desperate need of both. Despite a pounding headache, she crawled out of bed. Her legs were wobbly and she could barely sustain the weight of her body. Using every ounce of strength she had, Alicia showered, threw on the first outfit she touched, and sluggishly stammered out to the car. She needed to get out of the house before her depressed state of mind convinced her that life wasn't worth living; she decided to go to work.

All eyes were on her as she walked into the office. Since she hadn't bothered to iron her clothes and hadn't put much effort into combing her hair; the diva she exemplified to perfection was missing in action. Normally, it was her beauty, bright smile, and sweet fragrance that grasped everyone's attention as she walked by, but today she was drab and unappealing. Her disheveled appearance was a shock to everyone and before she made it to her desk the whispering rumors had already started to swirl.

Alicia plopped down in her seat. She was unaware of the stares and whispering. On a normal day, she would've never left the house looking that way, but her mind was still in turmoil over Marlon. Alicia fumbled through stacks of paper on her desk. She was trying to get her mind in the right place. There was a bottle of Tylenol on her desk. She popped two into her mouth and waited impatiently for them to work.

For an hour, Alicia looked over the same piece of paper. She would read a couple of lines down, then her mind would flash to the look on Marlon's face when he caught her in bed with Meme or to him passionately kissing that woman at the mall. Tears kept forming in her eyes and she fought hard to hold them back. Maintaining her composure at work was harder than she thought it would be.

Caught up in torturing herself with painful memories, Alicia didn't hear her boss asking her to come in his office. He startled her out of the torturous visions by banging on the desk. "You look a mess. It is obvious you're still not feeling well. Take the day off, get some rest over the weekend, and come in on

Monday feeling refreshed. I appreciate you trying to tough it out, but you have to take care of yourself." He ignored Alicia's protests and walked away.

Alicia was glad he had mistaken her grief for sickness, but did not want to go home and sit in an empty house. She took her time gathering her things and when she finished, a deep sigh rolled off her lips and she headed out the door.

She took the long, scenic route, stopped to get something to eat, and drove as slow as she possibly could to prolong the inevitable. She considered going to her parent's house, but she still hadn't told them that Marlon had left her. Telling them meant she'd have to explain why and she was not prepared to divulge all that information just yet.

As she pulled up in front of her house, Alicia's heart fluttered. Marlon's car was parked on the street. She threw the car into park and rushed into the house. Excitement over him finally coming home gave her tunnel vision and she paid no attention to the car that was parked directly behind his. She had no idea of what she was going to say or do, but she knew this was her last chance to convince him to come home. Alicia stopped dead in her tracks. Several bags and boxes were strewn across the floor. A few were taped and tied shut, and the open ones were half empty. Alicia rifled through the open boxes with tears in her eyes. He was only there to pack his things. Deep down, she knew this day was coming, but having his things in the house gave her hope that he might come home to stay.

Alicia stood preparing herself to see Marlon, but what she saw was infuriating. Marlon came around the corner and following close behind him was some strange woman. Alicia watched as Marlon tried to shield her by stepping between them.

Latrice blurted out, "If you love me, you will stop hiding me from her." Alicia's heart raced and time seemed to move in slow-motion as she waited for Marlon's response. He looked her straight in the eye, wanting her to fully understand that he loved someone else, and stepped to the side.

"Latrice, this is Alicia…My ex-wife."

"Ex-wife," the term tore into Alicia's heart and she snapped. Lunging toward Latrice, Alicia grabbed a fist full of her hair. Marlon tried to jump between them, but Alicia's fingers were locked into place. Latrice reached around Marlon and slapped Alicia across the face. Before Marlon knew it, arms were flailing and swinging all around him. One caught him in the eye and he stumbled back, which gave them the space they needed to go for blood. Alicia let go of Latrice's hair to use both hands to beat her down, but it back fired. Latrice rushed her, knocking her to the ground. Latrice had an advantage; she was raised in the hood and grew up fighting. Alicia had been a church girl all her life and the first time she had raised her hand in violence was the day Marlon caught her cheating and she slapped Meme.

"Get off of me you home wrecking slut." Alicia struggled to get free, but Latrice used her body weight to pin her to the ground.

Latrice laughed, "From what I hear, you're the slut that wrecked this home." That statement further fueled Alicia's rage. Sweat poured from her body as she fought to get free. Latrice sat firmly on top of Alicia and continued to wail on her face. Tears formed in Alicia's eyes. The pain and the helplessness she felt was beginning to get the best of her. She was on the verge of crying until she managed to wiggle an arm free. Grabbing one of Latrice's arms, Alicia did the only thing she could think of. She yanked Latrice's hand toward her mouth and bit down on the side of it as hard as she could. Latrice momentarily cried out in pain, but quickly recovered and with all the force she could muster punched Alicia in the jaw.

Marlon had recovered from the jab to his eye and saw his past and his future trying to kill each other. He was pissed off and fed up. He picked Latrice up and sat her on the couch. Then he picked up Alicia, carried her into their bedroom, and shut the door behind them. A tinge of jealousy pricked Latrice's heart. She couldn't believe Marlon chose to comfort Alicia over her, but when she heard yelling coming out of the room, she felt better about his choice.

"Latrice was right. You are the slut that wrecked this home. You have no right to be mad. I brought her here to help me pack, but you brought someone here and slept with them in our bed. You want to fight someone, go find that woman you slept with. If you ever put your hands on Latrice again, I will personally see to it that it is the last thing you ever do." Alicia stood in front of him with tears streaming down her face. Several times she opened her mouth to plead her case, but the look on his face warned her not to say a word. His words were like daggers flying out of his mouth. Defenselessly, she stood before him as his words cut into her flesh leaving scars that would probably never heal.

Marlon felt his anger getting out of control and took a few deeps breaths to maintain control. "I know you're hurting. It was not my intention to hurt you. I just came to get my stuff. We have our meeting with Pastor Hawkins tomorrow. I promise I will listen to everything you have to say then, but right now I need you to stay in here while I finish up. I will have Latrice wait in the car if that makes you feel better." The way he behaved at their last meeting was embarrassing and he had been preparing his mind to deal with her. When he walked away, he was proud of the way he'd controlled his anger. Shutting the door behind him as he exited the room, Marlon rushed to Latrice's side.

"Baby, are you all right?" Latrice tried to absorb his warmth. His conversation with Alicia had quieted and she had begun to worry that she was convincing him to take her back. Now that he was at her side, al. her fears were laid to rest. Marlon chose her and that thought alone ignited the passion that she'd been quenching since they decided not to have sex. It had been weeks since their last intimate encounter and it was getting harder for her to refrain from seducing him. She knew how he felt about the sexual part of their relationship, and although she didn't agree, she loved him enough to respect his wishes.

"Latrice, baby." The affection in his eyes and the heat from his hand caressing her bare arm made her desire for him smolder. "I hate to ask you this, but I need you to wait in the car while I finish packing. I can't have the two of you in here fighting." Marlon saw the worry that flashed in her eyes and immediately reassured her that he was finished with Alicia. "I love you and if Alicia comes back in here and puts her hands on you, we all are going to make the eleven o'clock news."

Latrice chuckled at his words, but the seriousness in his eyes convinced her to wait in the car. She could feel his eyes burning through her as she walked toward the door. Before exiting, she returned his gaze, but concern was in his eyes, not need. As if sensing her question, Marlon stated with a possessiveness that startled them both, "Lock the car door. If Calvin shows up, I don't want to have kill him today either."

Fear dampened her face and Marlon made a beeline to her and escorted her to the car. He wanted her to feel safe at all times and he made it his mission to make sure she did. He rushed back into the house and quickly finished packing.

Marlon made a list of everything he needed that was still in the bedroom. One trip to the room was all he wanted to make; anything he forgot would just be left behind. He finished packing everything else around the house, stuffed it all into his and Latrice's cars, and dreadfully went back for the things in his former room. Their eyes met as soon as he entered the room. He hoped Alicia had fallen asleep, but she hadn't. Ignoring the longing in her eyes, he immediately started gathering the things on his list. Alicia watched him pack, hoping he looked her way or said something to her, but he didn't. Several times, she opened her mouth to speak, but the words escaped her. She had waited for him to come back in, planning to make him an offer he couldn't refuse, but now she was losing her nerve.

He had gone through the closet and his drawers, packed his collection of designer watches and cuff links, and then made his way to the bathroom. Suddenly it hit her, this was her last chance. She had already prepared her body by stripping down to nothing. The thought of wearing one of the many never worn negligees that she received at her bridal shower crossed her mind, but she figured foregoing clothes altogether was her best option. He always commented on the exquisiteness of her body and wished she'd let him see it more often.

With her mind made up to just go for it, Alicia hopped out of bed and followed Marlon into the bathroom. It was now or never; her plan of seduction was in full swing. Before he recognized what was going on, she was all the way inside the bathroom and had shut the door, standing in front of it so he couldn't leave.

"Alicia what are you doing?" When she didn't answer, he continued packing his things in the medicine cabinet. He threw his razors and herbal supplements into the bag and made his way to the door. Alicia didn't budge. Reaching behind her Marlon attempted to grab the handle, but she had a firm grip on it. He looked her square in the eye, not once acknowledging her naked state.

With a pounding heart, Alicia made her move. Her short stature caused Marlon to tower over her. Slowly she rose to the tip of her toes, slid her hands around his neck to pull his mouth down to meet hers, and as she covered his lips with hers he mumbled into her mouth. "Don't make a fool of yourself."

She froze. His words stole her nerve. She shrank back down to stand flat on her feet and rested her head on his chest. With her hands around his neck, Marlon was able to freely grab the door knob. He stepped around her, opened the door, and left without saying another word. Alicia was mortified. Her body, which he once looked upon with hunger, now had no affect on him. Her heart sank into the pit of her stomach as she watched him walk away. He was gone, she had lost him, and there was nothing she could do about it.

After throwing the last bag into the back seat of his car, Marlon signaled to Latrice that he was ready to leave. Latrice stared at his face, searching for a clue as to what had gone on in the house, but there was nothing. His expression held no sign of what had transpired between him and Alicia. She tried to give him the benefit of the doubt, but she instinctively feared the worst.

The silence between them as they carried the boxes into Marlon's room was killing Latrice. She tried to reassure herself that he loved her, hated Alicia, and the sexual part of his relationship with Alicia was over, but his sullen countenance terrified her. He was alone in that house with Alicia a lot longer than she cared for him to be. Despite all she and Marlon had shared over the past months, her mind couldn't help but wonder if he indulged in a little marital bliss with Alicia while she sat in the car looking like a fool. *He loves me and would never be unfaithful to me* was what she kept telling herself. But then again, Alicia was his wife and she was the mistress. He had every right to sleep with his wife, but she hoped to God he hadn't.

"Marlon." Latrice tried to control the shaking in her voice. She had been watching him unpack. The look on his face said something was weighing heavily on his mind. Whatever it was had him so entrenched in thought that he hadn't even noticed she was watching him. When he did not respond to her voice, she stood in his path giving him no choice but to acknowledge her. Their eyes met and she asked, "Is everything all right?"

Marlon nodded yes and tried to step around her. Instinct told Latrice other wise and she was not letting him off the hook that easily. "What happened while I was waiting in the car?" She saw the look of shame on his face and braced her heart for his response. She loved Marlon, and the thought of him sleeping with another woman, even if she was his wife, was gut-wrenching. Tears swelled in her eyes as she waited for his response. Was he still in love with Alicia? Or was it just a momentary weakness because they hadn't been sleeping together? Would she be able to get past it and continue their relationship? Wait… Did they even have a relationship?

Latrice was driving herself crazy as she waited for him to speak. She could tell he was trying to gather his thoughts, but if he didn't respond soon, she was going to scream. When he finally opened his mouth to speak Latrice closed her eyes, steadying herself for the blow. "Alicia came on to me. She cornered me in the bathroom and she was completely naked."

"Oh God." Latrice sank to the bed losing control of the tears she had been fighting so hard to hold back.

Marlon rushed to her side, "Nothing happened!" Her eyes jumped to meet his and the pain he saw in them melted his heart. "My wife stood in front of me with the same body that I have adored for years and I felt nothing. All I could think of was getting out of there so that I could get to you."

The same look of turmoil that was on his face earlier resurfaced and she knew he was getting to the root of his anguish. "I am no better than her, maybe even worse. She had meaningless sex, but I have fallen in love with you, have made love to you more than once, and every night I dream about doing it again."

Latrice interjected, trying not to let her mind linger on the fact he dreamed about making love to her again. "You are nothing like her. She broke her vow to you. We were only together once your marriage was over. I understand if you feel the need to end our…" Latrice hesitated, not sure if her next word was appropriate for their situation, but decided saying it would bring her some clarity. "…our relationship until your divorce is final. If it will bring you peace, I love you enough to respect it."

Marlon didn't even consider her suggestion. It was their relationship that gave him strength to get up every day. She had been the eye in the midst of his tornado. Chaos swirled around him, but in her presence he had peace. "You, being my lady, have given me all the peace I need. I just feel that my hatred for Alicia is no longer warranted and it is time to forgive her and move forward. How can I hate her for being unfaithful when I am now doing the same thing? And if she hadn't been unfaithful in the first place, I would have never met you."

Latrice didn't know if it was the wrong thing to feel or not, but his reasoning about their meeting touched her deeply. It sounded like he wanted to thank Alicia for cheating on him so that he could meet her. And calling her his lady definitely brought a little clarification. She was his lady. She felt foolish for assuming he had succumbed to Alicia's advances. Alicia stood before him naked, offering sex that would have been acceptable in the eyes of the Lord, but he chose abstinence with her instead of a quick, much needed release with his wife.

Latrice looked Marlon in the eye. With all sincerity she tried to convince him of the man she knew he was. "You are the kindest man I have ever known. You took care of me when you barely knew who I was. You loved me back into my right frame of mind. From what you told me, you tried to make things work with Alicia. She chose to be unfaithful even after you warned her that infidelity would end your marriage. So, your anger was warranted, but I agree it's time to move on. I don't want to see you hurting anymore."

Marlon nodded his head in agreement. He was ready to move on and he knew just who to call to make that happen. When their counseling was complete, he wanted the divorce to already be in motion. He wanted no delays in being able to love Latrice freely and called Paul to get the ball rolling. He wasn't a divorce attorney, but had all kinds of connections. He explained to Paul everything he wanted done and how fast he needed it done. "No problem," was the response he received before ending the phone call.

Marlon slid his phone back into his pocket and met Latrice's gaze. At that moment, his need to make love to her was more overwhelming than it had been all week. It had been his decision to end the sexual part of their relationship and he was having the most trouble with it. Several times, he woke in the middle of the night, climbed into bed with Latrice, and passionately kissed her awake. She received everything he offered until his hands ventured under her clothes.

She had immediately stopped him and put him out of her bed. He'd groan in frustration, but was obedient. In the morning, he'd wake up grateful for her strength.

Latrice moaned as she rested her head on his. "We can't. No matter how bad I want you, I love you too much to allow you to back down off of your principles." Over the past week, the love that made her crave his touch was the same love that helped her deny her need for him. Each day, it was getting tougher and tougher to quench the fire that radiated between them and she knew if she did not move out soon, her sexual hunger for him would override her good sense. Marlon knew she wasn't giving in and decided to change the subject. There was no point in torturing himself. She would be his soon enough; he'd make sure of it.

The corners of his mouth curved into a smile as he pictured her thumping on Alicia. "So, where did you learn to fight like that?" He couldn't help but laugh. He was mad as could be when his vision cleared up and he saw her fighting, but now looking back on it, he couldn't believe how she held it down. All this time he had been trying to protect her, but if he had let her loose on Alicia a long time ago he wouldn't have been so stressed out.

"It's not funny," Latrice whined, punching him in the arm. She rolled her eyes when Marlon clutched his arm, wincing in pain as he rolled around on the ground like he was in the worst pain of his life. She held back the smile that was trying to escape. When he didn't quit, she jumped on top of him and pinned him to the floor. "You better quit making fun of me before I give you a taste of what Alicia got." Latrice stared down at him, giving Marlon a look that said, "I am warning you." And when he did not stop, she said, "All right, you asked for it." She popped her knuckles and plunged her fingers into his under arms, tickling him into submission.

With swiftness and a power that instantly turned her on, Marlon flipped her onto her back and stretched out on top of her. Her heart pounded against her rib cage when she felt the bulge in his pants press against her thigh; she almost came apart. The hunger in his eyes warned her of his intent. "Marlon wait, please wait." With her last ounce of sanity, she begged him to stop.

His head dropped in shame, "I am sorry. I don't know what is wrong with me. I usually have more control than this." He helped her get up and then finished unpacking his things.

Latrice couldn't believe how quickly the atmosphere had shifted to a temperature that would melt their resolve to abstain from sex. She decided that first thing Monday morning, she was going to take the necessary steps to put some distance between them. She was going to find a job and get an apartment before they wound up tangled between the sheets in the throes of passion. He had given up trying to deny his desire for her and she would not be able to resist much longer.

17

Having successfully made it through counseling without ripping Alicia's head off had Marlon up early and in a good mood while getting ready for church. Pastor Hawkins had taken control of the session from the start and barely let them get a word in, Marlon was grateful for that. He opened the Bible and read scripture after scripture that revealed what God said about marriage and divorce. Marlon was with Pastor Hawkins, agreeing with every word as he explained that because of Alicia's infidelity, divorce was permitted, but his closing statement pissed Marlon off. Even now as it rang out in his mind, it was starting to put a damper on his good mood. "Just because the Bible says you can, doesn't mean you have to." Alicia's face, which had been dark and solemn during the whole meeting, lit up as the pastor spoke those words. Marlon glared at her from across the table giving her a look that said, 'The Bible says I can and I am', which quickly knocked the smile off her face.

Marlon shook the meeting from his mind, cranked Kirk Franklin up on his phone, clicked on his clippers, and continued trimming up his beard for service. For the first time in months, he was excited about going to church. He wasn't mad at Alicia and wasn't sleeping with Latrice. Things weren't perfect, but they weren't as bad as they used to be.

Latrice was stirred out of her sleep by the loud music blaring from the bathroom. She looked at the time and jumped out of bed. Marlon hadn't wakened her and she was determined to make it church today. After having to take a cold shower to douse the blazing inferno her dreams had ignited, she decided she was going to need a little help to resist Marlon. She made up in her mind that she was going to give her life to Christ and beg Him to help her. Latrice ran to the bathroom down the hall after grabbing an outfit from the closet.

Marlon was looking good, feeling good, and smelling good. The first thing he noticed was that Latrice was no longer in bed. Just as he headed out of the room to look for her, she ran right into him. She laughed, relieved that he hadn't left her. "Why didn't you wake me? I am going with you."

"I tried to, but you were knocked out." Marlon laughed. "I'd really like to know what you were dreaming about because I shook you, called your name, then you moaned with a smile on your face, and rolled over."

"Well, now you have to wait for me." She knew exactly what she was dreaming about and refused to let him know that he had been haunting her all night. She rushed around the room throwing on last minute accessories, brushed her teeth, put on some lip gloss, and was ready to go. Naturally beautiful women were Marlon's weakness. Make-up was fine for certain occasions, but he loved for a woman to be beautiful without all the bells and whistles that makeup added; Latrice was definitely that.

Latrice turned to tell him she was ready to leave and was in such a rush that she didn't notice him staring at her. His eyes roamed her body as he followed her out to the car. Pride swelled in his heart at the realization that this beautiful woman in front of him was his. She loved him so much that she abided by his religious convictions, even when he was too weak to abide by them. Yes, every exquisite inch of her belonged to him and he planned to enjoy her for the rest of his life.

Thanks to Latrice, they had arrived to church late. Foregoing their usual church, Marlon felt it best not to attend Zion Pentecostal Church until Calvin backed off. Instead, he drove to his mother's church. High Praise Apostolic Church was the church he grew up in and the only reason he'd left was to escape his womanizing reputation. Alicia's parents still attended the church and Marlon knew he was going to catch hell, but didn't care. Having to face them was inevitable and the sooner he got it over with the better. The only thing he didn't want to deal with was the smug, gloating stares from those who told Alicia not to marry him or the looks of 'I told you so' from those who said their marriage wouldn't last. Those who warned him that he would soon reap what he'd sown were going to get a kick out of the fact that Alicia cheated on him.

Just as he remembered, the church was packed. Everyone knew you did not show up late to a service at High Praise. The power of God moved early in the service and no one wanted to miss anything. Even now, as they were ushered to the seats his mother had saved, the presence of God moved through the sanctuary. Marlon remembered how he always thought the name High Praise was perfect for the church. Every Sunday, the congregation praised God like they were losing their mind and he loved it.

Latrice smiled as she looked around. Just about the whole church was praising the Lord. Dancing in the aisles, laid out on the floor, hands lifted in the air, tears streaming down their faces—High Praise was in full effect. The musician's fast tempo, high-energy composition matched the rhythm of the dancing feet. The drums beat into your soul, making it virtually impossible for you to keep still. The organ sent goose bumps down your arms, causing the fine strands of hair to stand up, and the bass guitar was that final push over the edge into no holds barred praise. Marlon flinched and Latrice was sure he was getting ready to join in the praise, but managed to keep his composure.

She wasn't as strong; tears ran uncontrollably down her face and before she knew it, she was on her feet with hands lifted into the air. She had no idea what to do or say; she had never felt this way before. Marlon stood next to her coaxing her to say 'thank you Jesus'. The words had barely left her lips before her tongue was taken over by the power of God. Marlon had explained being filled with the Holy Ghost and even after he showed her the scriptures, she was still a little skeptical. Now it was happening to her. Trying to resist was futile and Latrice gave in to the Lord. She came to church with the mind to give her life to Christ, but He had given something to her in return; His spirit.

For the rest of the service, Latrice felt like she was floating on a cloud. The hairs on her arm were still erect, she felt tingly all over, and tears threatened to roll down her cheeks. When they made the altar call for anyone who wanted to be baptized, Latrice was the first to stand. They took her to a quiet room, explained things that Marlon had already explained, and then directed her to the changing area. She changed into the baptismal clothes and her heart beat nervously as she made her way to pool.

The water was cold and her body trembled as she stepped into it. Reaching out his hand, the minister guided her deeper into the water. Her breath sucked in as the freezing water saturated the baptismal gown and slapped against her skin. Latrice scanned the pews for Marlon, their eyes locked, and he discreetly blew her a kiss. The entire congregation stood on their feet and a hush came over the sanctuary as the minister began speaking. "My dearly beloved sister, upon the confession of your faith in the death, burial, and resurrection of our Lord and Savior Jesus Christ, I now baptize you in the name of Jesus for the remission of sins and ye shall receive the gift of the Holy Ghost." As he leaned her back into the pool fully submerging her into the water, the minister proclaimed, "In Jesus name." The sanctuary erupted in applause and the same power that engulfed Latrice earlier donned her once again.

By the time she had redressed and returned to the sanctuary, service had been dismissed and she made her way to Marlon just as he was being greeted by an older couple. "Hey son, long time no see." Latrice saw the confusion on Marlon's face and wondered who they were. Their next statement widened

Latrice's eyes in disbelief. "Where is that wife of yours? Her mother and I miss her. She used to call or come by once a week and we haven't talked to her in months." They were Alicia's parents, and from the sound of things, they had no clue that Marlon and Alicia were no longer together.

"I am sorry." Marlon leaned in to kiss his mother-in-law on the cheek. "There are some things going on and it is Alicia's place to tell you, not mine."

"Is she all right? Is she sick?"

"No," Marlon assured. "But you have to hear it from her. I suggest you go by the house to see her." Marlon excused himself to go congratulate Latrice.

He tried to ignore the inquiring glances as he escorted Latrice to the car. He was sure they wanted to know where Alicia was and what his relationship with Latrice was, but knowing that Alicia hadn't told her parents about their separation made him leery of answering any questions. So he rushed to the car nonstop regardless of who tried to get his attention.

Once they were down the street away from scrutinizing eyes, Marlon turned to Latrice to explain. "I am sorry about not introducing you to anyone, but Alicia's parents kind of shocked me. I thought they knew and I was prepared for them to give me hell for hurting their daughter, but she hasn't even told them. I didn't want to introduce you as my lady and have them hear through the grapevine that you and I are together. I respect them too much to embarrass them like that."

Latrice brushed her lips across his as she whispered, "You don't have to explain. I trust you."

If he wasn't driving, Marlon would have given her the kiss he'd wanted to give her since he bumped into her in the hall before they left for church. Instead, he watched as she stared out of the window with a huge smile on her face. It seemed as though laughter was on the verge of bubbling out of her mouth. Marlon pulled into the driveway at his mom's house and curiosity got the best of him. "All right woman, out with it. What is so funny? You've been smiling like crazy for the past five minutes."

"Nothing's funny, I am just happy." She smiled even harder. "I haven't felt this happy in a long time. What I experienced at church this morning was amazing. I am still tingly all over."

Remembering how he felt when he received the Holy Ghost, Marlon chuckled as he walked around to let Latrice out of the car.

He was seventeen-years-old and all the other kids who had grown up with him in church had received the Holy Ghost years before. Discouraged and confused about why he hadn't received it, Marlon had long since stopped trying.

Girls became his main focus and he had already started to develop the 'ladies man' mentality. Then, one Sunday when he least expected it, the spirit of the Lord landed on him. Just as Latrice couldn't stop smiling, Marlon smiled for days after. He tried getting his act together, but he was young and his hormones took over. No matter what he did or who he slept with, he made a point to be at service to give God some praise.

Escorting Latrice into the house, Marlon pulled her into his arms. "The only bad thing about going to Higher Praise is that service is so long. I never have time to relax before going to work. Can I get you anything before I go?"

"No." Latrice rested her head against his chest. "Just call me later."

"Okay baby." Marlon kissed her forehead before releasing her. "I have to go, will you wait up for me or can I wake you when I come in?"

"Of course." Latrice cupped his face in her hands, guiding his mouth toward her slightly parted lips. She played with his lips nibbling and sucking, then brushed her tongue across his. Just as quick as she entered his mouth, she was gone. "Bye honey," she whispered as he left the house.

Latrice was in the laundry room, folding Marlon's clothes when Gloria finally came home from church. She intended to speak and let her presence be known, but what she encountered stole her voice. Gloria sat at the table, lips locked with some man. Latrice cleared her throat and eased further into the kitchen.

Gloria nearly jumped out of her skin and Latrice apologized profusely. "I didn't mean to scare you. I just wanted you to know that I was here. Please forgive me." Latrice tried to rush out of the room, but the man stopped her.

"You must be Latrice. Gloria has told me so much about you. I can see why my son is in love with you. You are stunning." Extending his hand, he greeted her. "Marlon Wright Sr., it is a pleasure to meet you."

Latrice stared in amazement. She could definitely see the family resemblance, but found it hard to believe that the good looking man that stood before her was old enough to have a son as old as Marlon. "Nice to meet you," she finally managed to say. Marlon Sr. flashed a soul-stirring smile and Latrice thought Gloria was a goner. The way he possessively held her while they kissed let Latrice know that Marlon wanted Gloria back; he was reclaiming his territory. If he gave Gloria half the charm he was giving Latrice, there was no way she'd be able to resist.

"Well if you don't mind, I have laundry to finish." Latrice giggled as she excused herself from the kitchen. She had interrupted their little tryst long enough. They needed privacy. Latrice looked back before leaving; Marlon already had Gloria in his arms and was moving in for the kill.

An hour or so later, Latrice heard the front door open and close, shortly after there was a knock on her door. "Come in." Latrice yelled from the bathroom where she had been washing her hair.

"Hey Latrice, can we talk for a minute?" Gloria sat on the bed, waiting for Latrice to join her. "Please give me your honest opinion. Is it crazy for me to take him back?"

"Well," Latrice sang, shocked that Gloria had came to her for advice. "I don't know why you guys split in the first place, but I do know that since you opted for separation instead of divorce, it couldn't have been that bad."

"You're right. We had grown apart over the years. We allowed work and the kids to prevent us from putting time into maintaining our relationship. When the kids were grown and moved out, we realized we didn't know each other anymore. There were no ball games or dance recitals to rush off to after work and we were forced to spend time together. It felt like we were strangers, and before long we were avoiding each other. We both love the Lord and didn't want a divorce, but couldn't stand the awkwardness. I have never stopped loving him and haven't so much as looked in another man's direction."

"Gloria, you guys sound like two love birds that have lost their way. What would make you second guess taking him back?"

"Well, about a year ago, Marlon and I started seeing each other. Just an occasional dinner, nothing serious, and then one day this woman showed up at my door saying that I had my chance with him and it was her turn. I felt like a fool and figured she was right. I had asked Marlon to move out. I missed my chance with him. So I stopped calling and ignored his phone calls. But it was about more than missing my chance. I felt so inadequate. That woman was young and beautiful, I couldn't compete with her. There will always be women out there trying to catch his eye, being with him is just setting me up for heartbreak."

"Let me ask you a few questions. If you don't want to answer that's fine, just think about them. Did you ever ask him who the woman was? Just because she said it was her turn doesn't mean he was giving her the time of day. Did he cheat on you before? A man doesn't become a dog overnight. If he had never cheated on you before, why would he start now? There have always been young, beautiful woman out there. Last, but not least, are you blind?" Latrice laughed. "That man loves you. He looks at you the way Marlon looks at me and I come unglued every time. No one has to tell me Marlon loves me. I can see it in his eyes and feel it in his touch. Don't you feel it?"

Gloria flung her arms around Latrice and sobbed. "I do feel it. I am such an idiot. Thanks for helping me screw my head on right before I made another big mistake."

"No need to thank me. Just go get your man."

The next morning, Latrice woke up bright and early to make a few phone calls. She tiptoed out the room so she wouldn't wake Marlon and made her way to the kitchen. Sitting at the table, sipping a cup of coffee was Marlon Sr. Latrice chuckled, thinking, *All right Gloria.*

"Good morning Mr. Wright. How did you sleep?"

"Better than I have in six years and, from what I hear, I have you to thank for it."

"No need to thank me. So will we be having coffee together more often?"

"If you're asking if I am moving back in, the answer is yes. Gloria said she had wasted enough time and did not want to live another day without me. I was not about to protest."

Immediately, the wheels in Latrice's head started spinning. "What are you going to do with your apartment?"

"I am not going to allow a lease to keep me from being happy, so I will probably buy out."

Latrice smiled. "Would you consider subletting it to me? I love Marlon, but I need to move out before we lose control."

"I understand, but from what Gloria tells me, it is safer for you to stay here."

Latrice plopped down in the seat next to him. "I know everyone is concerned, but I cannot hide forever. Please, I need my own place. I need to get back into the world."

"Okay baby girl." He soothingly caressed her hand. "I have already paid this month's rent. You can move in tomorrow as long as I can keep my furniture and everything there."

"That's perfect because I don't have anything." Latrice jumped from her seat and hugged him so tight he spilled his coffee.

After Marlon Sr. left, Latrice sat at the kitchen table with a smile on her face. The phone call she'd just made turned out better than she planned and she was well on her way to independence. She contacted the company she worked for before marrying Calvin and they were ecstatic to hear from her. It turned out that they had a pregnant employee who wouldn't be returning to work after the baby was born. All the applicants they had interviewed didn't seem right for the position and Latrice called right on time. They told her she could start tomorrow with her same hours and wage, which was more than enough to live independently. All she had to do now was tell Marlon she was going back to work and moving out on the same day: tomorrow.

18

Marlon stared at Latrice from across the table trying to think of a way to convince her she was making the wrong decision. His heart rate slowed as the words, "I am moving out," spewed out of her mouth. Not only was she moving out, but she was also going back to work. He searched his mind for the right thing to say, but all he could come up with was, "Why?"

Latrice affectionately squeezed his hands. "Because I love you." She tried unsuccessfully to swallow the lump of emotion that had formed in her throat. "I want you so bad that I am taking cold showers in the middle of the night to contain myself. It is only a matter of time before we cave."

"Moving out is not going to stop you from wanting me." Marlon knew she was right and she was only looking out for his best interest, but he still had to plead his case. He hated to even think about what could happen if Calvin found her. "You're not going anywhere," Marlon bellowed as he abruptly shot to his feet and turned to leave.

"Excuse me?" Latrice followed after him with her hands on her hips and indignation in her stride. "Don't talk to me like that. You are not my father or my husband…"

"You're right and since you brought it up, let's talk about your husband. Have you forgotten he is still trying to find you? I am trying to protect you and you are walking away from me. I can't protect you if I am not there."

Silence fell between them. Marlon glared down at her, his eyes warning her not to do this. Latrice glared up at him pleading for understanding. She saw the hurt that he tried to mask with anger, but she had to do this. It was no longer just about helping him abstain from sex; she now needed to abstain. When she whispered, "I can't stay," Marlon walked away shaking his head.

Over the next few hours, the house was silent. She remained in the kitchen to give Marlon his space. It took all the strength she had not to give in to his wishes. Her heart was hurting and she knew his was too, but he had to accept what she needed. Time seemed to drag on, but she managed to occupy her time with minuscule chores around kitchen.

With everything cleaned, Latrice stood in front of the refrigerator scanning the shelves for something to eat. Neither of them had eaten breakfast and she thought she'd make Marlon a little peace offering. As she searched for ingredients, she felt strong hands slide around her waist, hard chest press against her back, and smooth lips brushing across her neck. Her breath was caught in her throat and if he hadn't spoken first, Latrice would've given in to his will and cancelled her plans to move out.

Before the words could leave her mouth, Marlon apologized. As he spoke, the closeness of their bodies and his breath blowing across her neck sent a yearning between her legs, further confirming that moving out was the right thing to do. Leaning back, Latrice molded her body against Marlon. He tightened his grip and a moan escaped from her lips. *This is exactly why she is moving out.* That thought halted his pursuit. He came into the kitchen to apologize and give her his support, but just the mere closeness of their bodies made him lose control. From the sounds she was making, Latrice was worse off than he was. Marlon tore their bodies apart and retreated to a seat at the table. Latrice followed behind him and kneeled in front of him.

She tried to fight off the things her body was telling her to do. Marlon knew where her mind was and if she touched him, he wouldn't have the strength to stop her. He stroked the side of her face and she looked up at him. For the first time, he was seeing her struggle. It had always been him who was weak and Latrice extinguishing his fire. The hunger in her eyes helped him understand the urgency she felt to move out. Conceding defeat Marlon asked, "When are you moving out?"

The question snapped Latrice back into her right frame of mind. Her eyes blinked wildly when she realized what she was getting ready to do. She dashed to the fridge for a cold bottle of water. "I can move in as early as tomorrow and I start work tomorrow too."

"Tomorrow is kind of soon, don't you think?"

Latrice laughed, "I think I just proved that the quicker I move out the better."

Marlon couldn't argue with that. "Can I convince you to stay here and I move out?" The thought of her being alone at night was going to have him quitting his job to camp outside her apartment.

"Marlon, I can't live with my boyfriend's mother. I am a grown woman. I have to get my life back."

"Will I be a part of that life?"

"Always." For a moment, they stared at each other wanting to embrace, but both afraid of their bodies' reactions. He had to let her go to keep her in his life, but if he let her go, he could ultimately lose her forever. She was determined to leave and there was nothing he could do about it.

"Okay." He stepped away, breaking eye contact, and pushing those thoughts to the back of his mind. "Go get dressed, so I can take you shopping. You are going to need some new clothes for work."

Taking Latrice shopping was a bad idea and Marlon sat in the department store suffering the consequences. She modeled outfit after outfit and his eyes roamed across every inch of her, giving his approval. The sexy, form fitting skirts displayed her butt and the blouses accentuated the swell of her breast. At the sight of each ensemble, Marlon let out a low, virile growl. When she disappeared into the dressing room, the thought that she was a few feet away taking her clothes off made his mind run wild with fantasies.

When she came out and asked him to zip her dress, he took advantage of the opportunity and crushed their bodies together trailing his lips down the back of her neck. "If you model one more outfit, I am going to lose my mind."

Latrice leaned into to him to enjoy the gentle torture of his wandering lips until they heard someone approaching. Like two teenagers making out on their parents couch, they jumped. Latrice ran back into the dressing room and Marlon reclaimed his seat at the entrance. His breathing was still rapid and his heart pounded in his chest as he waved at the two ladies walking by.

Moments later, Latrice emerged fully dressed in the clothes she'd worn to the mall. Marlon stood to greet her, hoping she wasn't mad at him. To his surprise, Latrice wrapped her arms around his neck and took his mouth with a force. Forcing herself to stop, Latrice wanted to scream. Living saved was harder than she thought. It had only been one day and she was already having a hard time keeping her commitment. "Sheena was right."

"Right about what?" Marlon grabbed the other bags of clothes they'd purchased and headed for the register. That kiss had done something to him. Although it was brief, it was powerful and knocked him off balance. Marlon silently prayed for the strength to make it through this last night with her in the bed next to him without giving in to temptation.

"She said keeping my hands off the man I love would be one of the hardest things I'll ever have to do." Marlon sighed in agreement as they silently walked the rest of the way to the register.

Trying to ignore the heat radiating from Marlon's body as he stood next to her, Latrice cleared her throat to greet the cashier, "Good morning."

Marlon placed the bags down to fish his credit card out of his pocket. "Your little kiss has me trippin' and I am having a hard time getting it together."

Latrice turned her head in the opposite direction and acted like she didn't hear him. The ache at the apex of her thighs was overwhelming; she knew what he was going through. "I hear you, but we can't." Marlon nodded in agreement.

"What in the world?" Latrice saw the seductive look the sales lady gave Marlon as she passed his credit card back. She grabbed the card before Marlon could even touch it. Seeing the fury on her face, he jumped in front of her, grabbed their bags, thanked the lady for her help, and practically drug Latrice to the car.

Marlon put the bags in the trunk and when he hopped in the car, Latrice was still fuming. He laughed at her. "You are so sexy when you're upset." She couldn't help but smile. Marlon assured her that she was the only woman he wanted. Within minutes, what had started as a soothing kiss, escalated to much more. They both wanted to do what was right, but the slightest touch or kiss was like setting of a grenade. Desire exploded within them and it took all the strength they had to stop. As if possessed by an outside force, Latrice frantically tried to unbuckle his zipper. Marlon stopped her, whispering against her lips. "Don't start something we can't finish."

Latrice mumbled into his mouth, "Why is it so wrong if we do?" Before the words left her lips, she knew the answer to her own question. *It is better to marry than to burn.* Since they were both already married, abstinence was the only other choice. Latrice buckled her seat belt more so to keep from crawling into his lap than to keep her safe.

Calling his job on the way home, Marlon informed them that he would not be coming in. Tonight was their last night living under the same roof and he wanted to spend it with her. Marlon grabbed all her bags out of the car, made her climb onto his back, and he carried her into the house.

Marlon was so focused on the way Latrice's legs wrapped around his waist and the soft pecks she was leaving on his neck that he hadn't noticed his parents sitting cuddled up on the couch. "Son," The sound of Marlon Sr.'s voice brought him out of his trance. "From the looks of things, you two need to stay out here and watch this movie with us."

"What are you doing here?" Marlon was shocked to see his parents being so intimate.

"Your little lady didn't tell you?" Marlon Sr. asked, glancing at Latrice for clarification.

"No. I wanted you guys to share the good news." Latrice chimed in as Marlon placed her on her feet. He was now more curious than before.

Marlon Sr. grinned from ear to ear. "Your mom and I are back together and I have moved back in." It had been Marlon's prayer for years that his parents reconciled. He had talked with his father about it many times and he was determined to give his mother the space she needed. When he did finally convince his father to pursue her, she shot him down. Talking to his mother was pointless; she changed the subject every time he brought it up. So, he waited and prayed hoping his dad didn't give up.

Marlon hugged his father and whispered, "I told you good things come to those who wait."

Gloria watched with tears, and when Marlon turned to her asking if she was happy, those tears streamed down her face and she cried out, "Happier than I have been in a long time."

Marlon plopped down on the other couch and Latrice joined him. He did a good job at containing it, but his joy and excitement were bubbling over. He took it hard when his parents separated and didn't understand how two people who were obviously so in love would want to be apart. Now they were back together. The world was right—at least part of it. Marlon turned to lie across the couch, slid his leg behind Latrice, and pulled her down to rest her head on his chest. They adjusted their bodies for that perfect fit they only found with each other, and then settled in to watch the movie.

Just as they were getting into the movie, Marlon's cell phone rang. Without checking the caller ID, he answered and was sorely disappointed. "Alicia," he growled in frustration. Hearing that name and the tone in his voice, Latrice turned to face him, rubbing his chest to soothe him. The call was short and Marlon barely spoke two words. As Marlon hung up the phone, a smile touched the corners of his lips and he chuckled, "Today is turning out to be a great day." He placed his hand under Latrice's arms and slid her up across his body to join their lips; he wanted her to feel his excitement. When they parted, he explained. "Alicia just called to thank me for not telling her parents about what's been going on. Apparently, they just left her house where she confessed everything to them. They were furious and appalled at her actions, but it was best they heard it from her. Once anger subsided, they encouraged her to think rationally and stop hoping for me to come home. They told her that counseling is good for a relationship, but after infidelity it is pointless. They convinced her to quit playing games and sign the papers."

"And she wants you to come by tonight and pick them up." Latrice huffed.

"Stop." Marlon laughed, sensing the hostility in her tone. "First, the lady at the mall and now Alicia. Are you going to beat up everybody?"

Latrice whined, "Stop laughing at me. That woman wanted you. Don't let me get started on Alicia. Need I remind you of what she did the last time you guys were alone?"

"But you're the only one I want." His words shut her mouth, which he lightly kissed before continuing. "She is going to bring the papers to our session on Saturday. She wants to move forward, but there are some things she wants to confess first. Apparently, it is a big deal because she wants her parents to be there." Marlon couldn't care less about the meeting or who was going to be there. As long as he was getting those papers signed, he was content.

After a long kiss and his parents clearing their throats to get him to stop, Marlon snuggled Latrice into the curve of his body made just for her and they continued watching the movie.

The soft caress of Marlon's hands down her side lulled Latrice to sleep. Gloria and Marlon Sr. retired to their room, leaving their son on the couch flipping through the TV stations. It was only ten PM, which was still early for him, considering the late hours he worked. Finding nothing on TV, he turned it off and focused on Latrice. Her head rested on his abs, one hand was under his shirt, splayed across his back, and the other arm draped over his chest, finger tips slightly touching his neck. The warmth of her breath tantalized him. The inhale and exhale of her breathing created a smooth tempo.

Without second thought, Marlon gripped her backside, squeezing as he pushed her up his body. A few months ago, she would've woken up swinging, but now her body knew his touch. She woke up with a moan, ready to receive whatever he was offering. Instinctively, she spread her legs to straddle him and adjusted her head to meet his lips. The soft moans she released in to his mouth made him come unglued. With a quick adjustment, they were sitting upright on the couch. Latrice pulled Marlon's shirt up and yanked it over his head. She rubbed her hands across his scrumptious chest before latching back on to his mouth. Their kiss intensified as their tongues fought for dominance; the rotation of her hips became more frantic as the fight ensued. Marlon shot to his feet with Latrice in his arms and practically ran to their room.

Once inside the room with the door shut, Marlon laid her on the bed and then made his move to join her. As he climbed on top of her, that internal voice of caution cried out.

His head dropped in frustration as his conscience warned him to resist temptation. She had just given her life to Christ and here he was professing to love her, but getting ready to take her new found innocence. He groaned and backed away from her. Latrice took one look at him and knew exactly what was wrong. He had found his strength in her weakness. He was giving back the strength she'd given him.

"You better go to sleep. You have a big day ahead of you tomorrow." Marlon backed out of the door. The couch would be his bed tonight. Latrice just smiled. If she opened her mouth to say anything she would have begged him to come back and finish what he started. After he closed the door, she jumped up and headed to the bathroom for yet another cold shower.

<u>19</u>

Latrice had been working hard all week and had barely spoken to Marlon since the Tuesday morning when he walked her to the car when she left for work. Her body and her heart ached for him. Work kept her busy during the day, but the nights were horrible. No one could come by out of fear that Calvin was following them; she hadn't even told Camilla that she had moved out. She was miserably terrified of being alone in her apartment every night, but she toughed it out. After her first day of work, she met up with Marlon Sr. to get the keys and started moving her clothes in. She found a bat on the table with a note from Marlon, *I have put bats in every room; this one is for you car. Please promise me you will use them if the time arises. Be ready to protect yourself at all cost, Love Marlon.* Immediately, she called him to let him know that he was being paranoid, but he shut her down. Removing the bats was not up for discussion. After going back and forth with him, she gave in.

It was a Saturday morning and Latrice was up bright and early. Gloria had invited her over for breakfast, but breakfast wasn't her motivation. She needed to see Marlon before he left for his meeting with Alicia. Breakfast was at 10, and his meeting at 8:30, which meant she had to be at his house by 7:30 in order to spend time with him before he left the house. She was a woman on a mission and was up and dressed earlier than usual. She was so excited to see him that she pulled in front of his house at 7:15.

She slipped quietly into his bedroom. The room was empty and she could hear the shower while going in the bathroom. For a second, she thought about joining him, but it would defeat the purpose for her moving out. Instead, she made herself comfortable on his bed and waited for him. When the shower stopped and Marlon walked out the bathroom completely naked Latrice thought, *I am about to sleep with him again.* The perfection of his body called to her and before she knew it, her hands were all over him roaming up and down his torso. Seconds later, her mouth replaced her hands.

Marlon tilted her head back to look in her eyes, lifting her chin with his finger. He caressed her lips with his thumb. Although he wanted her, his self-control was back in tact. He gave her two quick pecks on the lips and stepped away. As he turned put his robe on, there was a knock on the door. His eyes widened when he saw who it was. "Hey baby girl, what are you doing here?"

"Mom called said she was making a big breakfast and wanted me to come over and celebrate her and daddy getting back together. She also said she invited your girlfriend, which shocked me. Aren't you still married? And if you had a girlfriend, surely I wouldn't be the last person to know."

"Well, you haven't exactly been the easiest person to catch up with lately," he chided.

"Well, tell me about her. Mom said you had finally given someone your heart. I tried to tell her that Alicia had your heart and she started mumbling some mumbo jumbo about you only shared your heart with Alicia, but have actually given it to this woman. You know I don't know the first thing about being in love, so I quickly tuned her out."

"We will be here all day if I talk about her and I will be late for my meeting." Marlon stepped to the side, revealing Latrice. "But you are more than welcomed to get to know her for yourself."

"I am sorry I didn't know you were..." The words died on her lips when she finally got a good look at the woman sitting on her brother's bed.

"Latrice, What are you doing here?" Now Marlon was confused.

They embraced. "She is my hairstylist," Latrice responded to Marlon's quizzical look. "I finally got the courage to leave my husband and the friend I reached out to for help is the sister-in-law of Marlon's cousin," Latrice paused, "I guess he's your cousin too. Well, everyone felt I should stay with them just in case Calvin came looking for me and that's where I met Marlon."

"Small world," Marlon smirked, as he strutted into the bathroom to get dressed while the ladies got reacquainted.

"Small world indeed," his sister mumbled under her breath.

By the time Marlon came out of the bathroom, Latrice and his sister were sitting on the bed, laughing and talking like old friends. Alicia had never gotten along with his sister, which should have been the first sign not to marry her. Watching Latrice interact with her made his heart swell; he almost hated to interrupt.

"Alright baby girl," Marlon kissed his sister on the cheek. "I have a meeting with my cheating, soon to be ex-wife." Just like that, fireworks went off in Latrice's mind as she remembered her last visit to the salon and the conversation she had with Marlon's sister. She was so caught up in the memory that she didn't realize Marlon had spoken to her.

"Baby, I am leaving. Will you be here when I get back?"

"Yes, I am sorry," she said, trying to hide the shock and unsure of how to handle what she knew. "Breakfast isn't until later. I just came by early to see you." Latrice stood on her toes to kiss him goodbye. She tried to give him all the strength she could for what would more than likely be the most trying day of his life. Marlon lifted her off the ground for better access. Latrice wrapped her legs around him and he groaned with approval. They walked arm in arm to the front door, lips locked the whole way. His tongue frantically roamed her mouth, absorbing all it could to make up for the days they'd been apart. Reluctantly, he put her down, and with a few lingering nibbles of her lips, he was out the door.

Latrice watched Marlon as he got in the car and drove off. Her flesh was hot and tingly, and her heart pounded a fierce rhythm against her ribs. "My god," she mumbled to herself.

"I would have to agree." His sister's voice chuckled from behind, quickly bringing Latrice out of her trance.

"We need to talk." Latrice turned and marched toward Marlon's room. "It was you and you better tell him today, or I will." Latrice commanded, slamming the door behind them.

"Excuse me, what are you talking about?"

"You know exactly what I am talking about. You are the trifling heifer that slept with his wife. I should slap the hell out of you for hurting him like that." The look of fury on Latrice's face made Meme flee the room. "Today," Latrice yelled after her.

Latrice anxiously awaited Marlon's return. She surprised Gloria with how well she could throw down in the kitchen. Between all the probing questions and shooing Marlon Sr. out of the kitchen, time had flown by. Breakfast was done and the table was set. They were just waiting for Marlon to come home so they could eat.

Meme avoided Latrice as much as possible, even hiding out in the bedroom until her mom sought her out and made her come help. They had barely spoken two words the whole time they were cooking. Occasionally, their eyes met and Latrice gave her a look that said 'don't think I'm playing'.

The front door slammed against the wall, causing pictures to fall off. Everyone in the kitchen jumped, confused as to what was going on. Marlon had swung the door open with such force that he nearly put a hole in the wall. Marlon march toward the kitchen and bellowed his sister's name. The ferocity in his tone was intense. He rounded the corner into the kitchen and his eyes locked onto hers. Latrice watched the exchange between the siblings and moved closer to Marlon. *Alicia told him.* The love for his sister that twinkled in his eyes just a few hours ago had dissolved. They were now filled with contempt and loathing. His tall, muscular body stormed into her face.

Marlon brought his face within inches of hers and grimaced between clinched teeth. "I just left my meeting with Alicia. Is there something you need to tell me?" Meme gasped for air. The rage in his eyes captured her voice and she couldn't speak.

"Tell me the truth," he barked, when she didn't respond; everyone in the kitchen flinched. "I called you after it happened and you pretended to be looking out for my best interest." Marlon grabbed her by the collar of her shirt and his parents scrambled to intervene. "In reality, you were looking out for yourself. You did not want me to go back over there and find you there."

"I am sorry. I wanted to tell you, but I could never find the right time." Her voice was a mere whimper compared to the depth of his.

"The right time?" The terror in his voice made Meme flee to the other side of the room. Marlon chased after her, but his father blocked his path. "It should have never happened. You're my sister." With those words, he banged on his chest. "If Alicia was going to cheat on me, it should have never happened with you. For awhile, I suspected you were gay, but I loved you and didn't want you to be hurt, so I never said anything. I waited until you felt comfortable enough to tell me, and this is how you repay me?"

Meme watched her parent's faces as they realized what Marlon had said.

"Meme, baby," Gloria pleaded. "Please tell me this is not true."

Meme tumbled to the ground crying hysterically. "Mommy, I am so sorry. I wanted to tell you a long time ago that I was a lesbian, but I was afraid you would stop loving me."

"Child, no one cares about that," Gloria paused. "Did you sleep with your brother's wife?"

When Meme confirmed that she had, Marlon puffed up in anger and made his way toward her, but Latrice was right there. She grabbed his face and tried to get him to focus on her. "Baby, please don't do this." She planted kisses all over his face while she wiped away beads of sweat.

"Sit down at the table and we can all talk." Her efforts were successful and Marlon sat at the table.

Latrice sat in Marlon's lap to ensure he didn't get back up. His body trembled with anger and the cold look in his eyes reminded her of Calvin. The only difference was that Calvin would have never backed down. She felt Marlon wrap his arms around her and rest his head on her back. He took slow, deep breaths and the trembling ceased.

She turned and whispered in his ear, "I love you and we are going to get through this together." When he nodded, she took charge of the conversation. She prayed first, asking God to be in control, and then looked to Meme, giving her permission to speak. "Start from the beginning, he has a right to know everything."

"A few years ago, after a horrible heterosexual relationship, I met this woman through Wayne. At first, we were just friends hanging out with mutual friends. One day, she kissed me and I was so starved for affection that I went with the flow, but I never expected I'd enjoy it as much as I did. I kept it to myself because I knew what you, mom, and the church would say. This is who I am and I won't apologize for it. But I'm sorry for the pain I have caused you. You have to know that I didn't seduce Alicia into this lifestyle. We bumped into each other at a club one night. I went to your house to make sure she kept my secret safe and she asked me to do the same. I wanted to tell you, but how could I when I was so afraid of my own secret coming out?"

Marlon's body tensed as Meme spoke and Latrice stroked his arm. Alicia had left out all the details and he didn't stick around to ask questions. It might have been easier to hear this from Alicia since he already hated her so much. Hearing it from the sister he loved was torture. Latrice tried her best to soothe him, but instinct told her the worst was yet to come.

"That first night, we sat and talked for hours. We talked more than we had your entire marriage and when it was time to for me to go, Alicia tried to kiss me." Marlon flinched and tried to stand up, but Latrice patted his hand and he relaxed. "I told her that nothing would ever go down between us. She apologized, and that was the end of it. Over the next week or so, she called just about every day asking me to come over. She claimed to be lonely and had all kinds of questions about these new feelings she was having. I went over a few times and we became friends. I don't know when it happened or how I let it happen, but she got under my skin. I was thinking about her all the time."

"That's when you should have backed off." Latrice had shocked herself with the angry disgust in her tone and bit her lip to keep from interrupting again.

"I tried…God knows I tried, but I was lonely too and I enjoyed her company. What I felt for her was unexpected and I rejected it at first."

"So, when did you decide to stab me in the back?"

Meme paused and looked to Latrice for help, but there was no support available. "After trying to stay away, I called and asked her to meet me at this club I usually hang at. We needed to talk and I really wanted to see her. We danced and things got a little heated, so I thought it best to cut our night short and I promised to come by that Sunday." Meme knew the rest of what she had to say could cause her to lose her brother forever. She hated herself for the choice she'd made and knew the only way she could live with herself was to be completely honest about what she had done. "I came over that Sunday and as soon as Alicia opened the door, I knew something had changed. When she told me that we needed to talk, I panicked. Contrary to what everyone might think, there is not a line of men or women waiting to take me out. I have never been in love so strong before, and when I fell for Alicia, I fell hard. She apologized for leading me on, but wanted to work things out with you. She went into the room and told me to see myself out." Emotions gripped her voice and it was merely a whisper as she confessed. "I followed her into the room and all but attacked her. I knew what to do to get her to cave in to my desires. She fought me at first, but eventually gave in."

Her sobs echoed throughout the house. For a moment, no one moved and no one spoke. Gloria turned her back on her daughter and sighed with contempt. Marlon Sr. went to comfort his baby girl. Marlon replayed that dreadful day over in his head. He remembered thinking that the night before, they had made love more passionately than ever and he had hoped it was a turning point in their marriage. It honestly had been. Alicia intended to break things off. That thought shook him and he needed to get some fresh air to clear his mind.

"I have to get out of here," he mumbled against Latrice's back.

"Where are you going?"

He shrugged his shoulders. "Is there anything you want to say to her?"

"I need to think first."

"Can I go with you?" Latrice stood and they left, leaving Meme in the kitchen to wallow in self-pity.

Latrice drove around for about an hour before jumping on the expressway to the beach. They drove in silence; she knew he had a lot to sort through and didn't want to distract him. They arrived at Belmont Park and Marlon exited the car. The beachfront amusement park was packed. The clank and rattle of the roller coaster, coupled with the excited shrills of its riders, were the first sounds Marlon heard. There was the wave house, miniature golf, arcade and midway style games, and the restaurants, but the most spectacular part was the beach itself.

It was a little after noon and families had begun to gather for their Saturday activities, but Marlon was oblivious to everyone around him. Latrice guided him around beach towels and blankets covered with sun bathing bodies and claimed a spot close to the water. The water flowed up to them, and then glided back out. Once they were sure they wouldn't get wet, they sat down.

Latrice coaxed Marlon's head into her lap and he adjusted himself to get more comfortable. The cool breeze coming off the water and the warmth of the midday sun was a perfect mix. The sun glared off the water and Latrice wished she'd brought her sun glasses. Marlon shut his eyes to take in the sounds of the ocean. The rustling sound of the ocean waves crashing against the shore, seagulls chirping over head, and the rhythm of Latrice's hand rubbing across his stomach were hypnotic. Inhaling a few gusts of fresh air relaxed his body and his mind. With his mind clearer, Marlon tried to process everything Meme had said. He considered everything he'd gone through since leaving Alicia. He had discovered that he didn't really love Alicia the way a husband should. The main question was, if Alicia hadn't cheated, would he still be with her? He was unhappy, she was miserable; would they have come to their senses and divorced, or would they accept a life of misery?

Marlon was deep in thought when Latrice's voice broke through. "Does anything that Meme said change your decision to divorce Alicia?" Marlon sat up, giving her a confused look. Latrice explained, "Does knowing that Alicia wanted to break things off with Meme and work on your marriage affect your decision to divorce?"

"No, she also confessed to sleeping with some guy at the club in his car. The crazy thing is, I took her out that night and saw her dancing with that guy and I left. What kind of husband does that? I practically gave her to him, but let me catch some man with hands all over you and it is lights out."

Placing her hand on his chest, Latrice soothed the anger that was starting to brew. "Why sit here tormenting yourself with all the nasty details then? Use this time to find a way to forgive them, because until you can do that, they have power over you."

Marlon let out an agitated sigh. "Alicia, I can forgive. She was just looking for the love I wasn't giving her; it doesn't excuse it, but I understand it. I am sorry that I couldn't love her the way she needed to be loved. Meme, on the other hand, I will never forgive."

"How can you say that? She was looking for that same love Alicia was and she found it." She ignored the menacing look Marlon gave her. "Put yourself in her shoes. What if being with me was forbidden? Would you be able to stay away? You knew we shouldn't sleep together and you did it anyway. Even when you said we needed to stop, you had a hard enough time staying out of my bed at night."

"I don't care about who she loved." He growled through clenched teeth and Latrice caressed his jaw to get him to loosen up. "Where is her loyalty? The day she saw Alicia at the club, she should have came to me and told me what Alicia was up to. She should've never spent that much time with her, let alone fall in love with her." His voice was escalating and the people around them were starting to stare.

"Marlon, stop yelling at me." Latrice tried to calm him, but all her efforts failed.

"Stop taking Meme's side."

Staring at him in disbelief, Latrice stood to her feet mumbling, "I am not taking her side. I'm just trying to help you make sense of this mess," as she walked away.

Marlon jumped to his feet apologizing. He grabbed her arm to stop her from leaving, but she snatched it away and ran to the car. Marlon followed behind her, berating himself for being an idiot. Latrice made it to the car, cursing herself for having short legs. She intended to get in the car and lock him out, but his long strides caught up to her and they reached the door handle at the same time.

Marlon hopped into the passenger seat and apologized profusely. When she didn't respond, he kissed her on the cheek and begged. "Please don't be mad at me. I can handle everything else that is going, but losing you is the one thing I can't handle."

Latrice softened and turned her head to meet his lips. They kissed until the tension left his neck and his head stopped pounding. "I am not going anywhere." She caressed his cheek as their kiss ended. "But please think about this. You have had months to deal with the fact that Alicia cheated. That is why it's so easy for you to forgive her now. When you first found out, you wanted to kill her. So it is only natural to have those same feelings toward your sister. Give it time. One day you will be able to forgive her. She is family and you can't just erase her from your life." Sensing that she had gotten through, Latrice started the car and backed out of the parking stall.

She wished they could spend more time at the beach, but Marlon was a little too volatile, and if he yelled at her again, she just might leave him stranded out there.

"I am going back to your mom's house to pack you an overnight bag. You can stay at my place tonight." Flashing back to their rendezvous earlier that morning, she pictured his naked body. She wanted him bad. "In the guest room," Latrice interjected. Just the thought of it gave her goose bumps. Marlon chuckled. Latrice watched him out the corner of her eye. The smirk on his face warmed her heart. The Marlon she knew and loved was still there under all the hurt and rage; he was still there.

In no time, they pulled in front of Gloria's house. Latrice warned Marlon to stay put and she ran inside to get his things.

"Marlon is that you?" Gloria yelled.

"No ma'am. It's Latrice." Latrice was shocked to see Meme sitting at the table still sulking. There was a bucket in front of her; she'd cried herself sick. Gloria and Marlon Sr. were doing all they could to soothe her, but nothing helped.

Latrice didn't know what came over her, but she was tired of Meme crying. It was time for some tough love. "That is enough." She walked over and grabbed her by the chin looking into her eyes with uncompromising fury. "You sitting here crying is not helping your case. You screwed up, now dry your face and deal with it." Latrice grabbed some napkins off the table and shoved them into Meme's hand. "You haven't earned the right to be a mess. Now your brother on the other hand, is a different story. He has been betrayed by two important women whom he trusted with his life. If anyone deserves to be a mess it's him," Latrice said, pausing while Meme straightened up and blotted her face. "Now, what you are going to do is give him his space. He is staying with me tonight, but when he comes home tomorrow, please don't be here. When he is ready to talk to you, he'll call." Latrice walked away without waiting for a response.

20

"Where is she? Where is she?" Calvin sat outside Zion Pentecostal watching everyone as they walked inside. He had been following Camilla for days, hoping she would lead him to Latrice, but there had been no sign of her. He'd sat outside her home, followed her to work, to the gym, to the grocery store, and every else she went. He'd even followed her to Sheena and Delisa's house and sat a few nights outside of their houses, but Latrice hadn't shown up there either. So now he was back to watching the church. He was sure they were being extra careful since he had found her before. He'd just have to wait it out; in time they would make a mistake, and this time Latrice would not get away.

The majority of Latrice's little rescue squad had already arrived and were probably sitting comfortably inside waiting for service to start when Paul arrived with his family. Calvin traced the scab encrusted on his arm as Paul walked around the front of his car to open the door for his wife. Calvin intently watched him help his wife out of the car. He found the whole display of affection sickening. How a man could buckle under the touch of a woman and fall all over himself to make her happy was idiocy to him. Only a weak man allows a woman to affect him in such a way.

Calvin wanted to ram him with his car and knock the cockiness out of his stride. Not a day went by where he didn't contemplate revenge, but Paul's threat had resounded loud and clear. His family was safe for now, but if he dared to interfere with him getting Latrice back, he'd risk it and teach Paul a lesson. For now, he had to stay focused and find his wife. If Latrice thought she could leave him and not reap the consequences, she was sorely mistaken. Her place was with him and only death would separate them.

Calvin sat in the parking lot for the length of the entire service, just in case she came late. He was at a loss for where else to look for her. It was obvious they had stashed her somewhere and no one had contact with her. He had an idea of who she was with, but had no clue who he was or where to find him. Calvin wanted to be gone before church was dismissed; he didn't want to chance being

161

seen. Just as he was about to start his car and end his stakeout for the day, a car pulled into the parking lot. He waited just to make sure it wasn't Latrice and when the driver stepped out, a smile spread across Calvin's face.

Pastor Hawkins hurried out of the sanctuary and into his office to change out of his sweaty clothes before his meeting. He preferred not to hold meetings on Sundays, but when working on other people's time, sometimes exceptions had to be made. He took the time to order dinner so they could eat while they discussed the matter at hand. He was meeting with the only members of his church that he considered friends. Not only would they be discussing important church business, but it was a rare opportunity to fellowship. Their busy schedules had prevented them from getting together as often as he liked. Having no wife and no kids made being such a young pastor a real sacrifice and a little lonely. Time with friends was invaluable.

He stepped into the fellowship hall and his heart warmed as he watched his friends, which he considered his extended family, laughing and talking. They were genuine, fun people; this was hard to find when you're a pastor. They respected him as the pastor, treated him like any other man, put him in his place like a friend, yet loved him like family. They laughed at him, cracked jokes about him, prayed for him, and gave him words of wisdom; he wouldn't trade them for anything in the world.

Pastor Hawkins was greeted with affectionate hugs, fist bumps, and kisses on the cheek from the female members of his crew. They sat down, blessed the food, and enjoyed their meal before getting to business; friendship was first, business second.

Marlon sat in silence, hoping Pastor Hawkins didn't bring up Alicia, Meme, or their affair. No one else at the table new that his sister was the one that had lay down with his wife and he preferred to keep it that way. Marlon watched the other couples interact with a smirk on his face. Now he understood the constant petting and trying to sit as close as you can to someone without actually sitting in their lap, and all the whispering in each other's ears followed by blushing and giggles. When you find that mate that makes your heart smile, they become the only one that matters. Life isn't worth living without them. His smile deepened when he thought of his reason for living, a dark-skinned beauty whose heart he loved more than the firm curvy body it was cased in.

"It has been a long time since I have seen you smile like that. Do we have Latrice to thank for lifting your spirits?" Marlon nodded at Delisa as his smile beamed his answer.

"Latrice… what is going on with you and Latrice?" Pastor Hawkins jumped into their conversation from the opposite end of the table and all conversation in between stopped.

Marlon paused and asked, "Who is asking, Pastor Hawkins or Richard?"

"Which will get the truth?"

"I'd tell the truth to both, just different levels of truth."

"Well, tell Richard, but I reserve the right to respond like Pastor Hawkins."

Marlon chuckled. "You know it doesn't work like that. When we're boys, we're boys. When you're my pastor, you're my pastor."

"Today, I'm your boy who happens to be your pastor; now, tell me what's up."

With eyes unwavering Marlon considered Richard's reaction as he contemplated how much truth to reveal. *No need for details.* "I love her." Marlon sat back in his chair and waited for the barrage of questions.

"You love her?" Richard's brows rose in shock. He stood halfway up, then sat back down. His natural and spiritual personas were battling for dominance. Richard won and Pastor Hawkins took a back seat. "Don't be an idiot. You have too much drama going on with Alicia and Meme to be throwing someone else into the mix."

Marlon stared Richard down hoping no one inquired about the drama between Alicia and Meme. He knew they'd all heard it and all probably wondered what he meant. Using his eyes and body language, Marlon signaled for Richard to not go there, but it was too late. The words were hanging out there; lingering with confused faces hovering around it.

"What happened with Meme and…?"

"Not an appropriate conversation to have around the kids," Marlon said, cutting Jaleel off before he could even get the question out.

"Speak so they don't understand or let's go outside."

Going outside meant questions that his wannabe big brother would demand answers to. "Alicia cheated with Meme."

Jaws dropped and forks hit the table; all eyes were on Marlon. No one moved nor spoke. Marlon continued eating like he hadn't just dropped a bomb on everyone. The heat from the burning eyes made him sweat, but he refused to make eye contact. Instead, he shoveled food into his mouth as if it were his first meal after months of starvation.

Everyone was at a loss for words. Jaleel opened his mouth several times to speak, but what do you say to someone who'd caught his wife having sex with his sister. Saying *sorry* or *it will be alright* didn't seem appropriate. One by one, they all refocused their attention on their meals. Pastor Hawkins, hoping to get the heat off of Marlon, thought it best to get to the reason for the meeting.

"So, I wanted to meet with you guys to discuss Brother Jason. He should be getting out of jail in a few months." Pastor Hawkins informed them of the crime Jason was convicted of and how everyone, including the prosecuting attorney, knew he was innocent. Since Jason wouldn't snitch, he went to jail. Then, he laid out a schedule of visitations he'd made. Hearing the details of Jason's case touched everyone, and by the time Pastor Hawkins had finished his speech, everyone was on board. They rejected the visitation schedule and decided they would all visit together. They wanted Jason to experience the bond of their brotherhood.

Marlon left the meeting still tense from the brief discussion of Meme and Alicia. He said goodbye, and fled to the car. He called Latrice from his car. He needed her to help quell his frustration before going to work. He left the parking lot, headed in the direction of her apartment, unaware that he was being followed.

Persistence had finally begun to pay off. All the hours spent parked in front of their houses, jobs, and church was finally being rewarded. They had no right to keep his wife from him. Any problem they had could be worked out, but first, he had to teach her a lesson. He followed the car at a safe distance where he would not be detected. He recognized the man Latrice had fled church with the second he stepped out of his car. If Camilla didn't have Latrice, he knew this man did. The way Latrice had held on to him gave Calvin all the answers he needed. Calvin saw the connection between them and assured himself that they both would pay. With one hand on the steering wheel and the other on his neck, Marlon tired to ease the mounting tension. Jaleel, Paul, Tim, and Richard were blowing his cell up, but he ignored every call. If he had to discuss his sister while driving, he'd probably wreck the car. Just the thought of her or the mention of her name upset him. Marlon pounded on his car horn, then, took a few deep breaths to calm his road rage. He was just a few blocks from Latrice and he knew once he got there her smile alone would soothe him.

Marlon had barely thrown his car into park before hopping out and running up the steps. He used his key to get inside and found her in the kitchen washing dishes. She was wearing a strapless sun dress that flowed down her curves to the floor.

"Baby, you look good." Latrice smiled as he stepped up behind her and wrapped his arms around her waist.

"Thank you. How was your meeting?"

"I wish I had taken you with me. Not only did I have to sit around and watch all those couples kissing and whispering sweet nothings to each other, but we managed to get on the subject of Alicia and Meme. I needed you."

Without him having to ask Latrice faced him and gave him the love, strength, and peace that he sought. His hands started to roam, but Latrice stepped back. "You better go to work before we get carried away."

"Can I come by after work?"

"Come by, yes. Stay the night, no."

"I guess I will take what I can get." He tried to get her lips again, but she gripped his shoulders, spun him around, and directed him toward the door. She walked him to his car, giving him a quick kiss on the cheek and waved goodbye as he drove away. Turning to walk back inside, Latrice had a weird feeling. She scanned the surrounding cars and apartment windows; she felt like she was being watched. Nothing seemed out of the ordinary, so she shook it off and went back inside.

"Bingo!" Calvin's eyes lit up when he saw Latrice. "You can run but you can't hide." He watched her kiss her boyfriend goodbye and contemplated running them down with his car. But what he had for Latrice would take time. He wanted her to suffer for every day he had to spend alone. So, he waited until she was back inside before starting his car and heading home. He didn't want to risk her boyfriend coming back, so that day she was safe, but soon she'd get what was coming to her.

21

Marlon continued his life as normally as possible. He tried not to think about his sister and his wife being intimate, but it wasn't any easy thing to get past. That first night, he had Latrice in bed with him. Although she made him sleep in a separate room, he'd gone to her in the middle of the night, pleading for her embrace and she didn't refuse him. She held him tight, stroking his head until he fell asleep. Now he was alone and sleep each night had been a fight. Every night, he wanted to beg Latrice to come over and just sleep, but he didn't trust himself. Although he was determined to abstain from sex, there was only so much a brother could take.

Even now, as he lay in bed, sleep was hard to find. Tossing and turning, he searched for a comfortable position. When all else failed, he got on his knees and prayed like he had every night that week. Marlon cried out in prayer as conviction touched his heart. He had allowed the burdens of life to make him step down from the man of God he used to be. Marlon intensely pressed his way to the throne of God. Praying with a vengeance, Marlon shook under the power of the anointing. A flood of tears streamed down his face and onto the floor. He confessed his sins, exposed his fears, uncovered his pain, and God responded by sending forgiveness, strength, and healing. All the anger, hurt, rejection, sorrow, and chaos that had been in his life since the day he left Alicia were consumed by the presence of God. By the time he rose off his knees, Marlon felt restored.

He picked up the phone and called his sister. Before she could say anything, he sincerely stated, "Even though I am still not ready to talk to you, I just wanted you to know that I love you." It hadn't been long since he learned the truth and he didn't know if he'd ever be able to get past it, but how could he expect God to forgive him if he wasn't willing to forgive? Acknowledging that he loved his sister was a good place to start.

Meme whispered, "I love you too," just before he hung up the phone. The simple act brought Marlon peace, and when he lay down, sleep did not elude him.

Moments after Marlon ended the call, Meme sat with the phone still to her ear. Tears trickled down her face and joy bubbled over within. She assumed she'd never get to speak with Marlon again, but here he was calling just to say he loved her. It felt like an eternity since their blow up and her banishment from the family, but she deserved it. Not only had she devastated her family, but her secret was now out and she had no one to lean on for support. She wanted to call her parents, but was too ashamed. She wanted to call Marlon, but was too afraid. To her surprise, Latrice called every day just to check on her, but Meme was too suspicious to accept her friendship. Latrice had thoroughly put her in her place the other day and Meme found it hard to believe that she was now interested in her well-being. A huge weight had been lifted and Meme no longer felt exiled.

Meme also slept like a baby and when she woke the next morning, she knew it was time to revive her carcass of a life. There were too many things left unsaid and too many skeletons still in the closet. It was time to stand up and be a woman and stop running scared like a child. She jumped out of bed, showered, dressed, and drove to her parent's house.

As she suspected, her parents were already awake. Marlon Sr. sat at the table sipping a cup of coffee while Gloria made his breakfast. Meme couldn't help but smile as she remembered walking into this same scene every morning as a child. She'd finish getting dressed and come dragging into the kitchen, racking her brain for a plausible excuse to stay home from school. Each morning, her father watched with a smile on his face as she formulated her need to stay home. With the all too familiar response, he'd kiss her on the forehead saying, 'I am going to miss you too, baby girl'. He never responded to her request, just dug into his breakfast and with a pouty face, Meme did the same.

Meme felt nervous as she entered the kitchen. This was her first time facing her parents since the blow up and she knew there was going to be an onslaught of questions. When they first found out about her sexual preference, they were too busy consoling her to ask questions, but today she knew there would be no stopping them.

"Good Morning."

"Hey baby girl, this is a nice surprise." He stood and snugly wrapped his arms around her. "Sit down and eat breakfast with me before I go to work, just like we used to." He tried to let her go and help her into her seat, but Meme buried her head into his chest and wouldn't let go. Sensing her anguish, he kissed her forehead again and reassured her that things were going to get better and the pain she was feeling was only temporary.

After their hug, Gloria had breakfast on the table and watched them quietly. The look on her face let Meme know that her mother was not going to be as comforting as her father and she instantly regretted coming over. Just like when she was a child, her mother waited until her father was finished eating and had left for work before she let Meme have it.

The first question out of her mouth shattered Meme's resolve to be a big girl. "What are you doing here? You know your brother doesn't want to see you."

"What, I can't come see my mother?" She averted her eyes to avoid the revulsion in her mother's glare.

"I always welcome visits from my children." Meme could tell she was trying to remain calm and appreciated the effort.

"Ma," Meme decided to speak up while she still had the nerve. "You guys are all I have. It is killing me that everyone hates me. I screwed up and I know it's asking a lot for you to forgive me so soon, but I need you guys." Tears gathered in the corner of Gloria's eyes. Getting her mother to forgive her meant Marlon would soon follow. She didn't care that the hurt was still fresh. She just needed to feel accepted again.

Patting the back of her daughter's hand, Gloria sighed. She couldn't disown or turn her back on her child, regardless of what she had done, but Meme was asking for a lot. "We love you and that will never change, but you need to understand that you have ruined people's lives. Not just some random person either. You have caused your brother so much pain that I really think it is too soon for you to be asking anyone to forgive you."

"I know it is asking a lot. Marlon may never forgive me and that is something I will have to live with, but you better believe I am going to do everything in my power to make things right."

"I don't expect you to make things right." Meme and Gloria froze when they heard Marlon's voice. He strolled across the kitchen and took a seat across from his sister.

Instantly, her head dropped in shame. There was a long pause. Meme knew Marlon was waiting for her to look up and acknowledge his presence and tears flooded her eyes. Without fully lifting her head, she made eye contact and was relieved to see that the hostility that was there the last time she saw him was gone. Although he still didn't look too pleased to see her, at least he wasn't spitting fire at her. "I am so sorry," she uttered, finally getting the courage to face him.

"You can save the sorry; it doesn't do me any good. Didn't I tell you last night I wasn't ready to talk to you?" Marlon didn't wait for her to respond,

"Okay, since you want to push me, let's talk." He slid his chair closer to the table and rested his arms across it. "You are a grown woman who, with open eyes, walked willingly into an affair with her brother's wife. No one forced you and, from the sound of things, you continued your pursuit after my wife tried to break it off. So please, save me the 'I'm sorry it was a mistake' speech."

"I know full well what I did was wrong. I allowed my desire to be loved to cloud my judgment. I take full responsibility for everything that went down." Meme reached out to hold his hand, but he pulled it back, giving her the 'don't even think about it' look. Her shoulders slumped at his rejection, but she persevered. "I know it is asking a lot, but almost as much as I need air to breathe, I need you to forgive me." The room fell silent. Gloria watched the exchange between her children and prayed Marlon didn't kill Meme.

The weight of Marlon's eyes on her made her lungs feel heavy and Meme was on the verge of hyperventilating when he finally spoke.

"Forgiveness doesn't come cheap and I am not even close to that point yet, but I have been thinking. Alicia and I were already in a bad place. We barely spoke to each other, rarely spent time together, and we were miserably unhappy. She even confessed to sleeping with some guy before she ran into you. It was only a matter of time before I found out and we would have divorced anyway." Meme took a moment to process what Marlon had said, hoping he did not pick up on her confusion. "I know now the problem was that I didn't love her the way a husband should love his wife." Marlon smoothed his hands down his face as he adjusted in his seat. "Don't get me wrong, I had strong feelings for her. She was my wife. I just couldn't give her all of me. She begged me to, but I didn't know how. Giving my heart to Latrice is like breathing. I don't have to think about it or try to figure it out. I just do it."

Meme smiled as she watched Marlon's face light up. She saw them together and had to admit she had never seen him so captivated with a woman before. The slightest touch from her calmed him when he had every right to be enraged. "I know…I saw you guys together. You are so lucky to have found each other."

"We are very lucky, but as happy as I am with Latrice, it doesn't make up for what you did." Marlon got up and walked away.

Gloria looked over at Meme and rolled her eyes with disgust. "Consider yourself lucky. Don't push him to talk, because next time he might not be as pleasant."

Nodding in agreement to her mother's warning, Meme grabbed her purse, rushed out of the house, and went straight to Alicia's. She hopped out of the car, rang the doorbell, and banged on the door; there was no answer. She stood there for almost five minutes knocking, banging, and ringing, then felt like an idiot when she realized it was a weekday and Alicia was at work.

"Well, I guess it is all for the best," Meme whispered to herself. There was no telling what would have transpired between them had she confronted Alicia. Then again, why was she upset? They weren't a couple. Meme knew she still had feelings for Alicia, but no matter how bad she wanted to be loved, she would not risk her relationship with her brother again.

Latrice sat at work about ready to pull her hair out. She lacked the focus to compile the reports for the upcoming staff meeting. Her boss had been hounding her for the past two hours for the reports and Latrice was so stressed out that she was on the verge of tears. The sleepless nights were wearing her out. She'd grown so accustom to having Marlon in the room with her that she could not sleep without the soft hum of his breathing. When she did manage to fall asleep, she'd jump up, swearing she heard a noise. No matter how tough she tried to be, she was still afraid Calvin would find her.

There was a knock on her office door and before answering, Latrice prayed it was not her boss again. When the door opened, she jumped from behind her desk and ran into Marlon's arms. He'd brought her lunch, but the force of her body smacking against him made him drop everything. Burying her face into his chest, Latrice tried to absorb the comfort that he gave her.
Marlon searched Latrice's face for some sign of what was bugging her. Sensing his question, she lowered her eyes to prevent him from seeing her weakness.

"I miss you, too," Marlon answered as he kissed her forehead. "Just remember, going back to work was your idea. I am capable and willing to provide everything you need."

I know, but I cannot allow a man to control my life the way Calvin did."

"Calvin is not a man. On his best day, he's not even half the man that I am." Leading her over to the desk chair, he sat down and pulled her on to his lap.

"If you are going to work, do it because it excites you, not out of fear. I don't want to control you by making you dependent on me for everything."

Latrice knew he would never try to dominate her life the way Calvin had, but independence was something she needed for herself. Until she met her husband, she'd been a strong, independent, black woman. Calvin killed that side of her, but Marlon had revived it. Never again would she sit around playing house while depending on a man for money. All she wanted from Marlon was his heart. Money, clothes, and jewelry she would get for herself.

"I am fine with working." She stepped away from him to retrieve their lunch. "We just need to find a way to see each other more. I am really starting to understand how Alicia felt. Not seeing you during the week is torture. Then, you still work nights on the weekends. It's not fair." Quietly, she unpacked their lunch trying to avoid his penetrating stare.

"So now you want me to quit my job the way she did?"'

"That is not what I meant and you know it."

"Well, tell me exactly what you mean, because I am trying my best to make this work. I have brought you lunch a couple of times. I get up early on Saturday, after working late on Friday night, to spend as much time as possible with you before my Saturday night shift. Please tell me what else I can do to make you happy."

"All that is great and I don't want to complain, but where is the romance?" Latrice silently nibbled on her sandwich, occasionally glancing at Marlon.

Marlon finished eating and walked to the door. Glancing back he uttered, "I hear what you are saying, but trust me, I'm trying hard to make this work. But the last time I checked, a relationship is two sided. Can you honestly say that you have put forth the same effort that I have?"

Latrice tossed the rest of her lunch in the trash and got back to work. He was right. When had she gone to his job or done anything extra to spend time with him?

Marlon drove home in a funk that stuck with him throughout the day. He was putting forth more of an effort to be with Latrice than he had put into his marriage and she didn't appreciate it. Their whole conversation was a little unsettling and he began to think that maybe his job was the problem. The fact that he even entertained the thought of giving it up for Latrice shocked him. Quickly, he shook the idea out of his mind and took on the same mindset that he had with Alicia. "I didn't ask her to quit so why should I?"

Marlon threw himself into work that night, spontaneously offering a chef's special that he'd prepared personally. With all the special orders that came in, he kept pretty busy—not giving himself a chance to think about Latrice. When he pulled up in front of his house and her car was parked out front, a smile spread across his face. She had come to see him.

He took his time coming into the house. He didn't want to seem too anxious. She wasn't in the kitchen or in the living room. Latrice was sound asleep in his bed. Noticing the overnight bag by the night stand, Marlon's smile deepened. He jumped into the shower, washed as fast as he could, and then joined her in bed.

Latrice had waited up for him as long as she could. She needed to apologize, but as the hour grew late, her eyes drifted closed. Being in his bed with his scent lulled her to sleep and she slept better than she had since moving out. She felt Marlon slide into bed next to her, but days of sleep deficiency prevented her from responding. Her eyes had finally found rest and were not about to give it up for anything.

When her alarm went off, Latrice rolled over in Marlon's arms feeling refreshed and rejuvenated. She tried to get out of bed, but he tightened his grip. "Give me fifteen more minutes. I haven't slept this good all week."

"Me neither." Latrice nuzzled closer into his warmth. "That's part of the reason I was being such a brat yesterday. I am sorry for the things I said. I do appreciate everything you are doing and I promise it will no longer be one sided, but please remember that besides my husband, you are the only man I have actually had a real relationship with, so forgive me if I seem a little ignorant about some things."

"Okay, now go back to sleep."

"I can't. I will be late for work."

Marlon groaned in frustration, but released her. "Alright, you get dressed and I will make breakfast." He patted her butt and kissed her forehead before rolling out of bed.

Marlon stumbled into the kitchen, greeted his parents who were having their usual morning breakfast, and started preparing something simple for Latrice.

"I had a nice talk with Latrice last night. I really like her." Gloria sipped her coffee as she watched her son scramble eggs.

"I really like her, too," Marlon mumbled.

"Well, I think she more than likes you. I know things aren't fully over with Alicia, but don't let Latrice get away. Alicia was all wrong for you, but Latrice, on the other hand, is something special."

Marlon kissed his mom on the check. "I wish I had listened to you when you told me not to marry Alicia, and I assure you, I will not let Latrice get away."

"Good. Maybe I will get some grandchildren in the near future. Lord knows with the path your sister is headed down, she is not going to give me any."

"Grandchildren? Oh my God. You sound like my mother. I can't have a conversation with her without it ending with her pleading for me to make babies." Latrice walked into the kitchen, kissed Marlon on the cheek, did the same to his parents, and then whispered in Gloria's ear, "I want nothing more than to give you grandchildren." Latrice winked at her as she made her way back to Marlon.

"You're not leaving before breakfast?" Marlon whispered, while nibbling her ear.

"No, but I do have to leave soon."

"Can I bring you lunch later?"

"Sorry, I am having lunch with some clients today, but I tell you what," she turned her head giving him better access to her ear. "What if I come down to the restaurant tonight? It is Friday. I can stay late and we can have dinner together in your office."

"That sounds good. Come at about seven. That will give me enough time to set up."

She wolfed down the eggs and toast, put some finishing touches on her outfit, and was out the door.

C

ole stood in the doorway of Marlon's office watching him setup a table for two. It was a small intimate table with enough room to enjoy your meal, but close enough to touch. There were two candles for a center piece, but spread far enough apart to not obstruct his vision. The table was clad with a beautiful, white table cloth and a bottle of wine was chilling on the side. The setup was simple, but elegant.

From the day Marlon took over as Executive Chef, Cole had respected him and had begun to consider him a friend. Over the past five months, he'd watched his boss and friend go from being a great person to work with to being a grouchy old man who nitpicked over everything. He was beginning to worry, but now not so much. Marlon's bad moods had tapered off and he was the happiest Cole had ever seen him.

Cole stepped into the office, "What's the special occasion?"

"Latrice is coming for dinner. It is very hard for me to take off on the weekends, so she agreed to meet me here." Marlon added the final touches to his table, trying to avoid Cole's inquiring eyes.

"If my memory serves me correctly, isn't your wife's name Alicia? If I am out of line, feel free to say so, but we are friends and I am curious about what's been up with you lately."

Marlon studied Cole's face; he was most certainly out of line. Who in their right frame of mind would just come out and ask a question like that?

Marlon laughed, "You are absolutely right. My ex-wife's name is Alicia. About five months ago, she was unfaithful and I caught her in the act. Two months after that, I met Latrice and she was everything I needed at a time that I needed it most. I fell in love with her and I don't apologize for it. The only thing I regret is wasting so much time being angry with Alicia. My divorce should have been finalized way before now, but I couldn't stand to be around her long enough to go through the process. But now she has signed the papers and I couldn't be happier."

Their conversation was cut short when Latrice appeared in the doorway. Marlon's face lit up when he noticed her and Cole turned to see what had caught his attention. Seeing that his guest had arrived, Cole quietly excused himself. They were so focused on each other that neither of them noticed his departure.

"Hi," Latrice whispered, as she entered the office and shut the door. Her stomach had been doing flips all day in anticipation of their date. When he stood to greet her, his white polo shirt pulled tight across his chest. The silhouette of his immaculate body made her breathing heavy. When he placed his hands on her waist, pulled her close, and pressed their lips together, she thought she might pass out. His smooth, caramel skin, tall, finely constructed physique, and deep, sensuous voice that had invaded her dreams were here all in the flesh. Latrice slid her hands up his chest, circled them around Marlon's neck, and he groaned in satisfaction. They had to figure out a way to see each other more often or he was going to lose his mind. The few times he'd taken lunch to her job were unfulfilling; he wanted and needed more. He needed her in his home and in his bed in a way he had never needed a woman before. The sight of her standing in his doorway instantly made him salivate. Her tight, red dress hugged every curve; the v-cut neckline drooped down just above the navel, leaving very little to the imagination, the color radiated against her dark, chocolate skin, her wavy hair draped across her shoulders, and her scent was intoxicating. His dreams were nothing compared to reality.

Marlon escorted her to the table. "Are you hungry? Order anything you want, as much as you want, and Cole will make it for us."

"I am starving, but I want you to cook for me."

Marlon shook his head; how could a woman be cute and lustfully sexy at the same time? Cooking wasn't part of his plan for the night, but if that's what she wanted, he would not deny her. "Okay just let me change my shirt." Marlon pulled his shirt off and tossed it on the couch.

Latrice tried to resist, but couldn't. Before she knew it, she had followed him across the room to roam her hands all over his chest. Her mouth replaced her hands, kissing, licking, and biting her way down his chest to his abs. Marlon hissed with approval, but stopped her before things got out of control.

"Marlon," she moaned between each breath. "Is this real love or is it just a sexual chemistry?"

"Is that really what you think?" He apologized as he wrapped her in his arms, "I am sorry if that's how I make you feel. I never want you to feel like that." Searching through his pocket, Marlon pulled out a tiny black box. Lifting the lid he sincerely stated, "It is about so much more than sex to me and I want to spend the rest of my life proving it to you. Will you marry me?"

Staring down at the diamond Latrice couldn't breathe. Tears streamed down her face and her voice abandoned her. Seeing her speechless, Marlon continued to let her know how much he loved her. "After everything I've been through, the thought of marriage should leave a bad taste in my mouth, but because of you it doesn't. I want nothing more than for you to be my wife and I promise to love you for the rest of my life."

Latrice caressed his face. Her voice was raspy and unsteady as she tried to formulate her thoughts into words. "I love you more than anything, but I can't accept this." The hurt that flashed in his eyes was indescribable. "I can't dishonor the love we share by wearing your ring while legally married to someone else. When I put this ring on my finger, it will symbolize my total devotion to you and there will be nothing standing in my way to say 'I do'." Latrice closed the box and placed it in the palm of his hand. "On the day my divorce is final, ask me again and I promise my answer will be yes."

Marlon's heart was heavy. He tried to convince himself that she hadn't said no, but then she didn't say yes either. Trying not to let his hurt show, he slipped the ring box back into his pocket and finished changing his shirt. She loved him and wanted to marry him; he would just focus on that.

Eventually, they made their way out to the kitchen and Marlon made them a wonderful meal. From the salad to the dessert, Latrice enjoyed every last bite. She ate so much she could barely move and her belly bulged in that tight red dress. Although she didn't want to leave, they both knew it was for the best. Marlon walked her to her car and kissed her good night. Before driving off, Latrice rolled down her window and asked, "You do understand why I can't wear your ring; don't you?"

"Your loyalty is one of the qualities that I love most." He smiled, backing away from the car as he pulled out his phone and dialed her number. Hearing her phone ring, Latrice shook her head as she answered, "Yes."

"You won't let me follow you home, then you have to talk to me until you get inside your apartment with the door locked."

"Marlon that is not necessary."

"It is not up for discussion."

Latrice complied, knowing it would put his mind at ease. They talked and laughed the entire ride and when she pulled into her complex, she tried to end the call, but Marlon refused. Even when she complained about having too much to carry, he refused to hang up and told her to get the important things and leave the rest. Shaking her head, she climbed out of the car and opened the trunk.

The only thing she really needed was her briefcase. She grabbed it and froze. She heard a voice calling her name from behind. She didn't need to turn around to know who it was. "Oh my god," she whispered into the phone.

The fear in her voice was apparent and Marlon was on his feet heading toward the door. "Latrice what happened?"
"It's Calvin, he is here. Please come help me." Before she could fully turn around Calvin back handed her across the face. Her phone flew out of her hand and slid across the ground. Latrice screamed as she tried to get away, but her shoes prevented her from running.

Marlon could hear her screams through the phone and his blood boiled. Marlon swore under his breath, "If this fool harms Latrice in any way, this will be his last night living." Marlon floored it all the way to Latrice's house. He ran every light and stop sign that he came across.

Deciding that listening to her while she endured hell was doing nothing to help; Marlon hung up the phone and called the police. The 911 operator pissed him off with all the questions and when she asked, 'Are you sure she is in danger', he hung up the phone. He was halfway there and prayed he made it in time.

Latrice cowered away in fear, but Calvin was right on her heels. He grabbed her by the arm and spun her around, then smacked her across the face. Blood oozed from her nose and into her mouth. The taste of her own blood caused her to snap. That moment, she affirmed within herself that if he was going to kill her tonight, she wasn't going out without a fight. As he cranked his arm back, Latrice gave him a quick jab to the mouth. Shock halted his movement and Latrice popped him in the mouth again. The realization of what she's done hit him and fury lit his eyes. His tongue snaked out licking the corner of his mouth; he tasted blood.

His vehement strides made Latrice regret her actions. She'd hit him twice and now she had to pay. He was stronger and faster than her, so she had to be smarter. In her haste to get away from him, she allowed him to separate her from her car. The bat Marlon gave her was in the trunk and she had to think of a way to get past Calvin to get to it. Latrice slipped out of her high heels and took off running. Ducking in front of a parked car, Latrice glared at Calvin. He stood at the opposite end of the car watching her like a hawk. He made his move toward her and she ran around the car in the opposite direction. If she could just keep a car between them until Marlon got there she would be fine. He worked twenty minutes away; she had to play it safe until he got there.

This game was played many times when she was a child. Hiding behind a car to avoid being tagged always worked, but childhood memories did not prepare her for what Calvin did next. He proceeded to walk across the top of a car. Latrice's eyes widened as he made his way toward her. He towered above her glaring with such intensity that she almost urinated on herself, but now was not the time to be afraid. Latrice hiked her dress up and as fast as she could ran toward her car. Calvin hopped down and the thud of his feet hitting the ground startled her, but she kept running.

His footsteps were getting closer and she started to panic. Just as she made it to her car, Calvin was on top of her. The trunk was still open and she grasped onto the car with one hand. He gripped a handful of her hair and tried to pull her away from the car, but she held on tight. She could feel hairs being ripped from her scalp and screamed in agony, but held on. With her free hand, Latrice searched the trunk for the bat. Calvin enlisted his other hand to smack her across the face as he spit obscenities at her. When her hand slid along the slender handle of the wooden bat, Latrice felt like singing the Hallelujah Chorus. She gripped the bat firmly, let go of the car, and before Calvin knew what was going on, Latrice had spun around and was swinging the bat into his ribs. He buckled against the car and Latrice backed away. Apparently she hadn't hit him hard enough, because he almost instantly recovered and came after her. He lunged toward her and this time, with all the strength she had, Latrice swung the bat. The hard wooden bat collided with his head. Instantaneously, Calvin's movement halted and he dropped to the ground.

Latrice waited for him to get up, to move, or do something, but he didn't. She crept toward him with her hands firmly wrapped around the bat. She kicked his foot then jumped back, but nothing happened. Making her way around toward his head, Latrice stopped mid-stride. His eyes were as wide as could be and bloodshot red. Blood ran from his nose and pooled on the ground underneath his cheek. His body tensed as he fought for oxygen. Latrice watched in horror and the dinner she just shared with Marlon spewed out of her mouth. The struggle left his body and she dropped the bat, screaming as loud as she could. Frantically, she ran to get the cell phone Calvin had knocked from her hand. Latrice tried to call 911, but before she could Marlon, pulled up.

Marlon stopped in the middle of the street, threw the car into park, and rushed to Latrice's side. He was so relieved to see her alive, he could barely breath. Her body was drenched in sweat and blood still dribbled from her nose, but she was alive. He wrapped his arms around her, wanting to absorb her pain. "What did I do? What did I do?"

Marlon saw Calvin lying motionless on the ground with a bat next to him. "You fought for your life," he whispered, as he tightened his embrace. He let her cry into his chest and pulled out his phone and called the police.

Within minutes, several squad cars and an ambulance made their way into the apartment complex. Marlon placed Latrice in his car and greeted the officers when they arrived. He gave them the rundown of what happened, what he had heard over the phone, and informed them of the restraining order. Just as they were making their way toward the car to speak with Latrice, an elderly lady emerged from the shadows.

"Excuse me officers, can I speak with you for a moment?" Her steps were slow and unsteady. Her frail body shook with each step. The few, short steps seemed to take all the energy she had and she had to catch her breath before she spoke. "I hope you are not going to put that young lady in jail. I saw everything. I should have called you, but I was in shock over what I was seeing and wasn't thinking straight. That man was beating the hell out of her and she tried to get away." She relayed everything she saw, and Marlon listened intently.

The muscles in his jaw twitched as he clenched his teeth. He looked over at Calvin. The EMT's had rushed to his aid, but it was too late. They placed a sheet over him and called the coroner. His cold, lifeless body lay in the street. He'd finally gotten what he deserved. Latrice no longer had to live in fear; he could never hurt her again.

The neighbors had started filing out of their apartments, curious about the flashing lights. Some were mortified, but they all watched just the same. They watched as Latrice gave her account of the nights events. News crews arrived and a few people rushed over for their fifteen seconds of fame. A few more witnesses stepped up to say they saw everything, well able-bodied men and women who stood by watching Latrice get beat down and did nothing. Not a shout out the window, not a phone call to the police; they did absolutely nothing. Marlon understood not wanting to get involved. He had heard stories about innocent bystanders and good Samaritans becoming the victim, but an anonymous call to the police never hurt anyone.

Growing tired of the onlookers, Marlon made his way to Latrice's apartment. He packed her a suitcase; there was no way he was letting her stay there tonight. If he had his way, she would have never moved out in the first place. Although she had good reason, he felt it was too soon. She wanted freedom and to stop living in fear. With Calvin gone, she could truly have what she wanted.

Marlon went back outside carrying the suitcase. Latrice was in the car, Calvin had been taken away, and the officers stood in a circle talking in the middle of the street. Marlon tossed the suitcase in his trunk and went to speak with the investigating officers.

"Is everything alright? Are we free to go?"

"We are finished for tonight. Her story lines up with all the witness accounts and, given the restraining order, it sounds like a classic case of self-defense. Make sure she gets a good night's rest and bring her down to the station tomorrow."

"Can I ask you a question? Is this typical, to have so many witnesses and no one lift a finger to help?"

"You're lucky witnesses stepped forward at all. Most won't lift a finger and won't say a word in your defense. Latrice is very fortunate, although, we probably would have come to the same conclusion of self-defense. Having all these witnesses makes the process much easier."

Marlon thanked the officers for their time, shook their hands, and headed to the car. Latrice rode the whole way with her head in his lap. Her wails filled the silence in the car. Stroking the side of her face, Marlon prayed for her strength. He did not want to think about what he would have driven up on, had he not convinced her to put the bat in her car. She had told him it was excessive and refused to put in there, but he wore down her resistance. The drive from his restaurant to Latrice's apartment had been the longest drive of his life. If he had shown up and the tables were turned, and Latrice was the one lying lifeless on the ground, he would definitely be in the back of the squad car. There would have been nothing or no one there to stop him from beating the life out of Calvin. Tears formed in Marlon's eyes at the thought of almost losing Latrice and he did nothing to hold them back.

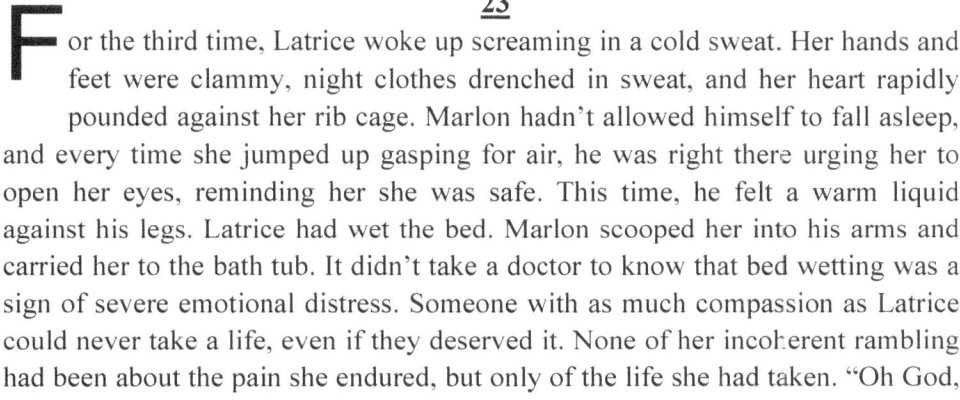

23

For the third time, Latrice woke up screaming in a cold sweat. Her hands and feet were clammy, night clothes drenched in sweat, and her heart rapidly pounded against her rib cage. Marlon hadn't allowed himself to fall asleep, and every time she jumped up gasping for air, he was right there urging her to open her eyes, reminding her she was safe. This time, he felt a warm liquid against his legs. Latrice had wet the bed. Marlon scooped her into his arms and carried her to the bath tub. It didn't take a doctor to know that bed wetting was a sign of severe emotional distress. Someone with as much compassion as Latrice could never take a life, even if they deserved it. None of her incoherent rambling had been about the pain she endured, but only of the life she had taken. "Oh God, I didn't mean to hurt him," she cried out over and over.

"Baby, look at me," Marlon tilted her chin toward him and cleaned her face with a wash cloth. "If you did not defend yourself, you'd be dead. So whenever you start feeling bad about what happened, think about that." She continued to cry, but as fast as the tears fell, he wiped them.

"What am I going to tell his family?" Her cries grew into intense wailing. "In a few hours, I have to call them. I can't tell his mother I killed him."

"I will handle everything. You don't have to worry about anything." Marlon finished washing her then laid her in the other bed.

After placing the soiled laundry in the wash, Marlon sat at the table with his and Latrice's cell phones and prepared to make phone calls. The sun was beginning to rise and he wanted to contact everyone as soon as possible. His first call was to Camilla; he needed her to come over as soon as possible to help with Latrice. Twenty minutes later, she showed up with Sheena, Delisa, Paul, Tim, and Jaleel. He was glad Paul had sense enough to bring her old cell phone, because the prepaid one he'd given her did not have any numbers stored in it.

Latrice woke again in a cold sweat, but this time Marlon wasn't there. When she came to, she heard voices. She put on Marlon's robe and followed the voices into the kitchen. All talking ceased when she stepped into the room.

"Good morning," Latrice said, pausing to clear the phlegm from her throat, but it was no use. Her voice was raspy from hours of crying. Camilla grabbed her by the hand to help her into a chair, but she opted to sit in Marlon's lap instead. He snuggled her against his chest allowing his hand to stroke her back. He whispered into her ear and she nodded her responses. His parents and sister had now joined them in the kitchen and he wanted to make sure she wasn't overwhelmed with all the eyes on her.

When he was sure she was comfortable, he continued the previous conversation giving her a rundown of what was being discussed. "I have spoken with Latrice and Calvin's mothers, they will notify the rest of the family and both are trying to get on the next flight out here." Again Marlon whispered in her ear, "Your mom was relieved to hear that you are okay. She has been worried sick for months. Apparently Calvin contacted her, trying to find out where you were and she had been calling your cell. When you didn't answer or call back, she feared the worst."

"I also spoke with the district attorney's office on my way over and he assured me they aren't going seek criminal charges, but I hired the best criminal defense lawyer just as a precaution," Paul added, as he poured himself another cup of coffee.

"Also, Delisa and I will be working with Ms. Stewart on funeral arrangements. So we need to know if you had life insurance," Camilla asked.

"No we don't, but Calvin does have a will. He told me if anything happened to him, I wouldn't get a dime and that all his money was going to his mother. You may have to wait until she gets here to pay for things, but if you look through my phone, Alistair Fuller is Calvin's lawyer. Contact him to let him know what's happened and maybe he can release some funds to get started." Latrice softly spoke, never lifting her head from Marlon's shoulder. She spoke when spoken to and Marlon translated when others couldn't hear her.

Paul grabbed her cell and stepped out of the room to make the necessary call. Within minutes, he returned stating that there were funds set aside for funeral expenses, but Mr. Fuller had strict instructions not to divulge the contents of the will until one week after the funeral. They scheduled a meeting for later that day so Paul could pick up the check.

Marlon spent the next thirty minutes delegating duties to everyone in the kitchen. He wanted the days leading up to Calvin's funeral to be as stress-free as possible. Latrice wasn't to lift a finger. By the time he was finished, everyone was clear on what their responsibilities were and headed out the door to get started with the funeral arrangements. Before walking out, each man turned to his woman and planted his lips on hers. Marlon watched each exchange with full understanding. He knew firsthand how just the thought of being away from the woman you loved could turn a grown man into a lovesick adolescent.

After the visitors left, Marlon turned to his mother and sister. Without saying a word Gloria knew what he needed. "Go lay Latrice on the couch. Meme will watch her while you shower. I will make us all breakfast."

Meme sat on the side of the couch stroking Latrice's back, wishing she knew more scriptures that would help Latrice. Instead, she decided to speak from her heart. "You know my brother loves you, right?" Latrice turned to look at her and Meme ignored the puzzled look on her face. "Seeing you like this is eating him up inside. When a real man loves a woman, her pain is his pain and he won't rest until she is no longer hurting. Over the next few days, he may be overprotective, overbearing, and might downright get on your nerves, but don't push him away. Let him love you through this. I know I am probably the wrong person to say this, but after all you guys have been through, you deserve to be happy with each other." Meme knew she was the cause of everything Marlon had been through and probably should have kept her mouth shut. Had she not acted on her feelings for his wife, he would have been spared months of heart ache. On top of all that, she had never really experienced the love of a man to speak on its effects, but had watched her brother with enough women to recognize how devoted he was to Latrice. "I know you are not comfortable with what you did, but I'd much rather be here consoling you for what happened to Calvin than consoling my brother after losing you. He has lost enough already. I am glad he didn't lose you last night."

Those words made Latrice sit straight up on the couch and she flung her arms around Meme's neck. They embraced for a while as tears ran down their faces. Marlon had pretty much told Latrice the same thing about it being her that could have died instead of Calvin and it did nothing to lift her spirits. Picturing Marlon lying on the couch inconsolably sobbing into the pillows over her death made Latrice want to shake this funk for his sake. Even if she had to fake it, she would not allow Marlon to see her grieve Calvin's death.

Marlon walked into the living room. "Is everything alright?"

Meme jumped to her feet. "I am sorry I wasn't trying to… Um you know. She was upset," she stuttered, while nervously fidgeting with her outfit.

"I know you weren't trying anything," Marlon pulled his sister into his arms squeezing her as tight as he could. "You know I love her too much and would hurt you if you tried that." He laughed, but was dead serious. She could thank Calvin's death for saving her from months, possibly years, of getting the cold shoulder, because right now Marlon was too grateful that all his family was alive to hold a grudge.

Latrice was too busy motivating herself to a smile to notice what Meme thought Marlon had assumed when he saw them hugging. As soon as she heard his voice, her mind said, *straighten up and dry your face*. When he finally came to her, she managed to do a pretty good job. She stood, plastered a fake smile, kissed his cheek, and took his hand as he escorted her into the kitchen for breakfast.

Marlon kept nodding off to sleep during the entire breakfast. He had been awake for over twenty-four hours and his body was begging for rest. Marlon talked Latrice into laying down for a nap and snuggled up next to her, hoping she'd fall asleep so he could rest. Latrice was afraid to sleep. While awake, she could pretend that she wasn't still horrified over what she'd done to Calvin, but if she allowed herself to sleep, her nightmares would surely give her away. Marlon pulled her close, prayed for peace in her dreams, and then kneaded her back and shoulders until her eyes shut. Marlon finally laid his head down and was out like a light.

They woke up a few hours later. Marlon felt rested, but could have very well slept through the night. The kitchen was beginning to fill up with the same visitors they had that morning. Latrice still seemed to be attached to Marlon's hip, but at least her face was out of its hiding place against his neck. Everyone gave her the rundown of their progress on the funeral preparations. They wanted things done as quickly as possible, so Latrice could move on with her life. The one thing that put a genuine smile on her face was the news that her mom would be arriving in a couple of hours.

Pastor Hawkins arrived with Chinese takeout. Latrice managed to remain pleasant through the entire meal. Tears lingered behind her eyes, but she managed to smile when spoken to and even laughed at a joke here and there. Along with the food, Pastor Hawkins brought a light-heartedness that was desperately needed. Everyone was walking on eggshells to avoid sending Latrice spiraling into depression, but Pastor was his same fun-loving self, and they all appreciated it.

He laughed, talked, and prayed for almost two hours. Before leaving, he turned to Latrice with deepest sincerity, confessing something none of his church members knew. "Every day, I pray for the Lord to bless me with a woman I can spend my life with and for the life of me I don't understand why some men abuse the treasure God has given them." As fast as his guard came down, it was back up to once again hide his inner most desire. "Remember, God is the giver of life, and it is only he who can take it away. Nothing happened last night that wasn't in God's will." Leaving those words with her, Pastor Hawkins stood to his feet, said his goodbyes, and was out the door.

Shortly after the pastor left, the front door opened; it was Marlon Sr. returning with Latrice's mother. She leaped out of Marlon's lap and ran to the front door. Before her mother could even get her coat off, Latrice was all over her, seeking that motherly nurturing that she'd been missing. When Sylvia finally wrapped her arms around her daughter, that is exactly what she gave, the compassion and strength only a mother can give her child.

"Mom, I have missed you so much."

"I missed you too. I wish you would have called me sooner. I should have been here for you."

"I know, but it was not safe." Latrice took her mother's hand and led her into the kitchen. After all introductions were made, Sylvia sat at the table. She had questions she needed answers to.

"I appreciate everything that you all have done to keep my daughter safe, but somebody please explain how this happened. Why wasn't there someone with her? You knew he was after her and you dropped the ball."

"Mom, please." Latrice looked around the kitchen, at the people who had put their lives in danger to ensure her safety. She was embarrassed by her mother's insinuation. "They did everything they could to keep me safe. It was my fault that I was alone." Shaking her head Latrice took a seat next to her mother. "Jaleel and Delisa opened their home to me and treated me like part of their family. Marlon sat with me all day, talked to me, and made me feel safe. Everything was great until Calvin followed them to church and found me. Then Gloria opened her home to me, but by that time I had fallen in love with Marlon. Although we tried, we found it extremely hard to keep our hands off each other." Latrice quickly mumbled through that part and rushed on before anyone had a chance to ask questions. "When I accepted the Lord as my savior, I knew I had to do something to help us both live holy." Latrice noticed all the shocked faces. Because of their need to sever all communication, she wasn't able to share the news of her being filled with the Holy Spirit. They had only learned that she had moved out when Marlon called to tell them about Calvin's death. "So, when the opportunity arose for me to move out, I jumped at it. Marlon was not happy and he tried to talk me out of it, but I did not see any other way to keep our feelings for each other in check." Latrice sighed at her stupidity and how the whole situation could have been avoided. "Even last night, Marlon begged me to let him follow me home to make sure I made it safely, but I was so set on being independent and getting my life back that I told him no."

Sylvia looked around the kitchen smiling and making eye contact with everyone until her eyes finally landed on Marlon. There was no smile offered to him. Instead she gave him a disappointed scowl as her eyes alternated between him and Latrice. "So, do you love her, too?" She asked, finally resting her eyes on Marlon.

"More than I ever thought possible." Marlon held Sylvia's gaze. He was not going to be intimidated into backing off of what he felt for Latrice. The sooner she understood that the better. When she finally averted her eyes, Marlon stood and exited the room.

"Are you alright?" Tim followed him out of the kitchen and stopped him just before he rounded the corner to go into his room.

"Yeah, I'm good," he lied. He was already feeling guilty for not following Latrice home last night. Every time he looked at the scratches on her face, he felt nauseous. Sylvia coming in and accusing him of not doing everything possible to keep Latrice safe made him feel even worse.

"Well, just keep your head up. My first encounter with Camilla's mom was similar to what you are dealing with. Be firm and stand your ground. Let her know that nothing she can do or say will stop you from loving Latrice."

"Thanks, but Sylvia is right about one thing." Marlon turned his back on Tim so he wouldn't see the tears forming in his eyes. "I should have been there. She had just left my restaurant and I wanted to follow her home just to make sure she made it safely. Even though I felt in my gut that she wasn't safe, I let her convince me that I was being overprotective." A tear slid down his face.

"Don't beat yourself up over this. You know if Calvin would have seen you, he would have hid until you left, snuck into her apartment, and attacked her. He would have been even more infuriated if he saw you guys together and would have definitely killed her."

"He's right." Neither of them heard Latrice enter the room. "Please don't blame yourself for this. No one is to blame, but Calvin." The waterfall of tears that had dried up were flowing once again.

Crossing the room to her, Marlon scooped her up into his arms and carried her to the couch. He sat with her in his lap, allowing her tears to soak his shirt. When it seemed like nothing he said was stopping her tears, Marlon lifted her head and joined their lips. He didn't know if it was working for her, but it was sure lifting his spirits. A moan crept out of his mouth when she turned her

186

head to give him better access. His hands stilled on her waist when he heard Sylvia gasp in the background.

"Latrice, what are you doing?" She rushed over and grabbed Latrice by the arm, snatching her off Marlon's lap. "Your husband just died and you're up in this man's lap letting…"

"My husband?" Latrice couldn't believe her mother was trying to defend Calvin's honor and stopped her before she went too far. "He stopped being my husband the first day he hit me. So if you are going to refer to him, let's call him what he really is. That bastard used to beat the crap out of me." Latrice stood face to face with her mom. "What is wrong with you? First, you're mad because they didn't protect me from Calvin and now you're mad because I am in love with Marlon."

"I don't care what Calvin has done. You don't cheat on your husband. You do not touch another man until your divorce is final. He was your husband and God only knows what you two," she gestured toward Marlon, "have already done to disgrace your marriage. It is improper for you to behave this way."

Latrice opened her mouth to speak and Marlon stopped her. The look on her face let him know that she was about to let her mother have it for defending Calvin. "Sylvia, I thought you came here to support your daughter. The past few years have been rough for her. I, for one, am proud of her for finally getting the courage to leave Calvin. You are standing here berating your daughter for dishonoring a man who made her life a living nightmare. Maybe you should talk to her and find out what he did to her that finally gave her the strength to leave. I won't stand for you attacking her and I will ask you to leave." Marlon stared her down until he was sure his warning sank in. When she nodded, he led them to couch where they sat and talked. Latrice explained everything and by the time they finished Sylvia was sobbing just as hard as her daughter.

24

Alicia's eyes widened when she looked through the peephole and saw Marlon standing on her doorstep. She had called him to let him know she was doing some cleaning and found some of his things. She hadn't anticipated him just showing up, but she was pleasantly surprised. A smile that spread from ear to ear quickly faded when she saw Meme standing on the side of him. She shot Meme a suspicious side-look. She hoped their visit was peaceful, but her refusal to make eye contact made Alicia nervous. She could barely get the words out to invite them into the house.

Alicia escorted them to the kitchen and poured them a glass of lemonade without even asking if they were thirsty, then she left to get the box of Marlon's things.

"Thanks, but this is not why I am here. Please sit down so we can talk." Alicia reluctantly took a seat and Marlon continued. "I know this is awkward and I feel even more uncomfortable having to say this, but I have been doing some thinking. Life is too short to hold grudges or harbor hatred. So, I want you guys to know that I love you both and I forgive you." Alicia and Meme were both already sobbing uncontrollably and Marlon joined hands with both of them.

"Because I love you, I want you to be happy. I am amazingly happy and don't want to selfishly rob you guys of that same happiness. Alicia, my sister loves you. She risked so much to be with you. If you feel the same way about her, then you guys have my blessing to be together."

Alicia gripped Meme's free hand and brought it to her lips and gently kissed the back of it. "I'm sorry, but I don't." The flow of tears down Meme's cheeks increased and Marlon's eyebrow rose. "Before we hooked up, I was already so detached from the Lord that I was being led of my own selfish desires. I wanted Marlon to hurt the way I was hurting and I guess subconsciously, I saw you as a way to get back at him." Meme's head dropped and her breathing stalled in her throat as Alicia's words singed her heart. She tried to remove her hand, but Alicia had a firm grip. "Wait, please let me finish. It wasn't all revenge for me, but it wasn't love either. It went from revenge to curiosity, to having the lust of my flesh quenched. I desired you, but I didn't love you and I am sorry for hurting you."

Turning to Marlon, Alicia apologized again. "I know this makes you hate me all over again, but I am done living a lie. Lies made me lose the most wonderful person in my life and I will regret it until the day I die. Latrice is the luckiest woman in the world. I hope she appreciates you more than I did."

"If you are denying your feelings for Meme in hopes that we will reconcile, you can forget it."

"I would love to be with you again, but I am not delusional. I know we are over, but I have to be honest. Being with Meme has shown me that I am slightly attracted to women, and if Meme is completely honest with herself, she would admit that she is more than slightly attracted to men." Meme opened her mouth to protest, but Alicia stopped her. "I know you like women, but you forget you have shared some of your inner thoughts with me. Your secrets are safe with me, but just keep an open mind. When the right man comes along, you will abandon the softness of a woman in search of the hardness of a man. Don't allow this misconception you have of men to cause you to miss out on true love."

Marlon was at a loss for words as he watched their exchange. Meme seemed to know exactly what inner thoughts Alicia was referring to and seemed a little apprehensive about them being revealed. "What is she talking about?" His eyes pierced his sister as he waited for an answer.

When Alicia saw how uncomfortable Meme was becoming under her brother's scrutinizing gaze, she interjected for her. "Marlon, just give her time to figure herself out. She'll confide in you soon enough, but as for right now, please don't hold all of this against her. Every day we spent together, she struggled with the guilt of hurting you. The fact that she ruined your marriage ate at her."

Marlon took a moment to process what Alicia had said and when he realized what she had admitted to, he was livid. "The only way you would know that is if you guys continued to see each other after I caught you." This whole time he had been under the mistaken belief that their affair ended when he caught them. Marlon's eyes were glued to his sister as he spoke to Alicia. He spoke through clenched teeth in an attempt to constrain his anger. "All this time, all the phones calls and attempts to get me back, and you guys were still together?"

"I am sorry. I don't mean to cause anymore problems. I just assumed she had told you everything." Alicia felt guilty for making things worse, but was done with deception; Marlon deserved to know the whole truth. "Yes, our relationship continued after you caught us. The day you called and asked me to fast for our session with pastor was the day things were over between us."

Marlon recalled the day. He had almost gone to see her after work. He didn't bother calculating an exact date, but knew they'd been together for at least three months and that infuriated him. He stared at Meme, waiting for her response. When she didn't, he grabbed the seat of her chair and spun her around, forcing her to acknowledge him. "So it was a mistake, huh? I believe that's what you said. Well mistakes are things that just happen, but when you continue to do something, it's intentional." Marlon was just getting ready to tear into his sister when his phone rang. It was Latrice calling to tell him they had company. The sound of her voice lightened his mood and he remembered why he had come to Alicia's house in the first place.

Marlon looked at his sister, "You know what? This is not worth the stress anymore. I have a beautiful woman who I love more than life itself waiting for me to get home. Like I said at first, I forgive you both and I want you to be happy." With that said, Marlon got up and left. He and Meme had ridden together, but he left her sitting at the table with Alicia; she'd have to find her own ride home.

Meme and Alicia sat on opposite sides of the table in silence for minutes before Alicia came and gave Meme a hug which she readily accepted. "I am so sorry. I didn't mean to make this worse. I thought he already knew. I would have never put you out there like that."

"You know what Alicia, save that for someone else, because this whole situation is about you putting me out there. You didn't even have the decency to give me a heads up about coming clean to my brother. You put me and my secrets out in the open without considering how your sudden need to purge yourself of the lies was going to affect me."

Alicia was stunned, Meme was right. She never considered how her confession was going to affect everyone involved. "Then you sit here and say you never loved me and only lusted after me. How is that supposed to make me feel?" Her anger turned to pain and tears rolled down her face.

Alicia wiped the tears from Meme's face, then leaned in close and apologized for being so selfish. Meme slammed her lips against Alicia's. The kiss was so sudden that Alicia didn't know how to respond. Alicia sat there stiff, refusing to return the kiss. Meme tried to part Alicia's lips with her tongue. When she was through, Alicia sympathetically smiled and asked, "Do you need a ride home or did you and Marlon drive separately?"

Meme's head dropped in defeat. "I need a ride."

During the drive to Meme's apartment, Alicia's mind was tormented as she recalled the way Marlon's eyes lit up as he talked about Latrice. His heart was gushing with so much adoration that it over flowed and seeped out of his pores. She had never seen Marlon that love struck—not even on their wedding day. Alicia blinked until the tears stopped; she refused to shed another tear over the mess she'd made of her life.

Meme sighed as Alicia pulled in front of her apartment. She turned one last time to look at the woman she'd fallen in love with. She traced Alicia's jaw line with her fingertips.

"Goodbye," Meme whispered. There was such finality to her words that both women knew it would be a long time before they saw each other again.

"Take care," Alicia said, brushing her knuckles against Meme's cheek. Without another word, Meme stepped out of the car and shut the door.

Meme walked toward her apartment, hoping that Alicia would call her back, but there was nothing. Once she reached her front door, she looked back hoping to see Alicia standing outside the car. Alicia was gone. "It's all for the best," Meme said, trying to encourage herself as she stepped inside.

Marlon arrived at Latrice's house, still reeling in the shock of Meme and Alicia's relationship. He should have really been pissed, but Latrice was never far from his thoughts. Just thinking of how Alicia's betrayal brought Latrice into his life dissolved all of his anger.
There was an enticing aroma coming from Latrice's apartment; he walked through the door with a smile on his face.

His steps slowed when he walked into the living room and noticed all the visitors lined up on the couch. "Is everything alright?" Marlon scanned Camilla, Sheena, and Delisa's face for an indication of what was going on, but their expressions were neutral.

"Everything is fine. We just came by to finalize the funeral arrangements and Latrice did not want to start without you. She offered to cook dinner while we waited." Camilla smiled at the disapproval that flashed on Marlon's face. "I know she shouldn't be in there trying to cook enough food for all of us, but I am pretty sure you know how persistent she can be."

"Persistent isn't the word for it." *More like hard head*, he thought. Marlon shook his head as he gave out the proper greetings and then followed the aroma into the kitchen.

Latrice's heart skipped a beat when she turned and saw Marlon leaning against the door frame. He looked incredibly sexy and for the first time since Calvin's death, something else was on her mind. The intensity of his gaze seared her flesh. She didn't know whether to run to him or run from him. Even if she did, she doubted her legs had the strength to do either. Desire and fear immobilized her and had constricted her lungs to the point where the tips of her fingers began to tingle from lack of oxygen. Marlon reveled over the effect his presence had on her. As he moved toward her, her fidgeting increased with each step

"Latrice," Sylvia yelled—snapping her daughter out of her trance. She ran off to assist her mother, but Marlon intercepted her by the arm, spun her around, and kissed her passionately. Sylvia barked her name again, but this time Latrice didn't budge. For a moment, all the heartache and grief she'd endured over the past week dissolved. The only thing that existed was them.

Marlon set their bodies in motion. They glided across the kitchen floor in their best impromptu version of a waltz. The tempo of his feet matched that of his tongue as he assaulted Latrice's senses. Marlon led her out the kitchen and into the living room without missing a beat. Latrice's heart beat wildly and she was clueless to her surroundings until he broke their kiss and told her to sit down. She plopped down onto the sofa awaiting his next move. Marlon strutted back into the kitchen and it donned on her that he seduced her out of the kitchen. She shot to her feet with fury to tell him off, but when she opened her mouth nothing came out.

All eyes were on Latrice, and she plopped back down on the couch with an attitude. She looked to the other women in the room and all three of them burst out laughing. They had told her not to cook in the first place and warned her that Marlon would not be happy if he came home and caught her. "Marlon doesn't tell me what to do. He is not bossy like I recall them being." She pointed her finger at their husbands. Latrice ignored their teasing and continued to brood in silence.

"Aww, we're sorry." Camilla sat in her lap with Sheena and Delisa positioning themselves at her sides. They wrapped their arms around her and squeezed her tight until Marlon returned to tell them dinner was ready.

Marlon was concerned by seeing them huddled up. "Is everything alright?" He inquired as he rushed over to the group of women.

"No, you hurt my friend's feelings." Before Marlon could respond, Tim placed his hand in the curve of his wife's back and escorted her into the kitchen. Paul and Jaleel followed suit, giving their wives a look that said don't get involved. Latrice was right, their husbands were bossy, but it was only for what was best.

"What is Camilla talking about?" Marlon asked. Latrice ignored his question and stepped around him, following everyone else into the kitchen. "Latrice, I am sorry," he said, but she did not respond. She was furious over the way he'd handled her. He'd have to deal with the silent treatment until she realized he was only concerned for her well-being.

Marlon answered his vibrating cell and sat down at the table. "Meme, I don't want to talk to you." He ended the call.

"I take it your get together with Alicia and Meme didn't go too well?" Latrice's attitude instantly changed to concern.

"Why on earth would you meet with them trifling…?" Jaleel elbowed Delisa in the arm before she could finish.

Marlon's eyes roamed across the faces at the table. Jaleel was the only blood relative, but he loved them all like they were his flesh and blood. He could see that same love plastered on their faces as they tried to read his thoughts. His eyes landed on Latrice. Minutes ticked by as they silently communicated. When he broke eye contact and picked up his fork to eat, Latrice wanted to kick herself for opening her mouth and putting him in this uncomfortable situation. After only a few bites, he tossed his fork onto his plate, pushed back from the table, and strode from the room. Latrice jumped up and followed after him.

Catching up to him in the hallway, Latrice apologized profusely for putting him out there like that, but he declined her apology, stating there was nothing to be sorry for. He quickly relayed everything Alicia had said and when she opened her arms to comfort him, he willingly went into them.

"Baby, I am so sorry you had to deal with that by yourself. I knew I should have gone with you."

"No, you don't need the added stress, and that is the only reason I did what I did earlier. I want you to take it easy. I know you are feeling better physically, but…"

"You are forgiven and I don't want to talk about that right now." She walked back into the kitchen. That was pretty much the same response she'd given him every time he tried to discuss her nightmares and despondent behavior. Marlon sat and hoped everyone would let the previous conversation go, but Jaleel couldn't.

"So, what happened when you met with Alicia?"

"Can you just let it go?"

"No," Jaleel shot back. This time it was Delisa elbowing him in the arm.

Marlon hesitated, and moments later said, "A couple of weeks ago Alicia called and said she was ready to sign the divorce papers, but wanted to confess some things. We met at the church with Pastor Hawkins and that's when she laid it on me." Marlon stood from the table and grabbed his plate to dump food into the trashcan. He no longer had an appetite. "Today, in an attempt to put it all behind me, I picked up Meme, drove over to Alicia's, told them I loved them and that I forgive them, I even gave them my blessing to be together." Marlon shook his head at how ridiculous the whole idea was to begin with. "Then Alicia inadvertently revealed that they didn't just sleep together once, but the day I caught them was the first of many. My sister slept with my wife and did everything she could to keep me from going back over there after I stormed out. They continued to sleep with each other for weeks."

"What the hell?" Sylvia had sat quiet through the whole dinner, but could no longer control herself.

Jaleel tossed his napkin onto his plate, "I agree with Sylvia. Meme has lost her mind. When did she become a lesbian?"

Marlon shrugged his shoulders, regretting having to put his sister out there like that. Even now, with everything she'd done, his brotherly instinct still wanted to protect her. "I think she is just confused."

"And you were just ready to forgive her for destroying your marriage?" Jaleel asked.

"It's easy to let go of the past when your future is so beautiful." He glanced at Latrice. "I hated them both when I first found out, but I had a little help getting over it." Marlon pulled Latrice out of her seat and embraced her. "I would have never experienced this kind of love if they hadn't screwed up. When that sank in, forgiving them was easy."

Sylvia continued to shovel food in her mouth. The more time she spent around Marlon, the harder it was to find an excuse to hate him. He was a genuinely nice guy. She was actually starting to respect him, but she'd felt the same way about Calvin. As soon as Latrice had married him, the nice guy façade disbanded. He had isolated her so he could torment her and there was no way she was letting that happen to her daughter again. She was determined to see to it that when she got on the plane next week to go back home, Latrice would be sitting right next to her.

"Man, why didn't you call me?" Jaleel stood, still reeling from the shock.

"With everything that was going on with Latrice, I didn't want to risk the phone call. But Latrice was there when I confronted Meme, so were mom and pop." Marlon smiled at Jaleel's facial expression. His mother and father being at the same location at the same time had been a rare occurrence over the past few years. "I thought they would have said something to your dad by now, but my parents are back together."

Jaleel's eyes widened with disbelief. Gloria loved her some Marlon Sr. and no one ever understood why they'd separated, but it was good to hear they were back together. Jaleel hated hearing about the changes his family was experiencing after the fact. They were usually a close knit group, but with everything that was going on with Latrice, they had been afraid to contact each other. It was over now and he couldn't be happier.

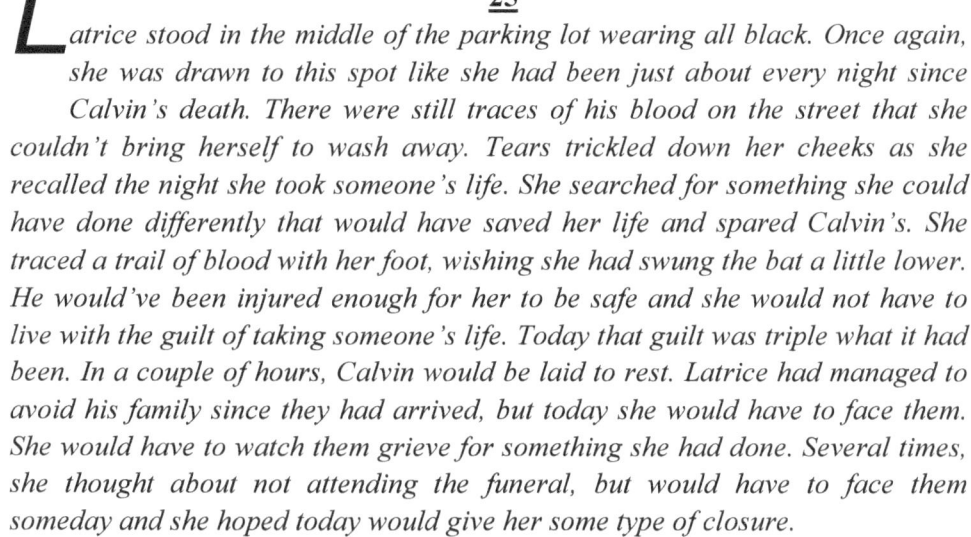

25

*L*atrice stood in the middle of the parking lot wearing all black. Once again, she was drawn to this spot like she had been just about every night since Calvin's death. There were still traces of his blood on the street that she couldn't bring herself to wash away. Tears trickled down her cheeks as she recalled the night she took someone's life. She searched for something she could have done differently that would have saved her life and spared Calvin's. She traced a trail of blood with her foot, wishing she had swung the bat a little lower. He would've been injured enough for her to be safe and she would not have to live with the guilt of taking someone's life. Today that guilt was triple what it had been. In a couple of hours, Calvin would be laid to rest. Latrice had managed to avoid his family since they had arrived, but today she would have to face them. She would have to watch them grieve for something she had done. Several times, she thought about not attending the funeral, but would have to face them someday and she hoped today would give her some type of closure.

The nightmares were just as strong as the day it happened. Only now, out of respect for her mother, Marlon wasn't in her bed to help her through it. He had compromised with Sylvia by offering to sleep on the couch when she demanded he stay at his mother's house. When the nightmares got really bad, Latrice would go lay on his chest. In the morning, she'd hear her mother fussing, but Marlon quickly put an end to it.

When she stood in this spot, she could see Calvin's lifeless body lying in the street with his eyes wide and blood shot. An eerie presence would surround her; Calvin's spirit was there to torment her. No matter how terrified she was, her feet were glued to that spot. She stood trembling and her chest heaved with each breath as her mind replayed the events in vivid detail. Flashing lights from police cars, the low hum of whispering neighbors, and the smell of blood and death were fresh like it was happening all over.

She was on the verge of hyperventilating when Marlon wrapped his arms around her. "Latrice baby, why are you doing this to yourself?" His voice snapped her out of her trance and she turned in his arms, wailing into his chest. Once again, he gripped her tightly in his embrace and prayed for her strength.

They were still standing in the street when Calvin's family arrived. Latrice's stomach twisted into knots as Ms. Stewart walked toward her. Breathing deeply, she tried to calm her stomach and her nerves, but it was no use. She let go of Marlon to dry her face and he stepped up to Calvin's mom and spoke. Latrice couldn't hear a word they were saying, but just the fact that Marlon was intervening soothed her nerves. There was no doubt in her mind that he was putting Ms. Stewart in her place, the same way he had done her mother several times during the week. When Latrice finally approached Ms. Stewart, her arms were outstretched to embrace Latrice. Her face didn't bare the expression of a woman filled with wrath, but was full of sympathy and shame.

"My dear Latrice." Tears rolled down her face as her arms wrapped around Latrice. "The people you have handling the funeral arrangements told me everything my son put you through. I wish you would have called me when everything started. I have always known what my son was capable of, but when I saw how much he loved you, I thought it would be different." She shook her head as she stepped back. "This is my fault. I should have forced him to get help before he married you." Before Calvin moved out of her house, Ms. Stewart had walked in on him a few times being abusive to women. He had even slapped a woman across the face at the dinner table for making a comment that he had deemed disrespectful.

"Neither of you are to blame. Calvin knew he had a problem and Calvin refused to get help." Marlon placed a hand on both women's backs.

Ms. Stewart relented, "Latrice, I have to warn you, not everyone is going to greet you with open arms. My other children adored Calvin and never witnessed the horrible things he did to the other women he dated. I tried to explain it to them, but their grief is too overwhelming for them to listen to reason."

Before Latrice could respond, Paul, Sheena, Jaleel, Delisa, Tim, and Camilla pulled up followed by two long black limousines. It was time for them to head to the funeral. Everyone piled out of their cars, including the remainder of Calvin's family. Latrice wiped the lingering tears, threw her shoulders back, and prepared her mind for whatever the family threw her way.

Latrice greeted Camilla and all of them with hugs and kisses. Then, she turned to Calvin's family. She wouldn't allow the scowls that awaited her to prevent her from being cordial. With extended hand, she approached them with a smile on her face, but her hand was left hanging in the air. Just as Calvin's sister fixed her mouth to cuss Latrice out, Paul intervened.

"I understand everyone is a little emotional right now, but I have something you guys should look at before we leave." He handed over a manila folder full of pictures. Calvin's brother and sister flipped through the folder and with each photo their expressions changed from anger and hatred to horror. Latrice knew exactly what was in the folder. She'd forgotten all about those pictures. Paul had insisted on taking photos of her injuries just in case they ever needed proof of the abuse.

"My brother did this to you?" When Latrice nodded, both siblings shamefully turned to their mother and passed her the folder. She declined to look; she already knew what her son was capable of. The air was thick with tension. No words were exchanged, only apologetic glances and nods of acceptance. Latrice breathed a sigh of relief. She had been dreading this moment all week and was ecstatic that it hadn't turned out the way she envisioned. Everyone piled into the limousines while Marlon ran upstairs to lock up and escort Sylvia downstairs.

The ride to the church was a lot shorter than Latrice had anticipated and when the limo stopped she wasn't ready to face Calvin again. Everyone started to climb out, but she couldn't seem to get her body to move. Marlon whispered in her ear, "You can do this. You need to go in there and close this chapter of your life. Just a few more hours and all the hell you have endured over the past two and a half years will be over." He gripped her hand, encouraging her to follow him out of the limo.

Latrice stood on shaky knees as she watched the pallbearers lift the casket out of the hearse. Marlon physically supported Latrice with every step she took. The church was practically empty. There were a few extended family members, business partners, and employees scattered through the pews, but not the crowd she was expecting to see. Perhaps everyone had seen through the front Calvin put on and saw the monster he really was.

Latrice sat listlessly through the funeral service. Pastor Hawkins was gracious enough to officiate over the service and perform the eulogy, but Latrice didn't hear a word he said. When it was her turn to say her last goodbye to Calvin, Marlon stood by her for strength. He placed his arm around her waist to support her wobbly knees. She knew Calvin's family was watching, wondering what her and Marlon's relationship was, but at that moment she didn't care. As she stared down at Calvin, her body trembled under the weights of grief and remorse. Her breath caught in her throat and nausea crept into her stomach. Her eyes bulged as she recalled the sight of his bloodied face struggling to breathe as the life drained from him.

Marlon called her name several times to get her to refocus on him, but it was no use. Her body was standing there, but her mind was gone. Marlon carried her out of the church; she was still unresponsive. He grabbed and shook her by the shoulders, and still nothing. He called her name and tapped her cheeks. Finally, she blinked and looked him in the eye. She crumbled to the ground and dry heaved onto the cement. She hadn't much of an appetite lately and her stomach had no substance to purge. Silently praying, Marlon continued to care for her. He cleaned her mouth and wiped sweat from her brow; then he helped her into the limo.

At the cemetery, Latrice opted to remain in the limo. She was on the verge of hyperventilating and her legs did not have enough strength to stand. While everyone else saw Calvin to his final resting place, Marlon remained in the car to calm Latrice. He caressed her, kissed her, and prayed for her, but all his efforts were futile.

Latrice understood defending herself that night was absolutely necessary. If she hadn't protected herself, she could've very well been the one being laid to rest. What she couldn't get past was the fact that someone's life had been cut short because of her actions. She lost control just as Calvin had so many times. Although he was motivated by anger and she by fear, she felt that she was no better than he was. She watched the family he left behind mourn and it was all because of her.

When they finally made it back to Latrice's apartment, Marlon helped her into bed and as he pulled the covers over her, she mumbled, "Please leave. I do not want you here." Marlon knew she was worn out and hurting, but he refused to leave. Sylvia demanded that he respect her daughter's wishes. When Latrice's muffled voice murmured through the covers, "I just need some time alone." Marlon had no choice but to respect it.

Marlon packed his things and reluctantly went back to his mother's house. He wanted to knock the smug look off of Sylvia's face, but it was pointless. He'd just have to deal with her attitude for a few more days and she would be gone.

Sylvia sat on the side of Latrice's bed pulling the covers back she stroked her daughters hair. If she could, she would've taken all her pain away, but this was something Latrice had to bare herself. All she could do was encourage her. "Latrice," Sylvia kneeled on the side of the bed to look in Latrice's eyes. "I know exactly what you need. You need to get away from here. There are too many memories. Every time you step outside you're reminded of that night."

"I know, but the only other place to go is the house I lived in with Calvin and I swore I'd never go back there."

"You could always come back home with me." She paused to let her offer sink in and Sylvia smiled when there wasn't an immediate refusal. She took Latrice's lack of protest to mean that she was seriously considering the idea. The only obstacle would be Marlon.

Latrice hoped she'd change the subject or leave her alone. When she felt extra weight rise off the bed and footsteps shuffling to the door she slumped into the bed and shut her eyes until keeping them closed was no longer forced. Sleep wafted over her and before long, her eyes were shifting rapidly beneath her lids as her dreams morphed into nightmares. This one was more vivid and terrifying than all the others.

> Keys jangled behind her as she walked down the dark, deserted street. It was eleven o'clock at night, but there was a thick fog that lingered as if the clouds were drifting to the ground. The jangling behind her became incessantly faster and louder. She racked her brain trying to figure out where she parked her car. Her heart raced with fear and within minutes, her feet joined the race. The thump of her heart, rattling of the keys, and the clacking of her heels on the hard cement set a rhythm that sent her anxiety into overdrive. The faster she ran, the longer the street became.

> Out of nowhere, Calvin called her name, instantly the rattle of the keys and the clacking of her heels halted. All that was left was the thumping of her heart, now joined with her panting. There was a wicked cackle in his voice as he called her name again. She spun in a circle, searching for a sign of him. She dreaded that he was lingering in a dark corner her eyes couldn't reach. Fear ignited her feet and once again she took off running. "You can't run from me," his voice cackled, giving her feet more fuel.

> She rounded a corner and ran smack dab into Calvin. Her body ricocheted off the massive wall of muscular flesh and she hit the ground. Remembering the many times he'd beat her senseless, she quickly stammered to her feet to flee from him, only to run right into another Calvin. Her eyes widened as she looked from one Calvin to the other. The first one was the Calvin she fell in love with; the second, the one who'd died in the middle of the street. The side of his head was caved in

with bruises aligning the side of his face. His eyes were bloodshot and blood oozed from his nose. One eye seemed to be dislodged and bobbed around in its socket. Both images donned the same depraved grin that sent a chill down her spine.

Searching the area with her eyes, Latrice looked for a way of escape only to find more Calvin's creeping out of the shadows. Each image was a replica of the original at a different point in their relationship. His image in every beating he had given her was etched into her mind and now here they all stood marching toward her drenched in sweat—each reciting the demeaning volatile words he spewed as he unleashed his fury upon her.

Latrice felt like the world was closing in on her as the likenesses made their way toward her. Within minutes, she was surrounded on every side. She saw the Calvin who stood at the altar on their wedding day, the Calvin who threatened to hurt her if she called her family, the one who caused the miscarriage of the only child she may ever conceive, and all the ones who physically and verbally assaulted her over the years. They all yielded their weapons of choice from bare hands to belts and chains, all which he used on her at some point.

Within a blink of an eye, a bat materialized in her hand. It was her against them. The original Calvin was the ringleader calling the shots for the assault to ensue. Before she could grasp a firm handle on the bat, they were all over her passing her back and forth as they slapped, punched, and spit in her face. She stumbled around the circle of men as each one exacted its rage upon her. When she finally dropped motionless to the ground bloody, bruised, and swollen, the Calvin she hated the most appeared. All the others backed away as he hovered over her. He tore her pants from her legs and without effort ripped off the flimsy fabric that covered her jewel. As he climbed on top of her, she struggled to keep her legs closed, but her weakened body was no match for him. Though her legs were easily pliable he purposely dug his nails into her thigh, drawing blood for his own pleasure. He impaled her with such brute force that tears formed in her eyes. He pounded into her as if trying to puncture her heart. His massive hand wrapped around her throat, gripping tighter and tighter as he approached his climax. Breathing was next to impossible and the struggle returned to her body as she bucked and squirmed for oxygen.

Latrice leaped out of bed, gasping for air. Her lungs burned intensely. She crawled across the floor to the bedroom door still searching for the oxygen to call for help. Tremors ferociously shook her body making it nearly impossible to move. When Latrice finally banged her head while attempting to stand, she was fully awake.

Latrice stumbled into the room her mother occupied trembling with sweat pouring down her face. "I thought about what you said and you're right. I need to get out of here, but let's leave in the morning. I can't take this any longer."

Sylvia pulled her daughter close. "You are making the right choice. Everything is going to work out just fine." She wanted to jump up and down, shout for joy, and do somersaults. *Latrice is moving back home and it didn't take as much work as I thought.*

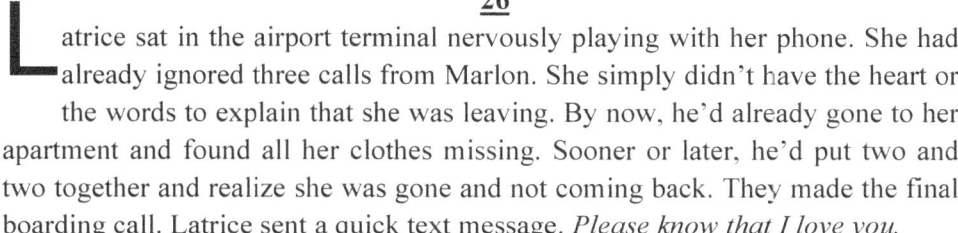

26

Latrice sat in the airport terminal nervously playing with her phone. She had already ignored three calls from Marlon. She simply didn't have the heart or the words to explain that she was leaving. By now, he'd already gone to her apartment and found all her clothes missing. Sooner or later, he'd put two and two together and realize she was gone and not coming back. They made the final boarding call. Latrice sent a quick text message. *Please know that I love you.*

Latrice powered down her phone, grabbed her carry on, and boarded the plane.

Marlon's heart sank into his stomach as he read the text. Instantly, he sent a text back.

Where are you?

He waited for a reply and when he realized there wouldn't be one, he sank to the bed. *She's gone.* Anchored with emotion, Marlon slid down to the floor. He was worried about what happened to make her leave, but as the time ticked by, worry quickly lost the fight. Fear hung around for a while. He was afraid he'd lost her—afraid of having to live without her. But in the end, it was anger that won out. He loved her and she had claimed to love him. How dare she leave like this? He had put his life on hold for months because he loved her and this is how she repaid him. Latrice turned out to be just like Alicia and Meme, taking his heart and stomping it into the ground. With that final thought, he stormed out of her apartment.

Marlon sped haphazardly down the freeway. Fire and emotions burned through his veins. At times like this, he normally called his sister, but the thought of her intensified the blaze. His foot leaned heavier on the accelerator and his car soared past the other commuters.

Sirens and flashing lights blared into his trance and for a moment he considered ignoring them, but thought better of it. Slowing his car to a stop on the right shoulder of the freeway, Marlon leaned his head back squeezing his eyes shut to fight back the tears threatening to fall. Losing Latrice hurt more than finding his wife cheating. When the female cop stepped up to his window, she must have seen the anguish on his face and decided to cut him a break. With the way he was driving, he should have been hauled off to jail for reckless endangerment. The pointed out several times, but wrote him a ticket for driving ten miles over the speed limit when he had to have been going at least thirty over.

Marlon pulled back into traffic and the tears began to pour. He arrived at his parent's house, packed up all his clothes, informed his dad that he would be taking over the apartment, and left without further explanation.

Halfway through the flight, Latrice broke down sobbing hysterically, "I can't leave him. What am I doing?" Her mind kept replaying the months they'd spent together, how he cared for her, and healed her by loving her. She remembered their lovemaking to the extreme that she could feel his hands caressing her. Most importantly, she thought of the long talks they had shared and the friendship they'd developed. Running away without talking to him was inconsiderate and he would never do that to her.

"Latrice, baby, calm down," Sylvia said, trying to console her, but it was useless. She wiped away her tears, but they poured out faster than she could wipe. A hint of remorse softened Sylvia's heart as she saw the depth of her daughter's love for Marlon. She realized what they had wasn't just some random rebound affair of two vulnerable hearts, but it was real love. She conceded to let her daughter go. "I understand, let's just consider this a long overdue visit. Stay for a couple of weeks and if you still choose to leave, I won't stand in your way."

Latrice nodded, laid her head in her mother's lap, and cried herself to sleep. There was nothing she could do in the air, but Latrice had no intention of leaving the airport. She had already decided to get off the plane and hop on to another. She was not going to waste any time away from Marlon.

Latrice stepped off the plane like a woman on a mission. Her feet were moving so fast, Sylvia had to run to keep up. Despite her pleas, Latrice refused to slow down. Desperately she searched for the ticket counter. She was so focused on getting back to Marlon she didn't see the group of people heading toward her. A shriek echoed in her ear, causing her to drop her purse, but when she saw where the sound came from, she smiled. The sight of her little sister, carrying a newborn, brought tears to her eyes. They were followed by her sister's husband she'd met overseas. Her sister passed the baby to her husband and ran to Latrice with outstretched arms. They collided into each other's embrace, holding each other for what seemed like an eternity. Along with her sister were her little brother and a couple of her aunts. The mini-reunion sidetracked Latrice and before she knew it she was walking, laughing, and catching up on the lives Calvin had isolated her from. She was so caught up in conversation that she walked right out the airport, forgetting her mission to get back to Marlon.

When she arrived at her mother's house, it was more of the same. Laughter and the aroma of barbeque greeted her at the door. She stepped inside, looked around at all the faces she hadn't seen in years, and once again was overcome with emotion. She made her way through the house greeting relatives and meeting new additions to the family, some by marriage and some by birth. She ate more than she had all week and laughed so hard that by the end of the day she collapsed on the bed in her old room and was out like a light.

Latrice had been too busy partying and having a good time in college to return home often and once she started building her career, visits where even less frequent. Then once she married Calvin, he outright refused to let her visit. She missed so much in the last nine years and was determined to get up to speed on everyone before she left.

For a couple hours Latrice slept like a baby, but before long, the nightmares showed back up.

Latrice mourned as she stood on the side of his grave. His casket had already been lowered into the ground and now her tears flowed from her eyes and plunged into the murky hole. The guests had left a long time ago and Latrice stood among strange mortuary employees who were finishing their job. Searching for solace and coming up short, Latrice released her last sob and cried her final apology before turning to walk away. She took one step toward her car and a hand popped up out the gloomy grave seizing hold of her ankle. Latrice screamed and tried to wiggle her way free to run toward her car, but the struggle only caused her to fall to her knees. The hand slowly and relentlessly pulled her toward the hole. She pleaded for Calvin to let her go, but his voice echoed, "I will never let you go."

Her struggle for freedom became more frantic as she dug her nails into the ground gripping for friction to stop her from sliding into the hole. Her efforts were pointless, steadily her body slid toward the hole, slowly creeping over its edge. In a last resort to stay above ground, Latrice dug her elbows into the ledge to keep her torso out of the grave.

She pleaded with the mortuary workers for help, but their response was to continue shoveling dirt into the grave.

"I will never let you go," echoed one last time before the hand yanked her ankle, causing her to fall backward into the dark pit.

Wailing, Latrice landed inside the open casket with her back against Calvin's chest. His arms, cold from death, wrapped around her and she froze. Fear took the fight out of her body and she whimpered as he whispered in her ear, "I will never let you go," then the lid to the casket slammed shut.

Latrice jumped out of bed in a cold sweat. She had fought so hard in her sleep that her covers and pillows were on the floor. She checked the clock. One in the morning in Atlanta meant Marlon was still at work. Even though he had been off work for a whole week to be with her, she knew he'd gone back to work. Latrice left her room in search of her cell phone and could've kicked herself when she realized she never turned it back on when she got off the plane.

There were several text messages and missed phone calls from Marlon, but only one voicemail that made her heart drop into her stomach. "Latrice, we promised that we would never hurt each other the way our spouses did. You walking out the way you did hurt more than anything Alicia did. I gave you my heart and you shattered it. I could have loved you through this just as I have these past few months. I hope you find happiness and peace, because that is all I ever wanted for you."

Latrice climbed back into bed gripping the phone to her chest. "Did he break up with me?" She asked herself. There was finality and a dismissive edge in his tone and after the third time listening to the message she concluded, "He broke up with me."

Tears flowed down her face in full force as she typed what would be her final message to him. *I got your message. I am sorry and I won't contact you again.* She curled up into the fetal position and cried her eyes out.

Marlon had spent hours in the kitchen of the restaurant trying to cook, but it was obvious he was off his game. After several burns and cuts, he retreated to his office. Cole had never seen him this distracted. He had a bottle of wine brought up and joined Marlon in his office. Marlon was never much off a drinker, but accepted the glass hoping it would take the edge off. They sipped in silence for several moments before Marlon offered Cole an explanation to his sullen attitude.

"She left me," Marlon grumbled, downing the contents in his glass then reaching for the bottle to refill it.

Cole's eyes widened with disbelief. He had just seen them together a little over a week ago and there was so much chemistry flowing between them that it was hotter in the office than it was in the kitchen. He was a confirmed bachelor and couldn't understand how Marlon had gone from a devastating break up to another committed relationship. He preferred to play the field. Marlon was the exact opposite.

"Did she say why?"

"Nope." Marlon downed the second glass of wine within seconds and poured a third. "I went to her apartment this morning. All her stuff was gone and she sent me a text saying that she loved me. I haven't heard from her since."

Silence filled the room. Marlon finished his third glass of wine and reached for the bottle again, but Cole beat him to it. "This is not the answer." Cole moved the bottle out of reach. "I know you are hurting, but getting drunk is not going to help you. You have to be thinking straight when she calls. Trust me, she will call. I saw you guys together and she loves you."

Marlon stood and turned his back on Cole. The dam holding back his tears was about to break, and he was not about to cry in front of his boy. "I hear you man. Can you give me a minute alone?" Cole saw the tears and gave him his space, taking the bottle of wine with him.

Marlon's cell phone buzzed in his pocket and his heart jumped hoping it was Latrice. He read the text and another tear trickled down his face. For the life of him, he couldn't figure out what had happened to make her leave. He knew the past week had been rough on her, but until the day of the funeral, they were closer than ever. He gripped his phone, staring at the keypad wondering what he should reply, but nothing came to mind. He typed, *I love you, please don't leave me,* but deleted it. Then he typed, *Why are you doing this*, but deleted that too. Unable to think of anything, Marlon placed his phone back into his pocket and marched to his car.

The drive home was a blur. Marlon didn't know how he made it home. He didn't remember stopping at red lights or stop signs, or even how fast he was driving, but he made it home safely. Buzzing off the three glasses of wine, Marlon staggered into the apartment numb to the pain of his break up. After a quick shower, he climbed into bed and was fast asleep.

In the morning, Marlon woke with a different mindset. He wasn't going to let Latrice go that easy and was determined to do whatever he needed to do to get her back. After having a taste of real love he didn't want to live without it, and refused to allow Latrice's fear and grief to destroy their relationship.

Marlon felt every drop of wine from the night before. He couldn't remember the last time he had a drink and his headache was definitely making him regret it. He had to get his mind to focus on finding Latrice. Hiring a private investigator crossed his mind, but he did not want to subject her to the same invasion of privacy that Calvin had. Every idea he came up, with he quickly shot down when he thought of how it would affect Latrice. He didn't want to be another man hunting her, tracking her every move like she was his prey. No matter how passive the plan, the root of it was tracking down a woman who at this point didn't want him to find her. He had to respect her wishes. He had already figured she went home with her mother, but until she called asking him to come, he would stay put.

The fervor and determination that he had arisen with quickly died. It had to be her choice to come back to him. The only thing he could do was make sure she knew how much he wanted that and how much he loved her. With that thought he picked up his cell and called Latrice again. With each ring, his pulse accelerated and when the phone clicked, he expected the voicemail, but Latrice's voice floated through his ear and settled around his heart. For a moment, he was at a loss for words. Everything he planned to say floated out of his mind the moment her voice drifted in. It was Latrice who spoke first.

"Marlon, I can't play this game with you right now."

"What game am I playing?"

"You dismiss me from your life in a voicemail and then…"

"Correction, you dismissed me when you left town without telling me." Marlon's anger over the situation had taken over and his voice escalated. "First, you put me out of your apartment for no reason, without any explanation, and then I come back the next day and you're gone." He sighed as once again his roller coaster of emotions shifted gears, anger out, sorrow in. "I am so tired of the women I give my heart to stomping on it." Marlon's voice cracked as he choked back his tears. "How did you think I would feel when I came back to the apartment and you were gone? Walking into that empty apartment hurt more than walking into my bedroom to find my wife screwing someone else. If you want out of this relationship, I am not going to stop you, but know that no one will love you the way I do." With that said Marlon hung up the phone.

He hurled his phone across the room shattering it to bits against the wall. Marlon was furious. The conversation had gone in an entirely different direction than what he had anticipated. He hoped she'd apologize for leaving and beg him to come get her, not accuse him of dismissing her and playing games.

For moments after the call ended, Latrice sat with the phone attached to her ear. Tears formed in her eyes, but never fell. Her body froze as her mind processed everything Marlon had said. The message he left replayed in her mind and she pictured him standing alone in the apartment trying to figure out where she was and came to a conclusion. *She screwed up.* His message wasn't dismissive; it was him trying to accept what he thought she wanted. *I hope you find happiness and peace, because that is all I ever wanted for you.* His words now rang louder and clearer than ever before.

Latrice dropped the phone, but quickly scampered to pick it up and called Marlon back. Once she hit the call button, she held her breath as she waited for it to ring, but it never did. The call went straight to voicemail. Latrice called several more times and got voicemail. She then resolved that he just didn't want to talk to her. Latrice decided to give him his space. When he was ready to talk, he would call and then she'd apologize and beg him to take her back. At least that was her plan, but over the next few days, Marlon didn't call and every time she called him she got his voicemail.

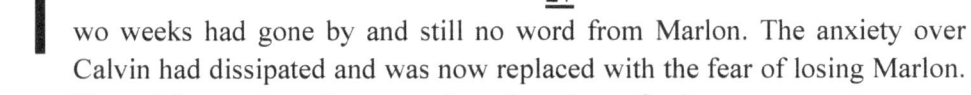

27

Two weeks had gone by and still no word from Marlon. The anxiety over Calvin had dissipated and was now replaced with the fear of losing Marlon.

The nightmares and tormenting thoughts of abuse were now gone. Depression was her new demon and it rode her morning, noon, and night. Even now, she pulled her head out of the toilet bowl and brushed her teeth, her heart ached for Marlon. Vomiting was now part of her morning routine. She was up at the crack of dawn, cried for about an hour, threw up, and pulled herself together for a conference call.

Mr. Fuller had shown up at her mother's house, stating he was now prepared to read the will. At first, she couldn't figure out how he had found her, but quickly realized that a man of his stature was very well connected and could find whomever he wanted. The news he gave her regarding Calvin's estate would have made anyone happy, but not Latrice. Ironically, Calvin had been bluffing when he said she would get nothing if anything happened to him. As it turned out, he gave her everything: houses she didn't know he owned, cars he never let her drive, his money, and his company which was the reason for the conference calls. With all the wealth she'd acquired, the most valuable thing Calvin left her was a piece of paper. The last thing Alistair Fuller gave her before he left was a note that Calvin had written before Latrice left him.

Dear Latrice,

If you are reading this, it means that I am dead and the monster that lives in me did not take your life. I know your life with me was horrible and at my hand you have endured hell. Please know that I have loved you from the first day I set eyes on you. I wish that I could have been the man you deserved, but no matter how hard I tried, I could not overcome the beast in me. Since I couldn't love you in life, let me love you in death. Everything I own is yours. The money, cars, houses, and my business all belong to you. I hope through them you can have the comfort and peace of mind that I could never give.

Love,

Calvin

That piece of paper alone did what nothing else could; it gave her peace over what she'd done to Calvin. She no longer beat herself up about protecting herself, but she had moved on to a much more gut-wrenching dilemma. She was head over heels in love with a man who wanted nothing to do with her. In order to effectively run her new company, she would eventually have to move back to San Diego, but couldn't bear the thought of living in the same city with Marlon and not being able to talk to him, hold, kiss, or even make love to him.

Latrice was glad it was a teleconference and not a video conference. Her eyes were red and puffy from all the crying and her skin pale from vomiting. Today it was the worst that it had been and Latrice decided that after the conference call, she would take her mom's advice and go see a doctor. Be it physical or mental, she needed help.

Latrice drug herself down to the kitchen and made a pot of coffee. The aroma alone perked her up a bit and she called into the office.

"Good Morning ladies and gentlemen. I know a few of you have been on edge regarding the security of your jobs and the direction the company will take under my leadership. Well," Latrice paused to take a long sip of her coffee. "Let me put everyone at ease. As long as you stay loyal to the company, you have a job. I know transition and change are very hard to handle, and if anyone feels they cannot work under my leadership or cannot adjust to change, speak now. We will prepare you a nice severance package and write you a glowing recommendation." Latrice paused again, taking an even longer sip of coffee allowing anyone to speak up. Despite her earlier mood a smile crept across Latrice's face at the lack of response.

"Good, I look forward to working with everyone. Starting Monday, I will be reviewing all personnel records that were sent to me. Then, I will be contacting you individually. At that time, I want your client profiles and portfolio summaries faxed to me. If, after reviewing them, I find that you are and always have been a loyal, team player you have my trust. I have already read through the files of employees who do not work directly with clients, so I will start with them. This will give everyone else an ample amount of time to prepare the information I am requesting. I suggest those of you who are considering leaving someone or certain information off your list to reconsider. I know more than you think and deception will cost you your job." With that said Latrice concluded the call, hoping the transition went smoothly.

For once, Latrice was grateful for every business dinner she had to attend, every file she had to review, and all the time spent cleaning Calvin's office. She had listened and learned more than she let on; now it was paying off.

Before they married, she had thoroughly researched Calvin and his company to get an understanding of what he did. When they started dating and he took her to a business dinner for the first time, she was intrigued by what she heard. From then on, she'd smile and was friendly with the business associate's wives and girlfriends, but always had one ear tuned to Calvin's conversation. After awhile, she was able to hold her own in conversation, should any of the men dare to address her. The first time it happened, Calvin sat back and watched with pride as Latrice eloquently answered every question the man had asked. After dinner, Calvin couldn't get her home fast enough and made love to her with the gentlest passion she'd ever felt. It wasn't rough or rushed, but it was deep, soul stirring, and ended with Calvin professing his love for her.

Latrice smiled at the memory; it was one of the few happy ones she had of Calvin.

She finished her cup of coffee, placed it in the strainer, and went up stairs to shower. Before entering her room, her brother poked his head out the room across the hall.

"Hey Tricey, how are you feeling?" The concern in his voice let Latrice know he'd heard her throwing up earlier.

"Right now, I feel great, but earlier this morning not so much," Latrice chuckled.

"I know. I heard you, and so did mom. She scheduled you an appointment at the clinic and made me promise to get you there, so if you could make this easy on me, I'd appreciate it."

Moms are nosy and always in your business, they say what they feel even when you don't want to hear it, but they are always there when you need them. "No fight. What time is the appointment?"

"We need to leave in about two hours."

Latrice agreed, stepped inside her room, and shut the door. Her eyes roamed the room. It was still decorated the same way it was the day she left for college nine years ago: pink and purple décor, a small stack of books on the dresser covered with dust, and Usher Raymond posters on every wall. He was the top R&B artist back then and if you'd asked Latrice, her future husband. She'd spend hours listening to his music and daydreaming about meeting him. She had managed to record every one of his videos and watched them over and over again, either fantasying or trying to learn his dance moves.

Latrice laughed out loud and shook the silly memory from her head. This time warp was not where she wanted to be and the more she looked around, she wanted her life with Marlon back. Latrice pulled out her laptop; she figured if she couldn't reach him on the phone, she could write him a letter. She typed herself up into an emotional frenzy, but was determined to finish. She knew she'd probably only have this one shot to convince him to take her back; the letter had to be perfect. Putting so much time into it left her with merely thirty minutes to shower and dress before her appointment. Stuffing the letter into her purse, Latrice rushed off to shower. By the time she exited her bedroom, her brother was standing in the hallway stomping his foot.

"I thought I was going to have to drag you out of the room."

"BJ Relax. I said I was going to the appointment. I just got caught up with something. Do you think you can run me to the post office after we leave the clinic?"

"If you just need to mail something, I have some stamps and we can drop it in the mailbox on our way so it makes the 2:30 pick up."

Latrice kissed BJ on the cheek and they were out the door. In no time at all, they'd mailed the letter, arrived at the doctor's office, been sent to the lab, and were now back in the waiting room waiting for the doctor to receive the lab results. Just as Latrice was starting to get restless, the doctor walked into the lobby with a smile on his face and a little white bag in his hand. Sitting next to her on the bench, the doctor announced loud enough for everyone to hear.

"Congratulations Mr. and Mrs. Stewart; you are going to have a baby."

Latrice sat straight up in her seat, her eyes wild with bewilderment. Her mind was racing a hundred miles a minute and the only thing she could think to say was, "That's my brother."

Seeing their expressions, the doctor toned down his exuberance. Speaking softly he relayed the usual speech he gave to the unexpected mothers to be that came into his office. Prenatal pills, take one a day, make a follow-up appointment with your OB/GYN, here is a paper about options other than childbirth and adoption if you so choose. He then shuffled out the room ten times faster than he'd sauntered in. Latrice grabbed her things and fled from the waiting room. By the time BJ caught up to her she was standing on the side of the car laughing with tears rolling down her face. He thought for sure she'd lost her mind; nothing about the situation was funny. Helping her into the car, he kept his mouth shut, but once he hopped into the driver's seat, he tested her sanity.

"I know this has to be scary. Your husband, the father of your unborn child is dead, but I promise…" the abrupt halt in her laughter interrupted him and the look on her face made him think that she had most definitely lost her mind.

"This isn't Calvin's baby."

"What?"

"I left Calvin months ago and up until the night he attacked me, I hadn't seen him except for a few minutes when he found me at church. If this was his baby, I would have known before now. This is Marlon's baby."

"Who in the hell is Marlon?"

Even his abrasive tone couldn't wipe the smile off of Latrice's face. "He's the man that took care of me after I left Calvin."

"More like the man that took advantage of you."

"Boy, drive this car. You are not my daddy." Latrice playfully punched him in the arm, and then relaxed into her seat. Closing her eyes, Latrice allowed her mind to replay every time Marlon made love to her wondering which time they'd conceived their child. Every time they were together had been unprotected and neither of them cared. Since she didn't use protection with Calvin, Latrice assumed that the miscarriage she had at the beginning of her marriage had affected her ability to have children. Now, she had a piece of Marlon inside her and no matter what his response to her letter. He'd always be with her.

Latrice spent the entire ride home reliving her sexual excursions with Marlon and she was in desperate need of a cold shower. She hoped she hadn't moaned out loud with her brother sitting next to her and rushed into the house to avoid hearing anything he had to say. Latrice high-tailed it into the house through the kitchen past her mother and sister with her brother close on her heels.

"Tricey wait. We need to talk." When she didn't stop, BJ enlisted his mother's help. "Mom, Tricey is pregnant."

Latrice spun around on her heels and went after her brother so fast that he barely had time to get away. "How dare you put my business out there like that? FYI Mom and I have already had this discussion about my relationship with Marlon. I hope whatever you were hoping to accomplish by putting me on blast is worth this butt whipping you're getting ready to get." She lunged at him, but her mother jumped between them. Latrice pinned her brother with a look that told him to watch his back and spun on her heels and marched out of the kitchen.

Latrice caressed her stomach as she pondered her next move. There was no question whether she'd tell Marlon about the baby, but when to tell him was the question. She didn't want him to take her back out of obligation to the baby. Marlon was an honorable man who would do just that, but Latrice wanted his love and therefore decided to wait for his response to her letter before telling him about the baby. A knock at her door interrupted her musings and she reluctantly told whoever it was to enter. Latrice sat up with a smile on her face as her sister walked in. Their relationship was one of brutal honesty and support. They were always upfront with each other, but would support the other's decision whether they agreed or not. Latrice knew her sister was about to give it to her straight, but had her back regardless. Deidre rushed over and wrapped her arms around her sister.

"You sure know how to shake things up around here. I haven't seen mom this pissed since I showed up at her house with a husband." She laughed at the memory as she kicked her shoes off to join Latrice on the bed. "I don't care what anyone has to say I am happy for you. You are going to be a great mother."

"Thanks, DeDe. Speaking of great mothers, you are doing a great job."

"Thanks. It's hard sometimes, but I couldn't have asked for a better father for my child." Deidre smiled at the perfect segue to the real reason she came to talk. "Speaking of the father of my child, tell me about yours."

"Smooth, real smooth," Latrice chuckled at her sister's subtlety.

"What? Would you rather me believe what mom had to say about him?" Latrice rolled her eyes, but prepared to defend her man against the lies her mother was telling.

"Well, I told you about the man who looked after me during the day. What I didn't tell was that we fell in love. He had recently left his wife because he caught her cheating. The first day I met him, I had just left Calvin. My face was bruised and swollen, I was hideous, but he told me I was beautiful. He agreed to look after me during the day since he worked nights, and the way he took care of me made me feel more loved than I have my whole life. He waited on me hand and foot and was so gentle. I don't know when it started happening, but the slightest touch or smile from him made me tingly all over.

Then, one day, he was going for a jog, I totally freaked out about being alone; he told me he wouldn't be gone long and walked out. He was gone for no more than two minutes before he came back in and wrapped his arms around me apologizing for upsetting me. I think I fell in love with him right then, but had too many issues to acknowledge it. Then, one day he had this stressful meeting with his wife and I offered a massage to help him relax. I guess I got too into it because I got a little turned on." Latrice laughed at the shock on her sister's face, but continued. "I ran out of the room, but he chased after me. After I explained how I was feeling, he laid me down and gave my body what it had been missing. Everything grew from there. The more time I spent with him, the less I thought about Calvin. I love him more than I ever thought possible."

"Trust me I know exactly how you feel. I fell so hard and so fast for my husband that I married him before I had a chance to tell anyone. But answer this, if you love him so much, why are you here?"

"Because I am crazy," Latrice laughed. "But I don't want to use the baby to get him to take me back. I sent him a letter explaining how much I love him. If he feels the same way and takes me back, then we will be a family. If he doesn't, then I will accept that and whatever involvement he wants in his child's life. I will give him a few days to respond, if he doesn't then I have my answer. We will be co-parents instead of husband and wife."

"Well, I guess I better start losing this baby fat so I can look good in my bride's maid's dress, because Marlon would have to be a fool to not take you back." The sisters talked for hours, reliving old times and renewing their friendship. Latrice felt like she had someone in her corner that would support her and Deidre was glad to have her sister back.

28

Marlon was at his kitchen table putting a SIM card into his new cell phone when the door bell rang. The past three weeks without Latrice had been torture. He couldn't eat or sleep, but still his pride wouldn't let him ask Camilla for her number. He wasn't even sure if anyone else knew Latrice had left, but didn't want to deal with all the questions, so he suffered for three weeks. He was so anxious to call her that whoever was at his door pissed him off before he even answered it.

The scowl on his face when he opened the door would have scared anyone off, but she'd seen it many times before and was prepared to see it today, "Good morning."

"What do you want?" Marlon turned his back on her and walked back into the kitchen.

"My brother back. I have been calling you for weeks and thought you were ignoring my calls because you were still mad at me until I talked to mom. She said you weren't answering her calls either. She's been worried sick. Then, this came in the mail and now Mom is freaking out." Meme held up an envelope. "Where is Latrice?"

"What is that?" Marlon sat forward in his chair and rubbed his hand across his face. He was quickly getting annoyed with his sister; she'd lost her right to be concerned about his life.

"It's a letter from Latrice and by the return address, she's in Atlanta. What happened?" Marlon snatched the letter from her hand and took it to his room to read in private.

Dear Marlon,

I broke my promise to never hurt you and I am sorry for causing you pain. Some would say marrying Calvin was the biggest mistake of my life, but I say leaving you was the biggest. Please know that my leaving had nothing to do with you or my love for you. Even in our separation, my love for you has grown. Just the simple thought of you still takes by breath away.

I left San Diego because I couldn't take the nightmares anymore and I thought a different environment would stop the torment, but I was wrong. For a while the nightmares intensified and I didn't have you to hold me. I am over the nightmares now, but can't bear the thought of living without you.

I have been trying to call you and beg you to forgive me, but I guess you've been too upset to take my calls. So, I am writing you this letter to make things clear. I refuse to lose the love of my over a misunderstanding or words unspoken. I LOVE YOU. I was crazy to have ever gotten on that plane or even to have entertained the thought of leaving. Mid-flight I had a panic attack when I realized what I was doing. I was going to come back as soon as I could, but then I got your message and misinterpreted it to mean that you didn't want me. But there will be no more confusion. Plain and simple, I want you in my life to have and to hold till death do us part. My heart and soul belong to you, should you want them, you know how to reach me.

Love Always,
Latrice

Marlon folded the letter and went to get his cell phone. He wasn't going to let another minute go by without letting Latrice know he wanted her too, but when he stepped into the kitchen his sister was still there.

Before he could give Meme a piece of his mind, she stood placing his cell phone in his hand. "I got you on the next flight to Atlanta. I don't know what is going on between you two, but you guys belong together. Go get her and bring her home." Not allowing him to protest, Meme gripped his shoulders and turned him around pushing him toward his bedroom. "Pack an overnight bag and I will take you to the airport."

Go get her. Yeah, go get her. He'd much rather see her and have this conversation in person than over the phone. Marlon quickly packed his bag. Within minutes, they were out the door and flying down the freeway to Lindbergh Field Airport.

"Marlon." Meme finally had him in a place where he had no choice but to listen to her and she was going to take advantage. "I need you to forgive me. I know I am asking a lot, but I can't live like this. I don't know what possessed me to do what I did and I am having a hard time living with myself." Now she had his undivided attention. "I get sick every time I think about how I betrayed you. I don't know how I expect you to get past this when I can't even get past it."

"I can tell you how it happened. You turned your back on the Lord and went searching for love instead of allowing him to bring it to you. I know you've met some really bad men, but they are not all bad. You only became attracted to

218

women after you made up your mind that all men were dogs. You used to love men and you will never convince me that you were just putting up a front to hide your homosexuality. If I ever find the man that hurt you, he will regret the day he was born." Tears flooded down her cheeks, but Marlon didn't let up. "I also know that this lesbian stuff isn't the real you. If this is how you choose to live your life then I will love and support you, but don't punish yourself or your soul mate by hiding out in gay bars. Come back to the Lord and let him heal you."

"I hear you, but it is so hard."

"I know, but you don't have to do it alone. I am here for you." He didn't know for sure that she'd been hurt by a man, he just spoke from instinct. There was a time when he had to lecture her on the type of men she was dating, warning her to be careful. Then one day she'd just stopped. Marlon recognized the change in her. She became more secretive about where she was going and who she was going to be with. In the light of everything that had transpired over the past few months, everything now made sense. Meme was hiding her new lifestyle.

Marlon gave her napkins from the glove box to dry her face. Meme tried to focus on getting her brother to the airport safely. She couldn't believe how close he was to knowing the truth about why she stopped dating men. She vowed never to tell him and made everyone else involved promise the same. As they pulled in front of the terminal, Marlon took a moment to reply to her original statement.

"I forgive you. When I get back, let's get together for lunch like we used to."

"I'd really like that," Meme sighed, and almost broke down into tears again, but managed to hold it together. "Forget about me and focus on Latrice. You have to convince her that she cannot live without you."

"That won't be hard at all."

Meme rolled her eyes at his cockiness, but Marlon wasn't being cocky at all. Based on the letter Latrice wrote, he was just speaking the facts. She'd been just as miserable as he had; there was no doubt in his mind that she'd return with him.

After having to practically strip at the security clearance and sprint to the gate Marlon made it just in time to board US Airways flight 163 departing at 11:00a.m. to Charlotte. He hated flying and eight hours of airplanes and airports was going to be torture, but being able to hold Latrice would make it all worthwhile.

As soon as the plane took off, Marlon got a little closer to God. The plane bounced around on pockets of air like it was a single engine plane or a crop duster. He prayed and pleaded, making all kinds of promises for God to steady the plane. When it finally leveled out, he opened his eyes, looking around to see if anyone saw him freaking out. Satisfied that he'd successfully concealed his panic attack, Marlon leaned over to stare out the window. Thanks to all the sleepless nights he had lately, he drifted off to sleep.

The plane arrived in Charlotte a little behind schedule and that hour and a half layover was almost nonexistent. By the time he found the gate and grabbed some Starbucks, it was time to board. Thank God that flight was smooth. They got up in the air, leveled out, the flight attendant offered drinks, and a few minutes later it was time to land.

The plane touched down in Atlanta at 9:30p.m. sharp and Marlon couldn't get off fast enough. His stomach was in knots as he grabbed his bag from the overhead compartment, fought traffic down the aisle, hopped on the first shuttle to the rental car company, rented the cheapest thing on wheels, punched in the return address from Latrice's letter into the GPS, and drove to get his woman.

Marlon was a bundle of nerves when he stepped onto the porch and rang the doorbell. He felt like a fourteen-year-old boy picking up a girl for their first date. He tried to quell his anxiousness, but nothing helped. At that moment, he realized just how much he missed her. When the door slowly cracked open, anticipation and joy filled Marlon's heart only to have it fizzle out when he saw Sylvia scowling on the other side. He was not in the mood for her or anyone else who tried to stop him from getting to Latrice.

"You better take good care of my little girl." She stepped to the side and allowed him to enter. After what Latrice had to deal with in her marriage, Sylvia wanted her daughter home so she could take care of her. Seeing how distraught Latrice was when she assumed Marlon wasn't going to respond to her letter was more than enough to convince Sylvia to let go.

With all the noise into the house, there must have been some sort of party going on. He could hear several different voices, but his heart held on to just one. The sweet sound of her voice and the sensuality in her laugh stirred him for the first time in weeks. He had to pause and put his emotions in check before walking into the room. As soon as he rounded the corner, all talking stopped and all eyes were on him.

Latrice felt his presence well before she saw him and when their eyes connected her breath caught in her throat. "What are you doing here?" She managed to say.

"I love you." He'd much rather have had this conversation without the audience, but if this is where she wanted to have it out, so be it.

"What took you so long to respond to my letter and why have you been ignoring my phone calls?" Latrice wanted to just go to him and melt into his chest, but she needed answers. She had already convinced herself that he wasn't going to call and had begun preparing her heart to get over him.

Marlon was done talking for now, he needed to touch her, hold her, kiss her, and then he would answer her question. Without hesitation, he stepped toward her and pulled her into an embrace. He seared her with a kiss that made her knees buckle. "Now, to answer your questions, I just got the letter this morning and I haven't been ignoring your phone calls. The last time we talked you pissed me off, I threw my phone, and it shattered. I don't have your number memorized." His words trailed down her neck with his kisses, her skin smooth across his lips, and her scent intoxicating. "I could have gotten the number from Camilla, but I didn't want anyone to know you left me."

Latrice clung to his chest, fearing if she let go she'd collapse to the floor. They were in a room full of her closest relatives, but as soon as Marlon stepped into the room everyone else ceased to exist. The second he touched her, all anger, frustration, and fear she'd felt over the past week dissipated and her love for him prevailed. The heat of his lips against her neck and the simple caress of his hand up and down her arm drove her wild. If she didn't reign herself in soon, her legs were going to be wrapped around his waist and everybody in the room would get an eye full.

Latrice gripped the back of his neck and pulled him toward her. The other hand slid up Marlon's chest and she prepared her mouth to devour him. A few nuzzles of his lips and a sensual moan rolled out of his mouth. Latrice smiled at his response and then went in for the kill. There was nothing gentle or passive about this kiss. Her leg was just creeping up his thigh when she heard several people in the background clearing their throats. Marlon finally ended the kiss, apologizing for their actions, but Latrice apologized for nothing.

"You must be Marlon," Deidre said, approaching with an extended hand. "I am DeDe, Latrice's younger sister." They shook hands and she pried him away from Latrice to introduce him to the rest of the family.

Marlon made his way around the house meeting aunts, uncles, and cousins. For the most part, everyone was friendly until he was introduced to BJ.

Latrice flashed BJ a look that warned him of what would happen if he opened his mouth and said anything about the baby. Thankfully BJ caught the warning and kept his mouth shut.

Once he'd met everyone, Latrice snatched him up before anyone had a chance to say anything else to him, "Come with me." She purred as she led him out the room. They walked toward the back of the house for more privacy. The sway of Latrice's hips had his tongue hanging out of his mouth and sent him into a lust-induced trance. *God help me*, Marlon thought as he put his hands in his pocket. He hoped that would help him behave, but when Latrice finally stopped walking and turned to face him, the tears in her eyes were enough to keep him in check.

Marlon opened his mouth to ask what was wrong, but Latrice put her hand over his mouth, preventing him from speaking, and with all sincerity pleaded for his forgiveness. "This entire situation is my fault. If I hadn't left the way I did. Three weeks of heartache and misunderstandings would not have happened. The night of Calvin's funeral, I had the worst nightmare. It felt like his spirit was trying to kill me in my sleep. I woke up out of breath and terrified. I wasn't thinking straight and thought moving away would put an end to my torment. I am sorry for not calling you first."

"You know what, yeah, I was pissed, but it's over now. Let's not dwell on it. I forgive you if you forgive me for allowing pride to prevent me from calling you." Marlon's hands made their way out of his pockets and slipped around her waist. Gradually, they crept under her shirt. He looked into Latrice's eyes, envisioning touching and kissing her the way his body craved. His gaze dropped to her quivering lips and he knew kissing her again would lead to the bed.

As if sensing his turmoil, Sylvia walked into the room. Marlon backed up and gave Latrice some space.

"I know you haven't seen each other in a while, but Latrice if you are still leaving in the morning, you should really spend more time with your family."

"This is your going away party?" Without waiting for an answer, Marlon led the way back to the living room. He'd let them celebrate all night if that meant she was coming back to San Diego. Trying to hide his excitement, Marlon took a seat on the sofa and pulled Latrice down next to him.

Latrice was irritated with her meddling mother. There was still so much that she needed to say. Marlon was going to be a father and she had no idea how he'd react to the news. He was married for four years and didn't have children;

maybe he didn't want any. Noticing the tension in her body and the distant look in her eyes, Marlon knew something was still bothering Latrice. He placed his hand on her leg, gently stroking her thigh. That helped ease some of the anxiety and she was able to sit back and relax.

Sylvia walked into the room bearing two cases of beer and Latrice sighed. *The party is just getting started.* Her aunt pulled out a deck of cards and BJ turned on some music. They were getting ready to have an old school, trash-talking game of spades. Latrice rolled her eyes. When the beer kicked in and someone's trash talking went too far, Marlon would see the worst side of her family and she was not ready for that. Spades plus alcohol equaled fights.

Their upbringing was very different. She was brought up with no form of Godliness, parents getting drunk on the weekend, family fights in the front yard, uncles smoking weed in the backyard, and someone hauled away by the police to detox. From what she knew of Marlon, he was raised in the church, which meant Sunday school, Bible class, and late-night church meetings; he was in for a rude awakening.

Latrice was just about to ask Marlon if he wanted to leave when Deidre asked, "Marlon, you want to be my partner?" Latrice was ready to interject when Marlon kissed the words off her lips and then joined her sister at the table.

Latrice prayed her baby left the table with his dignity intact. He was playing against her mom and aunt who were undefeated when partnered together. When Marlon said he had seven books in his hand, Latrice dropped her head in exasperation. *It is going to be a long night.*

Deidre asked, "Seven, are you sure?" You never ask the new guy to be you partner, but she knew how important it was for him to feel like part of the family. Calvin kept Latrice from them and Deidre didn't want the same thing to happen with Marlon.

Before Marlon could answer, Sylvia spoke up, "Quit talking the table. You said two, your partner said seven. Now bid nine and let's play the game." She sat back chuckling as she thumbed through her cards fanning them out.

Deidre and Marlon settled on eight and the other team six. With only thirteen books to be played, one team was going to come up short. Deidre had already accepted the loss and prepared her mind for her mom's gloating, but Marlon was confident as usual.

"Alright DeDe, let's show these old women what we're working with." DeDe snickered at the comment, but cut it short when she saw the look on her mother's face.

"Alright let's see if you still calling us old after we spank that…"

"Mom," Latrice jumped up to the table.

"What? He wants to be part of the family; I am just treating him like part of the family." Latrice knew it was true. If anyone else had made the comment, Sylvia would've responded the same way, but she still gave her mom a dirty look before taking her seat.

Marlon played the first card and Sylvia ate it up and took the first four books right off the back. From then on out, Marlon ran the table taking seven books straight. Then, Deidre ended strong with both jokers. Not only did they win the hand, but they got the nine books they originally anticipated, leaving Sylvia two books short and pissed off about it. It's hard to catch up when you're in the negative and even harder to talk trash when you're losing. Sylvia shut her mouth and tried to catch up, but Marlon knew how to bid his hand. One round, Sylvia and her partner were obviously dealt the better hand. The ninety points they scored was enough to significantly shorten Marlon's lead, but when the game was over, Marlon and Deidre came out on top.

Deidre screamed and high-fived Marlon like she was losing her mind. Latrice watched the whole game, shocked at how skillfully Marlon played. Deidre danced around, rubbing the win in her mother's face and everyone else's. Being the only one to beat the dynamic duo would give her bragging rights at every family function. She danced around her mother and stopped by her side trying to do the bump with her. Deidre wiggled and bumped her hip against Sylvia, but she was stiff as a board. "Come on Momma, help me celebrate," Deidre chuckled.

A night that usually lasted into the wee hours of the morning was now ending early. Suddenly, Sylvia was tired and needed to get some rest.

Latrice pulled Marlon down to the sofa as everyone else started to clean. "You know you're going to be a legend around here. No one has ever beaten them."

Marlon laughed. Deidre's celebration was strange, but now made sense. "Being a legend sounds good, but being your husband sounds even better." That same little black box that he'd given her a month ago was in his pocket. He wanted to give it to her as soon as he saw her, but she was angry with him, then he thought to give it to her when she led him out of the room, but Sylvia interrupted. Now he couldn't wait any longer. He pulled the box out of his pocket and placed in the palm of her right hand. "The first time I gave you this ring, you said couldn't accept it because wearing it while still married would dishonor our love." Marlon wiped the tears from her cheeks and opened the box. "We are both unattached and my love for you gets stronger and stronger as the days go by."

Movement around them had ceased and all eyes were on them. "Will you marry me?"

At her hesitation, Marlon was about to remind her that she promised to say yes, but at the risk of sounding ridiculous, thought better of it. His heart hammered in his chest as he waited for her response.

Latrice tried to stabilize her emotions and think clearly. "I love you, but we need to talk before I can answer."

"If you love me, what else is there to talk about?" Marlon unsuccessfully tried to hide his nervousness.

"Do you want children?"

"That's your choice. It is your body and I will never pressure you to do something you're not ready for. From what I've seen, pregnancy and childbirth strain a woman's body and I will never selfishly demand you do something like that if you're not ready. If you are never ready we can discuss adoption. I gave Alicia the same options and she wasn't ready for children either. I accepted it then and I will accept it now, but yes, I do want children."

Latrice wiggled her fingers in his face. "Yes, I will marry you." Marlon sighed with relief and slid the ring onto her finger. He hadn't prepared for the possibility of her saying no and she had him scared for a minute.

The moment the ring was on her finger the room erupted in applause, reminding them they were not alone. Everyone rushed over, offering their congratulations and when the crowd dispersed, Latrice grabbed Marlon's hand and placed it on her stomach. "I am glad you want children, because in a few months you are going to be a daddy."

Marlon snatched his hand away and sat up. "What did you say?"

"I'm pregnant," she stuttered.

Marlon's eyes dropped to her stomach and his hand slid across her flat belly. Covering his hand with hers, Latrice rested her forehead against his.

"We made a baby," she sang.

A smile spread across Marlon's face and you could hear the joy in his voice. "I'm going to be a daddy." It took everything in him to remain seated and not make a fool of himself in front of his soon to be in-laws.

Deidre hated to interrupt, but she was leaving and wanted to say goodbye. "Latrice, we're heading out, will you walk us to the door?"

Reluctantly, Marlon released her and watched her walk away. No sooner than she turned the corner, BJ plopped down next to him. Seeing the fire in his eyes, Marlon tried to ease the tension. "I have always wanted a little brother." He guessed BJ couldn't have been more than twenty-two years old and obviously hadn't mastered the art of holding his liquor.

"I already sat back and let her marry some fool I knew wasn't right for her and I will never forgive myself." He wasn't speech-slurring drunk, but if he finished that beer in his hand he would be. Marlon took the beer from his hand and put it on the table. "I won't let it happen again. At the first sign that you are not treating her right, I will be all over you."

Marlon laughed at this young buck's threat, but had to appreciate his protectiveness. "Well, let me put your mind at ease. With me, Latrice is safer than she has ever been. I don't want to hurt her or control her. I just want to love her."

"Well, you better, because I'd hate to have to throw these thangs on you." BJ jumped up boxing the air. He staggered backwards and tripped over the coffee table. Marlon leaped up to catch him, but was too late. BJ flipped over the table landing on his back. He turned the table over in the process, sending his beer, picture frames, and a crystal vase tumbling to the floor.

Latrice was standing on the porch having her own heated conversation with her sister.

"Girl, you did not tell me the brother was that fine."

I know, just the sight of him gets me all excited." Latrice fanned herself.

"I see," DeDe laughed. "That man walked into the room and you were ready to spread your legs right there in the living room in front of everybody. That's how you got knocked up."

Latrice gasped, looking around to see if anyone else had heard her sister. "If you hadn't stopped me, I might have." They clapped hands and fell into each other laughing. They were just getting started when DeDe's husband honked the horn.

"Alright, alright I am coming." She flung her arms around her sister. "I am going to miss you, please don't stay away so long again."

"I won't, I promise." Latrice released her sister and went back into the house. She walked in to the living room just in time to see her brother roll off his back. "I am not even going to ask what happened. You better have this mess cleaned up before Momma gets back." Latrice grabbed Marlon's hand and led him to her room.

So," Latrice smiled, as she kicked off her shoes. "We're getting married."

"So," Marlon mimicked her mood, "you're having my baby."

"Yes I am."

"Come here, baby." Marlon sat on the dresser and pulled her between his legs. "I am trying so hard to not make love to you right now."

"Well, seeing that it is after midnight and I have to be at the airport at 3:30 and haven't started packing, we have a lot of work to do to keep us occupied." Latrice retrieved her empty suitcases. "What time does your flight leave?"

"I don't have one. I wasn't expecting you to be leaving so soon. I guess I can try to fly standby on whatever flight you are on." Latrice pulled out her cell phone, called the airline, and purchased another first class ticket to San Diego. Aside from the new luggage set, a first-class plane ticket was the first thing she purchased with her newly acquired wealth. Clicking her phone closed, she saw the astonishment on Marlon's face. "Your fiancée is a very wealthy woman with houses, cars, and a very lucrative business. She can't have her man flying standby."

"He left everything to you?" Marlon stared wide-eyed at her revelation.

"Yes he did. It is all still a little overwhelming, but I'm pretty sure I'll get used to it. How do you feel about me being so wealthy?"

"I am not one of those men who have a problem with his woman making more money than him. I could use a sugar momma. I might even quit my job and take up golfing or something."

Latrice laughed loud and threw a pile of her clothes in his face. They packed her clothes and talked with the same light-hearted camaraderie that they'd developed over the past few months. By the time they finished it was time to head to the airport.

29

Three months later

The ink was barely dry on his divorce papers, but Marlon stood at the altar of Zion Pentecostal Church with tears in his eye as he watched his bride walk down the aisle. They both had been through all the hype of a big wedding and opted for a small, intimate ceremony instead. The church was moderately decorated with flowers around the altar and candles aligning the steps. Even their attire was less formal than a traditional wedding. Latrice wore a strapless, knee-length ivory dress that impeccably draped across her curves, flattering her baby bump. She would have married Marlon in her pajamas and slippers if she had to.

In their first weddings, they wanted everyone they knew to be there, the wedding party was huge, and they spent a fortune. But as Latrice walked down the aisle, there wasn't a church full of eyes on her. There was the soloist, Pastor Hawkins, her sister Deidre, Jaleel, their parents, and the one who mattered most, Marlon; everyone else waited for them at the reception. Slowly, Latrice made her procession down the aisle as the soloist sang his rendition of K-Ci & JoJo's, *All My Life*. The song was sung so beautifully, by the time Latrice stood before him, Marlon was in tears. Latrice wiped his tears with her own dampened handkerchief, and then slid her arm around his elbow as they turned toward the pastor.

"Marlon and Latrice," Pastor Hawkins opted to stray from his usual opening speech. "We are here today by the grace of God. The miracle of your union rivals that of the dead being raised. For two hearts that were once dead to love have been revived to love again. Hearts once lost, but now found; once blinded by hurt, but now they see. Pastor Hawkins continued with a prayer of unity, communication, support, and all it took to make a marriage work.

Latrice turned to Marlon and smiled as she recited her vows. They chose to write their own and she had no trouble finding the words to say. "I believe God created Eve from Adam's rib because the ribs protect the heart and today, I vow to protect your heart. You've given it to me and it is my most prized possession. I vow to support your dreams and nourish them like my own. I vow

228

to stand by your side during good times and bad. I vow to be your lover, your friend, and a mother to our children." She smiled, but when he recited his vows Latrice was crying profusely.

"You are a virtuous woman through and through and your price is far above rubies. I vow to treasure you like the precious gem that you are. You are more vital to my life than the heart pumping blood through my veins and I vow to give my heart to you and only you. You're the oxygen in my lungs that has given me life and I vow to share every day of that life with you. You give me strength to get up each day and I vow to give you that in return. My arms were made to hold you, my hands were made to caress you, and my lips to kiss you. I vow to do so for the rest of my life." Marlon barely made it through his vows and had to pause several times coaching himself to man up.

When he was finally able to kiss his bride, Marlon slid one arm around Latrice's waist, pulling her close and slid the other hand into her hair locking her in place, then entangled their tongues in the most heated kiss they'd ever shared. The kiss went on for minutes and nothing could stop them. That is until the little princess growing in Latrice's stomach chose that moment to kick for the first time.

Their bodies were pressed so firmly together that he felt it and jumped backed. "Was that the baby?" Marlon smiled and placed a hand on Latrice's stomach. Sure enough, his daughter kicked again. His heart swelled with love for his wife and leaned in to devour her mouth again, but Pastor Hawkins jumped in.

"I present to you Mr. and Mrs. Marlon Wright." He shook his head as he cocked a crooked grin toward his boy.

The first person Marlon saw was Meme as he walked into the reception. He knew not being invited to the ceremony hurt her, but he didn't want it tainted with memories of Alicia. With planning the wedding, preparing for a baby, searching for a house, and helping Latrice get settled in as the new owner of Stewart Investment Services, they hadn't the time to completely mend the fences.

To top it all off, she hadn't been invited to sit at the table with the family, and every time she made her way toward them to offer congratulations, Latrice would give her a look that said *don't even think about it*. The aggravation and tension swelled every time she looked at the head table with people who weren't even blood relatives seated around it. Before long, Meme was knocking back the champagne, hoping to relax and be happy for her brother from afar.

After three glasses of champagne, the tension eased out and the giggles eased in. Meme didn't become loud and obnoxious when drunk, she became giggly and playful. Anything remotely funny would send her into a fit of the giggles and the man staring at her from across the table was doing exactly that. Covering her mouth to muffle her laugh, Meme tried to focus on the best man's toast, but she could feel the man's gaze burning through her. She giggled out loud and was shushed by people at the surrounding tables.

Meme chanced another glance at her admirer and although she'd just guzzled a glass of champagne, her mouth instantly went dry. His gaze went from flirty to full on lust. The moment she sat at his table, his whole body was on full alert. Her scent wafted across the table, making it impossible for him to focus on anything other than her. He watched her drink champagne, wishing he could lick the drops that lingered on those full pouty lips. When she finally looked in his direction, her big green eyes caused his heart to flutter.

She laughed and turned her head to avoid him, which usually would have turned him off, but the more she giggled, the more intrigued he became. He watched her eat and she moaned over her first bite of wedding cake. He got up and made his way around the table to introduce himself.

Meme saw him coming and tried to figure out how to respond, but was still confused by her body's reaction to him. Her eyes bulged as she watched him walk toward her. His 6'4" muscular body towered over the seated guests at their table. As he approached, Meme tried to swallow the lump in her throat.

She shook his hand as he introduced himself and quickly turned back to her food thinking, just ignore him and he will go away. No such luck. He kneeled and placed his hand on her bare thigh and her body shook. His breath caught in his throat and he paused to enjoy the feel of her smooth, caramel skin. His hand crept further up her thigh and, now powerless, Meme allowed him.

"You are the most beautiful woman in here."

She giggled.

His hand crept.

She giggled.

"I am feeling you and I know you're feeling me."

She giggled.

"When you're ready to do something about it, I will be sitting right over there." His hand caressed the fullness of her lips.

She stopped giggling and he walked away.

Before he made it to his seat, Meme was up from the table and running from the room. He watched her fleeing, thinking he had screwed up by invading her space. After five minutes, she reappeared and locked eyes with him, then shockingly signaled for him to come. At least that's what he thought, but he wasn't about to sit around second guessing.

He exited the dining area and was just in time to see her enter the restroom. If he read her signals right, she would be expecting him. After he introduced himself, he realized she hadn't been giving him the cold shoulder, she was just shy. He was glad he'd decided to step up his game and approach her instead of moving on to someone else.

He knocked three times on the door and waited for her response. Slowly, the door opened and a seductively smiling Meme stood on the other side. "The coast is clear," she purred, allowing him to enter; she locked the door behind him. He usually didn't waste time kissing a quickie, but when he turned around Meme slammed her lips on his as if her life depended on it. He gave her what she wanted, but once he tasted the sweetness of her lips it was what he wanted too.

His mind kept saying *Foreplay is wasted time on a woman you'll never see again*, but the longer they kissed, that voice became softer and softer. He seriously thought about taking her to his place so he could enjoy this sweet-tasting, beautiful woman in the right setting, but didn't want to give her a chance to change her mind. He lifted her onto the counter and nuzzled her neck while unzipping her dress. The spaghetti straps slid off her shoulders and the dress pooled around her hips. He had done the one night stand thing plenty of times, especially at weddings, and was well prepared. Meme saw the foil packet the moment he took it out of his pocket. What she was doing became all too real and she choked.

"What's wrong?"

"I have never done this before."

He laughed, but seeing the sincerity in her eyes shocked him. "You're a…"

Meme nodded her yes before he could get the word out.

Instantly, confusion tilted his brow and he looked down at the beautiful woman before him and thought, *couldn't be,* but the look on her face let him know she wasn't playing games. *She is a virgin*. All the euphoric bliss came crashing to a halt.

"No, don't stop." Meme felt his retreat and didn't want this new found passion to end.

"I can't do this."

"It's okay, I want you to."

"I don't do virgins." He adjusted his clothing and fled the scene. He returned to the dining room and grabbed a glass of champagne from a passing tray. He impatiently searched for Marlon, so he could say congratulations and get the hell out of dodge. He was standing off to the side of the dance floor talking to his dad. He made a beeline toward him. Before he could say anything, his unhappy friend from the bathroom brushed passed him.

"Hey daddy," she said, kissing him on the cheek and did the same to Marlon. He choked on his champagne.

That's his little sister. He knew he screwed up by even touching her, but was glad he stopped when he did. Why didn't he know she was his sister? She should have been part of the bridal party or sitting with the family or something. That's what he usually relied on at these functions to keep these things from happening.

"Hey bro, I am going to take off. I just wanted to say congratulations." She turned to acknowledge his presence and the tears in her eyes constricted his heart. She nodded in his direction and took off before he could respond. Heading out of the building, she ran into April, Sheena's sister, and Candice, Paul and Tim's sister. They had heard about the drama she'd caused and could only imagine how hard it was to be at a wedding that you were only invited to out of familial obligation. They weren't close, couldn't even be considered friends, but had hung out a few times in the past.

They saw the look of anguish on her face and April instantly decided to rescue her from what had to be torture. "Hey Meme, Candice and I were heading out for some fun. You should join us." They had truthfully just arrived, but didn't want to be at this dry reception. Taking her silence as a yes, they grabbed her by the arm and left. Meme didn't protest; she needed something to take her mind off of what she had almost done.

He watched Meme walk away and thought to run after her, but quickly rebuked the idea and let her leave. He gazed in that direction long after she had left and was only brought out of his trance when he heard Latrice's voice.

"Are you alright?"

"Yeah, I am just a little tired." He looked at Marlon and was glad he hadn't noticed him staring at his sister. "I think I am going to head out."

"No," Latrice whined. "You can't leave before us."

"Speaking of leave," Marlon spun her around and molded her against him. "Why are we still here?"

"That's why I came over here. I am ready to go."

Just then, the wedding coordinator's voice came over the microphone announcing that it was time to say farewell to the bride and groom. Marlon grabbed his wife by the hand and led her to the exit. He was a man on a mission and the coordinator had to rush all the guests and the photographers to line up before Marlon drug Latrice out of the reception hall.

They walked through the path of guests who were flinging handfuls of rice. Next, Marlon and Latrice paused before entering the limousine to enjoy one last kiss for the cameras. Finally, they hopped inside and rode off into their new life together.

www.ingramcontent.com/pod-product-compliance
Lightning Source LLC
Chambersburg PA
CBHW050038180626
46810CB00002B/785